WARLORDS OF THE STEPPES

HORIZON
OF WAR

BOOK 3

WARLORDS OF THE STEPPES

HANNE

Podium

Copyright © 2025 by Hanne

Cover design by Thegreysun

Map by Arturo Gómez Martínez and diagrams by Leah Zink

ISBN: 978-1-0394-6811-5

Published in 2025 by Podium Publishing
www.podiumentertainment.com

Podium

WARLORDS OF THE STEPPES

Noma
Caladania
Tarraca
Centuri
Thiri
Human
Kehldin
Elven Satrapy
Sarmatia
Elearis
Halicia
Ekionia
Beastmen Confi

PEOPLE
Province of Brigandia
Province of Arminia
Inglesia
Tiberia
Arvena
MERCANTILE KINGDOM
Rhomelia
MPERIUM
Midlandia
Elandia
Korimor
Umberland
Ornietia
Edessa
Three Hills
White Lake
copola
South Hill
Korelia
Salceslia
NAVALNIA EMPIRE
Corinthia
Galdia
Lowlandia Plains
RATI
The Great Marshes

CHAPTER 1

SINEWS OF WAR

It was noon outside, but the sun couldn't penetrate the thick canvas of the tent. There was no ventilation openings, making the inside hot and humid. There, a Nicopolan-born lady sat upon a mat of dried grass inside of a wooden cage, her clothes sticking to her sweaty skin. Her mission to secure alliances with the cooperative Nicopolans had been discovered, and she had been captured.

Looking back, she had been too hopeful to think that the majority of refugees from Nicopola could be dissuaded from waging war with Korimor and her forces. These so-called refugees were, in reality, deeply influenced by the manipulative and ambitious Tarracan man, who was also ruthlessly competent.

The price for this misplaced optimism was the death of her accompanying guard—a smart, loyal, and resourceful man. He had died defending her, and Daniella blamed herself.

She licked her cracked lips and exhaled deeply, unbothered by the putrid stench emanating from the cage that had certainly imprisoned many more victims before her. After days of subsisting on watery gruel, she felt weak. Even water was hard to come by, and her dry lips bled easily. In her boredom, her fingers absently played with the dark brown beads attached to her belt. They looked like poorly lacquered wooden beads, but they were made of highly valued sucrose and hard biscuits, coated in beeswax.

These small, hard candies could give her a burst of stamina if needed. They wouldn't cure her hunger, but they could prove invaluable in certain situations. Aside from the candies, she had another item for defense: a thin, metallic garrote. It was tricky to use but could be similarly useful if an opportunity arose.

However, for now, escape seemed like a farfetched dream. The wooden cage was built to last, and possibly even sturdy enough to hold a beastman. Daniella stilled her thoughts and conserved her stamina, calmly maintaining awareness of her surroundings.

Despite days of isolation inside the cage, poor sanitation, itchiness from lack of hygiene, and debilitating boredom, her mind remained sharp. Many would succumb to despair, especially knowing their mission had almost succeeded only to be thwarted at the final stage. But even thrown into a cage with little hope of rescue, Daniella remained steadfast.

Ironically, her upbringing as a noble had prepared her for this kind of treatment. She remembered days when she had been confined to her chamber over disagreements with her family. In that solitude, she found strength and mental resilience.

Unbeknownst to her, the silence of her current confinement had empowered her further. Since yesterday, she had been replaying her last two battles in her mind: one against Lord Lansius, and the other as his ally. On both occasions, she had caught glimpses of her new lord's ingenuity.

She came to realize what made Lansius unique was his ability to understand the entire battlefield as a whole, to see the big picture.

That understanding sparked an undying conviction that rescue would eventually arrive. Lord Lansius wouldn't allow Korimor to fall. Not because the city itself was valuable, but because sooner or later, he needed to solve the Nicopolan problem before it ruined the entire western Lowlandia—a region he and his Grand Alliance certainly had a stake in.

And in this regard, Korimor offered him a great advantage: a castle, city walls, and a population that would gladly fight against the invading Nicopolans.

A smile momentarily bloomed on Daniella's lips. If her assessment was true, then she would have her justice against this Tarracan man—the charlatan who had fooled thousands with his rhetoric and false hope. The ruthless man had led innocents to live and die as brigands, had used them as mere stepping stones in his rise to power.

Her stomach groaned again. She held her knees to her chest, as though trying to stave off both cold and hunger. She carefully tore a small piece from her leather belt and chewed it. She had learned in her youth that the less fortunate did this to mask their hunger, but she had never imagined herself resorting to such measures.

The taste was earthy and bitter, with a strong, pungent smell released upon chewing. Yet, somehow, it provided some relief to her stomach.

Just as she was about to mentally shut down and save her alertness for the night, something happened outside. Hurried footsteps, calls, and shouting broke the silence. The noise didn't fade. Instead, it escalated into a full commotion.

The Nicopolan Side

Thousands of horses emerged on the southern horizon, casting shock through the Nicopolans' ranks, who hadn't expected any large military intervention from outside the region. Smaller advance groups also appeared separately, seemingly reconnoitering the area.

The men keeping watch shouted and clamored for everyone in the camp to take up arms. In a hurry, the Nicopolans haphazardly formed their battle lines.

Tension quickly filled the air as the cavalry from the opposing side advanced closer, kicking up clouds of dust.

"The attack is coming! The attack is coming!" one man shouted in fear.

Refugees had heard tales from Nicopolan mercenaries—survivors who had escaped the Coalition's doomed siege in Korelia—and these mercenaries had spread their tragic stories to anyone who wished to listen.

Now, upon recognizing the familiar blue and bronze banner, cries erupted. "It's him! That's the banner! The Black Lord is here!"

Many trembled at the sight of the Black Lord's banner. Some were so distraught that they fled the camp, seeking refuge in a distant forest.

Amid the chaos, Sergio, the Tarracan man, led his detachment of men onto the field. "A blue and bronze banner?" he asked the men flanking him.

"There are rumors of a powerful new lord in Korelia. They call him the Black Lord," one of them answered.

"Why is he here, so far from Korelia?" another inquired nervously, eyeing the large cavalry force amassing near their flank.

Sergio took a sharp breath. "Isn't it obvious? He wants the city." He then spun around to face his men. "Fear not these Lowlandian dogs. I knew they were going to interfere. Luckily, we're trained in anti-cavalry techniques."

His men sported nervous smiles as Sergio instructed, "Move the crossbow-men and the long pikes closer to the front. We're going to teach these outdated brutes some state-of-the-art warfare."

Out of eight thousand souls, four thousand men armed with spears, swords, sickles, or spades formed the Nicopolan battle line. Sergio also put enough men in reserve and positioned plenty to cover his other flanks.

With many experienced mercenaries under his command and a cavalry unit ready as a quick reactionary force, he felt well-prepared, confident that the odds were in their favor.

Korelia Side

After having rendezvoused with Sir Harold and Batu, who had completed their preparations, the relief force led by Lansius had undertaken a grueling three-day marathon ride to Korimor, each night traveling from the waning sun until the morning sun.

In record-breaking time, Lansius and his riders, along with a few hundred tribesmen, arrived on the outskirts of Korimor. Yet, even when joined with the elderly and children already stationed around Korimor, their numbers didn't exceed five hundred.

They made their numbers appear larger by tying their sleeping carpets, armor, and other baggage upward on the saddle, making them resemble riders atop their thousands of spare horses. The nomads aptly named this creation the *mirage warriors.*

They saw the Korimor city proper and its castle situated on a verdant hill, beside a flowing river. A large but crude encampment was also visible, not far from the river.

Lansius removed his mouth covering and cloak, then shook the dust from his hair and face. "Is that the encampment?"

"Yes, my lord, the scout confirmed it," said Sir Harold, riding beside him.

"I need to see it closer," Lansius stated.

"My lord, we're not in armor," the knight reminded him. Most of them were wearing padded jacks.

"Just a bit closer," Lansius replied.

"Riders, prepare for escort," Sir Harold shouted, readying them for contact.

Batu rode closer and suggested, "Noyan, let me take my riders closer. I want our presence to be felt."

Lansius quickly agreed but instructed, "Don't engage, and make sure not to get caught."

Batu smirked. "I'll be sure to maintain the illusion. This is the most fun I've had in a while." He then added, "I still can't believe you're familiar with nomadic tactics like this."

Lansius offered a faint grin at the compliment and saw Batu gallop off to lead his brethren toward the enemy camp's right side. "Dietrich," he called.

"Yes, my lord." An equally dusty man with a covered head and mouth rode forward.

"Get twenty riders and participate. Do not engage, but try to provoke the Nicopolans and see how many cavalry they've got," Lansius instructed.

"At once." Dietrich prepared his group and sallied forth.

Without saying a word, Lansius spurred his horse forward for closer reconnaissance. Audrey and the rest of the retinue followed.

Stopping at a safe distance, they observed the large Nicopolan encampment. Although the camp had no wooden fence or palisade, they used their carts and fallen trees as makeshift obstacles.

There was a series of large tents in the center, heavily guarded. "That's where they keep the supplies. Not bad," mumbled Lansius.

Audrey chimed in. "These aren't common refugees. Better not to underestimate them."

"The lady is correct," Sir Harold said, sharing her concern. "A simple cavalry assault wouldn't work, not with our real numbers."

Not a moment too soon, the enemy reacted to the Korelian and nomadic presence by sending thousands of men to form a circular battle line. The waning sun reflected off their metal weapons—spears, swords, and scythes—as if challenging the newcomers to attack.

Lansius also noticed a group of crossbowmen taking positions behind men armored with pikes. "They're competent, alright."

"Look, the city gate is open," Audrey pointed out.

"Our banner and White Lake," Sir Harold observed. "Must be Hugo and Sir Michael."

"Be on guard. No matter what the scouts say, don't get complacent," Lansius warned. Before he could say more, the heat seemed to suddenly overcome him. He coughed and tasted iron. Dizziness flooded him, and he saw red on his hand as he tried to cover his mouth. Before he understood what had happened, Audrey and Harold rushed toward him.

Nicopolan Side

The sun had finally gone down, and despite some cavalry activity, no follow-up action had occurred. Nervousness and anticipation ran high, but for many, burdened by hunger and fatigue, they clamored to return to their camp.

By now, even Sergio's closest aide was certain there would be no battle that day. In contrast, Sergio, recently briefed about the Black Lord by the survivors of the siege of Korelia, remained concerned and insisted that his men stay on the lines despite the falling light.

Only when complete darkness had settled, did Sergio allow a majority of his force to break formation. The thousands of men returned to their families and began to cook whatever meager food they had.

However, Sergio remained vigilant. Anticipating a night attack, he worked hard to convince his officers to allocate as many soldiers as possible for the night watch, but many believed his fear was unfounded.

"The enemy just arrived after a long journey; they should be wary of an attack from us, not the other way around," said one outspoken captain among his ranks.

"We're not only facing the newcomers. Don't forget the garrison in the city of Korimor," Sergio countered.

"The commoners are already starving on the few rations they have. Asking them to perform under these conditions might incite rebellion," another captain warned somberly.

"We'll give extra to those who take the night watch," Sergio conceded.

With such incentive on the line, they finally agreed to assign a third of their force to night watch. To ensure participation and maintain discipline, Sergio and his staff planned for random patrols along the lines.

Many among his inner circle understood that the stakes were too high; they would rather exhaust their men than risk defeat. This perspective was increasingly validated as they learned more about the Black Lord's cunning and unorthodox tactics from the survivors of the doomed campaign to Korelia.

That night, restlessness pervaded the camp, with everyone gossiping about the new threat and growing fearful of the Black Lord. Every distant neighing horse and every unusual sound from nocturnal animals spooked them. Sergio himself couldn't sleep, choosing instead to keep watch, accompanied by a guard with a loaded crossbow at his side.

Fortified Camp Outside Korimor's Gate

Lansius awakened around the third watch. He saw unfamiliar ceilings and surroundings and sat up abruptly. A damp piece of cloth dropped onto his lap.

"A fever?" he muttered to himself.

He checked his forehead but found it normal. However, a slight headache lingered.

The wooden cabin had no door, only a heavy canvas, which was pushed aside as someone entered. "My lord, you're awake."

"Sigmund?" Lansius asked, recognizing the skald's clear voice.

Sigmund scrambled for something before returning with a jug of water and a cup. He approached and knelt before the bed. "Please, have some water, oh lord. Shall I furnish you with anything or anyone?"

Lansius took the cup but didn't drink. "Where are we?"

"We're inside a camp just outside Korimor. The place was built by Hugo when he arrived several weeks ago. It's fortified, and Sir Harold has arranged his men on defense."

Lansius breathed a sigh of relief. "How's Batu and his tribes?"

"He has camped farther from the city to allow his horses to graze."

"And the castle?"

"The city is ours, my lord. The current House didn't even demand to see Lord Omin."

Lansius furrowed his brow. "So, where is Omin now?"

"Sir Harold has kept him in a separate cabin. He seems calm and hasn't caused trouble."

Lansius nodded approvingly and drank from his cup. The water felt good on his parched throat, although hints of a strong metallic smell still lingered in his nostrils.

"My lord, try to get more rest. The night is still long, and I'll remain at your side," urged Sigmund.

Acting on his suggestion, Lansius lay down again. Indeed, his head felt light. "What happened to me? Last I remember, I was reconnoitering the Nicopolan encampment."

"You either coughed up blood or had a nosebleed and almost fell from the horse," Sigmund explained.

"Ah . . ." Lansius remembered feeling dizzy and coughing. "Must be the heat."

The skald smiled and said softly, "That's exactly what the physician has told us."

"I hope he didn't recommend a duck egg as a remedy," Lansius joked.

The skald chuckled. "Just some cold water and vinegar."

"That is surprisingly mild."

Sigmund chuckled at Lansius's comment. "Fear not, my lord, as I will keep you from the duck egg broth. Let music be the cure for your malady."

Lansius smiled, amused at the archaic words he used. And unexpectedly, drowsiness came easily. "Where's Lady Audrey?"

"The baroness is sleeping with Carla next door. She insisted on being at your side, but we convinced her not to."

"Excellent work, Sigmund."

The skald bowed his head graciously. "Put more trust in us, oh lord. Let us take some of your burden."

"I shall if I can give it to you." Lansius drew a deep breath. "Prepare your shoulders. By tomorrow, I think we'll have an act to play."

"Then I'll gladly play my part to the fullest."

Lansius was impressed by his eagerness. "Then lend me your ears before the dream takes them away from me."

Sigmund's eyes turned sharp, his face serious.

"Tomorrow morning, the Nicopolans will likely send an envoy. They'll either try to curry favor, offer a deal, or intimidate us. When that happens, I want you to prepare everyone in my vicinity to play along with my act. If I say 'let's make a party,' then let's make one."

The skald nodded, and Lansius continued. "If I say 'let's bring a big cauldron and boil a person . . .'"

Sigmund raised an eyebrow but refrained from commenting.

"I want you and the rest to not hesitate at my command," Lansius explained. "We can't afford to be seen making empty threats. If they try to intimidate us, then we will counter with an equal measure."

Sigmund quickly understood the intention.

Lansius drew a sharp breath and reflected. "When we are weak, we cannot afford to appear so."

* * *

The words piqued Sigmund's interest. "Sir Michael said similar things when I met him," he noted. "He feared that after enduring famine, hunger, and conflicts, the Nicopolans will only understand the language of strong action or violence."

"He's wise to come to that conclusion," Lansius said with renewed interest. "Sigmund, could you please arrange a meeting with Sir Michael and Hugo at dawn. I need all the intel I can get."

"Certainly, my lord."

"Unsavory as it must be, we must try to talk it out, because the only other option is the ultima ratio," Lansius muttered grimly, thinking about just how many lives would perish from both sides if they resorted to battle.

CHAPTER 2

WHITE PIECES

Dawn had just broken when Sir Michael and Hugo slipped through the city gate and arrived outside the cabin. The cool wind was blowing, and the grass was wet with morning dew.

Sir Harold finally emerged from inside and invited them in. "The lord wishes to see you."

"Am I allowed to bring my sword?" Sir Michael asked, as he was not part of House Lansius.

"Is there any reason not to?" Sir Harold countered with a grin.

The one-eyed knight chuckled, pleased with the implied trust.

"Don't worry. He's perfectly capable of killing us both," Hugo jested, then entered first.

Sir Michael entered and saw Lord Lansius sitting on a folding chair behind a small table. Lady Audrey sat beside him.

"My lord," Hugo and Sir Michael greeted him. The latter added, "We welcome you to Korimor."

"Deputy, Sir Michael," Lord Lansius replied. "How are Korimor and its people? Do they oppose you?"

"No," Hugo reported. "At least not openly. But the issue of food rations is ongoing."

Lord Lansius nodded. "How about House Omin?"

"The House consists only of Lady Hilda and her young son. They pose little threat," Hugo reported. "I must say it's not really a surprise. With the baroness as their new head of House, they're essentially an extension of your own House."

His words prompted Sir Harold to add, "I suppose they're open to the idea of becoming part of the most powerful House in Lowlandia." His comment elicited a few smirks and smiles.

Amused, Lord Lansius glanced at Lady Audrey, who responded, "I'll meet with Lady Hilda today and secure their support."

"Don't promise them anything except safety, good land, and a monthly allowance. Take their son as a squire when he's of age," the lord instructed. Then he turned to the two commanders. "What's the situation with the city's supplies?"

Hugo looked at Sir Michael, who reported, "The city is fortunate that the previous lord maintained a large cache of food. The records show that he consistently bought from and used Three Hill's reserves during his campaigns. However, even with last year's harvest and the current rations, the granary won't last through the winter."

"He is indeed cunning," Lord Lansius commented of Omin.

"Perhaps we can use him instead of sending him back to the dungeon," Lady Audrey suggested.

The lord mulled over the idea. "If he's not too proud, I could place him under someone. But he needs to earn our trust first." Realizing the conversation had strayed, he added, "Let's set this issue aside for now. What are your thoughts on the Nicopolan situation?"

"My lord, first of all, I need to inform you that Lady Daniella has been captured," Hugo reported somberly.

The lord drew a deep breath but motioned Hugo to continue. He knew from the last message that she had attempted to broker peace, and it was indeed risky.

Hugo continued, his voice heavy with regret. "The enemy is keeping her alive and wants to use her as a hostage."

"Bargaining tools," Lord Lansius muttered. "Do we know the reason why she attempted to talk?"

"She said the Nicopolans are fractured. It's unlikely that everyone agrees on besieging a walled city like Korimor."

Lord Lansius understood her intention, but alas, it had failed. "How do you think we should solve these Nicopolan problems?"

Hugo and Sir Michael exchanged glances, and the latter spoke. "I think we should levy the populace. That way, we'll have the numbers required to meet them on the field. I believe that our cavalry should suffice to flank them."

"It'll be a good battle," Lord Lansius admitted. "High casualties from both sides, but a victory nevertheless."

"My lord, how about subterfuge?" Sir Michael suggested.

Lansius's interest was piqued. "What do you have in mind?"

"Before Lady Daniella was captured, she reported that her attempt almost worked. The Nicopolans aren't under one leadership. While in general, they follow this Tarracan man, there are mercenary companies that have joined in but have different loyalties. And not everyone likes the Tarracan man."

"So, she went there not to broker peace but to instigate a mutiny?" Lord Lansius asked.

Sir Michael nodded. "She found out that peace isn't possible if the Tarracan man is in the lead. The man simply wants to rule."

Almost everyone murmured, and the lord allowed them to vent their disgust.

Lady Audrey sighed aloud and lamented, "To use hungry people as a stepping stone."

"It's a bloody path none should ever take," Sir Harold responded.

Lord Lansius closed his eyes, comparing himself with the Tarracan man. Despite the contrast, he saw some similarities. He had battled Robert and taken Korelia for his own personal gain. He then stubbornly defended it, also for his own personal gain.

As if noticing his troubled mind, Lady Audrey placed her hand on his wrist. The lord glanced at her and nodded in appreciation.

"I hope I'm a better man than he is," he said openly.

"My lord, you surely jest," said Hugo, surprised. The rest also looked concerned.

The situation prompted Lady Audrey to say, "The Lord of Korelia is still recovering; please forgive his tactless jest. Perhaps, a duck egg broth could cure this ailment."

"No, wait—"

"There should be a stockpile in the city. I'll put up a petition right away," said Hugo.

"Or we can try the apothecary in the city. They should have potent medicines," Sir Michael suggested.

Lord Lansius suddenly chuckled and waved it all off. "No duck egg for me, on the pain of no pay," he threatened. Only then did they understand just how much the lord hated the broth.

With his retinue in line, the lord crossed his arms and said to Michael, "From your words, it seems possible to divide or turn the Nicopolans against themselves."

"Indeed, my lord, but it will require some finesse."

"Do you think you have it?" Lord Lansius asked.

"In commanding battles, I might be worthless, but in courtly matters, I believe I can hold my own," said Sir Michael confidently.

The lord sat in silence for a moment, pondering, and nobody disturbed him, knowing he was deciding on a plan. The shadows from lanterns hung around the cabin danced as the morning wind began to breeze.

He finally shifted in his seat and spoke. "Hugo, you're more suited for this task. At the first light, levy a thousand militia from the populace. Double their rations for the duration of the training. Make sure to only take the fit and people with arms, helmets, and gambesons."

"Yes, my lord," Hugo replied.

"Sir Harold," Lord Lansius called, and the tall knight stepped forward.

"Pick a hundred of the best from the existing troops from Korimor, their guardsmen, and their mercenaries. Meld them with your men. I want you to prepare them as crack troops in combination with our dragoon regiment," the lord continued.

"May I ask, what's their purpose?" Sir Harold asked.

"Possibly hostage rescue," the lord revealed. "If we want to divide them successfully, then chances are we'll need to rescue some families."

"That'll be hard to do," Sir Harold said without mincing words.

"The result may be bleak, but as long as they see us commit," Lord Lansius said, seemingly out of breath.

Lady Audrey readily reached out to him. "You're exerting yourself. Better finish this quickly and get some rest."

The lord nodded, seeing his men's concern. "At ease. Just fatigue. Let me outline that I wanted to try to avoid bloodshed. There's still time before harvest. I have discussed my plans with Sigmund; he'll be able to give you some pointers about what to do. The Nicopolans should send their envoy today or tomorrow."

"What if they don't send one?" Lady Audrey asked.

"Then I'll make them," Lord Lansius replied firmly.

Lansius

Within an hour, morning arrived in Korimor, and a crisp autumn breeze along with it. The wind carried a strong earthen scent, and there were more clouds overhead.

At first light, as ordered, Hugo and his men marched toward the city plaza and announced the recruitment of a thousand men. This announcement, with the promise of double rations, excited everyone. Word spread like wildfire, and soon many flocked to the plaza with helmets, swords, and gambesons.

While this was expected, there was also another movement of people. Propelled by the Lord of Korelia's presence outside, and the large group of allied tribesmen, the Korimors dared to venture outside to collect hay and firewood for the winter.

At first, the guardsmen allowed a small number of them, but before long, a large number began to amass at the city gates, and there was concern that this could turn serious. Sir Michael thus sent a message to Lord Lansius.

When the messenger arrived, the lord and the baroness were eating a light breakfast.

"Hundreds of people with carts could be a hazard if we need to defend against a sudden attack," Audrey voiced her concern.

Lansius nodded, then turned to his knight after sipping a bitter herb-infused concoction. "What do you think, Sir Harold?"

"Well, I say there's little harm, and if this baits the Nicopolans to move, then perhaps it's something we can exploit."

Lansius stifled a laugh at the knight's cunning answer. "Make some arrangements then."

"At once, my lord," said Sir Harold and left the cabin, taking the messenger with him.

After they left, Audrey asked, "You seem unconcerned with this. Is this within your prediction?"

"No. I didn't expect this, but it sort of aligns with my plan," he admitted.

Audrey offered him some sweet bread, and Lansius took a bite.

"Which part is aligned?" she asked after they finished with the bread.

"Well, I insist on staying here and not entering the city to try to provoke a response from the Nicopolans."

Audrey tried to fathom the reason.

"I want to break the sense of the city being under siege," he explained. "It's hard on morale. I want to encourage people to venture outside to gather food, hay, wild berries, or even to go fishing. Those activities will ultimately help the city."

"And this is exactly what happened," praised Audrey.

"No, I expected a dozen or tens of people, not hundreds. The Korimors are either too bold or desperate," he said rather worriedly. The situation inside the city might be worse than he expected.

Arriving at the city gate, Sir Harold personally ordered it opened, and hundreds of people armed with scythes marched out. They hurried to the meadows just beyond the city wall, working quickly to gather hay. Horse-drawn carts filled up and shuttled into the city almost nonstop.

Their livestock depended on it. Without good hay, the animals would neither fatten up for the winter nor produce milk.

Despite the bustling activity outside the walls, the Nicopolans did nothing. Frustration seemed to build up inside their camp, yet they launched no sorties.

After confirming the situation with his scout and Sir Harold, Lansius summoned House Omin. He was determined to use this opportunity to further his plan and solve as many issues as possible.

The issue of the transfer of power was particularly high on his priority list.

Despite his position, Lansius played little role except to witness Audrey take over her House's leadership from her nephew, a boy younger than Margo. The boy was only assisted by Hilda, his mother. Omin's wife was native to Lowlandia but was not born in Korimor.

Though she was already officially the baroness, with the symbolic transfer of the patent of Baron of Korimor and the key to the undercroft vault, Audrey assumed her new official title, styled the Lady of Korimor.

Audrey seemed stoic, emotionless as she took the items and gave them to Carla for safekeeping. Lansius at her side looked proud. Meanwhile, Hilda and her son seemed fearful and nervous until the lady guaranteed their safety and promised good land.

"We have moved from the castle and have transferred command of the guards to Deputy Hugo. But please allow me to retain some of my older retinue," asked Hilda.

"As long as you can afford it," said Audrey. "I'll give you a monthly allowance, but it won't be much, since we're at war. Do try to make it work."

Hilda then said, "We learned that my husband is here. Can we see him?"

Audrey almost allowed them, but Lansius cleared his throat and advised, "It'll be hard for him to be seen all dirty and dusty after a long journey. It's best to prepare him a bath and good clothes, as well as his personal barber and servant. Give them one day, and then tomorrow you can meet him."

"That is a kind suggestion, my lord. I shall do as you say," Hilda responded openly.

"A favor, if you could," Lord Lansius said.

"Please, if it's within my power."

"When you meet your husband tomorrow, please ask about his contingency plan in this situation. I might learn something beneficial to aid our situation. Rest assured, I would consider this a meritorious service."

Hilda understood his intention, expressed her gratitude, and left the premises. Not long after she returned to the city, a host of workers with carts carried three wooden bathtubs. The two largest were intended for Lord Lansius and the baroness, complete with hot water, flowers, and clean clothes.

The smallest of the three was intended for Omin, a sign of humility on their part.

Lansius gratefully accepted the gift and cleaned himself. After so many days without baths, the first time always felt good. His skin became supple, and his muscles felt relaxed.

As the baroness's squire, Carla politely took the flowers away and replaced them with herbal leaves she had gathered from the tribesmen. She had been taught by Cecile and Calub not to trust anyone too easily. Even insignificant things could contain poison that might harm her charge.

After cleaning himself and feeling refreshed, Lansius sat in his cabin-turned-command-center and received updates regarding the situation. He confirmed that the Nicopolans had done nothing but dig some pits as measures against a cavalry attack.

Next, he received a report from Hugo.

"More than enough have joined. Selection and training are ongoing. The anticipation is high," Roger, the squire, reported on behalf of Hugo.

Lansius nodded. From the window, he could watch Sir Harold condition his men to move speedily under his command and to retreat in an orderly fashion after achieving their objectives.

The newly formed dragoon regiment, the fast-moving footmen riding horses, would also participate. Lansius had yet to give them a role, but they would be vital.

Nearing midday, Lansius was about to survey the location, but Audrey and his staff urged him to get some rest to avoid a relapse.

Lansius lay down to rest, but a sense of restlessness kept him alert. Whatever had happened to him yesterday and this morning felt distant. Feeling better, he taught Roger how to make bird's-eye maps instead of sleeping.

Audrey entered the sleeping chamber. "Ah, you're awake."

Roger stood straight and bowed his head to the Lady of Korimor, surprising Audrey with the formality.

"Any new developments?" asked Lansius while putting down his quill pen.

"You're going to like this. We have an envoy," said Audrey.

Lansius couldn't help but smirk. "Who accompanies them now?"

"Harold and Dietrich. They're giving them the silent treatment," she replied.

Lansius nodded while feeling the weight of responsibility creeping on his shoulders. It didn't bend his tempered will, merely steeled his resolve.

He gazed at Audrey, feeling her trust in him. "Summon Michael and Sigmund. Let the Tragedy of Nicopolans begin."

CHAPTER 3

THE SONS OF NICOPOLA

The three envoys had been waiting in the midday sun. They had asked to find some shade, but the guards and knights gave only a lukewarm response. Thus, they settled to wait in an awkward and heavy atmosphere.

Suddenly, a young man exited, looked around fiercely at the three envoys, and spoke to one of the knights. "The lord is willing to entertain the envoys."

The tall and imposing knight grumbled, spat on the grass, and said to the envoys, "Well, you got your chance. Don't say I didn't treat you right."

The envoys hurriedly moved inside, welcoming the cool shade and sweet floral fragrance.

"Behold, the Lord of Korelia, the Protector of Korimor, the leader of the Grand Alliance, and the Noyan of the Lowlandia Tribesmen," a squire heralded.

The envoys bowed their heads in unison toward a man in brightly colored clothing slouched on a padded chair. Indeed, he had black hair.

"My lord, we Nicopolans bid our welcome to this area," said one of the envoys, an old but stout-looking soldier.

Another followed up. "What happened between the city and our people is unfortunate, but we're willing to make amends."

"Amends?" Lord Lansius laughed.

Seizing the moment, the third envoy brought forward a lacquered jewelry coffer. "Please accept a gift from our leader."

The two envoys looked excited, but the old soldier appeared anxious.

The lord's knight intercepted the intricate wooden box and broke the wax seal in front of them. When he opened it, a horrid pungent odor emanated from the box. The knight's eyes widened and turned fierce, sending the two envoys into panic. They gasped and shrieked in fear, nearly losing their footing.

The squires reacted quickly by drawing their swords, but the lord waved them off. "Let me see," he commanded indifferently.

"Don't let them near the lord," the knight barked at the squires. Then, more politely to his lord, "My lord, it's an insult."

The lord rose from his seat to take a look at the jewelry box. Meanwhile, the two envoys cowered in fear, while the old soldier visibly fumed.

"Ah, what a gift," the lord said, his tone surprisingly fascinated by the grotesque object. "Signet rings complete with the cut-off fingers. So intimidating."

"This is a preposterous insult. They should all be flogged," the knight declared.

"Oh, they'll have their flogs, but after I'm done with them," the lord said ominously. "I wonder what embalming he used to mask most of the stench." He then gazed at the envoys and asked, "Should I return the favor?"

Realizing the hinted threat, the two envoys dropped to the ground, their faces turning pale as they began to beg for mercy. Only the old soldier remained composed.

"My lord, please listen. I don't know about the content. I'm just a tradesman who dealt with Nicopolan nobles. Sergio instructed me to speak sweetly and present you this gift."

"My lord, I swear I didn't know. Sergio set us up. He must've wanted us dead," said another one.

"And I intend to deliver," the lord replied with bizarre enthusiasm. "This is a game I can't lose. He aimed to intimidate me, and I shall retaliate in kind."

The envoys were paralyzed with fear. The one who had offered the jewelry coffer began to weep, while the other trembled. At this point, the old soldier dropped to his knees as if pleading for mercy.

But the lord was far from finished. "My scouts found human remains in a cauldron in the forest. Perhaps I should boil you three alive." Madness flickered in his eyes, unnerving the envoys, who could only beg for their lives.

"No, wait," the lord suddenly exclaimed. "That wouldn't work. Sending cooked flesh to your leader would be akin to serving him a meal." He erupted into manic laughter, joined by his staff and knights.

The lord added, "I bet this Sergio will gladly chug a soup made from you three. He must truly despise you to have sent you here."

In desperation, one of the envoys threw himself at the lord's feet. "My lord truly knows. This Sergio, he didn't like us. He wanted us to die so he could control our families and followers."

Lansius coughed several times and returned to his seat. His squire readily offered a goblet of water, which Lansius took and drank. He then addressed the envoys, saying, "Gentlemen, I understand your plight. But to me, you're all already dead."

"My lord, please . . ." the envoy begged.

"You're mistaken," the lord corrected them coldly. "I am not the one who wants you dead but if I let you return unharmed, Sergio would likely become suspicious. He might conduct a sham trial, accuse you of colluding with me, and then execute you and your family."

Hearing the lord's explanation, the three envoys started to feel angry at Sergio's treachery.

The lord ignored their reaction and talked to his knight. "It's not a bad strategy, using my hand to kill them and gain their followers' loyalty. A dishonorable method, but who are we to judge?"

"My lord, my name is Servius," the stout old soldier declared, his strong voice capturing attention. "I'm loyal only to my legion, and I have influence over two hundred fighters."

"Oh, that must be the reason he wants you to die," the lord quipped.

"He suspected me of having contact with one of your agents," Servius tried to explain.

"Lady Daniella?" asked the one-eyed knight who just arrived.

Servius looked at the newcomer and sighed in regret. "Unfortunately, I never met her. But the ones working with her have been rounded up and killed. Many were people I have shared battles with."

The lord sized up Servius and asked, "Why don't you and your men stand up to him?"

"It's because I don't trust my own men," Servius replied, his voice laden with regret. "Sergio has a reputation as a savior. Time and time again, he has proven capable of bringing food to the table as long as people do exactly as they're told. This is why your agent's plan failed. Someone must've talked."

Servius's explanation made the other two envoys cower. Sergio, the Tarracan man, was a figure they feared and revered.

The lord let out a sigh. "I lost interest. Guards, take them out."

The envoys panicked and were about to beg again, but the knight stood tall, silencing them. Without turning, he asked, "My lord, how about their escorts?"

The lord rolled his eyes and replied hastily, "Let them watch."

The knights drew their swords, leaving the envoys with no choice but to accept their fate. The squires then tied them and covered their heads before sending them outside.

Nicopolan Camp

Drawn by a mix of dread and curiosity, the Nicopolans thronged to the east side of the camp, where they could watch a bizarre proceeding unfold at a distance. The three envoys, paraded on top of carts, were subsequently tied up. To everyone's horror, they were flogged mercilessly until all three fainted.

Despite pleas from multiple people, Sergio refused to send help, claiming, "This is what the enemy wants. They must have a force ready to ambush us.

While it pains me to see my trusted fellow Nicopolans being treated like this, we must endure."

As the crowd grew larger and more restless, he rallied them. "Sons of Nicopola, hear me out! This Lord of Korelia is a ruthless man. I offered him gifts worthy of high nobles, and yet he tortured our cherished envoys. What kind of lord harms a messenger? He is brutal, no doubt, and any attempt to resolve this amicably would be futile. But now is not the time to act. To move now would be to fall into their trap!"

His words put heavy pressure on the group that wanted to resolve the issue peacefully. Now, they had no counter-argument against Sergio's insistence on besieging the city.

Meanwhile, the three victims of Sergio's power play were kicked off the cart and left to fend for themselves. Only afterward did their escorts, who had stood by as witnesses, finally muster the courage to carry them back to the Nicopolan camp.

The rest of the Nicopolans also rushed to their rescue.

Sergio wore a face of regret and a pained expression, but deep down he was pleased. The only better outcome would have been for all three to die, but even this result sufficed. The brutal flogging of the envoys would deter anyone from voicing support for a diplomatic solution. He knew he had won this battle of wits.

Tonight, he would gather the council of Nicopolan leaders and ask for their total support to besiege Korimor. This new Lord of Korelia had to be dealt with before they could prepare a defense.

Sergio had enough crossbow bolts, long pikes, and heavy armor to execute a fairly recent strategy: the pike and shot. It would be something that a Lowlandian like Lord Lansius would never expect.

He planned to bait the Korelian cavalry and spring a trap, annihilating them in one go. This was why they didn't evacuate to the wooded area but stayed in the plains, despite the disadvantage and the opponent's large cavalry presence.

This seemingly massive tactical mistake from the Nicopolan side was in reality a trap. The same one that had worked against the knights of southern Nicopola and the Umberland cavalry. And now, the Nicopolans under Sergio had become experts at it.

Servius

With battered bodies, the envoys were brought back to the Nicopolan camp to a heroes' welcome. As expected, Sergio met them, pressuring them not to divulge his gift to Lansius, lest their beloved family members suffer a horrible death. Afterward, the three were led to their respective tents to receive treatment.

Servius lay face down on a bed of hay. His clothes were torn and stained brown with dried blood, as was his skin. His cousin ground medicinal herbs into a paste, while his aide provided him with wine to dull the pain.

Even without a proper whip, using just a straight wooden stick, the flogging had been painful and hard on the body. He couldn't even sit and simply tried to shake off the pain from his back.

After applying a thin layer of medicinal paste as an ointment, there was little else they could do but let the patient rest. Servius fell asleep only to awaken at sundown.

He drew a deep breath and smelled a strong iron scent inside his tent. His family was boiling their rations of watery gruel. Despite Sergio's rhetoric about how heroic the envoys had been, he refused to give their families more provisions unless they participated in the night watch.

Servius's family was bitter about Sergio but felt powerless against him. Worse, they knew that Sergio had planted spies to watch them.

Hearing his family talk about Sergio, Servius recalled the events of the day. He remembered sitting on the cart, his hands and legs tied, under a cloudy sky. Amid the creaking of cart wheels over uneven terrain and the sporadic whinnying of horses, he'd had an unexpected conversation.

Unbeknownst to most, Lord Lansius, in disguise, rode beside Servius's cart as the envoys were escorted to the field where they would be flogged.

Lansius's words still echoed in Servius's ears: "Do you know why I ordered this?"

Servius recalled that he'd wanted to spit, but mortal fear had made him shake his head.

"It's to save you from Sergio."

The words prompted Servius to do a double-take. The lord's tone was so different now—warm and caring—that Servius felt he was speaking with another person.

The lord continued, "Why did Sergio send you with that box of fingers? I think it's because he fears you. He needs you to die."

Servius could only exhale bitterly.

"You hesitated. You fear him," the lord pointed out.

"I do not," Servius replied firmly. "I fear for my family and my men."

"Then endure the pain. It's ironic, but this is the only way to keep you alive; otherwise, this Tarracan man will become suspicious and kill you outright."

"Why are you doing this?" Servius demanded.

"Do you want to save your family?" Lord Lansius replied, dodging the question.

Jumping to conclusions, Servius warned, "You want me to assassinate Sergio? That's impossible. After your agent's failure, it's difficult to even get close to him. He's surrounded by guards at all times."

However, the lord seemed to have another idea. "How many did you say are under your influence?"

"Two hundred," he replied. Then, after a pause, he added, "But if I make my move, another three hundred will join, along with possibly five hundred unarmed people."

"That'll do," said Lord Lansius, surprising Servius.

"I can't rush at Sergio, not even in the middle of your attack. He'll place me far away and put his men in my path."

"You don't have to. Instead of fighting, run to the woods."

The lord's words puzzled Servius. "Run . . . ?"

"Spread the word that you have a backup plan in the woods if Sergio fails in the war."

"But that still requires victory," Servius warned. "At least a decisive win to break the morale of Sergio's men. A rout won't happen if he's still alive."

"Then I shall defeat him," Lord Lansius declared with remarkable ease and conviction.

Even Servius was astounded by the man's conviction and couldn't help but warn him, "How can you beat him? He has the numbers and the supplies. Don't be fooled by the location of the camp; it's well-fortified. The men are well-armed and equipped against cavalry attack."

The lord replied with a faint smile, "It's true that he has greater numbers, perhaps even better fighters, and is better equipped to handle cavalry attack. However, that will amount to nothing. Just a tragedy waiting to happen."

The calm stemming from sheer conviction moved Servius, who had long sought to split ways with Sergio and his diabolical rise to power. "What will you do with the people under me if you win this?"

"Nothing but grant them the freedom to find a job and feed their families."

"My lord, we're not farmers."

"Then your men shall fight for me. Food in exchange for bravery in battle. This is Lowlandia; you won't find easy living here."

Servius heaved a long sigh but nodded.

"I suppose Sergio wouldn't plan for a general attack, given that his strong point is the camp," the lord predicted. "Fortunately, this will give you time to think. Remember this well: three days from now, when the night is burning, you must provide me with an answer," he warned sternly. "Fail to do so, and none of your men or their families will survive this war."

CHAPTER 4

TESTING THE WATERS

Korimor Castle

Inside a stone-walled chamber of Korimor Castle, a place that had witnessed countless strife, regime changes, and treachery, Lord Lansius sat alone, facing a stone table. A silver platter glistened in the midday sun streaming through the narrow windows. Despite the food situation, the staff had done their best to provide a savory menu for their new lord.

Carla stood guard. In Margo's absence, she had become the de facto food and wine tester. It goes without saying that living with the staff of a former opponent involved many risks.

Today marked the second day since Lansius's arrival in Korimor. Yesterday, he had met with envoys, which had resulted in a public flogging. He disliked the cruel punishment but understood its necessity.

His opponent, Sergio, was cunning and adept at scheming. The envoys incident proved that he could force Lansius to react against his will. Yet, that did not overly concern him. In war, cold calculation was paramount, and Lansius still felt he had the upper hand.

He carefully read the missive just delivered to him. It was from Omin, outlining his contingency plans against a siege. From this letter, Lansius learned a great deal. He had to admit that the man was a capable administrator.

Misguided, but capable.

However, he still harbored reservations about employing Omin. He felt the need for consultations with other lords in his alliance and his top retainers like Sir Justin.

Putting those thoughts aside, he shifted his attention to another report concerning grain rations and the new militia. Sir Michael had been invaluable in assessing the storage conditions and providing estimates, which helped Lansius greatly in understanding his real inventory.

Moreover, Sir Michael had also led a much-needed inspection of the grain storage as the traditional methods meant that the risk of mold was ever-present. In the face of scarcity, preventive measures were as important as rationing.

Time passed. Lansius yawned and stretched, feeling a deep ache in his bones from the exhausting marathon riding and nights spent sleeping rough. His buttocks and hips were still raw from the journey.

For days his only bed had been layers of rugs laid out in the open air. This harsh arrangement, coupled with the dusty environment, had led to a persistent shortness of breath, as well as a mild cough, and a sore throat.

Reflecting on it, the journey had been extraordinarily spartan. After departing from Korelia, they had spent several nights as guests in the yurts of nomadic tribesmen they encountered. Eventually, they rendezvoused with Sir Harold and Batu after days of traversing the northern corridor.

Batu was already prepared with his warriors and celebrated Lansius's arrival with a grand feast. However, beyond that point, there were no villages or yurts where they could seek shelter. Often this meant sleeping wherever they could find a water source, following eight- to ten-hour rides with frequent horse changes.

The journey was clearly excruciating. The only thing that gave Lansius solace was Audrey's resilience. As the more experienced traveler, she stepped in to care for him when he was at his lowest—prone to rants and easily irritated by everything around him.

Lansius glanced at Carla, who stood guard nearby. "Tell me, do you still feel pain from riding?"

"Just a bit, my lord," she replied.

"Ah, you're a tough one," Lansius complimented.

"Not at all, my lord. The baroness is even tougher. She resumed sword training this morning."

Lansius shook his head in disbelief.

Watching him, Carla continued. "It's as if the lady is pushing herself."

He raised an eyebrow. "Pushing herself?"

"Indeed, my lord. It seems she truly wishes to live up to your expectations."

"My expectations . . . ? Tell me, Carla, what are my expectations of her?"

Carla pressed her lips tightly together.

"Why do you hesitate?" Lansius asked, approaching the squire, who wore an embarrassed expression.

"It seems I've spoken too much, my lord."

Lansius chuckled, then moved to a red-cushioned daybed in the corner and slouched. No longer concerned about the ongoing gossip, he started to relish the bliss of ignorance. He had barely taken a deep breath when the door burst open.

Audrey entered, gulping from a water skin, clad in training armor she had found in the castle armory.

"My lady," Carla greeted.

Audrey waved her off and turned to Lansius. "I heard you've changed the plan?"

"Yes, I have a better understanding of the Nicopolan mindset. Our initial assumptions won't work," he explained, gesturing for her to sit beside him.

Audrey moved closer but remained standing. Lansius grabbed the water skin from her hand and drank slowly. The water burned his throat, a sign that he needed more rest and some honey.

"How's training?" he asked.

"Good. So, what's the new plan? I also heard you made some changes to the militia?"

"Nothing big," he reassured her, "I only removed able carpenters from the militia. I need to form a separate command for them, and I've placed them under Sir Michael."

"Mm, it seems you've given our friend from White Lake a lot of responsibilities."

"He's capable."

Audrey sighed and muttered softly, "Wish I could be of use . . ."

Lansius was surprised by the notion and turned to her, expecting a pout. However, Audrey simply looked back at him with a furrowed brow. "Why are you looking at me like that?" she asked.

To alleviate the awkwardness, Lansius coughed and then noticed something. "Drey, why are you still standing?" He motioned for her to sit next to him once again.

"I just trained," she replied, dismissing him.

"So? We often sit together after training."

"It's not as airy in here, and I don't want to trouble you with the smell."

"It can't be that bad," he argued.

"I also took care of the horses this morning, so I probably smell more than you think," she stated firmly.

Lansius chuckled. "I thought you hated me or something."

"Why would you say something like that?" she blurted out.

Sensing the atmosphere, Carla quietly moved toward the door.

After she left, Lansius whispered, "Why are you training so hard?"

Audrey hesitated before saying, "I'm revisiting my training from my master. I think she hid something in it."

"You mean she secretly trained you in magic?"

She shrugged. "I'm not sure, but some of her training methods are odd."

"Like what?"

"Like . . . oh, like this one." She sat on the ground, crossed her legs, and closed her eyes.

"I know what that is," Lansius said, recognizing the meditation sitting pose.

Audrey opened one eye. "Really?"

He nodded. "Does it have a name?"

"Not really," she mumbled and asked in return, "Does it lead to magic?"

Lansius rubbed his chin. "Not to my knowledge. Did your master tell you anything?"

"She said to focus, empty the mind, and feel the flows within you as you breathe."

Lansius continued to notice the similarity to meditation practices on Earth. "Tell you what, let me join you. Maybe we'll learn something from it."

While the lord and lady were winding down in the castle, the city bustled with activity. One thousand strong recruits were being trained. There wasn't enough space to gather them all, so training was being conducted in several locations. Hugo even had some of them marching on the battlements around the city to ensure their readiness.

Aside from the militia, the lord also commanded his retinue to gather all the able carpenters in the city and commissioned them to work on wooden structures. Although not complex, the sheer volume of the project was staggering. Two hundred carpenters and craftsmen labored intensely, depleting the city's timber stock in the process.

The woodcutters had also joined in, venturing beyond the walls to gather more timber. In the surrounding fields, people continued to collect hay. As work progressed farther from the walls, concerns about risks emerged. However, emboldened by yesterday's success, the people grew more daring.

There was a sense that the siege would soon be lifted and salvation was near.

In this regard, the carpenter took the lord's words to heart. The lord had emphasized that the better the structures, the more assured they could be of victory. Thus, they gave it their all. Luckily, the lord had requested simple but sturdy structures that were easy to construct and transport.

Finished parts were quickly loaded onto carts and readied for deployment. In addition, the lord had assembled a special team of a hundred people qualified for unique roles. Sir Michael was entrusted with their training, preparation, and instruction.

While work was underway, the Nicopolans unexpectedly marched out of their camp, steel glistening in the sunlight as it reflected off their spears, helmets, and armor.

The men on watch sounded the alarm, and riders were dispatched to warn those working in the fields to return immediately.

Nicopolan Camp

Truthfully, many mercenaries among the Nicopolans were reluctant to attack a walled city like Korimor. They lacked siege capabilities and had no desire to make the ultimate sacrifice.

Moreover, after the arrival of the Lord of Korelia, it seemed unlikely that the city would surrender. Many believed it would make more sense to negotiate for a portion of the harvest and depart peacefully. Even with their baggage train slowing them down on the mountain road, they could reach Nicopola safely before winter.

The journey was risky, but they had no alternatives. Camping in the open or in a hostile region like Lowlandia was out of the question. However, just that morning, Sergio had again urged everyone to seize the region by force.

In a fiery speech, he warned them to abandon the foolish hope that the city's lord would let them leave with any of his harvest. Sergio also stressed that even if they survived the journey home, they would face years of hardship and famine in ruined Nicopola.

In the end, Sergio pushed them to capture the city and claim the fertile lands around the hills. The Nicopolans, still fearful of facing another famine and allured by the prospect of finding an easy wintering spot, began to gather around his cause.

Without anyone daring to argue, Sergio swayed enough people that the rest had little choice but to follow. Thus, the Nicopolans prepared their weapons and donned their armor.

Under the midday sun, a four-thousand-strong Nicopolan force marched out. They assumed a wide formation and moved across the plains toward the city on the hill.

Their spirits were high, buoyed by the presence of Sergio and his elite, who were ready for an assault.

Korimor

Trumpets on the walls rang clear, alarming everyone in the city.

"An attack?" Audrey said, rising to her feet.

"Likely," Lansius replied, slowly getting up.

"You're expecting this?" she asked, suspicious of his lack of hastiness.

"Expecting?" He mulled over the words. "Well, it's within my expectations that they'll try to provoke us." Lansius walked to the heavy wooden table and shelved his notes as he spoke. "The Nicopolans don't have the capacity to conduct a siege."

"Meanwhile, we don't have the capacity to oust them," Audrey countered.

"A stalemate," he agreed.

She approached the table and cautiously suggested, "You know, the nomads might have a chance to make this work."

"Their camp is a fortified position. We'd lose a lot of horse archers to make it work," he stressed, then added, "I can't afford to lose them. It takes at least ten years to train a good archer."

"I sort of get that. Archery looks easy when they do it, but it feels unnatural when I try."

Lansius took a seat and waited patiently. Soon enough, a knock was heard at the door, and Carla entered. "My lord, enemy formations can be seen moving toward our camp outside the gate."

"How's the evacuation of the workers who ventured outside?" Lansius inquired calmly.

"I believe it's still ongoing, my lord."

"How many Nicopolans? Are all of them on the field?" Audrey asked.

"They say it's several thousand, but not all."

No chance to hit their camp . . .

"Well, I'd better check, just in case," Lansius said, rising to his feet. Audrey and their entourage followed him.

Lansius reached the battlements surrounding the city. Unlike in Korelia, here lush woodlands surrounded the hills before a sudden clearing some tens of meters from the wall. He glanced out, noticing the Nicopolan formation had advanced closer to the gate.

Hugo, who was also on the battlement, approached Lansius. "My lord, it seems we're under attack."

"Indeed. This Tarracan man is more than capable of sending people to their graves," Lansius replied grimly, and then added, "Can I trust you with defense?"

"Certainly, my lord. I believe you don't want me to chase?"

"Indeed. Let's not risk it. In time, Batu's scouts will notice and take action," he instructed.

Hugo quickly departed. Meanwhile, Lansius glanced at the city's interior. He saw hundreds of carpenters working and militias resting after training. Some looked up at him, and a crowd gathered below.

"I wonder what they think of me," he mused to Audrey.

"They'll think you a savior, if you can get them out of this situation," she responded.

"And if I can't?"

She took a deep breath and rested her hands on the parapet wall. "I'd rather not entertain such thoughts."

Lansius chuckled at her frank answer. Truthfully, the situation was worrying. While they could stay safe inside the walled city, that would only free the Nicopolans to harvest the field. His troops were also significantly smaller in number compared to the enemy, and unlike in the last battle, he lacked any advantage in crossbow numbers.

Furthermore, the wind in Korimor, as expected, was inconsistent. And with the Nicopolans camped close to the nearly ripened farmland, it was too risky to use fire.

Footsteps were heard from the staircase and soon a knight with a black eye patch ascended to the battlement. "My lord, my lady," he greeted gracefully.

"Sir Michael, you don't need to respond to the enemy's aggression. Please, continue your work," Lansius advised. He didn't want the preparation for the counterattack to be delayed.

"I understand, but I'm here to give a report," the knight stated his reason.

"Ah, then let's hear it," Lansius said, his mood brightening.

"The preparation is halfway complete. Currently, we're using some of the completed parts to train the militia."

"Well done." Lansius nodded, amused by the progress. "What about the supporting equipment?"

"The tools are ready. We've gathered enough sharp implements from the populace."

Lansius drew a deep breath, mulling it over, before suddenly announcing, "No changes then, we're on schedule."

Nicopolan Side

The Nicopolans under Sergio fought hard against the fortified camp outside the city gate. They opted to not storm the city outright, instead targeting a weaker position. Crossbow duels opened the battle before they grew close enough to switch to melee.

The lord's men countered the attackers' large numbers with wooden fences and a staunch, stubborn defense. Their crossbowmen on top of the walls played a major part in turning the tide against the Nicopolans. Whenever the Nicopolans focused their attack, the crossbowmen would loose their bolts to disperse the attackers, forcing them to take cover behind their shields.

The duel of crossbows continued, but due to the height advantage, it was a one-sided affair in favor of the defenders.

Attacking a well-fortified site was challenging, and the Nicopolans' daring attack achieved little. When their scouts alerted them of the approaching nomadic cavalry, they subsequently retreated.

Sergio allowed the Nicopolans to retreat in a disorderly fashion. He needed to bait Lansius's forces into chasing them. His entire strategy was to provoke a response and then fake a retreat to his camp, where he had hidden crossbowmen and his best men-at-arms.

It was a trap designed for the Korelians and their nomadic allies. However, the enemy's smaller force didn't take the bait. Disappointingly, the nomadic cavalry also halted their chase as soon as they noticed crossbowmen in the distance. Some became unlucky victims, but most escaped with their lives.

As a result, the Nicopolans suffered numerous casualties without achieving anything. The trap had failed, and Sergio led his men back to lick their wounds. Anticipating their shaky morale, he climbed onto a cart that formed part of their camp's makeshift wall. "Why do you look so dismayed?" he asked, addressing the returning troops. "This is not even a setback. It's all according to plan."

His claim attracted the attention of the men, who stopped to listen.

"Don't you dare take this as a loss. This is exactly what we planned for. There's no surefire way to win a war; otherwise, sieges would be over in a day," he said, glossing over the day's failure.

Sergio continued. "Believe me when I say we still outnumber them and are stronger than their combined might. Right now, the Lord of Korelia is trapped in Korimor. I bet he's busy trying to pack up and run."

His joke triggered laughter and mockery from the crowd.

"The more pressure we apply, the more likely he'll vacate the city and the castle. Soon, everything will be ours—warm bread, meaty soup, and clean shelter. Now, do you have the courage to endure?"

His men cheered.

"I ask again, do you have the courage to endure? There will be more challenges tomorrow and the day after," he warned them.

His men roared in agreement.

With just a single speech, Sergio effectively pacified his men. They would rest that night and mentally prepare themselves for another attempt the next day.

Sergio returned to his tent feeling genuinely excited about the challenge. Although he was generally short-tempered, he approached military matters with a cool head. To him, a strong defense was like a tough nut to crack. Today, he had observed several vulnerabilities in the Korelians' defense, particularly their reliance on reinforcements from the nomads.

That was something he could exploit and abuse.

He and the Nicopolans hadn't arrived here without struggle. They had experienced their own battles and challenges and had cracked tough defenses. That was why so many of these eight thousand people were loyal to him.

Sergio had seen enough of how the new lord operated his defenses. Enough to identify the nomadic cavalry as Lord Lansius's sole crutch, and tomorrow, he would cripple them.

CHAPTER 5

VEILED IN FLAMES

The tired and sleepy guardsmen rotated shifts as the night watch ended. Dawn had arrived, and the golden light breaking through the darkness marked the third day since Lord Lansius had set foot in the fields of Korimor.

Despite expectations, the lord still refused to sleep in the castle, choosing instead to spend the night in a humble cabin within his fortified camp just outside the gates. He aimed to keep his troops' morale high and reassure the people of Korimor that they were not completely under siege.

Inside the cabin, the lord and lady sat on a carpet on the floor, meditating. Although they had not gained anything from their previous attempts, they felt it was worth another try. After half an hour, they decided it was enough for the day.

Lansius munched on the breakfast bread Carla had brought them. After Carla had left, he asked, "So, did you feel anything?"

Audrey looked at her palm and shook her head. "I feel nothing has changed. Should I feel anything?"

Lansius chuckled. "You tell me. I've never been acquainted with a mage . . . no, wait. Technically, we know Hannei."

She shrugged. "But she hardly ever reveals anything about magic."

"Well, at least we're not tiring ourselves out," he quipped.

She found it funny and commented, "I guess I really do need a mentor."

Lansius whispered, "Are you thinking of accepting Sir Morton's advice?"

"Only if you feel that's the best course of action," Audrey replied.

Lansius nodded. "Let's discuss this when we have the time. Right now, we're stuck here."

Audrey nodded in agreement.

"But you should probably continue to do it," he suggested.

She furrowed her brow and asked, "Why? Is it beneficial?"

"Well, I read somewhere that it builds mental strength."

"Mental strength . . ." she mused. "Does it make me smarter?"

"Wiser," he corrected her.

"I'll do it, but only if you accompany me," she said, flashing a grin.

Lansius chuckled, acknowledging that meditation was easier said than done.

The two finished breakfast and went out to inspect the fences. There, the captains and lieutenants recounted the details of the battles. Even without their explanations, Lansius knew they had been hard-fought. There were many wounded and even some fatalities.

In the absence of Calub, Sir Michael was the one who kept records of the fallen and the wounded on their side. For an army to operate at its highest order, it was essential to record merits and compensate for bravery and sacrifice.

Lansius visited his men's camp and was pleasantly surprised by their whole-hearted welcome with big grins and jokes. Despite all the hardships and losses they had endured, the men remained optimistic.

Somehow, his troops had mastered mechanisms to cope with the violent nature of their business.

He was so impressed that he readily agreed when Audrey suggested ordering a keg of pale beer to be brought from the castle's supply as a reward. Immediately, the camp erupted into loud cheering.

Lansius then continued with his schedule for the day. He was inspecting militia training with objects newly made by the carpenters when the trumpets rang again. It dawned on them that another attack was imminent.

The men readily donned their armor and prepared their weapons. Meanwhile, Lansius and Audrey headed back to the battlements, their entourage trailing behind. There they met Hugo, who had been observing the situation.

"My lord," Hugo greeted.

"How many?" Lansius asked, observing the field outside.

"Almost the same, probably half of their numbers; some three to four thousand." There was plenty of concern in his voice.

Lansius felt the same and asked, "Do you need to take the levied men?"

"I'll take more of Korimor's guards for today. They're better trained."

Lansius nodded. Both understood that deploying the militia in high-risk battles would only result in senseless casualties. They would only consider such a move when their main combatants were at risk of exhaustion.

The rate of casualties and wounded was a significant concern for Lansius. Setting aside morale, he knew that his small force could not win a battle of attrition unless he retreated behind the city walls. However, doing so would cost him his strategic foothold and limit his ability to execute his plans.

Under no circumstances could Lansius afford to have his gate blocked.

"They're coming," said Audrey from his side.

Lansius squinted and saw the formations marching their way.

"If there isn't anything else, I bid my leave," said Hugo.

"I'll send for Sir Harold, Dietrich, and their men to assist you," Lansius promised.

"Gratitude, my lord." The deputy left to assume command for the upcoming battle.

Carla took a step forward and whispered, "My lord, are you sure about sending Sir Harold and Dietrich? Their men are your only protection inside the city."

"She's right," said Audrey. "I'm yet to fully trust the Korimor people."

"I've already given my word, and they're necessary to guarantee victory. Besides, at least I have you two at my side," Lansius said, and then sent a runner to summon Sir Harold and Dietrich.

Audrey sighed. "That kind of attitude will be fatal someday. Carla, please watch his back for me."

"Understood, my lady."

Lansius decided not to retort. Even he knew the risk.

Sir Harold and Dietrich arrived soon, and the two accepted the task after leaving ten select personnel as bodyguards.

With that settled, Lansius observed from the battlements as the battle unfolded.

The opening crossbow duel was fierce, and unlike yesterday, a part of the Nicopolans from the start aimed at the men on the walls, forcing Lansius and the rest to cover themselves with shields.

Underneath Carla's shield, Audrey commented, "This looks fiercer than yesterday's battle."

"The result might also turn out differently," Lansius responded.

"But Batu will also adapt and improve," said Audrey, kicking her crossbow's metal stirrup and reloading the bolt. She crouched, lined up her shot, and the crossbow jolted back as the bolt flew toward the target. By chance, her steel-tipped bolt struck a Nicopolan's loaded crossbow, causing it to break. The prod and string lashed out, knocking the crossbowman senseless while sending violent wooden debris flying around his vicinity. It caused a brief chaos before Nicopolans with big shields moved in to protect them from further attack.

"Good shot, my lady," Carla congratulated, while another bolt glanced against her shield.

"Gratitude, Carla," Audrey said, but then paused as she peeked at the horizon.

"What do you see?" asked Lansius, noticing her squinted eyes.

She looked at him. "Batu's cavalry is approaching."

Lansius rose to take a peek. "They're coming too fast. Are they trying to deter the Nicopolans from attacking? Did anyone relay such a message?"

"None. We would never dare to change strategy without consulting you," Audrey reassured him.

Lansius gazed at the enemy's formation; the fighting was brutal and loud. The Nicopolans were more committed than yesterday. It was hard to discern the mass of people even from above, and at first, he found nothing amiss. Meaning, the nomads' threat would once again force the Nicopolans to flee.

Then he was piqued by several groups of Nicopolans with long spears who were holding back from the fight.

Anti cavalry? But directed at our gates?

Lansius grew worried and glanced around, but his eyes couldn't find anything. "Get me someone with good eyes," he commanded.

Audrey volunteered while Carla called for her men to come closer.

"What are we searching for?" Audrey asked as two young men came up.

Lansius explained, "Go along the wall and look for groups of men hiding in the field, likely armed with long spears, pikes, or crossbows."

As the two ran along the wall, everyone else also joined in to help with the search.

"My lord, something glitters over there," one of the young men pointed out.

Lansius could hardly see anything, but Audrey's confirming nods suggested she had spotted something. He eyeballed the route the nomads would take to flank the Nicopolans and found the hiding groups conveniently placed in the middle. "They're aiming at the nomads!" he blurted out.

"By the Ageless," Audrey muttered, also realizing the extent of the ambush.

"Get me something to burn. Torches! We must send a signal," Lansius called out to anyone in the vicinity. Two men hurriedly ran toward the gatehouse.

"How about horns? Won't it work?" asked Audrey.

"Two signals are better than one," replied Lansius. He continued with instructions to the guards around him. "Gather a large cloth or some capes, along with spears and ropes."

As the men carried out his orders, Lansius confided in Audrey, "This Sergio guy got us. He's blocked our way out, so we can't send a rider to warn Batu and his cavalry."

Nomadic Tribes

Batu led his cavalry on a wide approach, not risking friendly fire from the on-edge Korimor defenders. He and his tribes had little love for this city. Yet, Lord Lansius had promised them that he would stop the raiding and slavery, and Batu placed his trust in him. The prospect of securing peace and vast grazing lands for the tribes was too beneficial to ignore, compelling him to shed blood once more under the blue and bronze banner.

Today, he and his one hundred and fifty cavalry—the real number of horsemen warriors he had—were en route to flank the Nicopolans. They were ready with their bows and had no intention of engaging in hand-to-hand combat. Their strength lay in horseback archery, aimed at softening the enemy and forcing them to retreat. He would only charge when the enemy was in disarray.

Unlike yesterday, they reacted sooner. Batu thought that Lord Lansius's small garrison would benefit from a shorter skirmish duration. He knew Lansius was planning something, and he intended to help keep the lord's troops fresh.

Riding with the wind around him, Batu and his men spotted a column of black smoke from the wall. The smoke confused them but didn't make them pause. They had seen the Nicopolans' formation and were busy chanting their war cries to pump their spirits higher.

Batu also heard a horn or trumpets from the wall and started to guess that something was amiss.

A fire? Did the enemy break through?

But the black smoke formed like small clouds, slowly rising to the sky. It wasn't billowing as it would if a wooden building were engulfed in fire. Batu shouted and signaled for his cavalry to slow down. He needed time to observe further.

Before all of his riders could react to his command, lines of men appeared out of nowhere from the tall grass, brandishing long spears and charging at them. Crossbowmen were also present, and bolts started to fly.

A rider in front shouted, "It's a trap!"

Batu responded instantly, "Spread out! Do not engage!"

His riders began to fall. Batu saw how the hiding Nicopolans had used dry leaves, grass, and dirt to prevent the sun from reflecting on their iron helmets and armor.

The nomads, in disarray, tried to fight back, leading to archery duels between the crossbowmen and the horseback archers.

The Nicopolans were ready with shields, while the nomads' horses—mostly without barding—were getting wounded left and right.

"Get them out, get them out!" Batu commanded his brethren. Some tribes were stubborn and hard to control; he and his tribes ended up galloping toward the separated groups to dissuade them from attacking further.

Bolts whizzed past Batu, narrowly missing him and his horse. Despite the imminent danger, he chose to be bold, racing against time as hundreds of enemies converged on their position.

He needed to pull his riders out; otherwise, everything would collapse.

Nicopolans Encampment

The Nicopolans successfully trapped and crippled the enemy's cavalry and Sergio was hailed as a victor. Although the skirmish failed to breach the enemy's defenses, the victory over the nomadic cavalry was seen as a significant breakthrough. Consequently, the threat of the enemy's horsemen was now greatly diminished.

They also recovered a dozen dead horses and butchered them for meat. Seizing the opportunity to galvanize support, Sergio distributed the roasted meat to everyone.

While meat from a dozen horses could hardly feed eight thousand people, and a large portion was cleverly allocated to Sergio's most loyal supporters, this act of generosity further emboldened his reputation.

The Tarracan man's reputation now eclipsed even that of the Black Lord of Korelia. Even survivors of the siege of Korelia began to support Sergio earnestly.

The Nicopolans ate heartily that day, sensing that victory was near. They believed the Lord of Korelia would soon pack up his belongings and leave the city for them to conquer at their leisure.

With the harvest at hand and a secure place for wintering, they had little to worry about this year.

For the first time in a while, many slept without worries in their dilapidated tents.

It was around the third watch, after midnight, when an eerie rumbling and hundreds of dots of light emanated from a distance. The Nicopolans awoke in a panic, scrambling to grab their weapons and don their armor in the dark. Slowly, they attempted to form lines around their camp as their superiors shouted commands.

As the Nicopolans scrambled to defend their encampment, the distant torchlight continued its rhythmic dance, growing larger and more menacing.

Sergio was finally awakened in his command tent and was angered by this unexpected development.

"Lights, hundreds of them," a scout reported immediately upon arriving, breathless from the east side.

Quickly donning his armor, Sergio headed out. Flanked by his men, he noticed the distant but approaching murmur of hooves against the earth.

"The nomadic riders again?" Sergio seriously doubted this could be the case. His trap had killed at least two dozen riders, which should have deterred them for good. It was well-known that the nomadic tribes lacked discipline and were even less committed to battle than mercenaries.

However, there was no denying the sound of hooves and the speed of the incoming riders.

"Cavalry!" shouted a captain, breathless and panicked as he spotted Sergio. "They've emerged from the darkness and are circling us—thousands of them!"

Sergio ignored the panicked captain and instructed his trusted lieutenant, "Wake the entire camp as orderly as you can." Then, turning to his other lieutenants who commanded the reserves, he added, "Don't get baited. Stay at the flanks. They'll want chaos, but let's give them a wall of pikes instead."

"Yes, Commander," they replied and dispersed to their separate commands.

Sergio looked up at the sky and found it was full of stars—a good night for a night attack. He climbed atop a carriage he used as a platform and looked beyond the perimeter of his encampment.

He saw hundreds of reddish-orange torches piercing through the fabric of the night. The radiant, fiery dots moved in one direction, slicing through the darkness as they danced. The sound, the sight, and the rumbling of it were otherworldly.

Feeling nervous about the size of the enemy force, Sergio made sure that his crossbowmen and pike-wielding infantry were ready behind the armed refugees.

"Hold your ground, and we'll win this," he said, rallying his men.

And thus, despite the confusion and fearfulness of the great spectacle before them, the men grew confident. The Nicopolans stood in line and maintained a large, almost circular formation. In a contest of wills, they stared down the thousands of riders who seemed ready to bare their fangs at them at any moment.

Meanwhile, on the opposing side:

"Sir, the nomads have encircled the Nicopolans," the lieutenant in charge of the lookout reported.

Sir Michael, caked in reddened mud, climbed the mound and confirmed the situation with his lone good eye. "Get the long torches out!" he commanded, and his men immediately sprang into action. They had been toiling in secret north of the city since sundown, working in near darkness save for the light from crudely made, one-sided lanterns with large covers.

This was the moment the thousand men—carpenters and militia alike—had been waiting for. With the nomads drawing the Nicopolans' attention, horse-drawn carts were now racing from the city gates to drop off their precious cargo. Time was running out; the nomads and their long torches would hold attention for only an hour, if not less.

With a steady stream of carts and the added illumination from the torches and lanterns, they worked quickly and diligently to finish the construction. Although it had only just begun to take shape, everyone present understood that they had reversed the flow of the entire conflict.

CHAPTER 6

WOOD SERPENT

Nicopolan Side

While many were awakened from their slumber in a state of panic, Servius awoke with a clear mind. Despite the pain from the broken skin on his back, tonight he was a man on a mission. With clear conviction, he strode through the darkness, a hammer in one hand and a lantern shrouded in damp, coarse cloth in the other.

The words from Lord Lansius echoed in his mind: "On the third day, remember to give your reply if you agree to my plan."

"How should I do it?" he had asked, to which the lord had answered, "Set aflame a small section of the camp, and I shall see it clearly."

Tonight, Servius planned to reveal his answer. It was risky, but he knew that living under Sergio's rule was equally dangerous. Moreover, Lord Lansius's plan hinged on Sergio's defeat. This meant that, aside from setting a fire, Servius wasn't taking on a big risk. His role was simply to lead as many people as possible into the forest once Sergio was overthrown. If this failed to happen, he would refrain from any action.

Steeling his old but stout heart once more, Servius walked with firm footsteps toward a specific location amidst the sea of tents. Approaching from the blind side, he saw a guard standing not far from a secluded tent, observing the thousands of riders circling their encampment.

He waited, observed, and found no one else in their vicinity. Setting down his lantern, he crouched toward the lone guard, who was entirely focused on the events outside the camp. The fiery spectacle and the thundering hooves were the last things on the guard's mind as Servius's hammer slammed into the back of his neck, breaking the spine.

The guard fell, dead. He'd had no chance. Servius wiped the blood on the dried grass and searched the body for keys but found none. Despite this, he entered the tent and faced the captured lady.

Lady Daniella stared at him from inside the cage and said, "I don't recognize you."

"There's not enough time. I promised Lord Lansius to go along with his plan, and I intend to free you so he may be more compelled to honor his part of the deal," Servius explained.

Daniella rose up. "Do you have the key?"

"Sergio must've kept it himself. I searched the guard, but he didn't have it."

"Then how do you plan to—" Daniella began, but Servius produced a pair of chisels and a smaller artisan hammer.

"It was hard to get these," he said, offering the smaller tools to Daniella, who grabbed them eagerly.

"Let me know if someone appears behind me," Servius instructed as he hammered the chisel against the area around the lock.

"Leave that to me," Daniella replied, working from the opposite side.

They attacked the sturdy wooden frame, chipping away little by little. Wood chips flew in every direction, and wood dust flew into their eyes, but they persisted.

After a long struggle, the frame began to show small cracks, and they redoubled their efforts. Even a cage designed to hold a beastman couldn't withstand two desperate humans with iron chisels and hammers.

The lock frame finally gave way, proving weaker than the reinforced frame on the opposite end that secured the heavy wrought-iron bolt.

Servius stepped aside as Daniella pushed the cage door open. It crashed to the ground with a satisfying thud. Without hesitation, Daniella rushed outside, pulling Servius along as they made their way to the darker, more concealed side behind the tent.

"Gratitude for getting me out," said Daniella weakly. "What's next?"

"It's best if we split up here," Servius replied, drenched in sweat.

"Understood. May I learn your name?" she asked.

"No, lest you get captured and tortured."

"Then we part here," said Daniella, who then stealthily walked toward the dead guard to take his hooded mantle and sword.

Servius moved slightly closer and whispered, "Be safe." He pointed in one direction. "The castle is over there, but the camp's weakest link is on the opposite side. Move quietly without a lantern, and they shouldn't notice you. Jump off the carts they used for barricades and crawl through the grass. With the nomads out there, I doubt they'll chase you, but beware of crossbowmen."

Daniella nodded. "Till we meet again," she said, disappearing into the night.

Satisfied that nobody had seen them, Servius returned to his hidden lantern. Seeing the small tallow candle still burning brightly, he began to set the remainder of his plan into motion.

Sergio

The unnerving scene of thousands of cavalry with torches circling and randomly attacking with arrows continued to unfold in the Nicopolan encampment. The attacking nomads brought no torches, surprising the Nicopolans with arrows from the dark.

This sneaky attack forced Sergio to instruct his men to be on guard at all times. Just when things seemed manageable, cries of "Fire! Fire!" erupted from the inner part of the encampment.

Many panicked, thinking the nomads had made a breakthrough. "Stay where you are!" Sergio shouted back. From atop a cart, he could see that only some tents were alight, not his precious supplies in the middle section of the camp, which was guarded by a separate command.

Returning to his men and lieutenants, he shouted, "Let them burn a few tents; I can replace them and make them better! Hold your ground. They want us to scatter. Let's not give them that satisfaction!"

His lieutenants readily ran to every section, relaying Sergio's orders. They were to keep their ground and let the non-combatants handle the firefighting.

The Nicopolans held on, despite the fire and the incessant attacks from the nomads. After an hour, the nomads' torches began to fade, and with them, their aggressive maneuvers. The tribal horsemen started to stray farther and farther away from the encampment. For a while, many Nicopolans feared a more severe attack was imminent. However, after several final volleys of arrows from the darkness, all went quiet.

Only then did Sergio rush a portion of his men to douse the fire. Another half hour passed, and it became clear they had survived the night. The Nicopolans rejoiced, as they were certain that the thousand nomads had disengaged.

Sergio remained cautious, but his men were convinced they had won this battle of wits. They thought not even the Black Lord of Korelia was invincible. Many believed their defenses were so strong that the nomads couldn't find a weakness to exploit.

Praise for Sergio's command echoed among the men. They began to mock the Black Lord as a mere upstart with black hair, considering him inferior to Sergio.

However, as the golden sun broke the darkness after dawn, the Nicopolans, with dreary and reddened eyes, began to realize they had been outplayed.

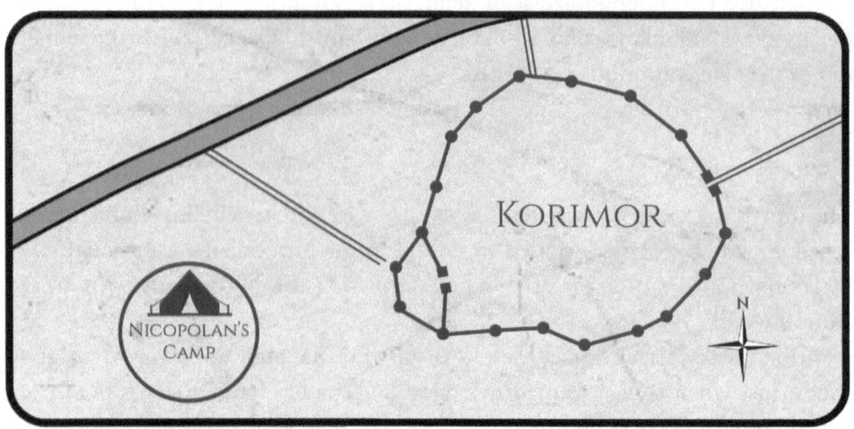

Battle of Korimor

It was easier to defend than to attack a fortified position—a fact well understood by both Lansius and Sergio. Initially, both sides had chosen to wait.

The difference was that Sergio could afford to wait indefinitely. He had access to water and nearly ripe farmland within his reach. The only factor that nudged him to engage in a minor skirmish was to bait Lansius into a decisive battle that would favor the Nicopolans.

Knowing this, Lansius did the unthinkable. Like Julius Caesar in the Siege of Alesia, he understood that results were everything. Thus, he took an unconventional approach, believing that adhering to conventional strategy would only squander opportunities for victory.

Armed with this mindset, and recognizing that the harvest, not the enemy's encampment, was the most crucial aspect of the campaign, Lansius decided to seize it.

Consistent with the strategy from *The Art of War*—when opponents are at ease, tire them; when resting, incite them to move—Lansius refrained from attacking Sergio's well-fortified camp. Instead, he brought a wall to their objective, forcing the Nicopolans to take action.

The long wooden wall, stretching from the castle to the river, protected a significant swath of Korimor's farmland from the Nicopolans. Just like the famed Sunomata Castle from Lansius's world, his wall was also built overnight using pre-constructed sections.

As soon as the construction began to take its shape, it presented a dilemma to the Nicopolans: attacking the wall meant incurring heavy casualties, but failing to do so would allow its completion, permanently denying them access to the farmland and its harvest.

Upon learning about the wall, Sergio was initially in disbelief, convinced it was merely an illusion. The idea that such an extensive wall, stretching from the city to the river, could be completed overnight was hard to fathom. It was simply an impossible feat of construction.

However, he quickly grasped the urgency of the situation. Soon, he prepared his troops, dividing them into three groups: The largest, comprising five thousand men, would assault the incomplete wall; a detachment of one thousand would protect the main army's flank; the remaining troops would guard their camp against potential raids.

He also formed a sappers group to start digging near the river, where the ground was softer, in case a siege was needed. Sergio even considered relocating his camp next to the river to minimize the risk of raids from multiple directions, but ultimately decided against it.

Understanding the stakes, Sergio allowed his men full rations for breakfast. Within an hour, the Nicopolans marched out, shields, spears, and crossbows at the ready, confident that their five-thousand-strong force could breach the hastily constructed and incomplete wooden wall.

Lansius

The lord had been present at the construction site since dawn. He knew his presence would boost morale and prevent a mass rout should the half-finished wall come under attack.

As the morning sun rose higher, both sides reached a critical juncture. Soon, they would learn if a thousand hastily trained militia, led by three hundred veterans, could withstand an assault by several thousand men.

At the moment, they were stockpiling spare spears and swords. They expected the battle to be hard. Unusually for Lansius, he had no crossbow superiority. Korimor did not have many crossbows or bolts stockpiled. While Hugo, and later, Lansius, had brought a fair number of them, they had expended many of them in previous skirmishes.

Hugo and Michael had tried to push for increased production and repair of recovered bolts, but it ran slower than expected due to a myriad of problems.

From atop the newly erected wooden tower, Lansius kept an eye out for signals from his scouts. Noting some activity, he acted on his instinct. Turning to Sir Harold, he commanded, "Stop the militia from their work. Let them have some respite, and bring in fresher men."

Harold nodded and relayed the order.

A man clearly couldn't fight after working all night, so Lansius had ordered them to work in shifts.

Now, the only ones still laboring were the seasoned carpenters who had pledged an oath to continue working until the site was overrun. Meanwhile, the rest of the carpenters were busy constructing another wall structure at a natural choke point to their rear.

While Lansius continued to observe the enemy camp, Hugo arrived with his men. He climbed the tower and greeted Lansius. "My lord."

"Hugo, I hope you and your men slept well, because today, I really need you all to put up a good fight."

The deputy nodded and took a moment to gaze around the site. Though the tower was only two stories high, it provided a good view of the surrounding area, which had been farmland until the previous night.

From their vantage point, it was evident that the wooden walls were not made of thick, sturdy logs typical of a proper palisade. Instead, they were assembled from timber, wooden planks, and various materials sourced from the town. These components were affixed to frames mounted on carts, forming a uniform, wall-like structure on one side.

Korimor's ample supply of horse-drawn carts made this strategy feasible. However, the extensive area to be covered meant there weren't enough carts to create a continuous line. Consequently, they were strategically spaced at even intervals.

Each cart was buried until half its wheels were deep in the ground, providing anchor points and foundations for these makeshift walls.

"What do you think—will the center wall withstand an assault?" Lansius asked.

"The training indicates it will," Hugo replied with conviction.

As they were discussing, another man climbed the tower. "Pardon my intrusion, my lord."

"Sir Michael. Do you bring reports for us?" Lansius asked with anticipation.

"Yes, the preparations are complete," said the knight with an eye patch.

"Including the gravediggers' work?"

"Indeed, my lord. They managed to do it."

Lansius sighed in relief as Hugo and Michael exchanged a firm hand clasp. The two had grown into close comrades.

"As planned, then," Lord Lansius said, with newfound strength. "Hugo will lead the defense at the center. I will hold the reserves. Meanwhile, our left and right flanks will be led by the baroness and Sir Harold."

Turning specifically to Hugo, he added, "I don't need to instruct you, but rally your men. Let them know that everyone must do their share in the fights, or Korimor won't stand a chance."

Hugo bowed his head slightly. "I shall relay your message and push them hard, my lord."

Having finished giving his orders, Lansius and Michael descended from the tower, leaving Hugo and his staff to use it for coordinating their troops.

Below, Lansius met up with his staff, as well as Lady Audrey and Sir Harold. He then instructed them, "Whatever happens in the center, stay true to your role. Do not, I repeat, do not worry about us in the center."

His firm voice struck a chord, their faces turning solemn.

"My lord, I shall take my leave," replied Sir Harold.

"Good hunting," said Lansius.

"Victory will be ours," said the tall knight confidently, and then he headed toward the right side near the river.

Lansius didn't need to rally his top retainers. Even before they had set out from Korelia, he had promised them a piece of farmland in Korimor as a prize for this campaign.

Audrey, already in her armor, looked at Lansius tenderly.

"I know, I'll be safe. Sir Michael, Sigmund, and the squires will be with me," Lansius reassured her.

"Sometimes I feel like I don't need to speak with you anymore."

Lansius broke into a smile. "Please don't feel that way. I love to hear your voice."

Audrey couldn't resist smiling. She took a step closer and whispered, "Don't exhaust yourself. Remember, this is not a fight worth dying for. We still have Korelia."

Lansius nodded. "I shall take that advice to heart."

Audrey took a deep breath. "I'll take command on the left side then. See you after this is over."

As they parted ways, Lansius and his remaining staff headed toward a tent in the middle of a farm. They were careful not to destroy the tall yellowing crops, keeping to a pathway between them.

"My lord, a question if you will," said Michael.

"What is it, Sir Michael?"

"Why don't you use ditches for this battle?"

Lansius could understand the origin of the knight's curiosity. "Digging deep ditches requires a lot of work and time. I doubt the Nicopolans would let us finish. But more importantly, there's the river," Lansius explained. "I fear they could easily dig a canal, connect it, and flood our trenches."

Trumpets rang out, cutting their conversation short.

"The enemy has made their move," Michael observed.

Lansius let out a bitter sigh. He had hoped that Sergio and his Nicopolans would hesitate for several hours, if not half a day. Unfortunately, his opponent was far more competent than he would have liked.

Too competent for their own good . . .

Lansius turned to the men who were following him. He scanned the faces of the squires and men-at-arms until he found the one he was looking for. "Sigmund," he called.

The skald stepped forward. "Is it time, my lord?"

Nicopolan Side

The six thousand Nicopolans marched toward the newly erected wall and stopped just short of the farmland. To advance farther would mean destroying the crops they had waited so long to harvest.

For people who had endured years of famine, the thought of trampling a field ready for harvest was unthinkable. Many began to question whether this was the right course of action.

Before their leader could urge them on, several riders emerged from the wooden wall direction, bearing a flag of truce.

The lead rider, clad in polished armor, shouted in a clear voice, "Hail, oh people of Nicopola! I bring words from the Lord of Korelia and the Lady of Korimor. All the farmland on this side of the wooden walls is yours to harvest. It should be sufficient to sustain you on your journey back to your home province."

The Nicopolans looked among themselves. Deep down, many wanted to believe it, but after the flogging of their envoys and last night's attack, they doubted the Lord of Korelia's sincerity.

Sergio observed his men with contentment; he was sure that speeches like this wouldn't sway them. He had done his preparation to steel their conviction.

The rider drew closer, his shield held tightly to his body. "Do not waste this offer. Stand down, and let us settle this amicably. Otherwise, there will be bloodshed. You cannot win. The Lord of Korelia has never been defeated in battle."

"Remove him from my sight," Sergio ordered, after noticing the subtle whispers, shaking heads, and confused looks among his ranks.

The rider persisted. "If you choose to attack, you'll be trampling your own share of the harvest. We won't be responsible for your hunger and death. I suggest you think this through. Do you want to cast your families into certain death just for your leader's glorious ambitions?"

However, this time, at Sergio's command, a group of crossbowmen rushed to the front, ready to fire.

"Nicopolans, is this your answer?" The rider bravely stared at them, still waiting for a response, but eventually gave up. He concluded with a cold threat. "So be it. You have made your choice. Your deaths are no longer our concern." He and his escort then retreated toward their wooden walls.

With that, the Battle of Korimor had begun.

CHAPTER 7

THE GRAVEDIGGERS' TRIBUTE

Nicopolan Side

The five thousand Nicopolans marched across the farmland, trampling crops that were almost ready for harvest. Slowly, they approached the wooden wall, shields at the ready.

As anticipated, crossbowmen from both sides opened the battle by exchanging volleys. However, the Nicopolans found themselves at a disadvantage, protected only by their own shields as opposed to the sturdy wall protecting their opponents.

Fearing he might lose the initiative, Sergio quickly issued the command to attack.

Almost immediately, Nicopolan forces attacked along the entire length of the wall. Scouts had informed them that the wall was not particularly tall, eliminating the need for ladders. Instead, they brought stacks of wood or crates to serve as makeshift climbing aids.

Although they resembled a disorganized swarm of ants, Sergio had strategically positioned his strongest contingent on his left side, near the river, targeting what he believed to be the enemy's weakest point.

He went to great lengths to ensure that, from above, the distribution of his troops would appear similar in number, effectively masking the significant differences in their fighting prowess. As an added diversion, Sergio concentrated a large number of his less-skilled troops to launch an assault on the center.

What they lacked in skill, they made up for in numbers, hoping to overwhelm the enemy.

Now, Sergio waited patiently with his reserves, his eyes level as he searched for any weakness in Lansius's defense. He considered three potential outcomes:

First, the walls nearest to the river could give way under the assault of his elite troops.

Second, the center line might buckle under the sporadic but intense attacks from thousands of men.

Third, the one thousand men he had left behind might successfully trap another flanking attack from the nomads.

If any of these events occurred, Sergio planned to unleash his reserves to decisively win the battle.

Hugo

The deputy and his men fought hard along the center wall. Clad in full plate armor, he struck out at anyone who dared to climb the wall. His footing was sure and firm, as the cart provided him a solid platform to move about. Spears or swords struck his head and shoulders several times, but this only angered him further.

Another wave of attackers approached, and Hugo rallied his men. "People of Korimor, this is your harvest! Your livelihood, the food for your families this winter—are you going to hand it over to them?"

Cries and shouts rose from the men around him.

"Stay with me! This is EASY!" Hugo ended with a forced laugh, mimicking a certain friend who used to boast like this in fights. "More harvest thieves are coming; let them know what Lowlandians do to thieves!"

With only five hundred men under his command, Hugo withstood the first wave of onslaught. He knew he just needed to wait and persevere.

Lansius

As the battle raged, Lansius was dispatching group after group to reinforce a portion of the wall that was in dire need of support. His reserves consisted of men still resting from their previous shift, but he had no other choice. With the Nicopolans deploying their vast numbers, sections of the wall were being overrun.

Before long, Lansius had exhausted his reserves, and he personally joined the fray to bolster their defenses.

He arrived at an overrun section with Sir Michael, Sigmund, Roger, and several other men. He watched as his men evacuated the wounded, leaving the dead and the gathering Nicopolans on the walls. The fighting continued, but the Nicopolans had enough numbers to assist as many men as possible in climbing over the wall.

Having a clear line of sight, Lansius stopped in his tracks, took aim, and pressed the lever on his crossbow. A bolt flew angrily through the air, striking an unsuspecting man in the back. The man turned in shock, his eyes widened with disbelief and horror, as he clutched his wound and stumbled away.

Lansius's attack prompted Sir Michael to charge forward with a spear. His thrust felled the swordsman who had challenged him. At his side, Sigmund lunged and swiftly dispatched another who had hesitated, with two precise strikes from his sword.

The fresh commotion, coupled with Lansius's personal banner being waved by one of his men, quickly drew attention. In no time, dozens of warriors from both sides converged on their position.

"I'll be fine, take them down," Lansius commanded the men around him, who sprang into action.

Lansius lowered his visor and readily engaged as his side was outnumbered. He squared off with a man whose eye sockets were sunken from hunger. Instinctively, he countered the man's reckless swing, feeling only meager resistance. With a calm breath, Lansius intercepted the next desperate strike with a deft parry, stepped forward, and drove his sword into the man's chest.

The man's wet and dirty gambeson soon turned an ochre color. He writhed in pain, but Lansius knew better than to let his opponent die an agonizing death. Gritting his teeth, he swung his left gauntlet into the side of the man's head, ending the pain in an instant.

He felt no regret, only the pain of necessity as he killed. In one swift motion, Lansius pulled out his bloodied sword, took one deep breath, and walked to the next assailant, poised to flank Sir Michael's blind side.

Using both hands, Lansius gripped his sword like a polearm and charged. The Nicopolan's eyes widened in realization, but it was already too late. Despite the man's futile attempt to block with his arm, Lansius's thrust found its mark, sliding into the man's chest near the armpit.

The man groaned loudly as the sharp point of the blade punctured his body. Within a few breaths, he began choking on his blood. Sir Michael came from the side and struck the man's head with both hands using the pommel of his sword, granting him a quick death.

"My lord—"

"Focus on the fight!" yelled Lansius to reassure him.

In front of them, Roger fought as if he were dancing, parrying, and countering with smooth, non-wasteful movements against multiple opponents. His armor, a plunder from the previous war, was bathed in red as he felled another man with a slash to the face. The man fell in complete agony, losing his nose and the soft tissues around it.

The squire wanted to deliver a coup de grâce, but more men were approaching him with spears and bardiches. Roger fell back, while Sir Michael and Sigmund readied their stances to protect their lord. Fortunately, the Korimors returned to the fight, invigorated by the sight of their lord in combat.

They soon clashed and regained the upper hand. Hugo must have noticed the fight, as crossbow bolts began raining down on the section in front of the wall. Soon, the Nicopolans who had climbed were all but slain to the last man.

It was unfortunate that in such an uneven battle, they couldn't afford to take hostages.

"My lord," called Sir Michael, excitement in his voice. "Our opponents' gambesons are soaking wet. Our plan is working!"

Lifting his visor, Lansius noticed the wet mud stains all over the slain men's clothing and boots. "So, the gravediggers have done it," he remarked gratefully. Humble as they were, the hundred strong gravediggers had proven their craft and worth.

Sir Michael proceeded to rally the Korimors around them, while Lansius retreated to the rear.

On the way, he flicked his sword to shed the excess blood. His heart felt numb, but his mind was briefly filled with silent prayers for the fallen. Memories from the Battle of Korelia and of Sir Callahan surfaced in his mind. There was no guilt, only the heavy weight of responsibility for the men under his command.

Lansius knew he wasn't fighting for himself. He was fighting for the people of Korimor, Korelia, and the entirety of Lowlandia. Only by securing victory here could Lansius move forward with his Grand Alliance, to usher in peace and stability throughout Lowlandia.

It was a future they had fought so hard for—a future where all Lowlandians, including him and Audrey, could live in peace.

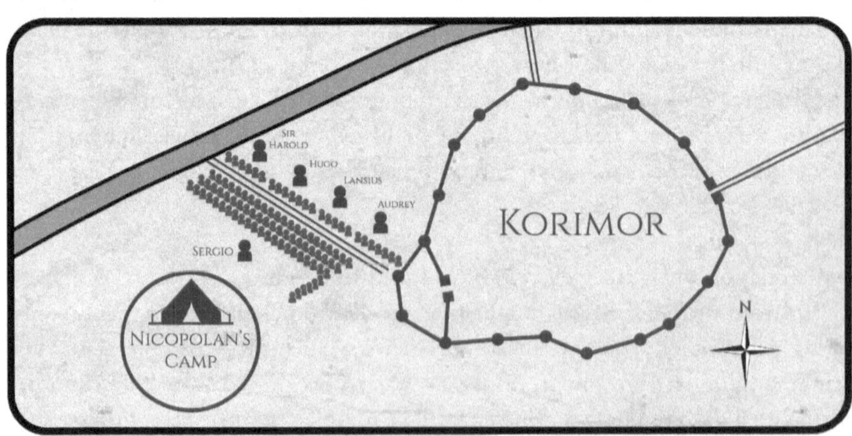

Nicopolans Side

The Nicopolan left wing had launched their assault on the far side near the river. Comprised of select groups of mercenaries, they fought hard to scale the walls, using logs and crates to aid them. However, the muddy ground proved more difficult than they had anticipated.

Contrary to Sergio's prediction that this would be the weakest point, they found it staunchly defended by knights in full plate armor, a healthy number of men-at-arms, and plenty of levied troops.

The rain of crossbow bolts was also fierce, pinning them down whenever it was unleashed. They fought in waves, attempting to breach multiple defense points simultaneously, but the muddy terrain hindered their progress and made everything slippery.

Still, they proved their worth by rallying on their captain and redoubling their efforts. Like torrential rains, the best of the Nicopolan mercenaries stormed the walls, chipping the defenses little by little.

Sergio noticed his assault was beginning to bear fruit. Several sections of the wall were overrun, and things were going better than he had expected. He had almost decided to commit his reserves to attack when progress suddenly slowed.

Initially, he hardly noticed, but then the advance ground to a halt. Gone were the energetic attempts to scale the wall. In their place were men, exhausted and caked in dirt and mud, failing to climb after encountering strong resistance at the top.

"Get the scouts! Why haven't I been briefed?" Sergio yelled to his staff.

Pulled by one of the staff, a scout hastily reported, "Some of the farms appear to be muddy. We suspect it's leakage from the river since the farms haven't been maintained."

Growing suspicious, Sergio decided to head to the front lines. As he drew closer, the air was thick with tension. Cries of command, words of encouragement, and the screams of men fighting with all their might filled the air.

His bodyguard helped him wade through the thousands of men waiting for their turn to climb. Suddenly, Sergio felt the ground soften beneath his feet. He stopped in his tracks, and his men quickly raised their shields around him.

Kneeling, he scooped up a handful of mud and realized it wasn't normal. He glanced at the yellowing crops around him; they showed no signs of long-term water submersion, which would have caused them to wither.

Squeezing the mud, Sergio realized it wasn't totally soaked, meaning it was recent.

"No . . ." he muttered under his breath, recognizing that his adversaries had likely altered the irrigation canals the night before. When the Nicopolans refused to back down, the enemy must have breached the canals connected to the river.

With the help of the existing irrigation system and the river's powerful current, the field on the Nicopolan side was effectively flooded.

Sergio saw his men struggling to trudge through the claylike mud, slipping and being hindered by its clinging to their limbs and armor. Worse, once they slipped and fell, their gambesons made of linen would absorb a lot of water and weigh them down considerably, further taxing their strength and stamina.

Frustration boiling over, Sergio wanted to scream, but he held back, aware his lieutenants were watching. Pushing aside his shaken emotions, he motioned for his lieutenants to approach.

He saw their young, eager faces and commanded, "Commit more groups! We can't let the attack falter. Send them in, send all we got!"

His young, brave Nicopolan lieutenants puffed out their chests and saluted, ready to obey. Meanwhile, Sergio's hands trembled. A pang of guilt and regret pierced Sergio as he sent them into the fray, but he knew he had no other option. If he didn't secure victory today, another opportunity might never come, and rallying this mass of people again would be near impossible.

Under the command of the young lieutenants, the assault boldly resumed.

Ingenuity suddenly struck the Nicopolans: Some began cutting the abundant crop stalks around them and throwing them into the mud to create better footing. The dried stalks absorbed water, and their coarse fibers acted like a fine, woven organic net. Seeing this, more troops followed suit, and the lieutenants ordered everyone to do the same.

"What are they doing?" Sergio asked in awe as the assault regained momentum and fighting erupted again along the wall.

Knowing this was the moment he had been waiting for, Sergio ran toward the rear of the formation to reach his reserves.

"Sergio, have you found the enemy's weakness?" his captain inquired.

"Soon," Sergio promised. "Now, ready your men. We either ride the wind of victory or die trying."

His captain, an old mercenary comrade who was fiercely loyal, grinned. Facing his men, he shouted "Men, ready to march! On my order!"

The horn-blower played an excited tone, repeated twice. Soon, another thousand battle-hardened Nicopolans marched toward the battlefield, trying to keep the scales tipped in their favor.

Lansius

The previous night, a group of gravediggers and farmers had been sent to alter the irrigation on the farmland opposite the walls that were being constructed. The job normally required many men and several days of work, but the gravediggers, with their sharpened tools, managed to complete it in just one night.

The plan worked superbly. After the initial two attack waves, the mud began to form in earnest, and the subsequent wave struggled, due to the slippery, clay-like mud. As the Nicopolans slipped and fell, the layers of linen in their gambesons or padded jackets greedily took on water and doubled in weight, making it especially exhausting just to move around in it.

"Just like Agincourt," Lansius muttered as he observed from a recently secured section of the wall. The quagmire that had formed on the Nicopolan side was clear for everyone to see.

The only difference is this ground wasn't freshly ploughed.

By flooding the area, he had not only stalled the enemy's attack but also trapped Sergio into either fully committing or retreating with significant loss.

"My lord, the runners from every section report that they withstood the attack," Sigmund reported.

Sir Michael chuckled, satisfied with how the battle had progressed.

"I hope our enemy will fall back. There's still remaining farmland for them to harvest," Lansius said to his staff.

"I believed that's the wish of many, my lord," Sir Michael expressed.

Lansius was about to leave his section and tour the rest of the wall when Roger called out, "My lord, the Nicopolans. They're doing something . . . they're fixing the mud."

Fixing the mud . . . ?

Lansius was stunned. "Is that even possible?" he asked, then looked to where Roger was pointing his hand.

After a brief observation, Lansius drew a heavy breath and shook his head. Many Korimors interpreted this as a bad omen, and their faces were immediately painted with concern and worry.

Noticing them, Lansius spoke. "Men, don't be so disheartened. In war, nothing ever goes as planned. There are always variations, which is why we make plans in the first place." He then added, "Even this is within my expectations!"

His words emboldened his men, especially the Korimor people, who looked at him with reverence. "My lord, please lead us to victory!"

"My lord, please save Korimor!" The soldiers' voices cracked with desperation, each man thinking of home and family.

Taking a rare moment, Lansius gestured for them to quiet down. He removed his helmet, looked at them with his deep brown eyes, and declared, "If you swear an oath of loyalty to my House, I promise you a victory that neither you nor your grandchildren will ever forget."

CHAPTER 8

THE REDDENED REAP

The battle had raged for an hour when the Nicopolan vanguard finally breached the Korimor wall defense. In an attack that exceeded expectations, the young Nicopolans demonstrated both ferocity and tenacity, shaped by their survival of numerous life-and-death conflicts arising from recent famines. Meanwhile, the men of Korimor displayed their stubbornness, hardened by generations of strife in war-ridden Lowlandia, but they were clearly outnumbered.

Lord Lansius's wooden walls, built atop half-buried carts, served as a formidable equalizer. His strategy of using existing irrigation channels to flood the area in front of the wall was a masterstroke; however, it wasn't enough.

Now, the three wooden platforms that the Korimor side had used as crossbowmen platforms were overrun and being captured. Despite their best efforts, they failed to contain multiple breaches in their defense, and soon more than a third of the center wall section was overrun.

Watching the Nicopolans fierce advance, the Lord of Korelia finally gave the order. "Blow the horn."

Deep, resonating trumpet blasts filled the air, echoing repeatedly. Horn blowers atop the city walls amplified the command, ensuring all defenders heard the directive.

In the thick of battle, Hugo recognized the dreaded signal: a call to retreat.

His lieutenant and fellow men-at-arms' faces obscured by visors, glanced his way, filled with questions and anticipation. Lifting his visor, Hugo shouted grimly, "Halt, halt!"

The troops instinctively tightened their formation, brandishing their weapons defensively. Cold sweat and fear struck deep into their souls.

"Remember your training!" Hugo commanded, capturing their attention. Methodically, they began to step back, pulling in any stragglers to form a solid spear line.

To the Nicopolans, it looked as though they were watching a hedgehog curl into a protective ball. Impressed by the Lowlandians' discipline, they opted not to engage and instead took the chance to catch their breath. With the immediate threat gone, they fully realized their exhaustion; their limbs felt heavy, burdened by the weight of their soaked clothes and gambesons.

Some turned to scavenge from fallen comrades and enemies for knives, helmets, dry boots, or waterskins, while many others tended to their wounded, if only to be present in their dying moments.

The rising sun intensified everyone's thirst. Many even considered drinking from the muddy puddles that seeped through the gaps in the wall, regretting that they had left their waterskins behind during the ascent.

However, the lull was short-lived. Once the young Nicopolan lieutenants had caught their breath, they started issuing commands to form a line.

They had no banner, but enforcers armed with wooden clubs began making rounds to ensure compliance. The thousands who had scaled the wall and were not tasked with dismantling it, slowly formed up.

Once the Nicopolans had amassed, their vast numerical advantage over the defenders became evident.

On the Korimor side, despite their impressively orderly retreat, the situation looked dire. They had lost their makeshift wooden walls, their most significant defensive asset in today's battle.

Meanwhile, for the hundreds of mercenaries who had fled from the battle of Korelia, this initial victory felt like the breaking of a powerful curse. It appeared that the reputation of the once-feared Black Lord was finally waning.

Lansius

The remaining Korimor men hastily abandoned the wall and retreated a hundred paces back. The morale took a plummet, but Lansius was grateful that there was no rout. The Korimor people under his command had proven to be courageous. Despite all the threats and the major loss, they still followed his orders faithfully.

Lansius saw Hugo approaching and gestured for his men to make way. Everybody in the center was now converging on his banner.

"My lord." Hugo greeted him with an open helmet. He was drenched in sweat, his armor had new dents and was stained in various places.

"How's things on your end?" Lansius asked.

"I apologize that the center line failed." His voice held bitter regret.

"Nonsense! You and your men fought courageously. Lift your chin, I expect nothing less than a proud face," Lansius declared to everyone in general. "Now, tell me about your men. Did you manage to disengage safely?"

With renewed confidence, Hugo reported, "We managed to form a wall of spears. No desertion."

"Excellent . . ." praised Lansius, without sounding excited.

"But how about on the other sector?" It was Hugo's turn to ask.

Lansius turned to one of his lieutenants, Sigmund, who reported, "The left and right wings are holding. They're outnumbered but able to form a defense independent from our center."

Hugo nodded thoughtfully, his respect for the other two commanders visibly renewed. He then looked back at Lansius. "My lord, I understand that you have prepared for this eventuality."

Around them, everyone could see the bundles of cloth and ropes scattered about, previously used to pack shields and spears. Drinking water and temporary medical aid were also present.

Lansius held his response, wanting to see where Hugo was going with his words.

"But is this truly sufficient? Shouldn't we consider evacuating?" Hugo continued, likely feared that the left and right wings could become ensnared.

"I've called upon Batu and his riders," Lansius replied, alluding to a contingency plan they'd discussed.

Hugo's worry seemed to deepen, a concern Lansius noted was well-founded: A mere hundred cavalry wouldn't be able to mount an effective counter inside the farmland. Lansius knew others doubted his willingness to sacrifice his crops. However, before anyone could voice their thoughts, yells from the opposite side indicated that the opponent had made their move.

Korimor born, Walter

With fifty years under his belt, thirty of which were spent in multiple battles, Walter and the other townsfolk believed they had seen it all. But watching a lord lead a battle and personally fight alongside common men was nothing short of spectacular.

The lord had dispatched his knights and men-at-arms to reinforce other sections of the walls, leaving himself without a regiment of knights for protection. Beside him stood just a lone knight, two squires, a bannerman, and several fighters.

Yet, this did not convey vulnerability. Instead, it fostered a deep sense of camaraderie and inspired all who saw. Here was a lord willing to shoulder the same risks as the commoners fighting beside him, a leader who stood his ground, even when the odds turned against him.

Lord Lansius had demonstrated his mettle by plunging into the heat of the battle, leading his small group against the Nicopolan vanguard at various points along the walls. Naturally, wherever his banner went, the Korimor men flocked to it, rallying around their leader.

Like the other people of Korimor, Walter had never expected outsiders to bleed for them. They were accustomed to being treated as mere commodities by conquerors, to be used and discarded on a whim. Thus, witnessing Lord Lansius and his entire retinue—including the baroness—take an active role in the city's defense was nothing short of a revelation.

Previously, many had expected the new lord to loot the treasury and flee. Instead, over the past few days, they had worked tirelessly to establish a solid defense. This image was further reinforced by tales of how the lord had ridden to the point of illness to come to the city's defense.

When most of Korimor had resigned themselves to the overwhelming Nicopolan forces, it was the lord's undying conviction in victory that reignited the people's will to fight.

What the lord had done during his brief tenure was unmatched in the war-torn region known as Lowlandia. For centuries, it had seen only wars, occupations, and rebellions, orchestrated and fought by countless usurpers and power-hungry tyrants. There had never been a true champion of the people.

Walter and the Korimor populace realized that although their lord, lady, and knights had much to gain from holding Korimor, there were simpler methods to benefit from the city without facing the vast Nicopolan army. One such strategy would be to burn the harvest, thereby denying the Nicopolans its yield.

Such a choice would starve the people of Korimor in hopes of driving the Nicopolans away—a tactic other lords would employ without hesitation. Thus, witnessing the lord's efforts to preserve the harvest endeared him to the people.

This was why, even in the darkest hour, Walter and his comrades refused to flee. They were determined to stand by their champion until the bitter end.

When the Nicopolans finally resumed their attack, the Korimor men held firm. Brandishing their spears and shields, they roared their battle cries and fought fiercely for their families, livelihoods, and a lord worthy of their loyalty.

From the elderly to young warriors, they traded thrusts and lunges of their spears against the more numerous Nicopolans. But passion alone couldn't substitute for numbers in battle, and casualties began to mount.

"Arghh!" Walter cried as a spear slipped through. The steel-tipped spear penetrated his gambeson. At first, it wasn't too deep, but as he staggered and tried to wrestle the spear out, his opponent thrust it deeper, causing Walter to bleed profusely.

The opponent withdrew the spear, and Walter dropped to a knee. His comrades to his left and right, locked in combat, were unable to assist him. Strength drained from him as he gasped and clutched the searing, stinging wound.

Amidst the yelling, screaming, and clash of swords and spears, Walter's thoughts drifted to his family. Trapped between two forces who brandished barrages of spears above him, Walter saw no hope. He felt his time drawing near.

Amid the pain, a smile formed on Walter's lips, still defiantly wishing for Korimor to emerge victorious.

Suddenly, he sensed a change in the air. Even in his weakened state, Walter noticed a distinct shift in the Nicopolans' ranks. Their formation began to crumble, their spear thrusts lacked weight and ferocity, and their shouts became sporadic and confused.

The tide was turning.

With a laugh and a deep breath, Walter mustered what strength remained. He reclaimed his spear, discarded his shield, and gripped the weapon with both hands. He found strength in his legs, and with a great roar, lunged at the enemy one final time.

The Nicopolan Vanguard

The young Nicopolan lieutenant watched in shock as his friend collapsed in front of him, his thigh pierced by a low thrust. Like him, his friend was just months away from turning twenty. But now, he would be forever nineteen as his face turned pale from blood loss.

Meanwhile, the perpetrator died with a satisfied expression.

What kind of monster is able to inspire a man to this degree?

But the lieutenant had little time for contemplation as another volley of ranged attacks rained down on their position. He shielded himself, fortunate to be spared, but another beside him fell, an arrow protruding from his shoulder.

Recognizing the long, slender shaft, he realized it wasn't a bolt. "Arrows! It's the nomadic bowmen!" he shouted, trying to warn his men.

Many hadn't carried their shields or had lost them, leaving them vulnerable to ranged attacks. And unlike crossbowmen who reloaded slowly, bowmen could release a rapid succession of arrows.

Panic spread among his ranks. "They have nomadic archers!" one cried, echoing the sentiments of others as they began to see whether they were allowed to retreat.

"Lieutenant, the men can't withstand this anymore!" his enforcer shouted, after enduring a relentless volley of arrows.

Before the lieutenant could respond, he felt a sharp impact on his mouth, knocking him backward. Blood poured from his mouth, his front teeth now missing, and an arrow was lodged deep in his throat. He could only gurgle in pain, his body writhing in agony, much to his men's horror.

His closest men and the enforcer tried to assist, but a rout had begun. And they were in no condition to care for anyone but themselves.

The two friends were left lying side by side, neither having reached twenty under the sun.

As the Korimor side began their counter-push, the Nicopolan vanguard hastily retreated to the wall while scavenging for shields or even helmets as protection.

Lansius

While the first part of his strategy failed to deter the opponent, the second phase successfully divided the Nicopolans' strength. Treating the wall as if it were a river, Lansius allowed a segment of the Nicopolans to cross, only to mete out heavy punishment once they had ventured far enough.

Lansius was baiting the enemy into the perfect killing zone. Separated from the main force, the Nicopolan vanguard, though numerous and aggressive, ultimately lacked support from their main army.

The Korimor men, with their phalanx-like formation, successfully kept the Nicopolans' advance in check while the newly arrived archers began their volleys with their famed recurve bows.

By integrating nomadic archers on foot into his line, Lansius had transformed the Nicopolans' numerical superiority into a weakness to be exploited. Here, the opponents had nowhere to run, and their retreat was blocked by walls.

While Batu had just over a hundred horse archers remaining, nearly all his tribesmen were proficient with bows. As a result, he could field two hundred bowmen on foot. Their sure footing made them even more accurate and deadly.

Facing such a densely packed enemy formation, even the younger, less-skilled archers found it easy to land damaging shots. Batu personally positioned himself among the Korimor formation, targeting and eliminating the opposing group leaders and commanders, instilling fear in the heart of the Nicopolan vanguard.

Before long, the Nicopolan vanguard reached their breaking point. Their formation collapsed, and they sprinted toward the wall.

The wall, which they had fervently attacked, again became their obstacle to escape. In a panicked frenzy, they scrambled to climb over it. With the chain of command in disarray, they failed to form any resistance. Many were either too exhausted to fight or paralyzed by fear of the nomadic archers, choosing only to flee.

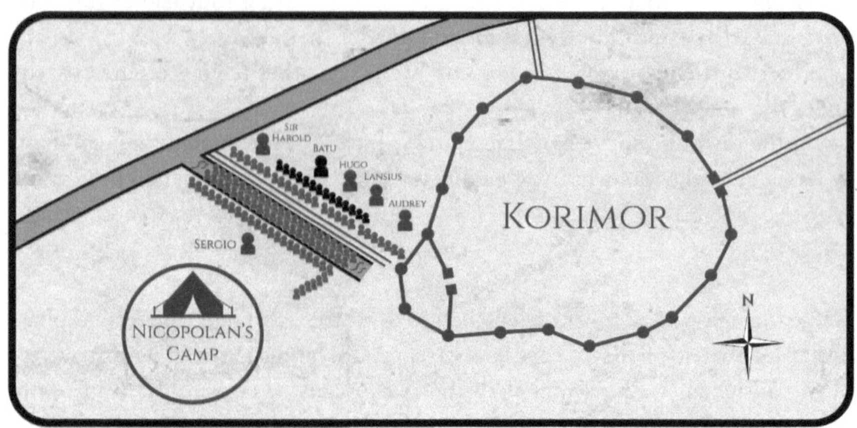

Lansius ordered his troops to pursue. While he didn't relish the slaughter, he had no other way to secure victory. Without hesitation, he commanded his men to inflict maximum damage upon the enemy.

A one-sided fight erupted near the wall, with Nicopolans perishing in large numbers to the relentless archery volleys they couldn't counteract.

In addition to Batu and his nomadic archers, Lansius accepted reinforcements from the city. Youths capable of wielding arms rushed to assist, having observed the battle from the city walls. To them, the fighters weren't faceless grunts, but kin—fathers, brothers, cousins, nephews, and uncles.

Lansius directed these newcomers to retrieve as many arrows and bolts as possible. Taking the field again, he readied his crossbow, helping to maintain pressure on the beleaguered Nicopolans as they desperately tried to escape.

The deafening screams and deaths from ranged attacks shattered the Nicopolan vanguard's morale. Meanwhile, the Korimors regained their momentum.

In a last-ditch effort, the Nicopolans managed to form a shield wall, but they were quickly challenged by Hugo and his veteran men-at-arms. Despite the line of shields, Batu downed another foe with his archery, while Lansius's bolt struck into an unfortunate man's exposed gut.

Still, the Nicopolans were a hardy people. Some of the fresher soldiers, having just scaled the wall and yet to engage in combat, rallied to lead a charge toward where the lord's banner flew.

Shit, I put too much pressure . . .

Lansius realized that cornering the enemy too hard would drive them to fight desperately in a fight-or-die scenario. But he had no time for regrets as he aimed and released his final bolt, striking down an approaching man clad in ringmail. Yet, this was just one of many advancing toward him.

Sir Michael, Sigmund, and Roger readily put themselves on the line, confronting those who preferred to die fighting rather than be hunted down like animals. With the support from the men of Korimor, they successfully halted the Nicopolans' advance.

After an intense bout of combat, which left Roger injured, the Nicopolans' will to fight waned, following significant losses. Despite their courage, they ultimately paid for their recklessness with their lives.

"Sigmund," Lansius called out, as the fighting waned around them. The skald retreated to his side, panting and drenched in sweat, clutching a pilfered enemy shield. Lansius confided in him, "Have I spilled too much blood?"

"No, my lord," Sigmund replied. "Perhaps we'll need to do even more to convince them to leave the region."

Only now did Lansius understand what Henry V must have felt during the famed Battle of Agincourt. Facing a significantly larger force, despite gaining an advantage, the English monarch ordered the killing of prisoners and hostages, out of fear that they might re-arm and join a potential counterattack.

Lansius faced a similar dilemma. Having barely recovered from the brink of being overrun, he lacked the manpower to properly guard a large number of prisoners. Moreover, unlike high-valued knights, nobody wanted to take the Nicopolans, mere refugees, as hostages, as they presented no incentive for ransom. Worse still, if another major assault occurred, the prisoners could re-arm and rejoin the fight.

A young boy, no older than twelve, approached Lansius from the side, holding four retrieved bolts. His helmet was comically oversized for his head, but his enthusiasm was unmistakable.

"Gratitude, boy," Lansius said. The child responded with an angelic smirk and hurried away to recover more bolts.

As Lansius reloaded his crossbow, he found himself wondering how a boy so young could stomach all the carnage that had unfolded around them. Turning to Sigmund, he confided again, "If I've taken too many lives, tell me. I don't want to be a mass murderer."

Sigmund quipped, "If that day comes, I'll gladly take that title from you, my lord."

Despite the grim situation around them, Lansius let out a chuckle.

The skald continued. "To be honest with you, my lord, you warned them. You knew your capabilities and tried hard to prevent this tragedy. Yet, they ignored your warnings. Now, they must realize they feared the wrong man. This Tarracan man's leadership must fail, or our situation will never improve."

Lansius took a moment to survey the scene, noting that many of the yellowing crops now had a shade of deep red ochre, tainted by the spilled blood.

He took a deep breath and patted Sigmund's shoulder. "Let's retake the wall while we still have the chance."

Soon, the trumpets rang excitedly. The order for general attack had been cast.

CHAPTER 9

COLLAPSING LINES

Sergio was in deep denial upon learning that his vanguard had been pushed back from the wall. He heard reports of nomadic archers being deployed over the wall. "How strange," he pondered aloud.

His words drew his staff's attention. Sergio continued. "If the opponent had their bowmen at the ready from the start, shouldn't they have rained arrows down from the walls?"

The staff members could only knit their brows in confusion. They, too, found it puzzling. Defending the wall with bowmen would have been a huge advantage.

"A lapse in judgment from the opponent's leader?" one ventured.

Sergio nodded. There was another reason, but he refused to acknowledge it. "This is nothing but a desperate move," he asserted. "Our opponent panicked after we drove them from the wall and called for any reinforcements they could get. It just so happens that the nomads answered his call."

His staff nodded in agreement, their earlier confusion vanishing.

"Do not be deceived. It's time to commit the next wave. We need to send more men before they push us back from the wall," Sergio commanded.

His orders were swiftly relayed, and the Nicopolans continued to muster column after column to the wall, oblivious to the worsening situation.

However, the men weren't blind. As their terrified comrades retreated, shouting warnings of the dire situation, they quickly realized the reality differed sharply from what their commanders had described.

For those midway up the wall, the view was clear; their comrades were being slaughtered below. No one wanted to jump into a hopeless situation, and soon the stream of people halted. Everyone hesitated.

Instead of crossing, they leapt down, refusing to obey commands, and wished to head back to camp. Before long, the columns stopped in their tracks, and everything bogged down to a standstill on the Nicopolan side of the wall. In contrast, more and more survivors successfully climbed back, many bearing scars and fresh wounds from battle.

The survivors, having discarded their drenched gambesons, wore only their tunics—dirty and bloodied. When confronted by the enforcers, a heated shouting match ensued. Overcome with rage, the survivors charged and maimed their enforcers. They had suffered enough and only wanted to return to camp. They knew they had been beaten and had set their priorities right.

On their way back, almost everyone they encountered inquired about the situation. The survivors explained and urged all they met to abandon the fight. Some, sensing that infighting was inevitable, readily offered their weapons, while others eagerly joined the retreat.

One commander attempted to stop them, but they shouted that they had paid their dues in blood. Realizing it could turn into a fight, the commander and his guards backed down.

When Sergio heard of this, he ordered his men to downplay the event, fearing it would exacerbate the situation. "I'll deal with them later. For now, focus on restoring order," he insisted.

"But, Sergio, we've sent the youths, and they returned bloodied. Now, the rest are frightened, they won't listen," one staff argued.

"Then find those who will!" Sergio snapped.

"The right wing is fresh and separate from the rest," someone suggested.

"Pull them," Sergio consented. "Now that we know the nomads are behind the wall, we don't need a thousand to cover our right flank."

The staff member quickly left to mobilize the right wing.

Sergio turned to his other staff. "Do whatever it takes to get the men to climb that wall and resume the attack. If we fail, we'll lose everything. Do you want your families to be cooked as meals?" he threatened, spreading unease and discomfort among the group.

Watching their lack of approval, Sergio raised his voice, "We burned the deal. We trampled the crops meant for us. If we don't win, how will we feed eight thousand men through winter?" he howled. "Those men, the very ones you commanded, will eat our hearts out. So, get out there and make them climb! Better them dying than us!"

Afterward, his staff and inner circle ran with renewed spirits to act on his command. Sergio himself approached the front line again and pushed the column into attacking, even to the point of brandishing his sword to make them obey.

Despite the stream of deserters, the men, fearing Sergio, pushed their comrades in the front to advance. But progress was slow.

The arrival of the men with long pikes and crossbowmen from the right wing changed all this. Sergio quickly took command of these elite troops, positioning them behind his other column.

"Climb, or we'll make you bleed!" he threatened in front of his loyal elites. With that chilling cry, the attack finally resumed.

Lansius

The lull in the opponent's attack allowed the Korimor force to regain control of the center wall. Piles of Nicopolan casualties were shoved aside, while the mortally wounded were mostly left to their own devices. A few who were groaning or screaming from pain were given a merciful stab to the heart or a blow to the back of the neck.

Hugo reclaimed the center wooden tower and allowed Batu's archers to occupy it, taking as many spare arrows as they could. Meanwhile, Sir Michael was organizing a new defense on the wall.

Inevitably, there were pockets of Nicopolans who surrendered. Even in their darkest hour, men wouldn't kill unless they truly had to. The surrendering men were brought to Sigmund, who led them to Lord Lansius.

Gazing upon the two hundred of them, Lansius, his armor stained with blood in various places, commanded coldly, "Kneel."

His words weren't forceful, but the Nicopolans heeded them, driven by the dark-haired man's fearsome appearance and formidable reputation.

"Raise your right palm, and swear to me an oath that you will not follow Sergio anymore," he demanded.

"We swear not to follow Sergio anymore," they chanted, almost in unison.

"The next time we meet, I will choose a leader for you, and you'll obey that person with your life. Swear this to me."

In cold sweat they responded, "We swear to obey the person that you choose."

"If your oath is true, then I shall find a way to feed you through this winter."

With wide eyes, the Nicopolans looked up to Lord Lansius earnestly. They couldn't believe what they had heard.

"If you dishonor this oath," Lansius added, then turned to Batu. This move looked ominous to the Nicopolans.

Batu stepped forward with a grim smirk. "If you dishonor your oaths, then all the tribes in Lowlandia shall hunt you down. We will find you, and when we do, we'll make a hole from your rear to your head, so precise and carefully that you won't die, despite the excruciating pain. We'll fill that hole with hot tallow, thread a large rope through as a wick, and turn you into living candles."

The men gulped, frightened by the unknown custom of the nomads, taking Batu's threat at face value.

Batu finished with, "The skies and my Noyan are my witnesses. Mark my words, this will happen."

Lansius was pleased with the creative threat. He glanced at the frightened survivors and commanded, "Now, drop all your gear and run north to the river. Hide until the war is over, and remember your oaths."

Sigmund and his men escorted the surrendering individuals north, toward the river.

Lansius was hesitant to shelter them, fearing they might rejoin the battle. He was aware that he had confronted only about a thousand Nicopolans, with another four to five thousand remaining. Yet, he anticipated a rout to happen soon.

Unlike in epic tales where every foe perishes in battle, in reality, even minor casualties can cause an army to flee. Historically, most medieval armies would rout after incurring just ten percent in losses, and almost certainly before the twenty percent mark.

Lansius felt that the Nicopolans were approaching this critical threshold. However, he wasn't solely relying on these hopes. He was also geared up for a prolonged battle.

Hugo returned to Lansius's side and saluted. "My lord, we've secured the walls. May I learn your instruction?"

"Prepare to defend. Have the boys collect swords and spears, but prioritize bolts and arrows."

"Acknowledged, my lord. But one question: Will it be a long fight?"

"I'm not a seer," Lansius replied lightly. "But let's assume it will be, unless the commanders on our flanks find an opportunity."

Hugo observed, "The opportunity seems to be present on our left wing."

Lansius looked to the far left. "The baroness's side?"

"Indeed. When I secured the tower, I saw that the Nicopolans had withdrawn their long pike wielders and crossbowmen from their right flank."

Hearing that, Batu spat to the side. "Those cunning bastards," he cursed.

The men Hugo mentioned had cost Batu dearly in yesterday's battle. "My condolences to your brethren," said Lansius.

Batu bowed his head a little in respect.

Lansius looked back at Hugo. "If our opponent is pulling their right flank, then the baroness might have a chance."

Roger suddenly stood up. "My lord, I should still be able to deliver a message to the baroness."

"I admire your courage, but you have more than just a broken finger," said Lansius.

Distinct whistling sounds echoed from the tower, alerting everyone. Batu's bowmen had loosed their arrows, and in return, bolts came flying from beyond the wall.

Nobody needed to be told that the Nicopolans were back on the attack.

Hugo heaved a sigh, while Lansius stared at the blue sky. Somehow, Sergio continued to defy expectations. Despite the large casualties and the near-rout situation, the Tarracan man had managed to regain control and resume the attack.

"Rally the men for defense," Lansius said to Hugo, "and this time, there are no more ruses."

The deputy nodded, and Lansius gazed at his ally. "Brother Batu, can I count on you again?"

"Till my bow is broken and my sword dulled," replied the tribesman solemnly.

Lansius was pleased and offered a customary drink that one of his squires carried. He shared the ale with Batu, Hugo, and the rest of the crew. It wasn't much, but the situation made it sweeter.

Hugo and Batu departed for their respective posts, and before long, fights erupted atop the wall. Assisted by Roger, Lansius donned his gorget, gauntlet, and helmet. Armed with a sturdy spear Roger found earlier, the Lord of Korelia strode to the wall, fighting side by side with his men.

Nicopolan Side

Threatened by Sergio's newly formed rear guard—comprising long pike wielders and crossbowmen—the Nicopolan attack surged with renewed vigor. They knew what Sergio was capable of. Although the rear guard were Nicopolans like them, they were nothing but Sergio's lackeys.

In total, three thousand men were pouring over the walls, haphazardly trying to climb or survive the onslaught of arrows coming at them. Many were wounded, and several were crushed or trampled in the frenzy. The situation was dire, but Sergio, driven by desperation, believed the battle could still be turned in their favor.

However, the situation worsened. The water had risen ever so slightly, but enough to swell the mud beneath. Now, with thousands on the move, the area before the wall had turned into a muddy swamp. Men struggled to trudge through the thick mud, striving not to slip or die from sporadic arrow attacks.

It was a matter of time before they could take no more. Finally, enough of them realized that Sergio was leading them to certain death. Gradually, they began to disperse in small groups, wandering and stalling for time. In hushed whispers, they hatched a plot. Then, seizing the opportune moment, they swiftly marched back and launched a surprise attack on Sergio's unsuspecting rear guard.

This bold act took many by surprise, but it was brutally quelled by a volley of crossbow bolts. Sergio witnessed the incident and moved quickly, trying to contain the problem, but his army had mutinied.

As the crossbowmen in the rear guard reloaded and the pike wielders still recoiled from the brazen surprise attack, more groups fled west toward their camp. Although many bore no ill will toward Sergio, they had no desire to die that day.

In just a span of several breaths, almost a thousand men made a run for it, evading the rear guard in two directions. Some were simply escaping the death march, while others followed their mercenary friends or family members who had decided it was better to loot their own camp and live as brigands.

Watching half the army flee, Sergio and his guards plunged into the fray to physically bar the soldiers from leaving. He caught several, shouted at them, and slapped one of them, but the rest simply ignored him and continued to flee toward the camp.

It was then that the harsh truth dawned on him: He had lost the battle. His rear guard, who should have prevented this, failed to act. Even the elites were unnerved by this sudden development. Despite Sergio's commands, as long as they were not attacked, they refused to retaliate.

Watching this unfold, a trusted aide at his side urged, "Sergio, we must return to camp. The situation is critical."

"But I've put your uncle and his men to guard the supplies," Sergio snapped back.

"I can't truly trust even them," the aide countered strongly. "Our supplies might be the first they loot on their way out."

"Bah!" Sergio grew angry. But deep down, he recognized the possibility was real.

Casting his pride aside, he commanded, "Get the rear guard and anyone still loyal. We return to the camp, now!"

Without hesitation, Sergio and his elites left the battlefield, leaving the rest of his men to serve as a buffer against possible enemy counterattacks.

He had forsaken the hope of ever winning this battle. Now, his lifeline was clear: Secure the supplies. If he still had the food and spoils, then he could maintain an army and survive this major defeat. Even with as few as a couple hundred men, he could safely escape Korimor, or even form a raiding party and cross the Great Plains into prosperous Midlandia.

It would be tough to make the crossing and organize a base camp in Midlandia, but it was better than being trapped against a formidable foe.

However, his dreams were quickly shattered. A section of the wooden wall on the right side parted, opening like gates. And like a vulture sensing dying prey, the sons of Korimor marched through in high spirits. They were no more than two hundred, along with several riders, but the thousands of Nicopolans in the field had no heart to fight.

Wherever the Korimor went, the Nicopolans dispersed. The few hundred tore through the lines without fear and kept charging straight toward Sergio's banner.

Sergio saw the risk, but he couldn't lose his banner. The rear guard halted their march back and spread into their line formation.

Against hundreds of brandished spears at the front and crossbowmen at the flanks, the Korimor slowed their approach. Everything seemed under control. However, more Korimor men poured through the opened section.

It was akin to watching a building catch fire and collapse. Similarly, another section of the wall just crumbled. As Sergio's elite left wing fled the scene, several hundred Korimor readily emerged near the river through a similar opening in the wall.

But the worst was yet to come. The blue and bronze banner finally arrived from the right wall with hundreds of men and tens of riders.

Despite the situation, Sergio's face remained stoic, though his hands betrayed a slight tremor. He was trapped by his own acumen. To move would mean abandoning everything he had built, up to this point. And he knew he couldn't live without the success and reputation he had gained.

Unwilling to start anew and tempt the Lady of Fortuna a second time, the Tarracan man made his stand.

CHAPTER 10

THE GRIM REAPER

A trumpet sounded in the distance, blaring low notes in quick succession. Lady Audrey and her Korimor men halted their approach. They had been facing Sergio's rear guard, who outnumbered them nearly five to one.

Audrey dismounted and joined the men-at-arms on foot. "Dietrich, bring all the men-at-arms to me and reform the line," she instructed.

"But, my lady, the signal was to halt," Dietrich said, puzzled.

"It doesn't mean we shouldn't reposition and prepare for an assault. I'll be damned if the order is given and we're unprepared," Audrey explained.

Dietrich nodded and quickly relayed the baroness's orders. Soon, the two hundred men reformed their column, with Audrey commanding the veteran men-at-arms who had been with her since the fateful battle against Lord Robert two years ago.

Audrey was satisfied with the formation and ordered, "Rest. Sit on the ground if you need to. Now's the time to drink and catch your breath."

Almost all of her troops dropped to the ground to recover. By this point, there were no more stragglers in the field. Aside from Sergio's rear guard, the rest of the Nicopolans had retreated to their camp.

The heat of the day had caused everyone to sweat profusely, but the men were eager. Unlike their counterparts at other sections of the wall, these two hundred were still relatively fresh. From the start, the Nicopolans dared not to go against Audrey's position, as they were relatively close to the city wall and benefited from the protection of the crossbowmen above.

"The lord's banner is approaching from behind," one aide reported.

Audrey glanced back and smiled, dabbing the sweat from her brow with the cloth Carla had provided. "What do you think?" she asked her squire.

"I think the lord is eager to unite the troops and offer battle," Carla commented, keeping her shield ready to protect her master.

"Sir Harold is also coming," Dietrich noted, observing their right wing approaching from the side.

Audrey chuckled and turned to her men-at-arms. "Boys, we've done so little today. Will you be content to let them take all the glory?"

The men chuckled at the verbal provocation. The lady's style of command was simple, direct, and down-to-earth. Her troops saw her as the Knight Baroness, always there among them and treating them with respect.

After receiving her benevolence for almost two years, the men-at-arms at her side would readily follow her anywhere. Now, the two hundred Korimor under her command were also thinking the same. They were already captivated by the baroness's imposing black armor, sureness of action, and confidence in the field of battle.

Wherever the lady went, her troops followed with unswerving determination.

Lansius

"Did they heed the command?" asked Lansius as they trudged through the muddy field.

Sigmund, walking in front of Lansius, glanced back and nodded. "Yes, my lord, my lady's column has halted."

"Good," Lansius commented. He didn't want Audrey's column to interfere with the Nicopolan rout, in case she applied too much pressure for the Nicopolans to potentially regroup and mount a defense.

Never interrupt when the enemy is making a mistake.

Lansius recalled one of the maxims in *The Art of War*. His aim was to provoke the enemy into a rout, not give them a reason to unite and fight.

Before Lansius's column could catch up with Audrey's, something unexpected occurred. The thousand men from Sergio's rear guard charged toward Audrey's column.

"By the Ageless," muttered Sigmund, and the sentiment was echoed by many nearby.

"Get Batu's riders out, and make haste!" Lansius roared, setting a hard pace as he ran. Hugo and his column let out war cries, quickening their march. The three hundred Korimor and one hundred Korelian men-at-arms charged forward, striding across the battlefield.

Behind them, Batu and his brethren had retrieved their horses and now raced toward the front line.

Lansius knew that both Audrey and Dietrich were excellent commanders, but they were also audacious.

This could backfire . . .

Even though he had anticipated scenarios like this, Lansius hadn't expected that Sergio would still command a thousand men—let alone elites equipped with pikes and crossbows. Despite being weighed down by his armor and short of breath, Lansius and his column pressed on, running.

Sir Harold's column was approaching from the right when he saw the attack unfold on the baroness's column. Though his men were fewer in number and low on stamina due to fatigue and injuries, he knew he had to rally them. The outcome of this battle could hinge on crushing the remaining Nicopolans.

"Lads, we've fought a static defense. I think it's time to stretch our legs. Fast march!" he commanded, and his men gave it their all.

Sir Harold watched as Batu's riders galloped past them, their allies soon coming within range for deadly ranged duels against the Nicopolans. However, the enemy's rear guard was already in disarray, so much so that their crossbowmen were preoccupied and unprepared for the approaching nomadic riders.

The disarray among the enemy ranks presented a golden opportunity for Batu's riders, who unleashed a rain of arrows on their exposed flanks. This nomadic ranged attack, coupled with the unexpectedly fierce resistance from the smaller column and the arrival of two additional columns, ultimately broke Sergio's rear guard.

Faced with overwhelming odds, the Nicopolans panicked and fled the battle-field. In their haste, they discarded their cumbersome long pikes and ran in the general direction of their camp.

Meanwhile, the two columns finally arrived alongside Audrey's column, greeted by cheers and celebrations. Lady Audrey and her men-at-arms had once again proven their worth. Their bannerman proudly waved the baroness's newly made banner, which depicted a charging black horse over a white shield.

Just like the lord's blue and bronze, the lady's black horse banner also claimed victory the first time it was carried through the battlefield.

"A blessed banner," Sir Harold murmured, catching his breath. Now, his column was in the process of regrouping, as many had lagged behind due to exhaustion from the sprint.

Off to the side, the tall knight noted that the lord's column had reformed. In contrast to their orderly situation, chaos reigned to their west within the Nicopolans' encampment. Thousands fled, resembling ants whose nest had been destroyed.

Korimor Side

Lansius drank from the waterskin provided by Roger. Within the damp confines of his helmet, the heat lingered stubbornly, even with the visor up. He stood tall, catching his breath and fighting off the nausea that the full-armor sprint had induced. His sabatons were caked with mud, and aches pervaded his body. Yet he was overjoyed by Audrey's victory.

Sigmund and Hugo finally cleared a path, and he caught sight of Audrey. They approached each other and met halfway.

"Are you injured?" Lansius asked, ignoring the glances from their troops.

"No, thanks to this armor. Took a bolt to the pauldron, but it didn't bite," she replied gracefully.

Lansius noticed new dents on her gauntlet and thigh plate but chose not to raise issues. He didn't know what she had done to overcome the enemy, but he knew that it was effective.

Results are results . . .

The study of her tactics would come later, at a more appropriate time. For now, he grabbed her left wrist and raised it high, shouting, "Behold, the Baroness of Korimor!"

Their troops erupted in cheers and whistles.

Audrey was smiling, her face flushed from the excitement around her.

Lansius wished the celebration could last longer but knew they were pressed for time. "Hold your celebration for now," he said to his men. "There's still unfinished business. Pray, gather your spirits once more and follow me to the encampment."

The troops responded with enthusiastic clamor. Hugo, Sir Harold, Sigmund, and Dietrich rallied their men. Afterward, they checked their equipment and replaced lost or broken items with whatever they could scrounge from the battlefield.

"Who will lead the wounded?" Sigmund asked Hugo as they convened.

"Get that squire, Roger, to do it. Time for him to get used to leading," Hugo decided.

Dietrich joined the conversation. "Deputy, sir," he greeted, his cheek and left ear bandaged and bloodied.

"What happened to you?" Hugo asked.

Dietrich touched his bandaged cheek and winced. "Direct hit to the helmet. Nearly cost me an eye."

Hugo breathed a sigh of relief. "You're one lucky bastard."

Sigmund chimed in. "It's fortunate that we have these confiscated armors; otherwise, many of us would be goners."

The staff nodded. Compared to the Nicopolans, the men from Korelia had the advantage of better armor.

"How did you win the fight?" Sir Harold inquired.

"Praise the lady," Dietrich began. "She had gathered the men-at-arms before the fight. When they charged at us, she ordered us to form a solid wedge—much like cavalry—and execute a focused counter charge. The Nicopolans relied too much on their long pikes, which became cumbersome once we closed in."

"That's impressive," Sir Harold praised.

"So they broke from just that?" Hugo asked, seeking confirmation.

Dietrich exhaled deeply, jogging his memory. "I saw it in their eyes," he began. "These Nicopolans were not in for a decisive fight. Our counterattack shocked them, especially since we aimed at their standard-bearer. Before we knew it, they began to break and flee."

The staff nodded at his explanation.

Dietrich continued. "The challenging part was surviving their initial volley of crossbow fire, which took down many . . ."

The sound of hooves interrupted their conversation. The cavalry, led by Sir Michael, had arrived. The one-eyed knight had been tasked with retrieving horses from the city stables. Now, the lord, the lady, and the knights could mount up and prepare for their final move.

While Lansius and his men were preparing to march, Batu and his riders were decimating the fleeing one thousand. It was a vendetta against the column that had trapped them the day before. With their arrows and blades, they claimed justice for their slain kin.

The Nicopolan elite were not even resisting; they were running away as fast as they could. It was a gruesome slaughter, and many were eventually captured.

Batu and his men scoured the area, searching for the elusive Tarracan named Sergio. However, despite all their efforts, neither Batu nor his scouts could determine where Sergio was supposed to be.

Sergio

The Tarracan man was drenched in sweat. He had run from the battle like a coward, a fact that deeply humbled his ego. When he reached the camp, it was in an uproar. Many were waiting for him, seeking his guidance and comfort. Sergio could only assure them that he had a plan up his sleeve.

It was a lie; he had no plan to save them. With the loss of his rear guard, there was no hope to defend this camp. Sergio had dispatched his most loyal men to secure the food supplies, hoping that not much had been lost. His only aim now was to collect his valuables and await the return of his men, so they could make their escape from this cursed place.

"Guards!" he yelled, but nobody answered. "They left . . . ? Spineless curs!" He discarded his soaked gambeson as he entered the inner part of his tent.

Upon seeing that his wooden chest was still locked, his anger subsided. The plunder he had amassed was significant. Feeling relaxed, he glanced at his bed. The clean sheets over the hay mattress and the lingering fragrance from burned incense made him want to rest.

He even considered taking a quick bath, the large bucket already filled with clean water. Sergio was tempted, thinking his thousands of followers would likely defend the camp long enough for him to escape if an attack came.

"Who knows when I'll be able to enjoy a proper bath again?" he muttered, not caring about the grim fate awaiting his followers.

"How about never?" came a surprise answer from behind.

Sergio was shocked and was about to turn around, but something snared his neck, and all he could do was grab the strong thin cord that tightened like a noose around his neck.

He was gasping for breath when a kick came from behind, forcing him to kneel on the carpet. He wanted to ask, to curse, to plead, but could only gasp for air and helplessly cough.

Daniella

Due to certain circumstances, Daniella ended up as the one who strangled Sergio, forcing him to his knees. The previous night, despite her newfound freedom, she had decided not to flee, choosing to hide instead. With thousands of tents available, she figured she could survive for a day or two by stealing food as needed. Fortunately, she only had to wait one day before her patience was rewarded.

She hadn't been idle while waiting. She'd disguised herself in pilfered garb and a hood. When Sergio went off to battle, she tracked the remaining people who had once been her cohorts. Daniella convinced them to join her in seizing this rare chance for vengeance. Lord Lansius's victory and the ensuing rout made it all easier.

By chance, she reunited with Servius, who had urged his family, friends, and allies to flee to the neighboring forest. Daniella asked him to join her. Together, they successfully infiltrated Sergio's tent, killing the guards and cleaning up the mess. However, the men froze when the Tarracan man returned. It was Daniella who broke the spell with her stealthy attack.

Now, the infamous Tarracan man was kneeling at their mercy.

Servius revealed himself to Sergio and declared, "It's time to answer for your crimes."

Daniella relaxed her grip on the garrote.

"You ungrateful wretches," Sergio coughed and gasped for air. "I kept you fed and alive all this time! I demand a fair trial!"

Daniella laughed. "And who will be your judge? The Lord of Korelia?"

Sergio trembled at the suggestion.

Others wanted to strike Sergio, but Servius blocked them. "It's not a bad idea. Let's present this man to Lord Lansius."

"Bah! Servius, the people outside will kill us and free him," one warned.

"The affairs of Nicopolans will be settled by Nicopolans," another recited the well-known saying.

Servius sighed heavily. "Fine! A trial it is. Let's make it quick."

One man stepped forward. "We trusted you with our sons, yet you sent them on pointless raids that did nothing to secure food."

Another took a key from Sergio's pocket and opened the chest filled with golden goblets, rings adorned with gemstones, and gold coins.

"This is what you're looking for, not food but richness!" he half-shouted at Sergio. "You sacrificed my brother, cousins, and nephews as if they were your private army. They died as thieves and robbers."

"You lured us with promises of food, only to feed us human flesh. We know, Sergio, how you butchered those villagers who surrendered to you. You're no better than a mindless beast!"

The accusations flew one after another.

Servius knelt and stared at Sergio coldly. "One of your guards assaulted my friend's daughter. When we reported it, you only laughed. Then the whole family died from food poisoning. Were you involved?"

Sergio could only stare back in response.

Unfazed, Servius continued. "You also sent me with two other envoys carrying a box containing embalmed fingers. Was that an attempt to get rid of us?"

This time, Sergio turned his gaze away.

Servius turned to Daniella. "You're also Nicopolan; you be the judge."

"Any defense?" Daniella asked, maintaining tension on her cord.

"I led you through famine, and this is my reward—"

One of the men, who had lost brothers and kin, shoved gold coins into Sergio's mouth. "This is the reward you sought!"

Sergio choked violently. Daniella had had enough. She whispered, "Remember the one you left to die under the sun? He said thousands perished because of your ambitions, not to mention the innocents you butchered just for your rise to nobility. Sergio, it's time you met them again."

Gasping for air, the condemned cast a terrified, bloodshot glance at his captors. But Daniella summoned her strength, and the struggle of the Tarracan man came to an abrupt end. His legs gave out, and his jaw opened wide, releasing gold coins stained with blood and saliva.

The fallout from his demise and the fate of the Nicopolans and the Korimor region would finally be decided.

CHAPTER 11

DIRTY END

The blue and bronze and the black horse banners marched confidently toward the Nicopolan camp, with the nomads on their left flank and the knights riding in front.

As they marched closer, more and more Nicopolans fled to the west.

"Should we give pursuit, my lord?" Hugo asked.

"No, maintain formation. The men are exhausted. Let's not over-exert ourselves," Lansius replied.

"A group of men ahead," Sir Michael called out from the vanguard.

Lansius narrowed his eyes against the distance, discerning a dozen figures hastening toward them.

"That's strange," Audrey observed at his side. "Perhaps, they intend to surrender?"

"I'll lead a contingent to intercept," offered Hugo, his hand ready on the reins. "With your leave, my lord?"

Lansius nodded. "Granted. Take Sir Michael with you. Inform Batu to have his men on standby, the situation is delicate at the moment."

The two spurred their horses forward, leading a column of armored cavalry across the field. Lansius watched as they galloped the brief stretch, swiftly encircling the newcomers before escorting them back.

Audrey's gaze lingered on Lansius. "What do you think they want?"

"It could be anything—an envoy wishing a truce, a discussion to stall time, or a trap."

Audrey nodded and spoke with a deadpan expression. "With you around, I doubt anyone could backstab us."

"I take that as praise," he replied.

"Certainly, my lord."

Both stifled chuckles as they watched Hugo and his riders approaching. The column was escorting a group who were on foot. Meanwhile, Hugo shared his ride with someone.

Sir Harold, always close at Lansius's side, was intrigued. As he had anticipated, he recognized the figure riding with Hugo. "Lady Daniella!"

The lady pulled down her hood, looking thinner but her eyes were filled with determination. She nodded respectfully and stepped off the horse. "My lord, Daniella reporting."

Lansius and Audrey were elated. "I thought we had lost you," Audrey breathed a sigh of relief.

"Are you free as part of the truce?" Lansius asked.

Another person stepped forward. "My lord, my lady, my apologies for interrupting," Servius interjected.

Sir Harold glanced at Lord Lansius, who nodded to allow the interruption. "Envoy, we meet again."

"I upheld my part of the bargain," Servius asserted.

"And I will uphold mine," Lansius replied.

Pleased by the reassurance, Servius added, "My lord, I was the one who freed Lady Daniella. However, she earned her merit on her own."

"Merit?" Lansius questioned.

Servius took a deep breath. "She convinced us to take down Sergio, and we succeeded."

Murmurs spread among the troops. The members of Lansius's staff looked hungry for answers but knew better than to interrupt.

"Is Sergio dead?" Lansius inquired directly.

Servius looked at Daniella, giving her the honor.

In turn, Daniella, now the center of everyone's attention, replied proudly, "By my own hand."

Lansius took a deep breath and glanced at Audrey.

"The battle is finally over," she remarked gratefully. Smiles and expressions of relief blossomed around them. Like wildfire, the news spread quickly, lifting the spirits of the entire army.

"My lord," Servius called for attention with a hint of trouble.

"Speak," Lansius commanded.

"My allies have moved to the forest as you instructed. However, Sergio's followers . . . they threaten to burn their hoard of supplies unless my lord allows them to leave with the provisions."

Lansius shook his head in disbelief. "This madness must end. Servius, send someone you trust. Tell your men to remain in the forest and arm themselves. And be wary of troublemakers."

"Yes, my lord." Servius bowed low and went to send a pair of messengers.

"Sir Michael, Deputy Hugo."

The two commanders approached. "You called for us, my lord?"

"Let's move forward. Be wary of crossbowmen. I wish to see just how mad they can be."

Under Lansius's command, the hundreds of troops and cavalry resumed their march to the Nicopolan encampment. Their advance caused the Nicopolans to panic. The flow of people who had been fleeing west had ebbed, and now completely stopped. Nobody fled anymore.

The remaining people barred the entrance with spears and pikes. Crossbowmen appeared on their makeshift wall. Several in plate armor warned from atop earthen mounds, "Do not come closer!"

Lansius reined in his horse, and his formation halted. His men and squires quickly formed up around him with shields and crossbows.

"My lord, let me handle the negotiations," Sir Michael stepped forward.

Lansius gazed at the native Lowlandian-born knight. "Take Servius with you and go with my blessing. Try to persuade them to send an envoy; I wish to talk."

"Gratitude for your trust, my lord."

"Sir Harold," Lansius called, "Have the knights accompany Sir Michael and Servius."

"At once, my lord," the knight replied.

Upon his command, a column of men, all in shining plate armor, bravely rode toward the camp entrance. Sir Michael, in the middle, bore a pike with a piece of white cloth tied to it, the signal for parley.

"What do you want?" a man shouted from the front.

"Watch your tongue; you're addressing a knight!" Like a thunder strike, a powerful voice came from one of Sir Michael's men.

It was enough to make most men shudder. Sir Michael guided his horse forward and announced, "I am Michael, knight of White Lake, under the command of the Lord of Korelia, who wishes to speak. I suggest you send your envoys immediately."

Under the blue skies of Korimor, Lansius and Audrey shared a drink. The midday heat in the plains was taxing, especially when clad in plate armor and arming jack. Everyone around Lansius was fatigued, drenched in sweat from the heat, but their eyes shone with determination to finish the fight.

His gaze turned to Daniella once again who stood not far from him. He motioned her to come closer and said, "I apologize for not being able to arrange a rescue party. I tried to form a special group for the task, but the situation was too risky."

Daniella, touched by the kind gesture, replied, "Please, my lord. I am the one who troubled you with my reckless plan—"

"Don't be," Lansius interrupted. "I applaud your courage and initiative. I could use such talents."

Daniella could only bow her head in respect.

Lansius looked at Audrey. "My lady, what do you think of having her as your captain of the guard?"

Daniella shot a nervous glance at the two.

"Nothing but gratitude," Audrey replied to Lansius with a smile on her lips, and then to Daniella, "We promised to ride together. Perhaps it's fate."

"Daniella, is this arrangement good enough for you?" Lansius asked.

"My lord, my lady, to be trusted in such a position is an honor. However, I fear there will be those who question my loyalty."

Audrey looked at her fondly and said, "You fought the Nicopolans for us. Nobody will dare to question where your loyalty stands."

Her trust caused Daniella to break into a genuine smile. "I, Daniella, will be forever loyal to your ladyship and lordship."

Once an outcast daughter of a noble, forced to live as a mercenary, Daniella had finally found a place to call home. She had once possessed nothing but memories of her former noble life; now, her resilience had paid off.

She would become a part of the household of the Baroness of Korimor. In Lady Audrey, Daniella found not only a leader worthy of her trust but also an incredible ally who could reciprocate that trust. To such a leader, she gladly pledged her loyalty.

After several tense moments, Sir Michael and the knights finally returned with five Nicopolans in tow.

"My lord, they have sent five envoys," Sir Michael reported.

"Well, let us receive them," said Lansius as he wiped his sweating face with a clean cloth.

"May I suggest offering leniency to those willing to submit?" Sir Michael proposed.

"Lansius nodded without hesitation. "The steward has advised me that many Nicopolans are excellent farmers, craftsmen, and scribes."

"Do you intend to recruit them?" Sir Harold inquired, rather surprised.

"I'm aware of your reservations about Nicopolans," Lansius reassured his knight. "But we'll need all the talent we can muster for Lowlandia and the Grand Alliance."

The rest of the staff smiled, contemplating their lord's far-reaching plans. Even Sir Harold flashed a grin.

The five envoys, all young men, then presented themselves.

"You stand before the Lord of Korelia, Protector of Korimor, and leader of the Grand Alliance," Sigmund announced to the envoys.

The envoys bowed, murmuring, "My lord."

Sir Harold and the knights stood imposingly, ready to act at the slightest provocation.

"You are here. But make no mistake, my interest is merely in satisfying certain curiosities."

"This is not to discuss a truce?" one envoy blurted.

"Truce?" Lansius feigned surprise, followed by an ominous chuckle. "It is far too late for that."

Lansius glanced at Sir Michael, who caught on and said, "In case you are unaware of your current situation. One, you are surrounded. Two, your troops have been defeated. Three, we know that Sergio is dead."

Without waiting for their reaction, Lansius pressed on, "In essence, you have been totally defeated. There are no grounds for a truce."

The envoys exchanged worried glances. One ventured, "We still have the food supplies."

"But I have heard that you're going to burn them," Lansius mused.

"That will be the case if my lord pushes us," the envoy countered.

"Oh, I shall," Lansius retorted. "As I've said, I am simply inquiring. My strategy remains unchanged."

The envoys grew noticeably paler. Another stepped forward. "We still have the baggage train, laden with gold and riches."

Lansius smiled mockingly at their naivety. "If you burn the food, then one way or another, you will die. After that, I can send my men to take the gold from your cold, lifeless hands."

The stark message sparked a hushed but chaotic argument among the envoys.

Lansius shook his head and said aloud, "You are all far too inexperienced for this. And certainly too young to die if I can help it. Do not tempt me further. Where are your elders? Hiding in safety?"

Sir Harold, Hugo, and the knights subtly tightened their circle around the envoys.

"Please, my lord," they pleaded. "Sergio is dead. We are without a leader. The crowds are splitting up."

"I presumed someone among Sergio's lieutenants had taken command," Lansius ventured.

"No, nobody wanted them." Another spoke up. "We only trusted Sergio, not his henchmen."

"Wise move," Audrey murmured at Lansius's side. She then addressed the envoys. "Do you speak for all inside the camp?"

"Yes, my lady. The people trust us over Sergio's lackeys," one replied in a hurry.

Another added, "We never loved Sergio, either. We followed because we had nothing to eat, and he was the only one who could feed us and our families."

Satisfied with the answer, Audrey turned to Lansius, who was ready to deliver the ultimatum. "Inform everyone in the camp that they are surrounded," he directed. "Remind them that I can encircle your camp just as swiftly as I made those walls appear overnight."

The envoys listened, some with eyes red from strain, as they committed his words to memory.

Lansius continued, "Lay down your arms, answer for your crimes, and surrender half of your supplies, along with the entire baggage train."

"What shall become of Sergio's remains?" an envoy asked nervously.

Lansius paused, turning to Sir Michael, who quickly suggested, "Should the Nicopolans see the Tarracan man as a hero, let them bury him. If they deem him a villain, his head should grace a pike."

The young envoys were momentarily divided before one spoke up. "My lord, we humbly request time to deliberate further, perhaps with one of your knights to mediate. We assure you of their safety."

"They may come with escorts, fully armed," added another.

Lansius showed no intention of being delayed, but Audrey leaned in, whispering, "It would be wiser to delegate this to someone else."

He knitted his brows. "For what reason?"

"They fear you too much. They can't even come up with a counter proposal, terrified that they might slight you. At this rate, they have no hope of bridging you and the rest of the Nicopolans inside."

Lansius hadn't expected that, but in retrospect, he had indeed won the battle that ultimately ended Sergio's life. To them, he must be the living embodiment of terror.

Callahan, my adversaries now see me as a conqueror. Is this what you wished for?
Memories of his lost mentor flashed before him momentarily.

"Sir Michael, Hugo," he called.

"Yes, my lord," they responded in unison.

"Let the troops rest. We will hold a deliberation to discuss the envoys' request. Get everyone something to drink while they wait."

Sir Michael had been prepared for this and had his men erect a small field tent for cover from the heat.

The staff followed Lansius inside, where he also invited Batu. He began, "Gentlemen, in light of the upcoming negotiation, I wish us all on the same page. Right now, the situation boils down to this: attacking them right now would invite a huge, unnecessary risk. If we're lucky, they'll flee. If we're not lucky, they may unite, and we'll be fighting desperate men who have nothing to lose but wish to make us pay dearly. I do not wish to turn victory into defeat."

The staff and allies pondered the lord's words.

"Then how do we proceed?" asked Audrey.

Lansius gestured to his staff to offer ideas, but none could answer.

"Against three thousand, it's difficult without sacrificing more men," Sir Harold commented.

"I could lead a night attack and burn their tents. Maybe that way they'll be more inclined to surrender," Batu offered.

"I don't want to overburden your brethren. Horse archers are hard to train," Lansius replied.

Daniella stepped forward. "Pardon me, but isn't this similar to the situation when we took the city?"

Her words made Hugo's and Sir Michael's eyes widen as they recognized the resemblance.

Lansius smiled. "Loss of leadership. External threats. And internal conflict. Well done, Daniella."

"Does that mean we only need to wait?" asked Audrey, referring to the strategy that had won them the city.

"No, waiting is for when we have nothing at hand and expect them to doubt themselves. In this case, we are in a better position," Lansius explained.

Audrey nodded. "Of course. We've just won the battle."

"The problem is," Lansius said, gathering their attention, "even if we win this battle of wits, how can we feed an additional three thousand souls?"

The staff drew a collective sigh, while Sir Michael added, "Based on my men's latest report, Servius's group and their families account for an additional one thousand. So, we're facing four thousand, my lord."

Lansius drew a heavy sigh. No matter how he looked at it, for the Nicopolans, this would likely end in disaster.

CHAPTER 12

GRAND STAGE

Lansius

After deliberation, Lord Lansius sent Hugo, Sir Michael, and Servius to broker a deal with the remnants of Sergio's followers. Aware of his still-precarious situation, he solidified his position by bringing Servius's group into his fold.

Riding to the western forest with a heavily armed escort, Lansius met with Servius's allies. It was a tense moment, but Lansius quickly reassured them with his words, and in turn, they swore fealty. They agreed to serve without pay in exchange for the assurance of food and shelter for themselves and their families.

The five hundred men were taken in as the new Nicopolan regiment. Lansius planned to integrate their families into Korimor and its surrounding villages and hamlets, promising protection as long as the regiment remained loyal. He further stipulated that the family members must work for the benefit of his House.

Having done all they could, the lord and lady retired to their field tent. Now, all that remained was to wait.

Nicopolan Camp

It was already midday, yet the fate of the remaining three thousand Nicopolans in the camp was yet undecided. Composed of Sergio's loyalists and common refugees from Nicopola, they were either too late to escape or had resigned themselves to their fate.

The meeting between the two sides had been delayed due to internal strife among the camp leadership. Tensions were running high, and despite this, Sir Michael still refused to promise them food or shelter, even if they swore fealty to Lord Lansius.

"It's out of the question," he declared. "This morning, you were given an offer, and you destroyed the crops my lord had graciously provided. You must own up to your mistakes!"

The new camp representative, taken aback, then asked timidly, "Can you at least allow us to depart from Korimor with a share of our own supplies?"

"Only to those who could ransom themselves," Sir Michael responded.

His answer seized the Nicopolans' attention.

"But don't even think to take it from the baggage train," the knight warned. "That belongs to the war victor. For those who cannot ransom themselves, they must answer for their crimes."

"Can you guarantee safe passage to those who can pay?" the new camp representative asked again, to the mockery of the crowd, who felt betrayed. Clearly, only the top-ranking loyalists, who had been given a share of the loot by Sergio, could afford the ransom.

Sir Michael decided to play hard. "My lord commands both heavy and light cavalry that could hunt you down at his whim. And let's not overlook the nomadic horsemen under his command, who excel at hunting on the plains. So, tell me now, what guarantee do you seek?"

The answer embarrassed the new representative, but Sir Michael wasn't done with his sarcasm. "Shall we have the horsemen to slaughter their horses to give you that guarantee—that we won't give chase?" He highlighted the absurdity of their demand.

Before anyone could retort, the knight pressed on. "The tribesmen would slaughter you for less than this foolishness. Heed my words, forget about ransom. Right now, the only action you can take is to trust Lord Lansius's judgment. And be certain of this—he has never broken his word."

Murmurs erupted among the Nicopolans. Even his adversaries could not deny that the Black Lord had always been true to his words.

Seizing the moment, Sir Michael stood with the poise of a seasoned orator and addressed the crowd. "What transpired this morning should be clear for all to see. Make no mistake, the Lord of Korelia doesn't make bluffs—he makes guarantees. Thus, I urge you to place your trust in him. And mark my words, Lord Lansius is a far better leader than the Tarracan man who has deceived and exploited you for his personal gain."

"But what will he do to us? We don't have food, and if you can't provide us with any, how are we to survive?" shouted one from the crowd.

"Have faith!" Sir Michael responded with confidence. "My lord has confided in me that he has a way, should you prove loyal and resilient enough to endure hardship."

The response invigorated the crowd. Like the most insidious of poisons, hope had taken hold of their minds and souls.

"There is still time before winter. Now, are you with us, or do you still follow Sergio?" asked Sir Michael.

Sir Michael's speech acted as a catalyst, prompting the common Nicopolans to turn against Sergio's loyalists. Increasingly, groups of men broke away from the perimeter and moved toward the supplies—the heart of the issue—where they taunted and threatened one another, weapons drawn.

Witnessing the near-inevitable end, Sergio's loyalists knew better than to prolong the losing situation. To avert their ruin, they quickly agreed to surrender the supplies to Sir Michael, on behalf of the Lord of Korelia, in exchange for protection.

The news of the agreement spread rapidly, and the Nicopolans from both factions, albeit reluctantly, ceased hostilities.

Immediately, Hugo and his select men took command of the camp, firmly planting the blue and bronze standards on the ground. With this act, the Battle of Korimor had finally been won.

The death of Sergio, the infamous Tarracan man, coupled with the raising of the blue and bronze banner over the Nicopolan camp, marked the end of a conflict that had claimed more than a thousand casualties.

Despite rumors casting doubt on the Lord of Korelia's worth and insinuations that he had fabricated his reputation, the Black Lord ultimately triumphed. Those who had doubted him were now steeped in shame and fear, bracing for the punishment that awaited them.

In the aftermath of the battle, Hugo organized several hundred security guards, led by Servius, to maintain order in the camp. Cautiously, they began to disarm everyone.

The three thousand Nicopolans, having acknowledged their crimes of invading and besieging Korimor, agreed to offer their labor as war reparations. The specifics of this labor would be determined later, as the lord had not yet deliberated upon Sir Michael's proposal.

To demonstrate their sincerity, the Nicopolans voluntarily placed Sergio's head on a pike for all to see.

Meanwhile, a separate group under Servius's command rounded up tens of Sergio's close associates, notorious for terrorizing refugees and committing atrocities during Sergio's reign. These individuals would face execution or exile, but Hugo, suspecting the lord might find them useful, had them taken to the dungeons.

Before the day's end, under the vigilant supervision of Hugo and Sir Michael, the Nicopolans relinquished their weapons, dismantled their makeshift defenses, and transferred half of their supplies, along with Sergio's baggage train, to the castle.

The lord allocated the supplies between his newly formed Nicopolan regiment and the people of Korimor, alleviating their hunger. Today, the rationing ended, and Korimor buzzed with renewed life, open for business once again.

Behind the scenes, more complex developments were taking place. For their services, the lord and lady bestowed the steppe plains east of Korimor upon Batu and his allied tribes. During their victory celebration, a hundred tribesmen pledged a blood oath before a grand pyre in the presence of the Noyan and his esteemed lady.

In a ceremony laden with rites, they swore that they, their sons, and their grandsons would safeguard the safety of the plains and remain faithful to House Lansius.

Content with their vows, the Lord of Korelia granted them permission to pursue the fleeing Nicopolans. This decision was primarily based on his concern that the armed fugitives might turn to banditry, threatening the safe passage of trade and goods to and from Korimor.

At the same gathering, Lansius called upon the city officials, urging them to swear an oath never to allow raids or slavery, under penalty of death. Each official took the oath solemnly, under the watchful eyes of both the citizenry and the nomads.

That night, Lansius had forged a new alliance between the two communities, in the hopes of preventing future conflicts among his subjects.

Lansius

The next day, atop the gatehouse, the Lord of Korelia sat cross-legged on a fine carpet, sheltered from the sun by an overhead field tent. His eyes were focused on the point where the nomadic landscape gave way to the fertile lands surrounding the hill of Korimor and its adjacent river.

Lansius was enjoying this private moment with his wife. There were no guests, only Carla, Sigmund, and the castle musicians, who played their strings and flutes, evoking a rhythmic sense of calmness. As was customary, the ensemble included no drums, but rather the soft jingle of the smallest tambourine. Large percussion instruments were uncommon in the era, yet the mood remained decidedly upbeat.

To freely pick a place to take my lunch, and to have musicians follow and play as I dine—this is absurd . . .

Lansius mulled over where life had taken him, sipping a mild brew of herbal leaves to soothe his persistent sore throat. The brew was bitter, yet the honey-glazed, golden-baked snacks, no larger than a coin, offered a sweet balance. It felt almost decadent in a region just recovering from famine, but his staff assured him that enjoying such delights was only fitting for a lord of his stature.

Lansius looked at his wife. The baroness was gazing at the farmland below; the daily activities of her people were of great interest to her. The people of Korimor had been working hard to rejuvenate the neglected fields. Some of the fields damaged by the battle might yet be salvaged with tender care.

The good news was that, despite all the wars, it appeared they were in for a good harvest this year.

The mood in the city was lively. The siege had been lifted, and normalcy returned. The Korelia market buzzed with life as trade resumed. From the poorest to the richest, everyone was busy preparing for the upcoming harvest.

Lansius felt content, if not thoroughly grateful. The city had been freed, the populace clamored for his name, and the death toll on their side was so low there was no call for a mourning period.

From downstairs, servants gracefully arrived with silver plates set on silver trays. Carla and another member of the staff checked the food for trouble and poison before it was served. All the while, the musicians maintained their harmonious melodies.

Lansius surveyed the feast before him: spiced skewered lamb, freshly baked flatbread, a medley of olives and seasonal vegetables, rich cheese, and fish grilled to perfection. The staff had outdone themselves, preparing a meal so lavish and complete it surpassed any they had enjoyed for days.

A victory, a city that supports our rule, loyal staff working diligently, and a loving wife by my side . . . what more could I ask for?

He concealed his smile, cautious not to disturb his wife, who was still enraptured by the sweeping view before them.

Perhaps it's because Korimor is hers. There's a deeper attachment—something she never had with Korelia . . .

Lansius couldn't help but be amused until he noticed the bruises marring her lower arm. Despite her assurances, Audrey had sustained more than mere bruises; there was swelling on one of her limbs from the battle as well. He had heard reports of the baroness fighting like a hungry lioness, leading her men like a pride of lions against the Nicopolan elite rear guard.

While worried, Lansius also felt an overriding sense of pride in her accomplishments. Audrey was no longer just an adept rider but had proven herself on par with other senior knights in their ranks, becoming another capable field commander in her own right. Just as Lansius had outgrown his past roles as a clerk, Audrey had outgrown her past roles as a squire.

And he found the combination of baroness and field commander to be fearsome, exactly what he had wished for—a growing power at his side. Pleased, Lansius breathed in the scent of autumn. A chill in the air signaled the coming of the harvest, and the landscape was teeming with life: birds, foxes, even moles.

More than winning, what Lansius truly cherished was the return of peace to the land. With Korimor secured, its resources, talent, and manpower under his command, and the Grand Alliance at his back, suddenly many doors of opportunity swung open before him.

Now, he could explore realms and enact policies previously beyond his wildest dreams. Even solving how to feed the four thousand Nicopolans seemed possible if he played his cards correctly.

As if echoing his thoughts, Sigmund and the musicians reached a crescendo in their performance, the harp's strings resonating with vibrant anticipation, the flutes sounding a jubilant herald. It was as if they were celebrating Lansius's ascent to the grand stage.

CHAPTER 13

ACCOLADE

The music, the field tent, and the high position of the gatehouse shielded Lansius from witnessing the grim aftermath of yesterday's battle. He knew his staff tried hard to protect him from the unsightly procession of the Nicopolans, who were collecting and transporting their dead to be buried in mass graves just outside the fertile grounds.

However, being put on a pedestal did not mean he could stop reflecting on the situation. The flight of crows overhead, on their way to the feast, reminded Lansius that death was always near.

A plan is only good if we act upon it . . .

Sooner or later, he would have to demonstrate how he could feed an additional four thousand souls through the winter. The Korimor harvest alone would support fewer than a thousand extra, and it might strain their grain market.

Despite the end of hostilities, tensions between the Nicopolans and the people of Korimor remained high, fraught with distrust, leaving Lansius with scant options to resolve the crisis.

Similar to their limited food production capabilities, the city and its surrounding community could, at best, host a thousand for wintering. That was his hope, at least. He would face significant trouble if social conflict arose; therefore, he planned to keep a close eye on reports of dissidents and crimes.

Fortunately, the other groups, the nomadic tribes, were less demanding. Content with the grazing grounds east of Korimor, they only wished to take the captured men and a portion of the loot as their prize.

Lansius agreed but on one condition: The captives would not be treated as slaves. Instead, they were to work as shepherds or in other labor roles for nine years—the time necessary for an infant to grow enough to assume the work of the fathers or relatives they had lost.

Aside from the immediate issue, Lansius was also troubled by the situation in Umberland. The mountainous gateway between Lowlandia and Nicopola remained uncertain. Not even Servius was aware of the conditions there, many months after their departure. There was fear that other Nicopolan groups might have followed into Umberland. The fate of the castle town itself had yet to be ascertained.

As these thoughts preoccupied Lansius, Audrey savored the meal, taking a bite of skewered lamb and flatbread. It was then that she noticed Lansius had not touched his food. "My lord, is something troubling you?"

"Mm . . . ?" Lansius masked his surprise at her inquiry.

"You haven't touched your food," she said, her voice tinged with concern.

Her reaction, coupled with the situation, reminded Lansius of an old tale he once read, and he couldn't resist chuckling.

Audrey furrowed her brow, prompting Lansius to ask, "Would you like to hear a story about a young king and his advisor?"

"This comes out of nowhere," she protested, but then, with a spark of excitement, she added, "But do tell."

Lansius smiled. "In an ancient kingdom, there came a day when a newly crowned king visited his trusted advisor. During their lunch, the young king left his food untouched, lost in thought. Concerned, the advisor asked if he had made a mistake. Only then did the king reveal his worry: I am merely an untalented man; how can I possibly keep my kingdom intact?"

Audrey looked at him intently, and Lansius continued. "The advisor, relieved that he had not erred, recognized that the young king was wise to ponder the state of the kingdom, and responded."

Adopting as regal a voice as he could muster, he recited, "If a talented ruler is surrounded by talented people, he will be a king above kings. If a less talented ruler has capable people around him, he will still maintain his kingdom as a prince. However, a ruler who is not talented and is surrounded by equally unskilled individuals will surely bring disaster upon his realm."

Audrey stared into the distance. Realizing that Lansius had stopped speaking, she asked, "Is there more to the story?"

"I believe so. The news spread that the new king was so concerned about recruiting talented people that he forgot to eat his lunch. Before long, skilled individuals from far and wide came to offer their services to the king. Because of this, the kingdom remained strong for several generations—until his descendants forgot to heed this wise lesson."

Audrey nodded her head and remarked, "It's a wise story . . ."

"Indeed," Lansius agreed, reflecting on himself. "Audrey, despite what you may think of me, I'm not that talented—much like the young king in the story."

"Humble, are we, after the grand victory celebration last night?" she asked with a smug expression.

Lansius chuckled. Last night, everywhere they went, people chanted their names affectionately. The Korimor people toasted to their health and their ever-lasting rule.

Audrey licked her lips and adopted a more serious expression. "I understand why you wanted to recruit talent from the Nicopolans."

"From any place," he corrected her. "We need people skilled in various crafts. From fletchers who make arrows, to individuals familiar with clay making for pottery and roofing, to statesmen who can assist us in governing the realm."

"Realms," she corrected him with a sweet glance. "I haven't paid my dowry, so I've decided to give Korimor to you."

"Drey . . ." He rejected the idea.

"Lans, the town, the castle, even the House . . . you'll have more use for them than me."

"I'm honored, but it's your House."

She looked at him longingly. "I'm a simple shield maiden. I'm not talented enough to run a city."

"You've used my own story against me," Lansius lamented.

"Praise me, for I have been a good student," Audrey quipped.

He laughed at her jest, as all the while the beautiful melodies of string instruments and flutes continued to fill the air.

"Accept it. Otherwise, I fear that someone will exploit me sooner or later," she suggested.

"I doubt anyone would dare to cross the famed war baroness."

"That's the thing. I'm good with battle, but I know nothing about leading a domain or managing the coins."

Her words made Lansius ponder. "The city isn't mine to take, but I can manage it on your behalf," he said, finally finding his appetite and taking a bite of the skewered meat.

Audrey sighed with relief. "Then, I shall keep Korimor for our sons."

Lansius was intrigued. "Sons?"

"Yes, I doubt you'll settle for just one," she replied, resuming her meal.

The way she stated it so plainly made him stifle a laugh. "How about a daughter as charming as her mother?"

"I'd rather have a daughter as charming as Lady Felicity."

Lansius picked the best-looking olive and offered it to her. Audrey accepted it with her mouth, savoring the buttery taste of the pickled fruit. After a moment, she said, "Lans, how does it feel? You're now the lord of two baronies and the leader of a Grand Alliance."

"My title means nothing if you're not happy."

"Who says I'm not happy?" she protested. "I'm overjoyed." She took his hand and caressed it. "It's I who fears that you're not happy."

"Me . . . ?" Lansius asked, surprised.

"Once, you told me that you wished to live far from the city—in a village or up in the forest. Do you still wish for that?"

Lansius chuckled, the words reminding him of simpler times. "I admit, I did say something to that effect."

With a tender gaze, Audrey asked softly, "Where is home, Lansius?"

The music from the skald's harp and other musicians became even more uplifting, as if they were on the verge of a great adventure.

Lansius met his wife's gaze; her fierce eyes were directed at him longingly. "This is home," he assured her. "Wherever you are, I'm home."

Korimor Castle

It was the second watch when Lansius heard knocking at the door. Audrey was the first to get up, blade in hand.

"My lord, my lady, I apologize, but Roger is in critical condition," explained Carla from the other side of the door.

Audrey opened the door to a slit and asked, "How bad?"

"The physician told me that they might need to amputate his hand," Carla replied worriedly.

"The sword hand?" Audrey turned grim. For a squire to lose his sword hand would be the end of their career.

Lansius appeared behind Audrey and asked, "I'm guessing the physician asked for our permission?"

"Indeed, my lord. They're waiting at the castle's infirmary."

"Guide us there. No need to wake anyone else," Lansius instructed.

Roger lay on the sickbed, sedated but mumbling and groaning in pain. His skin was pale, his fever unrelenting, and some spots on his right hand were turning black.

Upon seeing Lansius, the physician blurted out, "My lord, we mustn't tarry. The man's life is in peril."

"But it's the sword hand," Carla protested on behalf of her friend.

"Better the hand than his life," replied the tired physician.

"Give us some room," said Lansius, and they obliged. He inspected the hand himself and was taken aback by the severity of the infection.

Gangrene has set in . . .

The broken finger from the battle had led to a nasty infection. "Have you got the poppy milk?" Lansius asked.

Before the physician could answer, Audrey interjected, "Wait, leave us." Lansius looked at her, puzzled.

Carla, the physician, and his aide left the chamber.

"What are you doing?" Lansius asked in a hushed tone, watching as Audrey carefully inspected the hand. She then held her palm just above it, not touching but seemingly hovering with purpose.

"Recite the verse Hannei used to chant," she urged. Lansius slowly realized her intent.

"I don't remember, and we don't have time. The flesh is rotting; he needs immediate treatment."

"I know this sickness. Trust me, we have time. Just recite something from your language. It's Roger's best shot."

Lansius racked his brain and recalled the only prayer he could remember. "Our Father, who art in heaven, hallowed be thy name . . ."

Audrey blinked in surprise as Lansius uttered the unfamiliar language. She tried her hardest to recite the tongue-twisting words. However, despite her best efforts, even after half an hour, there were no changes to the hand.

She exhaled deeply, and Lansius comforted her. "You've done your best."

"No remorse," she said before calling back the physician, who returned with the town's best barber.

The barber brought his sharpest tool and, as was the norm, performed the amputation cleanly and with ease. They were fortunate that only the little and the ring fingers needed to be removed.

Hearing this, everyone breathed a sigh of relief. With two fingers and a thumb remaining, Roger might still be able to wield a sword, though his grip wouldn't be as strong.

"There are ways of using a strap connected to the wrist to improve grip strength," Lansius reassured Carla and Audrey.

Keen to avoid causing a commotion as more castle staff curiously peeked in, eager to be near their lord and lady, Lansius and Audrey decided to retire to their bedchamber.

"I feel foolish," Audrey admitted once they were alone.

"For a baroness to care deeply for her squire is praiseworthy," Lansius replied.

She sighed. "I'm just a fake one."

"Hush," Lansius said, drawing her close. "I won't allow anyone to belittle my wife."

She looked up at him. "Not even myself?"

"Especially not yourself."

Audrey managed a small pout. "I'll heed my lord's words then."

He continued to embrace her. "He'll be alright. He's receiving the best care available in Korimor. Just like the last time with the spear wound, he'll return stronger."

"I'll train him harder. He's been too careless and reckless," she resolved.

Satisfied with her response, Lansius gently suggested they rest, mindful of the long night and the important day awaiting their two Houses tomorrow.

Korimor

On the third day following their victory, the Lord and Lady of Korimor held a knighting ceremony. For many in their retinue, this honor had been a long time coming.

Hugo, attired in fine white linen and a red robe symbolizing purity and readiness to shed blood for their realm, knelt in the Great Hall before Lord Lansius. The assembled staff watched solemnly.

Initially, Lord Lansius had suggested that Lady Audrey, the one who held the baroness's patent to knight Hugo, since he had not yet received his. However, Hugo had personally requested Lord Lansius, declaring, "Patent be damned. I want the man who led us to victory to knight me."

This sentiment resonated with the staff, bringing an additional challenge to Lansius, who had scrambled to memorize the lines since early morning. Despite being officially registered as a knight of the Mercantile Kingdom, Lansius had never been formally knighted. While not required to memorize the lines, he feared botching this important event.

Carla was now reading the list of Hugo's achievements, detailing the battles he had fought under the blue and bronze banners. Once the embellished records were complete, Hugo solemnly made his vow of honor, loyalty, and bravery.

Afterward, Lansius took the sword offered to him on a silver tray. The ceremonial sword was heavier than the usual arming sword, intricately etched and decorated. He gently tapped the flat side of the sword on Hugo's right shoulder, then on the left. "Rise, Sir Hugo. May you serve the House with loyalty and honor."

Following Hugo, Daniella was also knighted. Unlike Hugo, she had personally requested Lady Audrey to confer the title.

The event also celebrated Sigmund and Dietrich, who received their formal titles as captains. Roger, still recovering in the infirmary, and Carla were formally titled as squires to the lord and lady.

In addition, rewards and prizes were given to Sir Harold, Sir Michael, and Servius for their large contributions in battle.

This week would mark Sir Michael's last in Korimor. With the campaign concluded and their pockets filled with coins, his riders longed to return to White Lake. For them, the last few weeks had been a grand adventure. They had started as a relief force for Korelia, but ended up taking Korimor and fighting against thousands of Nicopolans.

Their victory would bring back honor and prestige to White Lake and Lord Robert.

The knighting ceremony also established a clear distinction between House Lansius and House Audrey. In House Lansius, Sir Justin and Sir Hugo served as marshal and deputy, respectively. In contrast, similar positions were intentionally left vacant in House Audrey.

Instead, for overseeing security and the troops, House Audrey relied on the role of captain of the guard, held by Dame Daniella, assisted by Captain Dietrich as the Master of the Horse, responsible for the cavalry.

Carla and several staff members were also transferred to House Audrey. This arrangement enabled House Audrey to maintain complete independence during emergencies, as it already managed its own expenses, paying its own troops, officers, and other essential staff.

Council Chamber

After the celebration and lunch, due to pressing matters, the two Houses convened for the first time. The council chamber in Korimor, larger and more grandiose than Korelia, boasted a marvelous round table, its surface lacquered to a high-gloss finish.

"You should ask Sir Michael to stay," Audrey suggested, once they had settled down for the session.

Carla and Sir Hugo turned their gaze toward them.

"What made you think that way?" asked Lansius.

"He's reliable and matched your wits well."

Lansius nodded in agreement, also believing that Sir Michael had become indispensable. "What's your take on him?" he asked Sir Hugo.

"Well, he's one of the best we have in terms of court-related manners. He's also a well-rounded knight. I count myself as his friend," Sir Hugo stated.

"You said it yourself, you lack talent. There's no need to wait for Nicopolan talents to prove themselves," Audrey urged.

"But he's Lord Robert's vassal," Lansius pointed out.

Suddenly, a distinct sound from outside interrupted their discussion, drawing everyone's attention.

"Weapons clashing," the deputy observed, quickly rising and heading for the door, with Carla following close behind.

Outside, Sigmund was sprinting alongside the guardsmen. "We have sightings of intruders."

CHAPTER 14

INTRUDERS

Korimor

People were still celebrating the accolade ceremony when several armed men barged into the castle, quickly breaching security and clashing with the guards. The skirmish reached the courtyard. The lord and lady watched the scene unfold from above. They were barred from descending, as Carla had blocked the stairs, following Sir Hugo's orders.

"Twenty men, they said? I only see four," Audrey observed, loading a crossbow.

"We're not sure, my lady, but the intruders have reportedly defeated at least a dozen guardsmen," Carla replied.

Now, the fighting was intense near a small iron fence that separated the garden from the rest of the castle complex.

The lead attacker skillfully used his broadsword to loosen the metal hinges, almost like using a crowbar. Noticing his intent, the guardsmen quickly rallied and pushed against the heavy iron fence, attempting to trap him. However, the attacker, displaying remarkable strength, managed to hold back the falling fence with just his left hand.

And then in an extraordinary feat, the attacker forcefully pushed the iron gate, causing it and the guards leaning against it to topple over.

Watching from above, Lansius was astonished by the display of superhuman strength. Carla behind them gulped while Audrey remained sharp, possibly feeling challenged by the extraordinary display before her.

By chance, the attacker looked up and noticed Lansius and Audrey at the window. "Fuck, you two really are wed!" the man roared with laughter, effortlessly deflecting an incoming attack.

Lansius's eyes widened in recognition. Audrey sighed and put away her crossbow. "Get them to stop. He's one of us . . ." she instructed a confused Carla.

"But my lady—" Carla began, only to be cut off by Lord Lansius shouting, "Anci, you bastard! What are you doing here?"

Anci's laughter echoed through the air as he tackled the nearest guard. The other guards, unnerved by his overwhelming strength, opted to maintain a safe distance.

"My lord, Sterling, your squire is here," another voice called from below.

"Sterling . . . ?" Lansius's tone was full of doubt. "Why is he here too?" he asked, turning to Carla and Audrey, who appeared equally bewildered.

"Why are you hiding your face?" Audrey asked.

"I beg your pardon, my lady, the helmet's jammed!" Sterling replied while trying hard to remove the headpiece.

"Just stay there. We're coming down," Lansius shouted at them. Led by Audrey, they descended the stairs.

Meanwhile, the guards, upon recognizing the names, widened the distance between themselves and the intruders. While they might not have remembered Anci, Sterling was certainly a familiar figure to the Korelians.

As the lord and lady appeared, Anci removed his helmet with a flourish. "Archibald, at your service."

Audrey called out, "It's really you, Anci." She stood beside Lansius and Carla, with the rest of the castle guards surrounding them.

Anci smiled. "Are you a consort or a lady now? The innkeeper in Korelia gave me quite the tale." He chuckled.

"Innkeeper in Korelia, you say?" Lansius's interest was piqued. "Put down your sword; you're scaring everyone."

"Apologies, my lord. Just some morning practice," Anci replied, tossing his sword and helmet aside, seemingly without care. Two young men behind him caught them. "They're my squire and servant," Anci boasted. "And guess who I found in Cascasonne?"

The man with the stuck helmet stepped forward. "The visor's jammed, but my lord, I assure you, I have no part in this."

Anci couldn't help but laugh.

Lansius sighed, well aware that this was typical of Anci's antics. "Sterling, good to see you walking again."

"Gratitude for your lordship's mercy in sending me to a healer," Sterling said.

Suddenly, thundering footsteps echoed from the entrance. "There they are!" Sir Hugo shouted as he arrived with Dietrich and the rest of the men-at-arms stationed in the city.

"Slowpoke!" Anci called out, catching Hugo by surprise.

"Bastard! It's you!" Hugo exclaimed, immediately recognizing Anci.

"I heard about your knighting, so I came to see for myself!" Anci declared as he charged toward Hugo.

The two clashed in a wrestling bout, but Anci effortlessly tossed Hugo into the garden, stunning the onlookers. Dietrich rushed to aid a visibly shaken Hugo.

"Something's off with him," Lansius remarked to Audrey.

"His strength is almost like that of a Mage Knight," she nervously agreed.

Sterling turned to them. "Traveling with him, I still can't figure out if he's a man or some fell beast in disguise," he added, his voice muffled by the jammed helmet.

"Not even a fell beast is that strong," Audrey remarked.

Lansius shook his head. "Just what happened in the capital?" he wondered aloud. "Oi, Anci, let's talk over snacks and drinks." And then to Carla, he said, "Could you arrange that?"

"At once, my lord," Carla dutifully responded, though her expression showed disapproval.

"It's okay. He might look tough, but even he is wary of Hannei," Lansius reassured.

"Hannei? That cursed mage is here?" Anci suddenly crouched, scanning the area cautiously.

Audrey chuckled at Anci's reaction.

Feeling the need to move the discussion, Lansius urged, "Come, let's talk inside. Otherwise, we'll draw more attention."

Council Chamber

The lord and lady dismissed the destruction caused by Anci as a security test. The guardsmen who had been bested voiced little complaint, especially after receiving compensation for their injuries. Many who knew Anci were thrilled by his visit. With the matter settled, the lord and lady proceeded to the council chamber.

Lansius was still dressed in his celebration attire from the accolade ceremony, while Audrey wore her black gambeson over her robe, her sword resting neatly on the wooden bench beside her. Anci, comfortably still in his armor, joined them at the round table.

Hugo, having fortunately landed on soft ground, suffered no injuries except to his pride. Now, the recently knighted man sat beside Anci, with Carla standing behind him.

Sterling had been sent to the blacksmith, accompanied by Dietrich, to have his jammed helmet removed, a casualty of his scuffle with one of the guardsmen.

"So, how's the capital?" Lansius initiated the conversation.

"It's glorious! I had sword bouts almost every day. Lots of tournaments, both formal and informal." Anci chuckled. He then glanced around, seeming to recall something. "You okay, sir slowpoke?"

"Never felt better," Hugo replied with a load of sarcasm.

Anci chuckled again. "I said I'm sorry. I thought you'd be heavier."

"Your strength is uncanny. Did you eat a fell beast's heart or something?" Hugo complained.

"Ah, never tried that. Though I almost fought one," Anci replied, casually munching on a fruit.

"How did you manage to send me flying?"

Anci chuckled. "I didn't go to the capital just to run errands. I'm also on a quest to strengthen myself. And as you know, there are ways to gain strength, either naturally or unnaturally."

Anci's cryptic answer was met with a grumble from Hugo.

"So, how's Lord Arte's mission?" asked Lansius, trying to put the conversation on track.

Through Anci's occasionally incoherent ramblings, Lansius understood that the mission to the capital had been successful. Lord Arte's bid to reclaim Arvena was sanctioned, and Bengrieve's bid for Lansius's baron title had also been approved.

He then silently expressed his gratitude to the men and women who had made this possible.

The diplomatic gymnastics must be crazy . . .

Lansius couldn't fathom the favors owed and the bribes necessary to achieve all this. However, not everything was cause for celebration.

"On our journey, we found the towns and villages in Elandia lifeless. Bandits are on the prowl, and the local lords seem to be losing their grip," Anci reported.

Lansius listened intently.

"Even armed convoys are being ambushed. Bah, I couldn't find a moment's peace there!" Anci added somberly. "The villagers I had saved on my first trip had turned into brigands by the time I returned from the capital. They blamed the bad harvest. But that didn't explain why they killed a nobleman's wife, so I had no choice . . ."

Lansius poured ale into his cup. "Drink up," he offered gently.

Anci gulped it down.

So the situation in Elandia was already bad before the Nicopolans even showed up . . .

Sadly, there was little they could do to help. Despite Lansius's newfound prestige and power, he was just a minor player in a backwater province.

"So, you got knighted?" Audrey interjected with a lighter question, casually munching on a morsel of bread, ham, and lettuce.

Anci showed a smug expression before answering, "I won the jousting tournament, and Lord Arte knighted me afterward."

"Ha, good for you!" Audrey smiled, genuinely happy for a fellow Arvenian's success, despite her Centurian origins.

Hugo raised his cup to honor Anci, who nodded respectfully.

"So, has Lord Arte returned to Midlandia?" Lansius inquired.

"Yes, he's sorting things out in Midlandia. Oh, and their marriage got approved, so I'll be heading back to Korelia to fetch Lady Felicity."

"Just you and the squires?" asked Lansius.

"Nah, in about two weeks, officials from the capital will arrive in Korelia. The entourage and escort for Lady Felicity will be part of the officials' convoy," Anci elaborated.

Lansius leaned back in his sturdy wooden chair. "So, my baronial patent is finally coming."

"A word of caution, though," Anci added. "Lord Arte mentioned that, given the circumstances in the Imperium and your recent victories, they might want you to intervene in the Elandia/Nicopola conflict."

Upon hearing this, Hugo and Carla exchanged troubled glances, and Lansius sighed deeply. "Lowlandia doesn't have the capabilities to wage war out of province. We don't have the manpower or the logistics to support it."

"I find that hard to believe," Anci remarked.

"Let me clarify: We don't have the capabilities to wage war outside Lowlandia and actually win."

Anci grinned and chuckled. "Well, now that Lady Audrey is a baroness in her own right, I doubt those officials will be able to pressure you much."

Lansius gave a thoughtful nod.

"My lord, are you considering a return to Korelia to welcome them?" Hugo inquired.

"No, our priorities lie here in Korimor. We need to figure out how to sustain an extra of four thousand people through the winter," Lansius said, more to himself than to his staff. Then, turning to Anci, he asked, "What's the word in the capital about the emperor?"

Anci's grin widened. "Do you really want to know?"

Lansius nodded. "The rumors are many, and I need the truth."

Anci chuckled. "You're lucky to have asked me. I was sought after by many factions, and they were quite open with their secrets," he boasted. "I wasn't exactly a white knight. For the right price, I'd accept invitations and, let's say, resolve disputes in duels . . ."

Hugo shook his head in disapproval but remained silent.

Leaning in closer, Anci continued. "And let me tell you, behind closed doors, they speak of the Imperium and the Ageless as if they're already dead . . ."

Lansius silently drank his ale, offering no response.

"From what I've gathered, it's likely that the Ageless One is no longer with us. Yet, the ministers and the Imperial bureaucracy continue to maintain a facade. Meanwhile, the nobles, like vultures, are busy carving up the Imperium: making alliances, countering, and impeding their rivals. It's as if they expect the Imperium to fall anytime soon."

"How utterly foolish of them," Lansius finally commented. "The end of the Imperium isn't going to be pretty, or clean. We'll have a succession crisis followed by strife before the strongest can claim as the successor."

Lansius's dire outlook prompted Audrey and Hugo to take a sip of their drinks.

After a brief pause, Hugo ventured, "What do you think of Lord Arte's chances of reclaiming Arvena?"

Anci looked squarely at Hugo. "Even with Midlandia's backing, Lord Arte admitted it's a longshot. But it's a blood feud, and you know how these things go."

Lansius exhaled deeply. "Sometimes, I wonder when things will start to improve for us. Will it take ten years? Or perhaps twenty?"

"Twenty? I'll probably be dead by then," Anci lamented half-jokingly.

Audrey chuckled at his remark. Unexpectedly, Hugo retorted, "Please, die alone. I still plan to raise my kids and keep them away from unscrupulous men like you."

Hugo's coarse joke managed to draw laughter from the rest of the council members. The laughter was a welcome reprieve, as their nerves had been strained by the dark tidings from the capital.

From Anci, Lansius learned about the situation outside of Lowlandia. Unfortunately, Anci had no information about his family from Bellandia, mentioning he hadn't met Lord Bengrieve, despite traveling to Cascasonne. When asked how he met Sterling, Anci explained that their meeting was coincidental, as few were traveling to Lowlandia, making it likely for people like them to encounter each other.

Despite Hugo's insistence on putting Anci in the dungeon, Lansius gave them accommodation in a guest house, entrusting Sir Harold and his men with security.

Dame Daniella returned to the castle as soon as she heard about the security breach. However, Lady Audrey instructed her to return to her task. Lord Lansius wanted her to ensure that the newly formed Nicopolan army had a functional administration and was well motivated to march.

Priority was given to repairing the carts, as the lord wanted them in good shape for transportation. Given the limited number of draft horses, only well-functioning carts that wouldn't overburden the animals were allowed.

As for the Nicopolan men, a fitness selection reduced their size from three thousand to two thousand. Those who didn't make the cut, along with the civilians who couldn't be integrated into Korimor, were designated as camp followers.

Servius's contingent of five hundred remained an independent regiment, acting as military police in case the much larger army became involved in a mutiny.

Thus, there were currently two distinct Nicopolan groups: Servius's Nicopolan regiment and the larger Nicopolan army.

The castle's study chamber was occupied only by the lord and lady.

"Nicopola, Elandia, Tiberia," Lansius mumbled, standing and observing the map on the table.

"Still thinking about them?" Audrey asked from a chair overlooking the window.

"I don't want to, but I can't help it," he lamented.

With the agility of a big cat, Audrey moved up behind him and gently encircled her arms around his waist, leaning in to whisper in his ear, "You better focus on things we can handle."

"But they're all interconnected. Without Elandia—"

"That's a problem for the people in the capital. We're not the Lord and Lady of Elandia."

Lansius caressed her hands and nodded. "Good point."

"Glad to help," she quipped, nestling her face comfortably into his back.

"What's with the sudden affection?" he asked gently.

"Why, don't you like having a sweet and affectionate wife?"

Lansius chuckled. "Drey, what's on your mind?"

"Aside from you on top of me?" she flirted.

Lansius blinked. "I must warn you, I'm bad with temptation."

Audrey giggled and released her hug. She sat on his chair and leaned in. "So, my lord, when will you make your move?"

"When the troops are well-rested," Lansius replied, recalling the recent report from Three Hills about Umberland that had solidified their decision. "That reminds me, I need to send word to Korelia. Also, I have to meet with Sir Michael to convince him to stay."

"It might be better to send a letter directly to Lord Robert, asking him for a favor," Audrey suggested.

Lansius raised an eyebrow. "And that favor would be Sir Michael?"

Audrey nodded. "I heard Lord Robert still hopes for Sir Michael to marry into his family. I think he might agree to attach Michael to our forces, seeing it as a better opportunity for him to distinguish himself."

"That's quite an insight . . . You're getting good at this," praised Lansius.

Audrey's expression turned smug, then quickly serious. "Lans, there's one thing I still don't understand: Will there be food in Umberland?"

"Unlikely." Lansius shook his head. "And that's precisely why we can't wait until harvest. We'll march as soon as we're ready."

CHAPTER 15

IMPERIUM IN IMPERIO

The land south of the Great River ripened, appearing as if a blanket of gold had been spread over the countryside. The fall of 4425 had arrived, and it should have been the merriest time of the year. However, for the Arvenians under Lord Gottfried's control, there was only preparation for war.

Men from Bellandia were among the thousands of Arvenians recruited for the upcoming campaign. They were encamped near the Arvena-Tiberia border, and tensions were running high. While the Arvenians were reluctant participants in this conflict, they felt pressured to demonstrate their loyalty.

Worse yet, rumors were circulating that the emperor was dying. These whispers were embellished with claims of Lord Gottfried attempting to rescue the dying emperor from the clutches of evil ministers. However, the Arvenians weren't buying it.

Although they were shocked by the news that the Ageless was dying, the memory of how Gottfried had killed the previous Lord of Arvena and his family remained fresh in their minds. There seemed to be no good reason for Lord Gottfried's actions, other than to seize Arvena for himself. Thus, the Arvenians generally viewed their new overlord with distrust.

Hans, a young lad in a gambeson, entered the tent in a hurry. "Marc, did you hear? Another marching order has been issued."

"So soon?" Marc groaned. They had just made themselves comfortable.

"It's possible that they're not going to wait for the harvest," Darren, the butcher's son, commented.

Hans and Marc sighed as the three of them began to pack their belongings. Marc and Darren hailed from Bellandia, while Hans was from a neighboring village. The three were levied troops, lightly armed with spears, helmets, and thick clothes serving as gambesons.

A muscular man with a graying mustache peeked from outside and asked, "You lads heard of the marching order?"

"Connor," Marc exclaimed excitedly. "Indeed, we just heard it. What's the news on your side?"

"I'm on an errand," he explained, offering a lump of waxed parchment to Darren, his son.

The trio was ecstatic. Darren quickly went outside to their campfire to cook the red meat while they still had the chance. Hans followed and nudged Darren playfully. "It's a good thing your dad's a well-known butcher, eh?"

Darren could only respond with a proud grin.

Connor entered the tent before replying to Marc, "Yeah, the news isn't good. They're moving us away from the villages and marches. I guess they're not going to use us to help with the harvest."

"You think they are going to send us into war?" Marc asked.

Connor's response was only to exhale sharply. He took his wineskin and offered, "Wine?"

"Don't mind if I do." Marc gratefully took a sip of the spiced wine. The paleness in his cheeks from sleeping rough turned into a healthy red.

The two talked briefly about the situation and what news Connor had about Bellandia.

"It's a good thing that your mother and sister aren't in the village anymore. Life is hard with all the food and grain quotas."

Marc sighed, knowing that, as vegetable farmers, they had limited means to fulfill such quotas.

Darren and Hans returned with sizzling meat on a skillet.

"Eat well," Connor said with a grin.

The three used their knives and devoured the steak.

Marc noticed Connor looking at Darren with worry. "Don't you worry. When the time comes, we will protect Darren, I swear it—on this piece of good meat." The sudden declaration prompted laughter from the others.

Connor chuckled. "I love it when the bribe works."

"But really, you should ask them to put Darren as a clerk. He can calculate. That way, he'll be working with the command staff, much safer than here."

Darren groaned. "Stop it, Marc. I'm not as good as my teacher. I calculate slower than a snail moving."

Connor sighed bitterly. "If only he were here to mentor. Perhaps we could save more youngsters from becoming footmen."

"Well, not even Lansius can save me. I am far too stupid to be taught," Marc joked. "It is always spear and shield for me."

Before they could continue their banter, the sound of horns echoed in the distance.

"That's the call to assemble. Better hurry," Connor said to Marc and then to Darren, "Take care. I'll visit when I'm on another errand."

The trio quickly tidied up after their meal, grabbed their gear, and headed to the designated assembly field. The sun shone brightly as thousands of Arvenians formed up next to their northern army counterparts.

Chateau de Cascasonne

Seneschal Bengrieve's preparations were complete. He and his private army would march west to maintain order along the Elandia-Midlandia border. Southern Elandia was in turmoil after the famine-stricken people from neighboring Nicopola province had raided the land in search of grains or livestock.

However, instead of focusing on static defense along his province's border, Lord Bengrieve and his staff had a different plan in mind. Recognizing the challenge of maintaining a watch at the border, they aimed to seize a strategic castle in Elandia, intending to keep all fighting confined to Elandian soil.

Externally, this strategy was to prevent the conflict from spilling over to Midlandia, but in reality, they planned to claim the land and castle for themselves. Like other lords, Lord Bengrieve had no intention of aiding the Imperium without personal gain. Moreover, he doubted that the high court would dare antagonize him and Midlandia, given their dire need for support against Gottfried.

The situation was ripe for taking advantage of. However, Bengrieve was cautious not to overreach. With the affluent Saint Candidate Nay swaying the masses and the Lord of Midlandia's position vacant, the region faced potential jeopardy.

The region's stability was far from set in stone; it was akin to sitting on a three-legged chair, each leg of a different height, creating an imbalance that could easily topple. Bengrieve understood this precarious situation perfectly.

Thus, he wielded his army like a double-edged sword, each side pointed at his enemy from both within and without.

"Please excuse me, my lord," the steward interrupted, finding Lord Bengrieve sitting in his lavish garden outside the chateau, enjoying the sunset.

"What's the urgency?" Lord Bengrieve inquired, motioning his squires to give them privacy.

"Lord Gottfried has made his move against Tiberia."

"Before the harvest? Are you certain?" the lord asked calmly.

"I've confirmed it from two different sources."

"What about our border with Arvena?"

"Our scouts have infiltrated Arvena but found no military buildup at the border."

Bengrieve mused, "It seems that Gottfried has respected his promise."

The steward raised an eyebrow. "What is your plan then, my lord?"

"If nothing is amiss, then we'll depart for Elandia in three days," Bengrieve declared.

The steward bowed his head. "Understood. But, how about young Lord Arte's wishes?"

"Let him be," Bengrieve answered without hesitation. "Gottfried never asked about or mentioned him. And Midlandia hasn't formally endorsed the young lord of Arvena."

"Not to overstep my position, but is it wise, my lord? When he finds out that we backed an insurgence, Gottfried might use this as a pretext for hostility."

Bengrieve smiled. "I keep a dagger at Gottfried's back, just as he keeps one behind mine. The only difference is the size and sharpness."

"It doesn't seem like he has one behind you," the steward ventured.

"Then he'll fall, and I'll be the one to uproot his evil intentions from the Imperium's soil." Bengrieve chuckled at his rhetoric. "I doubt Gottfried is that incompetent."

"Your position is solid, my lord, save only for the ongoing succession crisis. Perhaps if you—"

"Don't worry. I have a better candidate than myself for that role," Bengrieve interjected, knowing that his staff wanted him to take the position as the Lord of Midlandia.

The old steward bowed his head respectfully.

"Ah, my guest has arrived," Bengrieve observed, watching a squire escort a woman.

"Then, I'll excuse myself."

"I don't mind if you stay. It's only Hannei."

"Understood." The steward then moved to a more appropriate place, close enough to be within earshot, yet far enough to maintain discretion, ready to offer advice as needed.

"Lady Hannei, please take a seat," Bengrieve offered from his seat.

"Gratitude, my lord," Hannei responded, taking her place on the wooden bench opposite her master.

"I apologize for keeping you in this chateau for so long, but the situation is rapidly evolving."

Hannei bowed her head, signaling her acceptance. She understood this wasn't a genuine apology but rather a formal way to initiate a discussion.

"You said you're here on an errand?"

"Yes, my lord. My charge, Lady Felicity, has arrived safely in Korelia and wishes to stay there. I'm here on behalf of the Lord of Korelia to bring his squire to a healer and to deliver his letter."

Bengrieve nodded; he had already received and read the letter. "And what are your plans after this?"

"Should my lord release me from my charge, I wish to retire to my hometown," she articulated, echoing the words she had practiced.

"Very well, I release you from your charge. Your contract is fulfilled, and I'll reward you accordingly."

Hannei bowed deeply in response. However, instead of dismissing her, Bengrieve handed her a missive, and Hannei rose respectfully to accept it.

"It's the latest report from Lowlandia," he explained.

She read the missive, expecting something major, but found nothing noteworthy. Puzzled, she read it again.

"Well?" Bengrieve inquired.

"Pardon, my lord, but I couldn't find anything—"

Bengrieve sighed. "Those two are married."

Hannei furrowed her brows. "Lansius and Audrey? Indeed, they are, my lord."

"Why didn't you mention this in your reports?" the lord asked in frustration.

"B-but, my lord, this humble servant already did mention it. My report stated that the two are enamored," she explained, nervously.

"Enamored . . . ?" Bengrieve shook his head, falling into deep contemplation. "Yes, you did write something to that effect . . . It's just that I never expected . . ."

Hannei squinted. She had never seen Bengrieve at a loss for words and became suspicious of Audrey's true identity.

"Lansius should marry Lord Robert's daughter, not Lady Audrey. I have plans for her," the lord lamented, fury evident in his tone.

It was only then that Hannei understood the issue. If Lansius were here, she was sure he would tell her: "In this day and age, nobles marry not out of love, but out of necessity and alliance between Houses." She vaguely recalled one of his stories about young Romans who often married wealthy widows for support. He had mentioned someone named Octavian or Augustus, who married a woman already pregnant by her first husband. This marriage was a strategic move for wealth, political connections, and legitimacy.

Bengrieve asked for and drank some spiced wine, seemingly attempting to quench his overwhelming emotions. However, his disdain was unmistakable. "Why do even smart men like Lansius behave illogically? This is absurd!" he exclaimed, raising his voice.

Hannei flinched and lowered her gaze, aware of how powerful and terrible Bengrieve could be.

The steward stepped forward. "A word, my lord, if you wish to hear it."

Bengrieve gestured for him to speak.

"My lord should remember the letter from the current Lord of Korelia brought by Lady Hannei."

"What about it?"

"The letter is full of praises and hopes for my lord's support. I doubt the person who wrote it has any seditious plans behind your back."

Bengrieve grumbled. "Perhaps he's even darker than Gottfried," hinting at his distrust.

"I doubt it, my lord. It's more likely that the current Lord of Korelia simply *doesn't know*."

Bengrieve took a deep breath and nodded. "Perhaps this is but a coincidence . . ."

The steward nodded. Meanwhile, Hannei, visibly anxious, was eager to ask but knew it wasn't her place.

Bengrieve leaned back in his chair and turned his gaze back to Hannei. "Is Lansius loyal?"

"Lansius is Lansius. He has fooled other lords in battle and defeated them. I doubt I could fathom him. However, from my observation, there's no indication that he's disloyal to you, my lord," Hannei answered spontaneously.

Bengrieve seemed pleased. "And why is that?"

"The Lord of Korelia needs an ally, and you are the most able and understanding benefactor anyone could wish for."

Bengrieve smiled at the praise, but replied, "I wonder if your sweet words will change under the nectar of truth."

Hannei gulped and could only look down.

Bengrieve stood up. "I'll march west in three days. I shouldn't worry about some lord from Lowlandia. However, let it be known that he has taken a prize greater than he's worth."

Korimor

In a move that shocked everyone, Lord Lansius announced his order to mobilize. He explained to his staff that they couldn't afford to wait for the harvest, due to the deteriorating situation with the Nicopolan refugees; there was simply no solution to be found in Korimor.

Upon hearing the announcement, the castle and the city immediately buzzed with activity to prepare for the upcoming march.

The recently knighted Sir Hugo was appointed steward of Korimor. To maintain order, Lord Lansius stationed two hundred of Servius's Nicopolan regiment to ensure Korimor's loyalty to his House. While public sentiment was generally favorable, he did not want to risk the city succumbing to rebellious tendencies.

Sir Hugo's new position came with a personal cost. This appointment meant he had to postpone his marriage until next year. However, the prestige accompanying the role, coupled with the absence of a more suitable candidate, made the decision easier for him.

While waiting for the army's two-day preparation for mobilization, the lord and lady organized a special banquet to send off Sir Michael and his White Lake cavalry. The cavalry, having completed their mission and recovered from the battle, were set to return home the following day.

Despite the food situation not yet improving, with the harvest still a week away, the castle staff successfully managed to prepare a modest yet lively banquet. The Great Hall of Korimor was filled with feasting, music, and laughter.

"Sir Michael, please extend my gratitude to the Lord of White Lake," Lansius expressed to the honored guest seated next to him.

"Certainly, my lord. On behalf of Lord Robert, please accept our gratitude for the share of the baggage train and the spoils from the city."

"It's within your rights. You earned it," Lansius replied with a smile. Audrey then asked, "Sir Michael, are you sure you don't want to wait until the harvest festival?"

"I'd love to, my lady, but the men are restless to return home. Please excuse their manners."

The lord and lady chuckled and raised their cups, followed by Sir Michael and the others. They drank and enjoyed the music and lively atmosphere.

"A letter if you will, for the Lord of White Lake," Lansius said as the festivities began to wind down.

Sir Michael respectfully took the sealed letter. "I'll ensure my lord receives it."

"Sir Michael, know that the doors of my House are always open to you," Lansius said.

Sir Michael bowed. "It's an honor, my lord."

Suddenly, noises from outside interrupted the banquet. Dietrich and Carla escorted in three men, who turned out to be Batu and his two relatives. Sigmund, the skald, sensed that something was off, and the music stopped. However, despite the urgency of their actions, Batu showed no sign of hostility, only a proud and joyful expression.

"My Noyan," he called out as he approached.

The lord and lady descended from their high table. "Batu, what brings you here?" Lansius asked.

"A messenger from my tribe just came. They said, my first wife delivered a healthy baby boy!"

The room erupted in congratulations for Batu, the new father. Cheers were raised to salute the fortune of their honored ally.

"What wonderful news," Lady Audrey said, pouring spiced wine into a silver goblet.

"Brother, congratulations on your son," Lansius said, offering the goblet to Batu.

"My Noyan, my lady, this is a great honor," Batu replied, overwhelmed by everyone's well wishes.

Audrey pondered for a moment before deciding on the most heartfelt wish: "May the boy and mother stay healthy."

Caught up in the moment, Batu raised his goblet and took a hearty gulp, his action met with cheers from the crowd.

"I'm here to ask for the Noyan's blessing," Batu declared, addressing the room. "I plan to name him Lancius."

Upon hearing this, Lansius let out a chuckle, and the crowd erupted in another round of delighted cheers, proud of the name Batu had chosen. "May he rule the plains as an honorable warrior!" someone called out, eliciting nods and smiles from the others.

"I feel unworthy," Lansius admitted, but the lady pulled his arm and whispered, "It's a good name. You should feel honored."

"I do," Lansius reassured her with a smile.

"Noyan, may the boy inherit some of your battle skills," Batu insisted.

Lansius exhaled, and the crowd fell silent. "May Lancius, son of Batu, only know peace and never need to use his skills in warfare."

Hearing this, the crowd and Batu rejoiced. Sir Hugo, Sir Michael, Dietrich, Sigmund, and Carla all took turns to congratulate the new father. Sterling, who had resumed his position at Lord Lansius's side, returned from the castle's cellar with extra spiced wine and ale to refill everyone's cups and goblets. It was truly a day to celebrate.

The lord and lady, along with their grateful staff and allies, were savoring their brief respite, uncertain of when they would meet again. Soon, they would embark on their campaign to the west, not knowing what fate awaited them there.

CHAPTER 16

CHAMPION OF THE IMPERIUM

Korimor

Who would've thought that the fearless intruder was the current Knight Champion of the Imperium? Moreover, such a highly esteemed champion was on a friendly basis with the lord and lady. People were abuzz with this newfound revelation, their respect for the lord and lady reaching an all-time high despite the order to mobilize.

Wherever the Arvenian knight and his squires went, people flocked to catch a glimpse of the current Knight Champion. The title meant that Sir Archibald was the strongest knight in the Imperium, whether on horseback or on foot.

It was such a staggering achievement that, had it not been for the tight schedule, Lansius would have thrown a grand party to celebrate his friend's triumph. His friendship with Anci harked back to his previous world, where he had formed strong bonds with fearless, sometimes reckless, but unyielding players. He saw a similar spirit in Anci and felt he could trust his back to someone like him.

Since their arrival, his two squires had tirelessly spread the account of their master's victory in all the places they visited in the city. Anci himself frequented the best taverns in the city with a heavy escort from Sir Justin and his best men-at-arms, lending more credence to the squires' stories.

While it was hard to fathom whether the squires' story was true or heavily embellished, the crowd enjoyed a good story and treated the champion like a celebrity. Moreover, the tens of guardsmen who had fought Sir Anci were all too happy to embellish the story further, recounting Sir Anci's superhuman strength and unrivaled martial prowess in their fights.

The minstrels spun the story into an even greater one in their ballads. For all who were fortunate to be involved, the greater the story, the better the drink, the better the tips.

Spontaneous parties were held wherever he visited, and there were countless invitations for supper, lunch, and dinner, even hastily made proposals to marry their daughters to him.

Sir Anci was pleased to be treated like a celebrity. He hadn't expected his new title as champion to be held in such high regard so far away from the capital. But above all else, the Lowlandians respected strength.

However, as abruptly as he had arrived, Sir Anci decided to ride alongside the White Lake contingent as far as Korelia.

The next day at first light, Sir Michael and his White Lake cavalry assembled outside the city gates. The lord and lady were there to bid them farewell. Again, stealing the limelight was Sir Anci and his two squires, with people from the city flocking to send him off.

"You know, my only regret is probably not accompanying Lansius during his search for you. But at that time, I had lost so many friends, and the thought of confirming another loss was just unbearable," Sir Anci confided to Lady Audrey as they walked to his horse.

"If that's an apology, then consider it accepted," Audrey replied warmly. Although they weren't exactly friends, they had met on several occasions during their service to the previous Lord of Arvena and had briefly fought together, with her as Lansius's cavalry commander and him as the deputy.

Sir Anci chuckled. "Gratitude, my lady." Then, turning to Lord Lansius, he added, "My lord, thank you for the hospitality and the extra coins."

"It's the least we can do for your assistance," Lansius replied, patting the knight's shoulder. "I didn't expect the Knight Champion of the Imperium would ride to Korimor only to ask for permission to take Lady Felicity home. Also, our gratitude for bringing Sterling safely back to us."

"Small things," Anci remarked, laughing. "The warm welcome, the parties, and the heavy purse certainly made this extra trip worthwhile. Korimor is surely a fine city."

Lansius responded with a smile. "Please, ensure Lady Felicity's safety for me and extend my best wishes to Lord Arte."

"Consider it done."

Just then, Sir Michael approached with his squires. "My lord, my lady," they greeted.

"Sir Michael, please take care of Sir Archibald for me," Lansius requested.

The two knights exchanged slight head bows.

Anci spoke first. "I better say it now. No hard feelings? I believe we've met in battle before."

Sir Michael was amused. "It's common for knights to cross paths in battles. No hard feelings, Sir Archibald. In fact, I feel much safer knowing the Knight Champion of the Imperium is willing to ride with us."

Anci laughed at the compliment. "Please, call me Anci. My squires and I will trouble you until we reach Korelia."

"The honor is all mine."

Lansius watched the two and commented, "Seeing former opponents trading friendly banter like this, perhaps the Grand Alliance isn't so farfetched after all."

"The Grand Alliance is a brilliant idea, my lord. I shall use all my talents to make it happen," Sir Michael declared, with Sir Anci grinning beside him.

Lady Audrey, pleased with the declaration, said, "Safe travels, you two. Drink plenty, watch out for the sun, and take care of your horses."

The knights and their squires bowed to the lady of the city. "May fortune always follow you, my lady, my lord. I await good news from your western campaign," Sir Michael said, before motioning for his squire to bring his steed.

"When will you leave for your campaign?" Sir Anci asked Lady Audrey.

Audrey looked at Lansius, who replied, "If preparations are complete, tomorrow after breakfast."

"Why ask? Interested in joining us?" Audrey quipped.

Anci flashed a predatory grin. "Tempting, but I'm responsible for a noble wedding."

The three chuckled. Three years ago, they were merely unnamed commoners; now, their reputations had grown immensely. Lansius was known as the Black Lord, a reputation so frightening it could stop a crying toddler. Audrey had become the Baroness of Korimor with rumors of her possessing the Fell Beast's eyes, and Anci was celebrated as the current Knight Champion of the Imperium.

Their rise to power was unprecedented, but fate was a fickle mistress and might easily take it all away. Tomorrow, Lansius and Audrey would embark on a dangerous campaign to the west, while Anci was destined to fight an uphill battle in the upcoming Arvenian war.

The Elven year 4425 was yet to end, but Lansius was facing his third armed conflict of the year. From summer through fall, his small troops had engaged in the battles of Korelia and Korimor, and now they were preparing for the campaign to the west. Spirited as they might be, the continuous wars were beginning to take their toll on everyone.

Lansius himself quietly harbored doubts about his own health, yet he knew there was no choice but to personally lead this complex campaign. With Audrey at his side, he drew a deep breath, watching Anci and the White Lake riders sally south into the Great Plains of Lowlandia.

The following day, Lord Lansius led his House to march. The people of Korimor bid them farewell with mixed feelings. Many were grateful that the lord was taking the Nicopolans away, yet they were also reluctant to part with their new lady and lord protector. Their departure cast a gloom over the populace, who were just a few weeks away from celebrating their harvest festival.

Nevertheless, those from Korimor who joined the march were highly motivated. Just as he had done with the Korelians, the lord selected only those who could ride horses and use crossbows. The chosen two hundred were reformed into a new dragoon company.

Excluding the nomadic tribes, the lord and lady had arrived in Korelia with only a handful of heavy cavalry. Now, they commanded almost three thousand men, along with another thousand camp followers.

Before leaving, Lord Lansius summoned Sir Hugo to the castle's battlements.

"My lord," Sir Hugo greeted as he arrived.

"Sir Hugo, please, join me for a walk."

They strolled along the battlements, overlooking the golden swaths of ripened land soon to be harvested. "It'll be a good harvest," the lord commented.

"I shall do my utmost to assist the populace with their harvest," Sir Hugo replied.

"That is wise," Lansius praised. "We need all the grain we can get. Beware of pests and locusts."

"I shall keep a watchful eye."

Their walk brought them to another side of the castle, overlooking the vast plains of Lowlandia stretching into the distance.

The lord stopped and gazed at his knight. "Sir Hugo, our past had its complications . . . but I believe we've moved beyond that."

"My lord, I am part of your House. Your victory and grandeur are all I wish for," the knight replied earnestly.

Pleased with his reassurance, Lansius presented a letter to Sir Hugo. "Tonight, read this and think it over. It outlines two paths for you to choose from. Remember, there's no right or wrong. Both are equally wise."

Sir Hugo accepted the letter. "Gratitude for your trust. I will consider it carefully."

After their discussion, they returned to the gatehouse and descended the spiral stone staircase. Below, the staff had awaited.

"My lord, please return safely. I shall await your instructions," Sir Hugo said.

"Gratitude for your concern. Please, keep me informed of any developments." Lord Lansius paused and gave a small nod. "Then, until we meet again." He then joined the lady and their staff in a parade through the city, where the people of Korimor gathered to wish them a swift victory and a safe journey home.

The parade, though brief, was memorable, with the townsfolk offering drinks and wrapped gifts as snacks for the journey. Soon, they reached the city gate, where the army awaited their arrival.

For this campaign, Lord Lansius commanded:

20 knights, led by Sir Harold

30 light cavalry, led by Dame Daniella and Dietrich

30 nomadic horse archers and scouts, led by one of Batu's sworn brothers

150 dragoons from Korelia, equipped like men-at-arms and with crossbows

200 dragoons from Korimor, similarly equipped

300 Nicopolan regiment on foot, led by Servius

2000 Nicopolan army on foot

1000 Nicopolan camp followers

As instructed, the Nicopolan army and camp followers utilized the carts confiscated from the war, loading them with as many tents, tools, and weapons as they could find. They were aware that the lord anticipated multiple sieges and had prepared accordingly.

For supplies, they relied on what the Nicopolans had, which would last only three more weeks. Even with additional provisions from the city's granary, they could sustain no longer than a month.

The only saving grace was the freshly smoked fish. Korimor boasted thriving freshwater fishing in their river, and the previous lord had popularized smoked fish as a delicacy. Thus, the army's morale was quite high, as they could enjoy good meals during the early days of their march.

The lord rode toward the center of the formation and gave a small speech. "Fellow Arvenians, Korelians, people of Korimor, and Nicopolans. From now on, you are members of House Lansius. Once again, I promise to treat you as fairly as possible, given your seniority and past merits toward the House."

Everyone felt inspired by the lord's address.

The lord continued. "Since you are now members of my House, remember this well: No one is born or raised a hero, but everyone can walk the path of a hero. I'm sure you know the stories of the heroes of old. Yes, they're unrealistic. Yes, they're what the old women tell their children. However, the idea is pure and true! And victory tends to follow whoever is pure and true."

Now, even the staff was piqued by the speech.

"Remember the way of the hero of old: Be cunning, but honest toward the innocent. Be strong, but compassionate toward the weak. Be powerful, but respectful toward the law. Men, display this on your march, and people will see you as heroes. Display this consistently, and perhaps we'll redeem the blood we've spilled on this soil, so the Ancients will grant us another victory and protect us from hunger."

The men nodded solemnly. The Arvenians and Korelians were especially grateful for their past victories.

As it ended, the lord and lady, flanked by the knights and riders, led the march southwest. Thousands of people with hundreds of horse-drawn carts followed in high spirits.

"What did you speak with Sir Hugo about?" Audrey asked as they rode slowly, careful not to burden the footmen.

"Well, if he's going to be our right hand along with Sir Justin, then he needs to navigate power and temptation," Lansius replied, ensuring they were not within earshot of anyone.

Audrey squinted her eyes. "Lans, that's too cryptic."

Lansius chuckled. "I told him if he could resist temptation, he should seek advice from Omin and learn from him."

Her eyes widened. "Are you sure that's a good idea?"

"Your cousin is a smart man. It'll be a waste not to have someone learn from him."

"But, Hugo is rather ambitious."

"This is why I gave him two paths. One is the loyal path, where he does not need to meet with Omin. This path is also no less wise or smart. I call this the 'see nothing bad, hear nothing bad' path."

Audrey pondered. "So one path involves not meeting my cousin at all, while the other requires learning from him but at the risk of compromising his loyalty . . . Why push him into such a situation?"

Lansius broke into a smile. "I need to know his tendencies when in power. The wise warn that power tends to corrupt, and absolute power corrupts absolutely."

The Baroness of Korimor nodded deeply before quipping, "Am I in danger then?"

Lansius furrowed his brow. "Why?"

"Because you're the most powerful person I know right now, and you said you're bad with temptations." Audrey grinned as she said it.

Lansius chuckled ominously and retorted in a whisper, "I'll have you tonight."

"But we'll be in tents," she protested.

"No excuses."

Audrey shook her head, feigning trouble, but nodded in agreement. This led to a lighthearted banter that eased their tension on the slow march southwest.

Meanwhile, miles away from the main army, Dietrich was leading a forward scout team, establishing a surveillance net spanning almost half a day's journey. Behind him, Dame Daniella led a reactionary force.

Acting as the senior commander in the lord's army, Sir Harold kept watchful eyes on the surroundings. He was concerned about remnants of the Nicopolans who might attempt to raid their baggage train. Although it was a slim chance, given that many feared the famed Black Lord and cowered at the sight of the blue and bronze banner, Sir Harold took no risks.

As a commander, his experience as a traveling knight proved to be invaluable. Well-versed in travel logistics, Sir Harold was adept at planning by utilizing available information and limited resources. Furthermore, during his brief tenure under Lord Lansius and Batu, Sir Harold had learned to be meticulous and paid great attention to detail.

He learned to utilize the scouts to their fullest abilities and to prepare an adequate reactionary force as a countermeasure. Sir Harold was also constantly on the lookout for safer routes and better places to camp each day. His experience shaped him into the type of commander whom opponents would find hard to catch off guard.

Together with Dame Daniella, Dietrich, and Sterling, he worked tirelessly to safeguard the main army from potential ambushes and unpleasant surprises.

And soon, they would encounter their first surprise on the march.

CHAPTER 17

THREE HILLS VISITS

Three Hills

The Lord of Three Hills, Jorge, had summoned a war council to discuss the situation in Umberland. They had sent multiple armed parties to assess the situation. Jorge and his staff had personally little interest in the mountainous region, but now their survival depended on it.

If Umberland remained at the mercy of the Nicopolans, then thousands more armed refugees from Nicopola could arrive, with deadly consequences for Three Hills City.

"Our scouting group found Nicopolans camped in the village of Ardia," the steward reported.

"That's close to our land. Do we know their number?" the lord asked.

"The scouts believed it's almost a thousand."

Jorge drew a deep breath.

"Harvest is near; this could jeopardize everything," an old knight who was loyal to House Jorge lamented.

Sir Arius stepped forward. "I'll lead my contingent and the Crimson Knights to deter them from the village."

"The fame of the Crimson Knights might be enough to prevent the villagers from fleeing, but can we actually win the fight?" the old knight pondered.

Jorge gazed at Sir Morton, who replied, "If you wish, I could send a small contingent of Black Knights to accompany Sir Arius."

He nodded at the suggestion and walked to the large glass window. After observing the bustling cities below, Jorge turned to his staff, asking with a hint of worry, "Do these Nicopolans really eat human flesh?"

The staff had no definitive answer.

Sir Arius, feeling the need to change the subject, asked the steward, "What about the Lord of Korelia and Korimor? Any new report?"

The steward hesitated for a moment. "We've received another report following the initial one, though I have my doubts about its accuracy. I'm still waiting for further verification."

"What does the report say?" Jorge pressed.

"It indicates that the Lord of Korelia is advancing with a sizable army."

This revelation caught everyone off guard. They had only recently heard of Lord Lansius's conquest of Korimor, a feat presumed to have involved a fierce battle against eight thousand Nicopolans, with Lansius commanding merely a thousand. A victory in such a scenario seemed nothing short of miraculous.

"Could you repeat that?" Jorge asked, his voice a mix of doubt and hope. Even he, who held Lansius in high regard, did not expect him to mobilize again so soon after such a brutal fight.

"The Lord of Korelia is on the move," the steward repeated and quickly added, "The report might be erroneous, though. Its contents are . . . hard to believe."

"What makes you think so?" inquired Sir Arius.

Turning to the young knight, the steward replied, "The report claims the Lord of Korelia is leading over three thousand men, which seems exaggerated."

Instead of agreeing, Sir Arius flashed an amused grin and turned to the old knight beside him, who was once his mentor. "Do you think the Lord of Korelia might have incorporated the Nicopolans?"

The knight, with arms crossed, delved into deep thought. "It's a stretch, but not beyond the realm of possibility. He could have enticed them with promises of food or safety. However, the real challenges lie in how he would sustain them and the issue of their loyalty."

Sir Arius turned his gaze to Sir Morton, seeking his perspective.

Sir Morton, the Mage Knight, simply shrugged. "Incorporating former opponents into the ranks would require an overwhelming victory."

Reflecting on their last encounter in battle, Jorge let out a chuckle as he moved away from the window and returned to his seat. "That's precisely why he's the undisputed leader of this Grand Alliance," he mused thoughtfully.

The steward implored, "My lord, please, let's wait for confirmation."

Their discussion was abruptly cut short by the distinct sound of knocking. The door opened to reveal a weathered but unassuming figure, recognized as the head of their scouts. "My lord, we've encountered the advance party of the Lord of Korelia. They assured us there's no cause for alarm. The Lord of Korelia plans to pass near Three Hills City to purchase winter gear," he reported.

He then added, "He'll be accompanied by a sizable army and intends to encamp within a day's travel from the city to avoid causing any commotion. Still, we'll keep a vigilant eye on their movements."

Jorge barely concealed his amusement, shaking his head in disbelief. "He must be reading our minds," he commented, noting Lansius's apparent anticipation of their concerns.

Sir Arius and Sir Morton were equally impressed by Lord Lansius's foresight.

The head of the scout discreetly took his leave, not being privy to the ongoing discussion. Once he had departed, Jorge turned to his staff and inquired, "What should we do now?"

"Clearly, we must adhere to the etiquette befitting nobility. Let's extend an invitation and host a grand banquet in his honor," Sir Arius proposed.

"Any objections?" Jorge asked, turning his gaze toward the steward, the old knight, and Sir Morton.

The three other staff members voiced no objections.

"What about the village of Ardia?" the steward reminded the council.

"I'll go, but Sir Morton should stay," Sir Arius said. "Although I admire the Lord of Korelia, he's dangerous, and I want our Mage Knight close to my lord at all times."

Sir Morton gave a nod of acknowledgment as Lord Jorge inhaled deeply. "What difference does it make?" He turned to his staff. "If the rumors hold any truth, that man took Korimor in merely a staring contest. And now, he's triumphed over eight thousand with a mere thousand, also swelling his ranks to three thousand. What chance do we stand if he sets his sights on conquering us?"

His staff did not share Lord Jorge's nihilistic view, yet they shared his nervousness about the prospect of facing the Lord of Korelia again. The consensus was clear: He was far too formidable an adversary for direct combat. If one wished to challenge him, one would need to employ intrigue and uncover his weaknesses, and such strategies would undoubtedly require close proximity and time.

"If he could achieve so much with just a few hundred men . . . now commanding three thousand, just imagine what he can achieve," Sir Arius observed thoughtfully.

"In that case, it would be prudent to divert his focus to Umberland," the old knight wisely suggested. Meanwhile, the steward chose to withhold his opinion.

Three Hills, Lord Jorge

Five days had passed since they sent a messenger inviting Lord Lansius to the city. Sir Arius and his Crimson Knights had departed for Ardia to counter the escalating Nicopolan activities. Today, the Lord of Three Hills attended the small council meeting. The steward had swayed him into believing that Lord Lansius's army would only spell trouble for his domain.

"Even if the harvest is as good as last year, we can only expect a marginal surplus. There won't be enough to feed thousands," the steward stated.

Jorge leaned back in his chair. "I know that our granary is almost empty because of the last war, but there must be something we could do."

"My lord, the city has only a little to spare," the steward replied. They knew that the lord wished to be supportive of Lord Lansius's cause. Yet, a sense of distrust lingered among them toward their supposed alliance leader, particularly regarding his abilities beyond the battlefield.

"What about trade?" The old knight tried to give counsel. With Sir Arius's absence, he was the only one who could, aside from the steward. Sir Morton, though in attendance, seldom participated.

"After the fallout from the siege of Korelia, I doubt South Hill will be willing to assist us. Now, it depends on their merchants and whether they had enough harvest."

Jorge gazed thoughtfully at his steward. The news of a significant Nicopolan presence within Lord Lansius's army had spread, sparking fears that the approaching forces would either seek supplies or demand to purchase grain at low prices—both prospects equally worrisome.

Furthermore, with the harvest yet to begin, they anticipated that Lord Lansius's army might camp near the city, exerting pressure to meet their demands.

Like it or not, Jorge found these fears justified. Although he had grown to like and trust Lansius, his priorities lay with his domain. A famine could severely strain his rule, potentially even inciting dissent among his ranks. This concern was rooted in his past experiences; after all, it was precisely such circumstances that led to his loss of Korimor and South Hill. The haunting thought lingered in his mind that a similar fate might unravel his control over his last domain.

That very same day, an envoy accompanied by a squire from the Lord of Korelia arrived in Three Hills, bearing unexpected news.

"Lady Daniella!" Lord Jorge exclaimed, his surprise evident as he caught sight of her standing beneath the grand chandelier in the guest hall.

"My lord, I'm relieved to see you well," Dame Daniella greeted warmly, recalling their time fighting under the same banner last season.

"The last I saw you was in the forest. I'm glad you made it out. How did you end up with the Lord of Korelia?"

"I wasn't captured. In fact, I was in Korelia when discussions about the Grand Alliance were underway. Now, I serve as the Lady of Korimor's knight captain."

Lord Jorge noticed the bright and good-looking squire behind her. Her change of allegiance unsettled him, yet he couldn't help but respect her rapid advancement, a testament to her new master's appreciation for talent and merit—qualities he also cherished. Collecting his thoughts, he asked, "What message do you bring? Does it pertain to the invitation?"

"Yes, my lord. The Lord of Korelia and the Lady of Korimor respectfully decline the invitation."

The reply took them by surprise.

"But why?" the steward inquired first. "Where else will your lord and lady wait out the harvest if not in the city?" He had been hoping that they would stay in the city, separated from their army, which could potentially give Three Hills leverage over their decisions.

Dame Daniella responded with a smile. "My lord believes that a foreign army stationed near a city creates unnecessary strain and tension. With the harvest not yet arrived in Three Hills, his appearance would only lead to price gouging and speculation, harming all parties, especially the community."

The steward sighed in relief, realizing this was probably a good outcome. "Your lord is wise to make such a decision," he acknowledged with newfound respect.

Meanwhile, Lord Jorge exchanged knowing glances with Sir Morton, who smiled faintly. Both were reassured of Lord Lansius's abilities.

"Pardon me," the old knight interjected, "You haven't answered: Where will your lord and lady stay before the harvest?"

"My lord, lady, and the army aren't stopping," Dame Daniella revealed, causing a stir. She added, "They're heading south as we speak. I'm here to gather winter gear, spiced wine, and crossbow bolts."

"South? To South Hill?" Lord Jorge interjected.

"Yes, my lord. They have unfinished business with the Lord of South Hill."

This left Lord Jorge and his staff dumbfounded. They were too focused on the issues of Umberland and their city.

"He has the pretext, but it's overly ambitious," the steward lamented. "And what about Umberland?"

"The supplies are for Umberland," she explained, prompting murmurs of disbelief.

"But you said they're marching to South Hill?" the steward demanded an explanation.

"Yes, we expect quick results," Dame Daniella clarified with a faint smile. "The lord and lady will likely celebrate the harvest festival in South Hill and then proceed to Umberland."

The steward, caught off guard by the response, was rendered speechless. Meanwhile, Lord Jorge couldn't help but chuckle, deeming the idea audacious, almost to the point of absurdity. "Attacking South Hill and expecting a swift victory? That would be a jest if we weren't talking about the Lord of

Korelia," he mused, shaking his head in bewilderment, yet with undeniable fascination.

He continued. "I do hope Lord Lansius isn't biting off more than he can chew. Dame, must he not be weary from constant warfare? This would be, what, his third campaign this year? And now he's already plotting a fourth?"

"It's difficult to say," she responded contemplatively. "The Lord of Korelia's victories, though hard-fought, only resulted in a small number of casualties."

The Lord of Three Hills nodded thoughtfully. "And what of his plan for South Hill?"

"Regrettably, I am not privy to that information. The Lord of Korelia is known for keeping his strategies close to the chest."

"I see . . ." Jorge nodded, acknowledging the careful nature of his ally.

"I am only aware of his plans concerning the upcoming grain deal," she disclosed.

"A grain deal?" the steward interjected, his suspicions seemingly confirmed. "Are you intending to purchase grain to sustain the army?"

"After the harvest," she reassured him.

The steward shot a glance at Daniella and launched into his rhetoric. "Even Three Hills doesn't produce such an excess. To buy enough grain to feed three thousand, essentially half a city's population through winter, would create an enormous burden."

Daniella turned to Sterling, prompting him to step forward. "As the personal squire of the Lord of Korelia, I must correct you, Maester. We are not here to beg for grain, but to offer assistance."

"Assistance?" the steward responded with a hint of sarcasm.

"Pardon my directness," Sterling began, "but my lord believes that, given the Nicopolans' strength and numbers, no nobleman in Lowlandia could singlehandedly seize, fortify, and hold Umberland. Currently, we find ourselves in a precarious situation. Without additional support, even the spoils from South Hill would likely prove insufficient for the upcoming Umberland campaign."

This insight into Lord Lansius's thoughts captured everyone's attention. Lord Jorge gestured to the squire to continue with a wave of his hand.

"The lord also confided that without the Grand Alliance, Three Hills alone would likely face costly wars against the Nicopolan marauders. Thus, he trusts that his assistance will be welcomed with open arms. If this isn't the case, then I'll inform the lord and lady so they might reconsider their plan."

Lord Jorge exhaled deeply, concern evident on his handsome face, which diminished his usual charm. While he was personally inclined to assist, Three Hills had limited resources to offer. Could he risk a famine to support Lansius in the Umberland campaign? Would his council even allow such a decision?

Not aiding Lansius might jeopardize their only chance against the Nicopolans' threat. Yet, to give support risked inciting rebellion within his own ranks. Each option carried the risk of potentially catastrophic consequences.

Now, the fate of the Grand Alliance and Lowlandia hung precariously on Jorge's decision.

CHAPTER 18

FALSE MESSIAH

It was evening on the seventh day of their march. Soon, they would arrive at the closest point to Three Hills City. Since the main army was laden with the confiscated baggage train, almost everyone assumed the lord would purchase food in Three Hills City and solve all their food problems. However, this was certainly an unrealistic hope.

"Why can't we just purchase food in Three Hills?" Audrey asked, alone with Lansius in their tent, waiting for Carla to bring their supper.

Lansius folded back a copy of his letter to Sir Justin in Korelia and tucked it into his pocket. "Well, we'll buy food from Three Hills, but not now. And certainly, it won't be enough to last the entire winter."

She looked surprised. "We don't have the money?"

"We have the money," he reassured her. "But if we purchase that much, then we will ruin Three Hills' economy, and I do not want to be hated by our future ally."

Audrey furrowed her brow. Lansius had already briefed his staff on this matter, but only Sterling seemed to grasp the concept. The rest of the staff simply chose to trust Lansius's plan. Sir Harold had once said he would rather cut down a tree with a blunt axe than ponder what caused market prices to rise or fall. Although educated enough to avoid blaming merchants, the knight preferred to deal directly with farmers, bakers, and other producers.

Meanwhile, Sigmund would play ballads about shopkeepers and fair market ladies, yet excuse himself when asked about market matters. Carla would politely avoid discussions on the issue, claiming she was too busy ensuring security.

Aside from Sterling, perhaps only Dame Daniella could comprehend the issue, but she was busy managing the Nicopolan contingent and the camp followers. Thus, Lansius was glad that Audrey was genuinely trying to understand.

She'll be a good baroness . . .

Lansius offered another explanation. "If we buy as much food as possible from the city, then food prices will rise sharply, right?"

Audrey nodded, grasping that much.

He continued. "If the food prices rise sharply, then how will the city folks and the poor buy food for the upcoming winter?"

"Ah," she exclaimed in understanding.

He elaborated, "Footmen, guardsmen, and their families, also less fortunate farmers or laborers who had a rough year. Moreover, they just suffered a major defeat in Korelia, so I assume many are in a bad position for this winter."

Audrey seemed to catch the general idea before she suddenly stared at Lansius. "Why the gaze?" he asked.

She looked away. "Nothing. I am just surprised that you think that far to worry about the lives of people who are not even your subjects."

Lansius found her remark amusing. "Am I crazy for thinking about them?"

Audrey crossed her arms and pondered. "That is beyond me. But perhaps that is why you are able to achieve all this. So don't let my words bother you."

"Drey, I trust you the most. Let me know if I'm going too far."

She tilted her head, appearing to ponder deeply. "I will try. But really, I am only good with swords and horses, not words."

Carla entered the tent with her aides, bringing bowls of warm food from the field kitchen. Despite some expectations that the lord would hold a daily feast like in the Great Hall, Lansius opted for a simple meal like common travelers to reduce the burden on his kitchen staff. Clearly, preparing for a feast during a journey was a tremendous effort.

As the lord set the example, his staff and army followed.

Out of nowhere, rumors began to swirl that the lord and lady were cleansing their spirits for the upcoming battle on behalf of the Nicopolans, who had gravely erred by consuming human flesh. These rumors found fertile ground as servants confirmed that the lord and lady subsisted on modest fare, akin to commoners. Consequently, many began to see them in a different light.

More than respect or admiration, those who had witnessed their impossible victories, seen the fruits of his labor and grasped his grand plans, grew deeply devoted to the cause. They congregated, driven not by monetary gain, the thrill of battle, or mere survival, but by a sincere desire to aid Lord Lansius in fulfilling his destiny.

Many believed he was marked for greatness. His black hair, once a symbol of foreignness and mistrust, had transformed into a revered omen from the Ancients. His wife, initially thought to be a mere squire but later revealed as a baroness, was now perceived as an undeniable harbinger of greater destinies.

In Lowlandia, as in the rest of the Imperium where organized religion was abolished by the decree of the Ageless One, superstition still thrived. The people began to regard the lord and lady not merely as nobles, but as beings transcending ordinary mortals. Many speculated that the lord might have the Grand Progenitor's blood in his veins.

Despite being on the march, the Lord of Korelia's long-range scouts, who traveled days ahead in the direction he had set, had gathered a fair amount of intelligence. He wasted no time reading their reports whenever he could.

Based on their information, he contemplated sending his cavalry to march ahead. The decision needed to be made now before his intentions toward South Hill were laid bare. However, he was yet to receive reports from Three Hills, and currently it was still too early to expect a response from Korelia.

Audrey returned to the tent and informed, "We're going to break camp."

"Yeah, sure. I'm prepared," Lansius replied, checking his gear.

"What's the news from Dietrich?" she asked, cleaning her face with clean water from a copper basin.

"Lots of interesting facts. I might even need to alter the plan."

Audrey's interest was piqued. "What changed?"

"South Hill is not only unprepared, but they're also in worse shape than I expected. Just like the captured men said, the Lord of South Hill has little redeeming qualities, aside from his tight grip on power."

"No surprise there," she said as Carla entered and began to pack the things inside the tent.

Lansius quietly approached Audrey's side. "What do you mean?"

"He was once a knight under Lord Jorge and was trusted to defend South Hill, but he decided he was better than Jorge and led his House in rebellion . . ."

Lansius nodded, recalling the story of how Three Hills lost all the neighboring regions and how Lord Jorge was called the Fool of One Hill.

"Is this what you meant by 'power corrupts'?" Audrey asked.

"Indeed, power tends to corrupt. In the case of the Lord of South Hill, power revealed his true nature."

Audrey looked concerned.

"I doubt we're so blind as to misjudge Hugo that badly. Besides, his hold on power in Korimor is questionable, and his troops' loyalty is not to him," Lansius reassured her. "If you're that worried, you should stay behind," he teased.

She quickly pouted at the suggestion and exclaimed, "No. Titles are just names. I'd rather lose the city than not be by your side in battle."

Lansius chuckled and was about to praise her, but Carla was everywhere, packing for travel. He ended up taking Audrey's hand, guiding her to a folding seat, and caressing her shoulder. "Don't worry about Korimor. Focus on the problem ahead of us."

"South Hill then. What will you do to him?"

"It depends. If his defense is strong, then I'll extort what I can. If it's not . . ." He shrugged and quickly added, "Whatever we do, we only have limited supplies, and Three Hills' assistance isn't guaranteed."

Audrey uncharacteristically groaned and looked at the tent's ceiling. "Why is it always a struggle for us?"

Lansius patted her arm. "At least now we have the numbers. South Hill probably has less than a thousand men."

The revelation turned her frown into a smile.

Chateau de Cascasonne

The wind outside was raging, heralding the changing of seasons. Hannei stood alone, gazing out the window. Though mages possessed the ability to see through the night like beastmen, she sought not to see anything but to appreciate the dark beauty of the night, which bore a certain void-like quality.

Memories of Bengrieve's year-long, subtle interrogation still haunted her. The *truth nectar* had forced her to spill everything she knew about her world's history.

Bengrieve had shown keen interest in the Renaissance and the Victorian eras, not just for the steam engine and industrial revolution, but also for the shifts in government models and its economy. In their meetings, the diminishing role of nobility and the concept of nationalism were also recurring subjects.

This was why Hannei had distanced herself from Lansius. The more she knew, the riskier it became. She realized she was just an ordinary girl with basic historical knowledge, whereas Lansius was a juggernaut who could recite *The Art of War* and detail the campaigns of Julius Caesar and Genghis Khan.

She feared that Bengrieve could learn too much, endangering the Imperium and everyone.

Despite being favored amongst the retinue, Hannei didn't fully trust Bengrieve.

The man isn't evil, just too powerful and cunning for his own good.

That was why she was relieved when, two years ago, Lansius left a meeting with Bengrieve without arousing suspicion, not even needing to mention his amnesia. She was even more relieved when Lansius was sent to Lowlandia and ended up staying there.

Truthfully, even when escorting Felicity to Korelia, she had intended to keep Lansius at a distance to protect him from Bengrieve. Yet, her warnings about the situation outside Lowlandia drew them closer. Fortunately, their benefactor didn't seem concerned. Somehow, Bengrieve hadn't suspected anything about Lansius's origin.

The cold wind paused momentarily before returning with greater force, creating a howling sound as it swept past the towers.

Hannei shivered. Years had passed since she left the Progentia continent and its labyrinth. Now, she felt weak and aimless, drifting from task to task, trapped in the employment of a powerful lord. She couldn't blame Calub, who had introduced them; she needed Bengrieve's protection.

She wasn't a member of the Mage Guild, and some powerful families might be tempted to use her. It was ironic that she felt safer in a continent filled with monsters than in one filled with humans.

"Should I sail east again and settle there?" she asked her reflection in the glass window.

Hannei had the means to live comfortably, but beyond the labyrinth, there was little else to do there. The region was dotted with small city-states along the coastlines, subsisting more on traditional fishing than trading.

Without skills in apothecary, crafting, or baking, starting a business seemed out of reach. This had been her dilemma before meeting Tia, the little girl now sleeping peacefully in her bed. Tia was intelligent and could assist her significantly in various tasks.

A thought struck Hannei: to ask Tia to leave everything behind and sail east. In a few years, Tia would complete her education. Hannei resolved to propose the idea after her graduation.

She would neither force nor manipulate Tia. If they were to leave for Progentia, it would be by the girl's own decision. In doing so, Hannei once again tied her fate to someone else's choice, just as she had done before: first to her savior and mentor, then to Felicity and Calub, and now to a little girl.

The evening before the lord's departure, Bengrieve summoned Hannei to a private dinner with just them and a squire. They enjoyed a meal together, a change from their previous encounters, with Bengrieve treating her more amicably.

"The steward mentioned your inquiries about the current situation," Bengrieve began as they sipped their after-dinner drinks.

"I merely wish to learn, my lord," Hannei replied.

Bengrieve smiled. "Ask away, Lady Hannei. You play an important role in my plans."

Hannei resisted the urge to furrow her brow. "I'm grateful, but I feel unworthy of being part of such an important plan."

"Don't play the fool with me," he said with a faint grin. "I march tomorrow, so indulge me with my request."

Hannei pondered for a moment. "About the emperor. Is it true that the Ageless One is no longer in this world?"

Bengrieve's smile stiffened. "You know I keep a close watch on the military movements around the capital. Despite the crises in Nicopola and Elandia, there's been no movement."

Hannei nodded, recalling the briefing from the steward. "But, my lord, as you said, there's been no movement."

Bengrieve's pleased expression deepened. "No movement is a move in itself."

Only then did Hannei begin to grasp what he meant.

"No movement means the Imperial House cannot trust anyone with military command, fearing they might not relinquish control and potentially lead a coup."

Hannei felt a growing nervousness. "Is the Imperium heading into a succession war?"

"Lord Gottfried will ensure it. His forces should be crossing into Tiberia as we speak, and he won't stop until he reaches the capital. That's the plan, assuming Midlandia commits troops to Elandia."

Hannei grew uncomfortable at the revelation. She wasn't privy to such information. "Does this mean we're cooperating with the Lord of Brigandia?"

"Cooperation implies a partnership, which can be misleading. We are simply doing what's natural for us: expanding. The Imperium is too vast for its own good; fortunately, that means there's no need to vie for supremacy. With other lords, we can simply choose to coexist," Bengrieve explained.

Hannei swallowed hard, her mind racing.

Why is he telling me all this?

At this point, the lone squire sensed it was prudent to exit the room and did so quietly.

Hannei, noticing the squire's departure, asked softly, "My lord, is it wise to entrust me with this insight?"

Bengrieve chuckled. "Things have happened and cascaded into this. Lady Hannei, now you play an important role."

"But, my lord, you promised to allow me to retire to my hometown," she reminded him nervously.

"And do what there? Waste your life? Marry? If you're considering marriage, how about Sir Stan?"

"My lord, I have no desire to marry."

Bengrieve leaned forward, his hands on the table. "Are you sure? This may be the crossroads of your life."

Hannei, believing that marriage was the crossroads, shook her head. "My lord, this servant does not wish to marry anyone."

Bengrieve's laughter unnerved her, as though he had anticipated her refusal. "Very well, I will honor your wishes," he declared viciously.

She shook her head in panic, realizing something was terribly off. "No! My lord, what do you mean?"

"You may not be the prime candidate, but you are equally perfect," he mused aloud.

Her heart raced as she processed his words.

"Yes, this is all a blessing in disguise," Bengrieve continued musing, more to himself. "Did the Ancients orchestrate this for me? How devious and yet, marvelous!"

"My lord, you're frightening me," she pleaded.

"Fear not, for you are the future leader of the Saint Candidate."

Hannei shuddered at the title. "Please, my lord . . ."

Bengrieve's laughter echoed as he strode to the window and flung it open against the dark sky, proclaiming to the wind, "The emperor is dead! Long live the virgin Saint *Messiah*!"

She stood, her hands trembling and her face pale with shock. In this world's language, there was no real equivalent to *messiah*, and the term Bengrieve used was the one Hannei had chosen when she retold her world's history. "My lord, what are you saying?"

Turning to her, Bengrieve explained, "We will transform Midlandia into a theocracy, mirroring one from your world's history. And how fitting that you shall be the leader."

Hannei felt weak and dropped into her chair.

Is this what he had planned for Audrey? To play as a false prophet? But why . . . ?

She felt sick. Meanwhile, Bengrieve walked toward her and bent his knees, placing his hand over hers. "With you as the messiah and me as the prime minister, we shall create a new kingdom in Midlandia."

The wind blew hard as if harboring warnings from the gods, yet Bengrieve was determined. "Imagine, an unshackled Midlandia Kingdom. We could lead the people to its full potential and achieve the unthinkable!"

With that declaration, Midlandia quietly cast the dice against the Imperium's survival.

CHAPTER 19

DULCE BELLUM INEXPERTIS

War is sweet to the inexperienced.

Fall of the Elven Calendar, 4425. Despite the ongoing succession crisis in Midlandia, at the behest of the Tiberia and Elandia provinces, which were struggling against Lord Gottfried's assault from Arvena, Lord Bengrieve decided to act, marching his troops to the border.

Externally, this action demonstrated Midlandia's loyalty to the Imperium. However, Bengrieve harbored an ulterior motive. In truth, he had secretly entertained an open pact with Gottfried by agreeing not to wage war or compete against each other. Therefore, Midlandia's move toward Elandia was essentially an annexation, veiled as a relief force.

The catalyst for this decisive move was a critical piece of information: the capital had not mobilized its army to resolve the Nicopolan crisis. Bengrieve interpreted the absence of military movement in the face of a major threat as a clear indication of the emperor's demise.

This revelation emboldened and spurred Bengrieve to accelerate his plans for Midlandia. Even the absence of Audrey, the person he saw as most fit for the purpose, did not stop him. Bengrieve settled on Hannei as his future head of state—a figurehead for the theocratic rule he deemed most effective for controlling the masses.

Meanwhile, outside Midlandia, at least three other lords saw through the Imperium's indecisiveness. Born into power and with little understanding of the horrors of war and the age of strife, these nobles maneuvered to advance their own agendas, treating the situation as nothing more than a game of politics.

Lord Gottfried had gained a foothold in east Tiberia and began spreading rumors that the Ageless One was dying and had been taken hostage by the

High Lords. As refugees traveled westward to avoid the war, the rumors traveled with them. This way, Gottfried successfully sowed chaos among the Imperium's populace.

With Nicopola, Elandia, and now Tiberia engulfed in turmoil, the Imperium faced its darkest hours.

New Korelia

"Dear Lord and Lady, your vassal, Sir Justin, writes to report on the progress in Korelia. I hope this letter finds you well. The building project for Korelia is progressing smoothly. The city wall on the western side is beginning to . . ." The marshal seemed to ponder about the correct words.

"To take shape?" Calub suggested, and Sir Justin motioned with his hand, prompting Cecile to write it down.

Sir Justin then waited for Cecile to catch up. "Now, what comes after the wall?" he muttered afterward.

Calub massaged his temple. "Well, we have reports from the newly opened farms, its windbreaker, and windmill . . ."

"I think we also need to report about the orphanage, guild hall, and bazaar," Cecile commented while jotting in her waxed tablet.

"I guess we can report on the orphanage," Sir Justin mulled. "But there is almost little to no progress on the other two."

"We also have the mud houses for winter, the duck project, and the market posts," Cecile offered more suggestions.

Sir Justin whistled at the suggestions. "You know, when I learned Sterling had arrived, I was overjoyed. I thought that I could just report all this verbally to him. So unfortunate that he left so soon to Korimor."

The other two chuckled upon hearing the confession.

"Well, he is with Anci, and he is always unpredictable," Calub commented.

"Which reminds me," Cecil said, "we have news of the coming of officials from the capital and the noble patent."

Calub leaned forward. "I think we should write that down first since it is the most important. That and the grain shipment from White Lake and the East Lowlandia Merchants."

Sir Justin nodded in agreement. "As long as Cecile can keep track."

"Let me add that to the draft. What else?" she asked.

Sir Justin pondered. "I want to report that the military training for levied troops using crossbows is progressing smoothly."

Calub added, "The spinning wheel device the lord ordered has also arrived. Also, Lord Robert had sent his staff to begin the work on his estate."

Cecile wrote what they had said on her wax tablet.

"There is also a . . . What should we write about the bathhouse?" Sir Justin asked with a big grin.

Calub chuckled. "A slight error?"

"A happy accident?" Cecile suggested.

The three chuckled at their own words.

"Don't worry, I shall take the blame," Sir Justin declared.

"No, you must not. I'm the one who gave the approval," Calub insisted.

Due to being overworked, both Calub and Sir Justin approved the Midlandia Mason Guild's proposal to prioritize the watermill and bathhouse. The two had only seen the watermill, not realizing it was part of a package with the bathhouse. As it turned out, the watermill, aside from grinding grains into flour, also functioned as a water pump.

The guild that built it was highly specialized, having constructed hundreds in Midlandia. They brought finished cogs, axles, and gears from their workshop ready to be assembled. With the help of local carpenters and masons, they built the first watermill with ease.

Developed in parallel with the watermill by another branch of the guild, the bathhouse's open-air section opened and quickly became an attraction. Although it lacked a heated section, essentially just an open pool, from day one it drew large crowds compared to its humble size. Visitors gladly paid for a respite in the clean pool and its sporting hall.

Rumors that the golden-haired Lady Felicity was visiting only sparked more interest. Women flocked to the bathhouse, eager to bathe their daughters in the same pool as the honored lady.

With the bathhouse proving profitable, the guild planned to expedite the completion of its heated section, thereby transforming it into a full-fledged facility. However, a problem arose: Korelia's small forest couldn't meet the increasing demand for firewood. It barely supplied enough for the castle and townsfolk during winter. Moreover, the forest was privately owned by the lord as a hunting ground.

Thus, one merchant group took the initiative and decided to import quality firewood from neighboring White Lake. When news reached Korelia that Korimor had been taken, another merchant group swiftly arranged a caravan to secure a firewood contract from that region.

The bathhouse inadvertently became the first economic powerhouse in New Korelia. It attracted two merchant groups, each vying to become the top supplier of firewood. Their quest for quality wood stimulated active trade routes between Korelia and two other cities, trading local goods and surpluses.

With each return journey, they also stimulated smaller economies along the way. Sensing an opportunity, villages and marches improved their inns and maintained stables to accommodate these merchants. Given the bathhouse's nearly year-round demand for firewood when it was completed, their regular visits were almost guaranteed.

The effect on the route to Korimor became even more pronounced. Traveling through Lord Lansius's new market post route, the merchants began to reap clear benefits from the available shelter, protection, water source, and hospitality. What was once a harsh and inhospitable route in the Great Plains turned into a bearable journey.

As for the tribesmen, after receiving their first guests, they began to recognize the profit potential. Coins, which were hard to come by, now flowed easily with each transaction. These coins were used as savings to purchase grains and secure their livelihood when the weather turned bad.

Thus, the tribes adapted to meet the travelers' needs. They put more work into making their renowned wool products, ranging from thick, durable socks that provided warmth on long journeys, to blankets woven with intricate patterns, offering not only comfort but a taste of tribal artistry.

Their woolen jackets, sturdy and weather-resistant, became a popular choice among the merchants and other travelers for their practicality in the often-harsh climate.

Additionally, they boosted the production of mare milk wine, a local specialty, to be traded for high-quality, almost smokeless firewood. The humble firewood, originally only intended to meet the demands of the bathhouse, turned into an unexpected linchpin in a growing trade network.

Sir Justin

The marshal strolled along the corridors with a relaxed gait, accompanied by his squire. His whistling brought forth a carefree, wandering tune that his little daughter liked. With Korelia now at peace, Sir Justin had invited his family from the safety of Midlandia. They were among the lucky few who had managed to escape from Arvena.

He couldn't wait to meet them and bring them to the manor house he had prepared. But before that, he planned to take them on a tour around Korelia. The new bathhouse was phenomenal, even boasting a private family section. The new bakery was also offering the latest patisserie trend from Midlandia.

As Sir Justin descended into the Great Hall with his mind drifting to his family, a messenger was waiting for him.

"Marshal, a letter from the lord," the man in weathered attire informed.

Upon hearing this, the marshal couldn't help but smirk. "Talk about coincidence," he mused as he broke the wax seal and read the letter. Yesterday, he had just finished his report and sent it, and now the lord had sent his own.

To Sir Justin, Marshal of the House,

I, the Lord of Korelia, command thee to release one hundred of the best-behaved men from South Hill that we have captured. Thou shalt send them to South Hill—

"South Hill!?" he exclaimed, gazing at the messenger. "You sent this from South Hill? By the Ageless, where is the lord right now?"

The rider grinned and proudly answered, "By now, my lord should have left the Three Hills region and is currently marching toward South Hill."

Hearing this, the marshal burst into loud laughter, drawing the attention of the servants and other castle staff nearby. "Did you hear that?" he asked his squire in sheer excitement. "The lord isn't in Korimor anymore. He's on march, to South Hill."

The news amazed everyone, and they began to crowd around. Meanwhile, his squire commented, "The lord is certainly spirited. Then what should we do, sir?"

Sir Justin returned to the letter at hand and explained it in plain language for everyone's benefit. "You'll send them to South Hill with enough escorts and using horse carts or simple carriages as much as possible so they could reach South Hill with haste. You're also to pack a hundred crossbows and bolts for the future campaign . . ."

He nodded in understanding and said, "It seems we have our work cut out for us." He then drew a deep breath and called, "Squire."

"Yes, sir."

"Summon Maester Calub, the captain of the guard, and the stable maester. Let's get to work. Lord Lansius is waiting."

South Hill

A young girl clad in simple brown garments, typically worn by the farming community, ran hastily along the dirt road, barefooted, her small brother's hand tightly in hers. Shouts and cries echoed from the direction of their humble home, but she did not dare look back. Her breaths soon failed her, yet she managed to put some distance between them and the lord's men.

Her brother pulled at his hand, feeling pain in his wrist. As they caught their breath, a group of minstrels on a journey stumbled upon them.

"What happened? A bandit?" the closest man in flute and bright yellow garb asked.

Panting, the girl warned amidst her breathlessness, "Do not go there. The lord's men are at it again . . . Just now, they were beating our parents."

The troupe, a motley crew adorned in colorful garb, turned tense.

The one who looked like a leader in red garb with a small harp slung across his back stepped forward and knelt. "Do not worry. You are safe with us. We'll protect you."

Another member expressed his displeasure openly. "But why? What could provoke them to beat the peasant so close to harvest?"

"The lord demands more time spent on his lands, but our own fields . . . they are being neglected," the girl boldly explained. "My brother and uncle went to Korelia and have not returned. We cannot tend to both, or our harvest . . . will fail."

The red minstrel nodded solemnly, understanding the gravity of the situation. "Without a good harvest, there will not be enough food for winter."

The girl nodded, her eyes darting back toward the direction of their home, fear and concern obvious in her gaze.

The leader motioned to his band. "I think we need to meet these men and play some music."

Ruckus and lively banter appeared out of nowhere until one said, "Sigmund, are you sure?"

"What, you are going to let these lords' men exact violence?" the red minstrel asked.

"No, but I do not want to get on the lord and lady's bad side."

The man named Sigmund smiled jovially and patted the sister's and brother's shoulders. "You see, Dietrich. That is why we have them."

"Oh, that's clever . . ." The one named Dietrich nodded.

Sigmund smiled. "Kids, we will help your parents." Then, to the rest of the group, he said, "Men, onward. Don't let anyone escape."

The men in bright clothing laughed and walked steadily with purpose. The children watched them, finding it bizarre to see a circus of colors with flutes and other musical instruments marching with determination and wide, sinister grins.

"But, Maester, you are only minstrels," she cautioned, while the boy continued to hide behind her.

"Don't worry, we are strong enough to handle bandits," Sigmund replied.

"But the lord has many men," she warned them again.

The skald chuckled while Dietrich patted the girl's head and spoke. "No worries. Soon we will have hundreds of friends. And tomorrow, probably more friends than you have learned to count."

CHAPTER 20

DESTINATION SOUTH HILL

Three Hills

The Lord of Three Hills treated Dame Daniella and Sterling as their guests and allowed them to stay in a guest house in the scenic part of the city. It had been almost a week, but the Lord of Three Hills still postponed their decision. The indecision was not expected, but not entirely surprising.

Fortunately, the envoy was allowed to conduct their business while waiting. Thus, Dame Daniella and Sterling had reviewed the city's bustling market for items Lord Lansius wished to procure.

Aside from grain, which would come later after harvest, other foodstuff, and winter gear, the lord also wished to purchase all kinds of backpacks for his army. His requirements were that the backpack should have two straps for each shoulder and a third to be tied around the waist. All the straps should be adjustable. The bag should be large enough to accommodate two helmet-sized objects and be capable of being securely tightened or closed.

As for the materials, there were no specific requirements. He accepted leather, canvas, or even woven baskets, as long as they fit his criteria.

Diligently, the two browsed the workshops and market, made purchases, and more often, ordered items to be tailored to their specifications. Throughout their negotiations, they were careful not to reveal the true quantity they were buying, to prevent price increases.

Slowly but surely, the two amassed a considerable stockpile of goods, stored in the guest house and its stable. The dame arranged for more storage space, and the guild readily rented her an empty warehouse.

Without wasting time, they began inspecting the building, as they had two cartloads of goods awaiting unloading.

"What do you think?" Dame Daniella asked Sterling beside her.

"Big double doors, wide enough for a cart. Brick walls, no holes, and not too damp. I think it's a good place," Sterling replied.

She nodded and motioned for her Nicopolan men to inspect. "Check the locks, attic, larder, and look for signs of rats," she instructed.

They nodded and proceeded. Her lieutenant returned and said, "We're going to need blankets. It's unsafe to leave a warehouse unguarded. Also, we'd better procure a cat."

Daniella agreed. "Yes, it would be shameful for all parties involved if our warehouse was compromised by vermin or thieves."

"Then I shall take three men and sleep here tonight. Is that arrangement satisfactory, Dame?" the lieutenant asked.

"No worries, I doubt the Lord of Three Hills intends any harm to me. However, our goods are another story. You should take more men from the guest house."

Despite their caution, news had spread about a party stockpiling a significant amount of long-lasting food, winter gear, and bags, enough to supply a village. Although they were not worried about price increases after placing their order, they couldn't shake off the concern that this might attract thieves or other unsavory characters.

Sterling climbed into the cart to take a peek and said, "But these are just wool coats, boots, woolen foot wraps, and bags. I don't see them as highly valuable items."

Daniella looked at him, deciding to educate the young man. "There's a simple trick to make them valuable."

Sterling furrowed his brows. "A trick to make these valuable? Is that even possible?"

The lieutenant grinned, seeing the squire's confusion, and revealed, "It's actually simple. Take enough and spoil the rest."

"Spoil the rest?" Sterling's eyes widened as he understood the implication.

Daniella explained, "Mercenaries deal with this kind of thing. Creating scarcity is a tactic. Once, a Nicopolan legion was ordered to burn a ripened field of barley, so those who stockpiled beer could sell it at higher prices."

Sterling looked disgusted, and the lieutenant patted his back. "You should learn as much as possible from us. The world isn't just about honor and duty. To truly protect your lord, you must be prepared to face the dirty underbelly."

"The bigger the city, the higher the nobility and its rich merchants, the nastier it gets," Daniella added.

Sterling nodded thoughtfully. "Even as a squire, I realized that people also fight in underhanded ways."

"Such is the world." The lieutenant smiled wryly. "Now, with me stuck in this place, please kindly escort the dame back to the guest house. It's almost sundown."

"Nah, I'll stick around," Daniella declared. "Go gather some food, lanterns, and blankets for the night. I'll be here, keeping watch until you return."

The lieutenant chuckled lightly. "I only wish to take some of the old man's role, but I'll heed your command."

Daniella offered a grateful smile, yet gestured for him to hasten his preparations. He nodded and departed with another man, leaving her with Sterling and a few men.

"The old man?" Sterling asked after the lieutenant's departure.

Daniella looked at Sterling with a soft expression. "He was more than a friend . . . not blood-related, but he raised and cared for me like a family. He passed away in Korimor, just before we set off on our march."

"My apology, Dame, and my condolences."

"Apology not required. He passed away peacefully a few nights after my knighthood ceremony. I hope he's at peace now, considering all he endured for my sake."

Sterling paused, choosing his words carefully. "Dame, these might seem like just comforting words, but as a squire and servant, I believe he was truly content to see you achieve knighthood and forge your own path."

Daniella nodded, her gaze drifting to the orange sunset nearing the high walls of Three Hills. "I've made many mistakes. How I wish I had heeded his advice more."

Sterling reflected quietly. Throughout his two years of service, he had encountered and observed many great individuals. Yet, behind their success and fame lay a trail of sacrifices and losses. Dame Daniella had mourned the loss of a father figure; Sir Hugo had delayed his marriage by another year; Sir Justin had been away from his children for two years; and perhaps most tragic, Cecile and Claire had lost their father.

As conflicts and turmoil persisted, both minor and significant sacrifices continued to be made. Sterling knew this all too well, having served alongside the late Sir Callahan and having nearly made the ultimate sacrifice himself.

"Dame, is it all worth it?" Sterling asked, his tone free of malice or judgment.

"Is what worth it?"

"The sacrifices we've made . . . will peace really come to Lowlandia?"

The dame offered a gentle smile. "Peace often comes at a steep price, but without it, there's only sorrow."

Sterling took her words to heart, valuing the insights of someone who had journeyed from noble birth through anonymity as a runaway, to a life as a mercenary, and finally to knighthood. Despite having known her only since the beginning of this march, he had grown to respect her unique perspective.

South Hill

At 51 years old, Gunther, the ruler of South Hill was still younger than the Lion of Lowlandia, yet his service in numerous campaigns for the Three Hills had left him scarred with wounds. These experiences did more than age him; they rendered him both vicious and brutal to those who opposed him.

Worse, two years ago, an old wound on his thigh became so painful that he needed crutches to walk. He turned to undiluted wine and small doses of poppy milk for relief, which led to emotional outbursts and sometimes even erratic decision-making.

Despite all this, Gunther still ruled with an iron hand, supported by his competent family who used their extended kin as knights and lieutenants to maintain their grip on power. However, there was no denying that the last campaign for Korelia was a grand fiasco and had become a challenge for his rule and prestige.

The coalition had been brokered by Lord Omin of Korimor to unite and repair relations with the Three Hills. Gunther had been a knight under Lord Jorge before he rebelled ten years ago. Officially, it was due to Jorge's incompetence, yet it was clear he seized the opportunity when entrusted with South Hill Castle.

Even in his old age, the Lord of South Hill felt no remorse. Gunther only intended to serve a worthy lord and would not say no to an opportunity. He had always lived by that creed.

But, as it turned out, Korelia wasn't an opportunity but a complete loss.

For weeks, only stragglers returned home. Out of almost two thousand, less than four hundred survived. The Great Plains had claimed their lives. Even for the natives, the vast expanse of the plains made it all too easy to become disoriented and perish from thirst.

The news came as a surprise, yet Gunther chose to ignore it. His indifference was not born out of foolishness, but from a deep-seated readiness to sacrifice them. He was rather pleased that his contingency plan, which involved sending only levies along with a hundred ambitious, non-blood-related officers, had proven useful.

Despite the huge loss, his smaller but competent men-at-arms were largely unscathed. Thus, he had little concern for external or internal threats. Not even the new acting Lord of Korelia's veiled threat of a Grand Alliance could sway his stance.

With his spies reporting that the Lord of Korelia was personally fighting in Korimor, he felt assured that South Hill would be safe for several more years. This would be enough time to build a significant force to deter sieges. For that, he needed to stockpile arms and supplies.

"Surely not even this Lansius can win battle after battle without replenishing his men and resources," Gunther muttered to himself as he walked through his fruit garden with the help of a crutch, a favored pastime.

"There." He pointed to a low-hanging fruit, its skin a vibrant mosaic of yellows and green. His servants promptly picked the succulent fruit for him, gently cleaning it in a bowl of water to reveal its glossy, sun-kissed surface. They then presented it on a silver platter.

Despite the pain, he forced himself to sit on the grass and let them place the tray beside him. He tasted the golden-yellow-fleshed fruit. It was sweet and aromatic. "It's a good fruit." He complimented the tree and its caretaker.

The caretaker bowed deeply, and the lord motioned for the fruit to be shared among his guards and servants. While violent toward those who wronged him, he treated his servants with respect.

He was about to ask his servants for assistance to stand when the head guard appeared.

"What is it? You look bothered, and I don't like it," Gunther remarked.

"My lord, there's a slight issue. I request permission to take some men and riders out."

"Explain," he said while still sitting on the grass.

"A small group of men is missing after inspecting a village to our north."

"Hmph, they probably indulged too much," he said, shifting his weight to the other leg to lessen the pain.

"It's been four nights, my lord."

Gunther sighed, conceding, "Then it might be a prelude to a peasant rebellion."

"My lord, I assure you, it's probably nothing."

"Then go and see it with your own eyes and report back. Take enough escort, but don't mobilize the troops."

The head of the guard bowed and left, leaving the lord to ponder the possibility of a peasant rebellion. "I've already lost so much, and now I might lose even more peasants." He lamented over the potential loss of productivity in his lands.

To him, peasants were too cunning for their own good. On multiple occasions, they were found slacking, failing to fulfill their end of the bargain. Left unsupervised, they would even harvest the best crops for themselves from the communal fields, leaving the lesser produce for the lord.

Now, with the failed campaign resulting in fewer men to work the fields, he suspected the peasants would stir up trouble.

While Gunther could accept some loss in yield, the peasants prioritizing their land over his felt like an insult. Harvest was approaching, and the fields left late for harvesting would surely be infested with vermin, potentially wreaking havoc on the entire region. Sooner or later, he would need to discipline them again with an iron grip.

Lansius

The Lord of Korelia stood inside a spacious tent as the first light of dawn cast a soft glow across the landscape. He leaned over a copper basin filled with water. With caution, he cleaned his face using the cool water, the chill more than enough to wake him.

Audrey, already clad in her marching gear, entered the tent and watched him with an alert gaze.

"I'm awake, just give me a minute to dress," Lansius said, reaching for a cloth to dry his face.

Without waiting, the Baroness of Korimor approached and helped him dress.

"You don't have to—"

"All my life I've been a squire, and last I checked, I'm still your squire. You've made me a consort—"

"Wife," he corrected her.

Audrey smiled and continued. "Wife and baroness, but that doesn't mean I shouldn't help you dress."

"Gratitude," he said tenderly as she diligently made sure that he wore his arming jack properly underneath the traveling attire, with the belt fastened enough to make it comfortable but secure.

"There, all set. Now what's left is just the armor."

"I think we can still skip the armor today." Even this close to South Hill, they remained undetected by the enemy. Their decision to use the nomads' route instead of the normal one, combined with Lansius's clever use of disguised scouts, enabled them to gauge the enemy's reactions effectively. So far, there had been no abrupt military movements.

"I'll make sure Carla is ready with your cuirass. Although we've made it this far, the castle is only two days away."

Lansius nodded, admiring his wife's gentle and caring side.

"Anyway, Lans. Congratulations."

He quickly squinted. "For what?"

"Well, I'm glad you're doing fine despite all the marching. This is the first time you've arrived somewhere without getting sick or becoming an annoyance."

He grinned at her direct honesty and teased, "Then kiss me, or I'll become a major annoyance."

Audrey shook her head but drew him closer with both arms and kissed him without hesitation. Just then, Carla entered with her aide carrying breakfast. Seeing their masters, they quietly retreated.

"No, come back," Lansius instructed, half-chuckling. "It's just a morning kiss."

That small innocent event spread quickly through the camp. For their men, the behavior of their lord and lady was a reassuring sign that the campaign was progressing smoothly.

Despite the weariness from long marches, the bruises, and calluses on their feet, thousands of men surprisingly found some enjoyment in the march. There was dust and pesky horseflies, but the weather was generally pleasant. Moreover, seeing the yellowing crops from afar, they were content, knowing the answer to their plight might be just ahead.

"The question is, how should we approach this? Do we send an envoy to announce our arrival and make our demands?" Sir Harold asked as they convened after breakfast.

"Wouldn't that just squander the element of surprise?" Audrey remarked.

Lansius let out a satisfied smirk, pleased to see that the concept of surprise attack had become second nature to her.

Sir Harold chuckled and reminded everyone in jest, "Despite our past victories, it's actually against noble decorum."

Lansius decided to comment. "Last I heard, I'm seen as a barbaric foreigner and a lord wannabe. So I might as well play the part."

The tall knight's chuckle grew louder.

Carla appeared in the tent doorway. "Urgent message from the forward scouts," she announced.

"I guess we've been discovered," Audrey commented, causing Carla to tense up.

"Let's not jump to conclusions. Please invite the messenger inside," Lansius instructed, without any hint of urgency.

Audrey's interest was piqued by his uncharacteristic calmness. "Are you planning something?"

Lansius almost chuckled at the thought. "No, but what's there to fear? For the first time, we have numerical superiority. If they want to come"—his tone turned serious—"let them."

CHAPTER 21

HEARSAY

Two Days' Distance from South Hill Castle

The messenger dressed in bright clothes but covered with an inconspicuous brown traveling coat entered the tent, knelt, and reported, "My lord, my lady, a message from Dietrich."

"Speak," Lansius instructed.

"'We rescued children and their families from rampaging guardsmen, capturing six men. None have escaped.' That's the message from Dietrich. He also ordered us to bring two of the most cooperative captives to you, under escort, for questioning."

Lansius nodded but refrained from commenting.

"When did this happen?" Sir Harold inquired.

"Four days ago, sir. It took us three days to find you."

"Have they discovered our intentions?" the knight continued.

"No, sir, at least not yet. The villagers are mostly on our side, and they believed the story that we're armed because of bandits."

Audrey asked, "I ordered Dietrich not to make contact. Why did he break the disguise?"

"Maester Sigmund encountered children on the run and took pity on them."

Audrey gazed at Lansius, who nodded once. "We'll record his mistake in the book, but that comes later. Sooner or later, we'll make contact, and this might be as good a reason as any." Then, turning to the messenger, he asked, "Tell me, what's the village like?"

"My lord, the village is sizable, with at least a hundred families."

That's quite a big community, especially in Lowlandia . . .

His original plan was to catch South Hill unguarded, block it from requesting reinforcements, and then send an envoy to stall for time while his army made ladders from the nearby woodlands. The discussions, despite having a fair chance of succeeding given the size of his army, would likely fail. When that happened, Lansius would launch a continuous day and night assault on the castle, which would also serve as a form of exercise before Umberland.

Of course, this plan was merely an initial strategy until he could gather more information about his opponent, understand the situation, and study the topography to formulate a better approach. He had learned about Lord Gunther and his character but had yet to find anything concrete about his military style or capabilities.

However, Sigmund's actions led Lansius to feel that he might have stumbled upon an unexpected opportunity. While he was certain that South Hill wouldn't attack to save a large farming village, he believed he could potentially provoke them into doing so. He stared squarely at the messenger. "Is it situated on a hill, or does it have any wide river or marshland nearby?"

"We didn't find any hill. There's a river, but it isn't wide, and there's no marshland. However, there is a forested area nearby."

Lansius thought of a plan. "Along your travel on the main route, did you encounter any other villages as large as this one?"

"We seldom found anything larger than small communes; they hardly have a tavern, let alone an inn."

Lansius nodded and remained silent for a while before calling, "Sir Harold."

"Yes, my lord."

"Interrogate the captured men for me. Ask them about the number of men-at-arms in their lord's service, and who's in charge of the military. Are they bold or confident? Do they gamble or like to boast? Do they like hunting or riding? I want to know what they are like, their likes and dislikes. I want to know everything."

"With pleasure." The knight smirked, recognizing that the lord was concocting a plan.

A Village North of South Hill

Two days after the messenger had brought the captured men to the lord's encampment, things took an unexpected turn. Contrary to what Sigmund had predicted, the lord didn't march his army to the village. Instead, he divided his forces unevenly into two groups, keeping them hidden away from any villages.

Before midday, the lord, disguised as a wealthy merchant, entered the village in a carriage, accompanied by a group of muscular, dangerous-looking packhorse drivers, porters, and caravan guards. Their arrival was met with surprise and a mixture of suspicion and coldness.

Soon, Dietrich and Sigmund recognized who was inside the cart and rushed to greet them, albeit in slight panic.

"My—" they both started, then exchanged a glance, unsure how to address the couple, since it was obvious that the lord and lady were in disguise.

Lansius waved them closer to the carriage window. "I'm Jans, and my wife is Jean. Easy to remember, right?"

"Yes, my—" Dietrich began but found himself unable to continue.

Quickly, Sigmund intervened. "We mean, yes, Maester Jans and Jean. So good to see you."

Audrey gave a small nudge of acknowledgment from inside the carriage.

Not to waste time, Lansius inquired, "Does this village have an inn?"

"Yes, it does. Please follow me." Dietrich quickly motioned to the coachman.

After the interaction, the villagers gazed at the convoy of carriages and carts, laden with goods, with newfound curiosity. The guards escorting them, common in protecting merchants, were notably well-armed, disciplined, and sophisticated in appearance.

"Carla," Lansius called to a woman riding a conspicuously fine horse.

She nodded slightly in her saddle. "Yes, Master."

"Split our group into three. Two should keep watch on the village's edge, particularly the road leading to the castle. However, keep your group close to the inn."

"Understood," Carla responded.

Audrey leaned toward the window. "Inform the lieutenants to allow their men to buy drinks and food, but to avoid causing trouble."

"Anything else, Master?" Carla inquired.

After a brief exchange of glances with Lansius, Audrey replied, "No, that's all for now. Best to keep things simple."

Carla nodded, signaling to the lieutenants, also in disguise, to gather around her.

The inn in the village was so small that the merchant convoy in disguise ended up renting the entire place after negotiating a discount. Lansius himself haggled the price while listening to the innkeeper's stories about the village and the region, all over a large order of food and drinks.

After a modest but merry lunch, they convened in the upstairs hall for a private meeting.

"The innkeeper looks happy," Dietrich commented, sitting on the floor. There were no chairs, as the hall was intended for sleeping, with travelers typically bringing their own bedrolls or simply sleeping with their jackets over their heads.

Lansius and Audrey's entourage ensured that folding seats were available for the lord and lady, but they too chose to sit on the wooden floor, out of habit. "So, what's the latest situation?" Lansius asked.

"My lord, have you questioned the men we've sent?" Sigmund inquired.

Audrey's small chuckle drew the attention of the others. Since it would be impolite to question the lady directly, Dietrich and Sigmund turned to Carla, who sat near the window to observe their surroundings.

Carla glanced at Lansius, who sighed deeply but nodded. With the lord's approval, she explained, "After the captured men realized they were in front of the Lord of Korelia, they were so frightened that they groveled on the ground, pleading for their lives. One even ended up emptying his bladder,"

Sigmund and Dietrich, amused, grinned sheepishly.

"Are any of you responsible for this?" Lansius asked.

"How could it be possible for us to spread such fear? Methinks, oh lord, your reputation in battle hath spread far and wide. Thus, even at the utterance of thy name, their courage doth falter and their bravery loseth its spirit," Sigmund praised smoothly.

"Oh, shut it," Lansius said, dismissing the praise. He understood it was natural for people to fear him, especially after the Battle of Korelia, where he had executed ambushes, fire tactics, and utilized nomadic cavalry. Despite this, he couldn't shake the suspicion. "Someone is fabricating questionable stories about me."

Audrey shifted in her seat, clearly uncomfortable with her disguise, before leaning toward him, "It's probably stories from people who survived the Battle of Korelia. It's only common for people to embellish stories of their victory or defeat."

Lansius could only nod.

"Is it really that bad?" Dietrich asked Carla, who replied, "One was sobbing hard and the other shuddered on the ground, clutching his wet pants."

Lansius sighed weakly, fully aware that as tales of his victory in Korimor and his notorious handling of the three envoys spread, his name would grow further in infamy. "By the Ageless, just what are they saying about me?" he lamented.

"The gossip is wild—" Dietrich started but stopped abruptly under the baroness's stern gaze.

"Go on," Lansius urged, but Dietrich only shook his head and muttered, "It's not good. I'd rather not say."

Lansius exhaled deeply before deciding it was time to focus. "Sigmund," he called.

Sensing the change in tone, Sigmund straightened his back. "Yes, my lord."

Lansius retrieved something from his inner pocket, placed it on the floor, and revealed a blank parchment. He then took a charcoal stick and began to draw on it. "Imagine this is the village. Now, where is the route to South Hill Castle? Are there other hamlets along the way? Any rivers, large farms, or orchards nearby?"

South Hill Castle

Undetected by Dietrich's men or the villagers, the South Hill senior guard and his men had successfully infiltrated the village outskirts and apprehended three men. From them, they learned about the suspicious traveling minstrels who had attacked the guardsmen. Sensing something was off, they decided to return to the castle with the three men in tow.

"Minstrels?" Lord Gunther shouted upon hearing the report during his court session. "Your men got captured by men with flutes and gitterns?" He burst out laughing.

The senior guard tried to explain, but an intoxicated Gunther chose to be merry, jesting, "Beware thee, for my zither is mightier than thy sword!"

The lord's uncharacteristic reaction provoked laughter from his entourage. The senior guardsman could only shake his head, and he decided to get a drink instead.

"Better to deal with minstrels than a peasant rebellion," the steward reassured him.

"They captured my men," the senior guard grumbled. "Their wives and uncles keep asking me about them."

The steward patted his colleague's shoulder and intervened. "My lord," he began, "won't this incident become an embarrassment later on?"

"Yes, it will," the lord unexpectedly revealed, capturing everyone's attention. "It could even encourage the peasants to consider rebelling against our rule," he added.

"Then what should we do?"

The lord chuckled and, without missing a beat, said, "It's just a village and men with flutes. Just send thirty men, and it'll be over. No need to embarrass ourselves further by overreacting."

The staff and the senior guardsman nodded, satisfied with their lord's decision.

Northern Village

With help from Dietrich and Sigmund, Lansius completed the crude map. There were two routes leading to South Hill City and Castle: one a direct path through open plains and the other a longer one passing through several hamlets. Unfortunately, there was no forest, marshland, or a body of water until South Hill City itself.

"Hmm . . ." Lansius rubbed his chin, finding no convenient place to position his troops for an ambush.

"Finding no good place to hide the troops?" Audrey inquired.

Lansius was pleased that his wife was starting to share his penchant for tactics. "That, and more importantly, I can't find anything to use as bait."

Dietrich observed quietly. A bold and brave cavalryman, he was not as adept at planning.

Sigmund, more comfortable with speaking out, put down his prized small harp at his side and suggested, "Can't we use the harvest as bait, as we did with the Nicopolans?"

"I doubt that'll work," Lansius remarked. "The Nicopolans were desperate to alleviate their hunger, but South Hill, from what we've gathered, is well-stocked."

Audrey recalled a quote. "A good castle always aims to have enough to last through winter and spring."

Hearing that, Dietrich scratched his head while Sigmund pondered.

"Time to be bold? Maybe we should start making ladders now," Audrey suggested.

Lansius exhaled sharply. "That's a last resort. I still want to avoid unnecessary bloodshed. Attacking a well-stocked and fortified castle is a bad idea. Any other suggestions?"

"The situation seems tough," Dietrich admitted.

Lansius clasped both of his hands behind his neck and stretched his back to relieve the tension. "We're running out of time," he warned his staff. "Soon, South Hill will send another group to search for their lost men. If we don't act now . . ."

"They'll detect our presence and will begin to barricade their castle," Audrey filled in.

Silence fell over the room, with only the muffled noises from the kitchen downstairs audible.

What Lansius aimed for was to bait a large portion of the South Hill garrison or even capture some of their key staff. If successful, this strategy could likely force them to capitulate, or enable Lansius to storm the castle with minimal casualties.

"We can also rule out using a ruse," Sigmund commented. "Everyone says Lord Gunther is cunning, even crafty, and suspicious by nature."

"He also doesn't like gambling and isn't superstitious," Lansius added.

Their initial expectations, based on word of mouth from sources outside of South Hill, turned out to be mere hearsay. While they had heard that the Lord of South Hill was old and violent, it emerged that his subjects viewed Lord Gunther as devious yet respectful, cunning, and possessing a strong sense of justice.

Looking up at the ceiling, Lansius noticed cobwebs and dirty wood beams. He had come here hoping to find something that would bait Gunther into sending his troops, but seeing the village for himself, he realized it was large yet mostly poor, offering little of value aside from its crops.

"My lord," Audrey called, and from her tone, Lansius knew she was about to say something serious.

"Yes?"

"Servius isn't here," she began calmly. "But even if he were, I doubt he would say no to your original plan to assault the castle."

Lansius gazed at his wife and felt her warm, almost reassuring gaze. "If I sacrifice the Nicopolans to gain a castle, then what's the difference between me and Sergio?"

Audrey's gaze intensified. "Sergio is dead. Daniella and Servius killed him. Meanwhile, the two only speak praises about you."

"It's not about that," Lansius muttered. What he actually meant was whether it was morally right to send people to their deaths if there were other means. However, for this era, such a concept was almost alien as sacrificing lives in battle was commonly accepted and part of their culture.

"My lord, apologies for interrupting, but what my lady said is true. Even in ballads, the hero doesn't always find a weakness. Sometimes, the strength of men is needed."

Lansius gave no answer.

"Should I summon Servius and end this speculation?" Audrey offered softly.

"No." Lansius rejected the idea firmly. "There will be days when all we can rely on is brute force, but today is not that day."

The room looked at him with anticipation, even Carla paying close attention.

"You have another plan in mind?" Audrey looked impressed.

"Two," Lansius revealed. "They're risky, but I have two other ways to win without attacking the castle directly."

"Tell us," Audrey urged.

"One option is straightforward. Appear at the castle and lay siege, but don't attack. Just wait for the harvest, take what is ours, and then leave South Hill."

"Ah," Audrey exclaimed. "Indeed, our goal is to acquire supplies, not necessarily to win the castle."

Meanwhile, Sigmund expressed skepticism. "My lord, to march this far with such a large army and not capture the castle . . . My apologies if this sounds rude, but it seems like a failed campaign. It could affect my lord's reputation."

"I know." Lansius drew a heavy breath. "It's also a wasted opportunity. Our pretext probably only allows us one chance to take South Hill, and personally, I don't want to squander it."

"Not wanting to squander this chance, but also not wanting to assault the castle," Audrey mused, feeling the contradiction. "Wait, you said there are two ways. What's the second one?"

"The second one . . ." Lansius hesitated. "Let me tell you this first. More than just provisions or the castle, we need South Hill to protect the Grand Alliance from famine."

His words captured everyone's attention.

The lord continued. "Korelia's position is strategic but doesn't produce enough food. Meanwhile, trade with Eastern Lowlandia is risky and unreliable. The surplus from Korimor will be used to support Umberland, which I foresee will consume a lot of resources for years to come."

Dietrich, finding this a bit odd, voiced his concern. "But South Hill is too far from Korelia."

"But not from Three Hills City, our biggest ally," Lansius reminded the cavalryman. "If we control South Hill, then Three Hills would be able to support us more, both in terms of the campaign for Umberland, or trade with Korelia."

Audrey leaned closer and asked, "If South Hill is this important, then why haven't you revealed this to anyone?"

"Because . . ." He looked at each of them. "I feared my own staff would push me to commit to an assault."

Audrey was taken aback, realizing the words were also directed at her. She turned to Dietrich and Sigmund, who both readily shook their heads earnestly. Sigmund pleaded, "My lord, my lady, we would never do such a thing. I doubt even your knights would dare."

Turning back to Lansius, Audrey's voice took on a formal tone. "My lord, our trust in you is absolute, as is your control over us. Please, have more faith in us."

Lansius hadn't expected such a strong response and couldn't help but break into a smile. "If everyone feels the same, then perhaps the second plan will work . . ." His words trailed off, but nobody dared to interrupt.

Then, with a decisive tone, he declared, "There's still enough time. Let's prepare the plan for tonight's battle."

"A battle?" Dietrich was the first to react.

"Yes," Lansius confirmed, a chuckle in his voice. "Tonight, we'll be battling hundreds of bandits in this village."

CHAPTER 22

SKIRMISHER

South Hill Castle

The supper feast in the Great Hall was lively, especially so close to harvest season. While wheat and rye were yet to be harvested, the wild animals in the forest had fattened, and the fruits in the orchards had ripened. Moreover, the barley, harvested half a season earlier, was now ready to be consumed.

The ale had been malted and fermented to perfection. It was rarely aged but consumed fresh to avoid spoilage. Along with plenty of food and good drinks, there was also music to keep everyone entertained.

Despite the disastrous campaign to Korelia, which affected the lives of two thousand men, hardly anyone here seemed bothered. Everyone present was either a firstborn or one of the fortunate with ties to Lord Gunther. They considered themselves the elites of South Hill society, and the failure of the officers who led the Korelia campaign only served to inflate their egos further.

They lived well in a region rife with strife, dining on white bread, fresh meat, puddings, and fine ale. Born affluent, the concept of famine was alien to them. In their view, famine was merely a consequence of peasant stupidity and laziness, a byproduct of weak discipline. These little landlords and their cohorts, who never tilled the land in their lives, ironically believed their role in life was to enforce obedience among the populace so that work on the land and tax obligations were fulfilled.

Amidst the lively laughter, a guardsman approached and leaned in to whisper to the senior guard at his table. The head of the guard appeared stunned, quickly glancing at his men, who nodded to confirm the news.

"Has something happened?" the steward beside the senior guard inquired, taking a bite of ripe, yellow-fleshed fruit.

"I'm not sure at this moment, but I'll inform you if there's cause for concern. Please enjoy the feast."

The steward nodded, and the senior guard rose and headed to the door, excusing himself as others inquired.

The next morning, the senior guard and the steward awaited the lord in front of his chamber. It was unusual, but they deemed it urgent. Yesterday, three of their men had escaped from the village and returned to the castle, bringing with them puzzling developments.

Following the three men, more than a dozen villagers seeking refuge also arrived. They too corroborated the reports about the village. The situation was so puzzling that the head of the guard had brought the issue to the steward, who suggested bringing it directly to the lord.

After a period of waiting, the castle guards watched as the squire finally opened the lavishly decorated oaken door, a sign that Lord Gunther had awoken. Bracing themselves for their lord's erratic temper, the senior guard and the steward entered, following the squire's announcement of their visit.

The lord's face turned to displeasure, thinking something bad must've happened. "How bad?" he asked.

"My lord, let's refrain from making such assumptions so early in the morning," the steward replied with a measured tone. "Three of our men have returned to the castle."

The lord furrowed his brow. "So the troublesome minstrels are gone?"

"Not quite. The men said they escaped when the village was raided," the steward explained.

"Raided?" Lord Gunther raised his voice. "By whom?"

"Our men reported bandits attacking the village," the senior guard replied.

"Bandits?" Lord Gunther's tone was full of doubt. "But there are no bandits in these lands. Have you heard of any?"

"This is the first time, but given our current situation, it's not too farfetched. Also, villagers who fled confirmed the same story."

Lord Gunther said nothing but gestured to his squire for some water.

"There are other things that might interest you, my lord," said the steward. "Before the bandits appeared, a group of rich merchants arrived in the village. The villagers who came to us spoke of carts laden with goods, heavy wooden chests, and dozens of hardy men for protection."

This piqued the lord's interest as he drank from his goblet of water, forgoing his medicine, since the pain in his thigh wound was manageable. He pondered. "If they had such protection, how could the bandits overcome them?"

"They said that bandits attacked at night. It was so chaotic that our men were able to escape."

Despite the steward's explanation, the lord harbored doubts. "For rich merchants to come to South Hill uninvited . . . This region hardly has anything special to trade, aside from rock salt."

The senior guard nodded readily. "Indeed. This series of coincidences, including the armed minstrels, rich merchants, and bandits, is all suspicious."

The steward, however, thought differently. With a knowing smile, he suggested, "My lord, have you considered the grain?"

"Grain?" the lord echoed, and then realization dawned. He recalled reports of rising food prices in the Three Hills, particularly after Korimor was besieged by the Lord of Korelia. "You're suggesting they are Lord Jorge's merchants? This is starting to make sense."

"Exactly, my lord. They must have been uneasy about their low supplies after the failed campaign and decided to procure grain secretly."

"But why clandestinely?" the lord mused aloud.

"Probably because the Lord of Korelia's Grand Alliance prohibits trade with non-members like us."

"Hmph, that Jorge still has clever aides." Lord Gunther chuckled.

"Not only does this explain everything," the steward continued, "but it might also prove lucrative."

The lord smirked. "The bandits might be tougher than angry peasants, but the potential wealth from those merchants should be rewarding."

The senior guardsman proposed, "My lord if you wish to capture them, allow me to lead the vanguard while you wait for the bannerman to summon the rest of the troops."

"Indeed, we had better make haste. Those bandits already gained a day on us," Lord Gunther agreed. "Then take a hundred men and go with my blessing. Win this, and I shall make you my marshal."

"At once, my lord," the senior guard responded confidently.

Lord Gunther

Unable to withstand the pain of riding, the lord chose to travel in his carriage. His nephew, who was in charge of the cavalry, had fashioned protection for the carriage and suitable barding for the horses. Even without the added protection, they were still flanked by a heavy escort of knights, cavalry, and men-at-arms.

Unlike those sent to the ill-fated Korelia campaign, these troops were the elite who had fought under Gunther since his days as a knight. Many were battle-hardened veterans and considered well-equipped.

"My lord, a report from the front," his captain announced from outside the carriage as they paused for a midday rest under the shade of a cluster of large trees.

Struggling against the effects of the poppy milk, Lord Gunther gestured for his captain to continue.

The captain relayed, "Our vanguard has located the bandits in the village. They seem unaware of our approach."

At this, the lord chuckled merrily. "It's fortunate they haven't thought to flee . . . Do we have an estimate of their numbers?"

"Approximately seventy, or perhaps under a hundred."

Euphoric from the poppy milk, Lord Gunther couldn't help but smirk widely. He then instructed quickly, "Let's wrap things up and make haste. Opportunity awaits."

With that, two hundred men, sixty cavalrymen, and a dozen knights prepared to advance. Despite the heat of the midday sun, they were eager, anticipating an easy victory.

Many assumed that the bandits were stragglers from the last campaign, likely Nicopolan mercenaries who couldn't return to Korimor due to the ongoing conflict. Like other Lowlandians, they had little respect for their neighbors, even harboring disgust for their mercenary tendencies.

Thus, the South Hill men-at-arms were in high spirits, eager to demonstrate their superiority. They were confident that not even the famed Lord of Korelia could defeat them at their best.

The main army, led by the Lord of South Hill, arrived at the outskirts of the village. Unlike the vanguard that could conceal its approach, the larger army, with its tens of horses, alerted everyone to their presence as they neared the village. This was not a lapse in judgment but a well-planned strategy.

En route, the lord had commanded the vanguard to circle the village and wait at the road leading out of the province. The vanguard would act as the mouse catcher, and the main army as the one to smoke out the nest.

The plan was proceeding smoothly, with their army closing in on the village unopposed.

However, the villagers' behavior was concerning. They seemed suspiciously afraid of the main army's approach, running away from them, despite the clear display of Lord Gunther's coat of arms on the banners.

The men at the front began to question amongst themselves about the villagers' odd behavior.

"Aren't we rescuing them from bandits?" one of the men-at-arms asked.

"Don't overthink. It's only common for peasants to be a bunch of cowards," his lieutenant said dismissively.

Meanwhile, Lord Gunther, inside his armored carriage, advanced steadily along the main route, flanked by his column. He was already pondering what to do with the rich merchants—whether they would offer enough gratitude or if it was better to declare that the goods were "gone" and blame the bandits.

"A good opportunity," he muttered merrily to himself, considering how the extra spoils could bolster his army against next year's threat from the Lord of Korelia.

His captain, riding alongside the carriage, leaned in through the window. "My lord, we've spotted the bandits. They're in chaos, attempting to erect petty defenses in the village."

The report left the lord overjoyed, and the double dose of poppy milk he had taken for this journey only heightened his feelings. He then inquired, "Have you located the merchants or their wares?"

"We've seen carriages and loaded carts hidden in barns and other buildings."

"Excellent!" Lord Gunther exclaimed, feeling immensely relaxed. "Now, Captain . . . unleash the men. Let them advance, but keep the cavalry by my side . . ."

"At once, my lord. But what about potential damage to the village?"

The lord's smile remained unchanged as he said, "Crush them if need be. They have harbored criminals and bandits. Now is a good opportunity to remind them of the Imperium's law, discipline, and their duty to me."

Village

The farmer's daughter ran breathlessly, passing through the villagers who watched her with curiosity. "Maester Sigmund," she cried as she found him.

The minstrel turned toward her, surprised at her sudden reappearance. "Hey, slow down. What's the rush?" he warned, reaching out to grab her, fearing she might fall.

Gasping for breath, she managed to say, "Maester, the lord's men—I saw many of them from our fields. You have to get out of here." Her tone was filled with urgency.

Unfazed, Sigmund scolded her. "See? You should've convinced your family to move away from the village like the others, at least temporarily. I'm part of the bandits, after all."

"B-but you don't look like bandits." She cried her heart out, choosing to believe her gut. "Please, Maester, run, they'll torture you."

Her response made the other supposed bandits around Sigmund chuckle.

"She's got a good wit," one praised.

"Bold too," another complimented.

The girl looked at them with a furrowed brow. "Why don't you run? I'm not lying, the lord's men—"

"I know. We know," Sigmund reassured her.

"The lord will torture you." Panic tinged her voice.

"I bet he'll try," Sigmund replied, his tone either fearless or foolish.

As if on cue, ruckus, shouting, and cries were heard outside the village. The villagers began to disperse, some to their homes, others to the adjacent woods. Observing this, Sigmund gestured to his men, signaling them to move.

The girl watched as a dozen men readily moved the newly made sharp wooden obstacles, *cheval de frise*, to block the road and pathways leading to the center of the village. The rest gathered around a cart and retrieved helmets, pole-axes, and even crossbows.

She gasped. "Maester, you really are bandits."

Sigmund laughed as his men provided him with his helmet. "You might want to stay somewhere safe. Don't you have friends around here? And where's your little brother?"

"He's with my mother," she answered, then quickly added, "Sir, you might be armed, but you only have this many. The lord has so many people."

Sigmund wore his helmet loosely on his head and patted the girl's brown hair. "I told you not to worry. I have friends more numerous than you could count."

"But you lied," she protested, her words catching the man off guard. "The bakers told me you have four of twenty friends. I can count that high."

Sigmund chuckled, impressed that the girl understood the method of counting by twenties, reaching as high as eighty. He knelt down and replied, "Worry not, lass. We still have a bandit king."

"A bandit king?" she echoed, her voice a mix of fear and anticipation.

"Indeed, a cruel bandit king." Sigmund sighed heavily. "Tasking me to defend this village with but these few men. Oh, Sigmund, how poor thy fate hath been."

Almost without warning, bolts began to fly from both sides. The girl barely registered the whistling sound as Sigmund scooped her up and rushed her to the open barn. "Get inside, and don't come out."

"Can I peek from the upstairs window?" the girl asked defiantly.

Sigmund, already on the move, didn't reply. He ran seemingly to assume command. His eighty men clashed with the first wave of South Hill troops.

The girl went inside the barn and found only an old donkey in the pen. She located a ladder, climbed it, and made her way to a window, only to discover it faced the wrong direction. Undeterred, she carefully moved the dried stacks of hay, searching for a vantage point. Her diligence paid off when she found a loose wooden board.

Peering through the gap, she observed the skirmish between the two sides. To her eyes, it was chaotic, with small groups fighting sporadically in different places. Others merely brandished their long spears, seemingly waiting for the correct time to engage.

The screams and shouts were disheartening. Even the old donkey was bothered and getting restless. It all quickly became overwhelming, and she instinctively covered her ears with her hands. Witnessing the lord's men limping or crawling to safety, she felt a sinking feeling.

Worse yet, several lay motionless on the ground. Nobody was helping or giving aid.

Then she realized that those had been left to die.

Her heart was beating fast, and sweat formed on her brows. The vivid carnage was vomit-inducing, yet it also strangely compelled her to keep watching. Amidst the brutal spectacle, she found herself silently asking the Ancients for Sigmund and his friends' safety.

Despite the man's claim of being a bandit, she chose to trust in her savior. Without his timely intervention, her father would have lost all his teeth again.

The last time it had happened was when her father and uncles were wrongfully accused of being part of a plot to steal crops from the lord's fields. They were beaten and lost nearly all of their teeth. They survived by subsisting on soup for nearly five years until enough of their teeth had regrown.

The lord's men said that punishment would instill discipline, but it only bred fear and resentment toward their lord.

Inside the village, the chaos continued, yet even to her untrained eyes, it was clear that the lord's men were stalled. They couldn't breach the village's defenses. Observing closely, she noted how Sigmund's allies moved with remarkable speed, applying pressure rapidly without waiting for commands and retreating without hesitation when needed.

The South Hills men struggled against these nimble and adaptable groups. The defenders seamlessly transitioned between melee and ranged attacks, baffling their opponents. They were also adept at feigning retreat, baiting the lord's men into vulnerable positions only to have another group launch a surprise flank attack.

Not just swords and bolts, but also throwing stones and hurling insults were part of their repertoire. The girl noticed that these fighters cannily used any available cover, contrasting with her image of armed men, whom she had imagined would stand proudly and openly in battle.

Gradually, the lord's men abandoned their assault and retreated. "They're beaten?" she whispered in astonishment.

The farmer's daughter found it hard to believe that Sigmund could have defended the village. Yet, her smirk faded as she saw the lord's men regrouping, launching another, more coordinated attack with additional forces. She also saw the lord's cavalry had gone from their original spot.

"It's far from over," she muttered to herself, clenching her fists so tightly that her knuckles turned white.

CHAPTER 23

BLACK BANDIT

The sound of a girl screaming was heard as the knights and cavalry charged toward Sigmund and his men's lightly defended position. Despite firing their crossbows, many of the untested skirmishers ended up wounded, saved only by their *cheval de frise*, or the tight and narrow streets of the village.

"I'm fucked!" one of the men groaned, his leg appearing to be broken by the recent attack.

"They're also fucked," Sigmund retorted, observing the two captured horsemen. More were wounded, but only two had fallen.

"Captain, let me gut them if they prove worthless," the wounded man rasped as his colleagues dragged him to safety.

"Stay alive; you can complain later." Then, turning to the rest of his men, Sigmund shouted, "We repelled them once, we can repel them again!"

Just like that, bolts whistled menacingly through the air as the fighting continued. Once again, the South Hill main column advanced on their position. This time, they proceeded with greater caution and committed all their forces, holding nothing in reserve.

Sigmund crouched and leaned against the wall of the wooden house. He passed his crossbow to the man in the best-concealed position at a corner, who then made the shot. After firing, this man exchanged his spent crossbow for a loaded one. This tactic allowed them to maintain rapid fire from a few advantageous positions, effectively slowing the enemy's advance.

Another group was pushed toward Sigmund's position. Spotting Sigmund, the young Korelian lieutenant called out, "Captain, we're getting pummeled."

"Take cover behind the building beside me," Sigmund instructed.

The lieutenant crouched and sat on the ground, his back against a nearby house. "We've spent our bolts. Besides, they're everywhere. We don't have room to maneuver."

"Go to the carts, see if you can find more bolts, and get halberds for everyone."

The lieutenant promptly began moving his group to the nearest cart, as instructed.

Watching them, Sigmund added, "And get your men to watch for the cavalry. They won't be gone for long."

How he wished that Dietrich, Sir Hugo, or Sir Harold was here. Only now did Sigmund truly feel what it meant to become a commander. Moreover, he was commanding the lord's latest creation, the skirmishers. While these men-at-arms with crossbows were proven capable, they needed space to maneuver, and right now, they were losing ground.

"Captain, a report!" a youngster called out from behind, pausing to catch his breath.

Sigmund quickly pulled the young scout's head down, fearing a bolt might strike him.

Once the scout was kneeling low, he hurriedly reported, "Another column is approaching from the rear."

"Ours?" Sigmund asked.

"The banner is South Hill."

"By the Ageless," Sigmund cursed as he reloaded his crossbow again. His men were looking at him, fear and doubt painted on their faces.

Sigmund shoved his loaded crossbow to the man next to him. "Don't get distracted. Keep sending those bolts."

His group returned to action, and Sigmund gazed at the young scout. "How many?"

"Groups of twenties, possibly a hundred, if not more."

The skald took a deep breath. "How long before we're surrounded?"

"Soon, Captain. They're moving unopposed."

"Isn't it better to reposition somewhere else?" the man next to Sigmund suggested.

Sigmund shook his head. "My gut tells me that if we try to move, then the cavalry will bear down on us."

The lieutenant's group had rearmed themselves with halberds and a few quivers of bolts. They returned just in time, as another group emerged from their hideout, pursued by dozens of South Hill's men.

"Have courage!" Sigmund yelled, donning his helmet and taking his spear, as he led his men into the fray.

Peering through a hole in the wooden wall, the girl watched with horror as Sigmund and his men engaged in a brutal battle. The clash of swords and the sight of bloodstained streets filled her with dread. Overwhelmed, she pressed her hands over her ears tightly to muffle out the loud shouts and screams.

Minutes of fighting felt like hours to her. She finally breathed a huge sigh of relief when it became clear that Sigmund's three groups had managed to fend off South Hill's attack. Yet, she was aware that this was not the last. Wherever she looked, the South Hill forces seemed to be gaining the upper hand against the bandits' defenses.

Now, Sigmund's men looked exhausted and seemingly wary of another cavalry attack on their position. Gone were their rapid attack and bait tactics. They were slowly losing their edge, and this deeply frightened her.

Worse, she heard different shouts from behind. At first, she thought it was just her imagination, but it bothered her so much that she waded through the dried haystack and returned to the barn's window. What she saw frightened her further.

A large column of men was marching from behind, their banners fluttering in the wind. "It can't be." She shuddered uncontrollably as she recognized her lord's coat of arms.

From her perspective, the Lord of South Hill had managed to maneuver a column of men to hit the bandits' weak point. As she observed, Sigmund had neither erected any wooden blockades nor positioned his men to defend the other side of the village entrance. Thus, the column was advancing steadily.

At this point, the girl lost all hope and simply sat in the corner, no longer wanting to witness or learn more about the unfolding situation.

For her, if reality was this bitter and bleak, then she no longer wished to know.

Sigmund rested his back against the wooden house, his breath ragged, his face and body covered in sweat. His men were no better. They had survived the attack, but their situation was dire.

Their only hope was the fact that two other allied groups were converging on their position. These groups had lost their checkpoints and had no more opportunity to bait and attack, yet with this number, they could fight as regular men-at-arms.

"Captain, our rear is blocked," the lookout reported.

Sigmund gazed at his men, who were eyeing him. "Listen. We should be able to create a box formation. Use the buildings' walls to our advantage."

"But it's seventy against a few hundred," warned the young lieutenant, who was resting next to Sigmund.

"The lord ordered us to stall for time." Sigmund raised his voice. "Come, let's assemble the damn formation!" He stood up and brandished his spear.

Slowly, the remaining skirmishers moved into a box formation, using the buildings' walls as their stronghold. Watching this, the South Hill forces reformed their combatants and approached from two sides—the vanguard from the north and the main army from the south.

Feeling trapped, many were feeling hopeless. "Where are the lord and lady?" one muttered.

"Captain, do you think they changed the plan without telling us?" another asked whilst standing in formation.

Sigmund shook his head. "I doubt they would do that."

"But that makes the most sense," the young lieutenant muttered timidly. "If they decided to rush the castle, they could easily secure the region."

"That means abandoning us?" another blurted out.

"Our lord isn't that kind of man!" Sigmund declared strongly. His conviction was enough to soothe his men's fear. "Recall how the lord has saved us again and again in battles."

The expressions on the men's faces began to shift, their fear diminishing as they recalled how the lord, even in wars, had always shown genuine concern for their well-being.

Sigmund knew he had captivated his audience. And like a good skald, he pressed on, "We've survived the Lion, the Coalition, and the Nicopolans. Our lord has never failed us. Let us show him our courage!"

The men in formation started to chant their nomadic-like war cries, steeling their hearts.

"For the Black Lord!" one shouted.

And then another replied, "For the Black Bandit!"

The cries further rallied the men. Due to their role in this battle as bandits, they had informally dubbed themselves the "Black Bandits," a tribute to their lord's hair. However, since no one had dared to seek permission from the lord, the name remained unofficial.

Then, as if to reward their conviction, a deep, resonant sound of a brass cornu, recently acquired in Korimor, was heard for the first time. Despite the distance, its powerful and penetrating sound cut through the noise of battle, delivering clear and haunting notes.

At first, nothing changed, but a small confusion emerged at the enemy's position. However, another cornu was heard from another side, and then another; only then did the enemy columns stop dead in their tracks.

Witnessing their opponent stopped, Sigmund and his men were filled with jubilation, cheering loudly. They watched as their allies arrived, not just in one location, but seemingly everywhere, all at once.

"It's the lord," one of them cheered, echoed by others.

Sigmund heaved a sigh of relief and patted the shoulder of his lieutenant beside him, who had let slip a few tears.

The young lieutenant smiled and nodded, his gratitude evident.

Although it took longer than expected, the Black Lord had now achieved total encirclement. His greater force had surrounded the entire village, along with the South Hill army. The battle entered its second decisive phase.

South Hill Side

"That is not possible!" Lord Gunther shouted angrily as he learned about the situation. Even the euphoric effect of the poppy milk couldn't ease his tension.

His captain was at a loss for words, while the squire diligently offered a tonic. The lord chugged the concoction of wormwood, mint, and rue, hoping to clear his mind.

A messenger arrived. "Captain, my lord," he greeted and reported, "our troops are requesting instructions."

"Just get them to return here. We need to protect the lord," the captain instructed.

The lord remained silent, offering no comment. Upon this cue, the messenger bowed deeply and hurried to his horse, racing back to the village.

"Get me the scouts. What army did they see?" the lord suddenly asked.

"My lord, we're still ascertaining—"

"Meaning you know things. Speak, or I shall remove you from command," Gunther snapped. At the lord's words, his armed entourage moved closer to the carriage.

"My lord, I only wish to do my due diligence. It could be a ploy by the bandits," the captain explained.

The lord's temper flared. "Reveal it to me. I command thee!"

Feeling cornered, the captain said in a hushed, reluctant tone, "It's blue and bronze."

"What . . . ?" came the puzzled response.

"The scouts reported seeing a blue shield with a bronze chevron," the captain clarified.

Upon hearing the news, the lord's strength failed him. He slumped in his carriage seat, feeling suddenly old and weary. His anger had gone, and in exchange the pain in his thigh throbbed relentlessly, seemingly unaffected by the poppy milk still in his veins. He remained silent, his face etched with an expression of shock.

The captain, anticipating such a reaction, swiftly assumed command. Reluctant to suggest that the lord or his entourage move closer to the village, his only option was to pull their columns back to defend their current position. Naturally, he deemed the lord's carriage as an ideal rallying point for the troops.

"Quick, bring me a horseman," the captain commanded. He knew his only hope was to regroup their forces. Once consolidated, he hoped the head of the guard might find a way to prevent a rout.

As his command was relayed, a cavalryman quickly rode forth. "Yes, Captain."

"Inform our vanguard of our situation," the captain instructed, "and ask them to retreat to our location."

House Lansius Side

Standing at the edge of the forest adjacent to the village, the Lord of Korelia watched as his men advanced toward the South Hill columns' position.

"My lord, acting Captain Servius has marched the Nicopolans with great strides. They will soon make contact with the enemy's main army," one scout informed him.

Lansius nodded in acknowledgment. Another scout knelt and added, "My lord, Sir Harold is leading his knights and cavalry to engage the enemy's vanguard column."

"Carry on," Lansius instructed. Their maneuvers were part of his plan.

Due to the skirmishers' small number and resilience, Lansius had successfully formed a complete encirclement of the South Hill army. Any other column might have failed spectacularly or suffered heavy losses in the process. However, periodic reports from the scouts had kept him informed of their situation, and Sigmund's column held against all odds.

The bait had worked flawlessly, and now the Lord of South Hill was within his grasp.

Thunderous hooves announced the arrival of the baroness along with her entourage, all armored and riding their prized warhorses.

"My lord, permission to capture their cavalry and their banner," Audrey requested from atop her charger horse.

Lansius gazed at her and gave a nod. "We're winning. Don't do anything reckless."

His warning made Audrey smile. "Gratitude, my lord, for allowing me the honor."

"Good hunting," Lansius responded.

As he said this, all of the staff standing around him cheered for the lady, the air filled with excitement and hope.

Audrey led the two hundred dragoons on a big hunt, while Lansius kept the remaining hundred, along with the nomads' horse archers, in reserve.

Today, Audrey would test the dragoons' mettle against the opponent's knights and cavalry.

In them, Lansius hoped to create a cranequinier brigade, a specialized mounted crossbowmen. With the skirmishers on foot and the cranequiniers on horseback, they would form a powerful combination, capable of harassing, provoking, and stalling the opponent until he could deploy his main attack.

These forces wouldn't replace the established mounted crossbowmen dragoons, but instead, provide more options and utilities on the battlefield.

Lansius looked at his staff and entourage. Some were new, having climbed through the ranks on merit, while others had been with him since the event in Toruna village. "Men," he called, and everyone in his vicinity looked at him with growing anticipation.

"I'm going to have a chat with the Lord of South Hill in person. Will you accompany me?" the lord asked.

His men responded with a chorus of chaotic but energetic reactions. They would gladly follow Lord Lansius anywhere. This battle was poised to be Lansius's fifth triumph. In just two short years, the unassuming teacher from Bellandia had become the most prolific warlord in Lowlandia.

Everyone present there was exhilarated. They had seen the strategy unfold and witnessed how the South Hill forces amounted to nothing more than a pebble on their lord's path to greatness.

CHAPTER 24

CRANEQUINIERS

Nicopolan Column

During their march to South Hill, the Lord of Korelia often spent time walking with his men on foot, claiming that riding all day was tiresome. And just as he had promised at the start of the campaign, he treated his men equally. Without any hesitation, the lord marched alongside the Nicopolans, with Servius proudly at his side.

It was clear from his interactions that the lord did not discriminate between his established columns and the newly joined Nicopolans. He repeated this multiple times, slowly gaining the trust and respect of the Nicopolans. While it might have seemed small and insignificant, his camaraderie and the fulfillment of his promise of equal treatment resonated genuinely with everyone involved.

Physically, the lord was an unassuming man, yet approachable and sincere in his actions. Unlike the charismatic noble born, who attracted people with their physical presence and elaborate clothes, the Lord of Korelia gave more of the impression of being a comrade in arms.

He wasn't stingy, pompous, or demanding like most nobles. He resembled the few nobles who didn't mind sitting and eating with their subjects. Beyond his strict military law, he was genuinely concerned with his men's well-being, as shown in his policies.

While he couldn't control the food situation, he made efforts to secure clean water, improve camp conditions, and even allow longer midday breaks so everyone could mend their footwear.

Despite their limited interactions, most Nicopolans came to view the lord as a trustworthy leader. His leadership felt natural because he had earned his victories and acted honorably, even toward those he defeated. Thus, despite his rather unassuming character traits, people were drawn to his presence out of admiration, eager to see and listen to him speak.

His men followed him not because of his rank or title, but because they believed he was the one who could truly protect them in these chaotic times. While other nobles would send their men to their deaths to settle petty rivalries, in Lord Lansius they saw hope. A way to escape from this time of chaos and turbulence.

This sliver of hope for peace was well-founded. With his recent victories still vivid in their minds, the long march south had once again proven the lord's canny abilities. Despite covering long distances, they were not rushed. The lord did not ask for a forced march, opting instead to maintain a steady pace. Yet, surprisingly, they covered significant ground each day.

Many of the former mercenaries realized that this performance was due to meticulous planning and expert scouting practices.

Currently, the lord had sent scouts as far as three days ahead. He also employed another group constantly looking for suitable places to build camps, along with alternatives. They looked for water availability, the height of the land, and food sources if available.

Thus, even though they marched at a steady pace, the blue and bronze army moved faster than most troops of their size. This feat was also attributed to the lord's humane treatment of his troops. From the start of the campaign, he had set aside dozens of horse carts for the injured or weakened men who couldn't continue the march.

For everyone involved, the thought that no one was left behind naturally boosted morale. Because of all this, and the fact that the lord and lady were personally involved in solving the Nicopolans' hunger crisis, the Nicopolans felt immensely grateful.

They had expected to be abused or treated as a burden to be discarded at convenience, but their new master proved to be magnanimous and treated them like first-class citizens.

Thus, when Lord Lansius asked his troops to continue hiding despite their arrival at South Hill, the Nicopolans complied without question.

Although eager to take the villages, as they were still on rations, they chose to endure it. Even the thousand camp followers chose not to escalate their complaints when Servius barred them from visiting the village.

Under the care of Sir Harold, the Nicopolans happily camped far from the village or any farmland and kept a lookout to avoid detection.

When they learned that the lord disguised himself as a merchant, the Nicopolans watched with a mix of curiosity and anticipation. Many believed that this was nothing but a scouting activity, while some thought that this was the start of an elaborate ruse to conquer South Hill with as little fighting as possible.

Village

Caught off guard by the sound of cheering outside, the girl's hope returned. She nervously took a peek outside and couldn't believe her eyes. A large force of unknown origin was mustering just outside the village and now encroaching inward.

She grew frustrated when she couldn't find the previous hole in the wall to peek through. Instead, she found a smaller crack, but it was enough to see Sigmund and his allies rejoicing.

"It must be the bandit king," the girl muttered as she recalled Sigmund's words. "So he wasn't lying."

She returned to the window and observed the bandit king's forces closing in. They were so numerous that the entire village was surrounded.

Suddenly, the old donkey made a hearty, infectious laugh, prompting her to peek out.

At the same time, the silhouette of someone appeared at the door. "Girl, where are you?" a familiar voice shouted from below.

She looked down and saw Sigmund. "Maester, I'm up here!"

The man looked up and grinned happily. "Climb down, hurry. I'm going to take you to the lord. I mean, the bandit king."

The farmer's daughter caught the word "lord" again and grew suspicious of the bandit king's true nature. However, her excitement led her to climb down as quickly as she dared.

Below, Sigmund was waiting for her, spear in hand, and helmet worn in a relaxed manner.

"Maester," she called out again as she ran toward him.

"Easy, I'm dirty and sticky," Sigmund warned her.

Stopping shy of hugging him like she would her uncle, she looked at the blood on his armor with great concern. "Maester, are you injured?"

"You're not afraid of blood? Never mind that, can you run?" Sigmund asked. "We might need to make haste. There's still danger out there."

"We're repositioning?"

"Clever girl," Sigmund replied, leading her outside where his men were already on the move. They had loaded their wounded onto three horse-drawn carts. Although there was space for the little girl, Sigmund didn't want her to see the gnarly wounds some of his men had sustained.

With urgency and heightened alertness, the skirmishers made their move. The South Hill forces had abandoned their attack, opening a path for Sigmund to lead his men to safety.

The Nicopolan Column

Three days after their arrival to the South Hill region, the Nicopolans received their commands. They donned what armor they had and fastened their belts. Despite being weakened by hunger, they were well-spirited for battle. After a short march, they were surprised at what they saw: the lord had unexpectedly used an elaborate ruse and lured the South Hill army into a trap.

This revelation thrilled the Nicopolans, who understood that a guaranteed victory awaited them as they surrounded the village as ordered.

Without wasting time, Sir Harold led his knights and cavalrymen in attacking the opponent's isolated column, which he perceived as the most significant threat. As the knights rode to glory, Servius led his select group of one thousand to descend upon the South Hill main column where Lord Gunther's banner flew.

Feeling grateful for the lord's fair treatment, the Nicopolans under Servius were eager to show their worth in battle. As their column rushed toward their opponent, the remaining Nicopolans at the back cheered hard for them. Deep inside, many harbored fears of being seen by the lord as unworthy, or worse, as deadweight.

Thus, Servius and his men doubled their efforts to secure a spectacular win. "Let us teach these South Hill backwater shepherds and farmers how the Imperium's finest condottieri fight wars!" Servius rallied as they reached the final distance.

The deadly whistling of bolts greeted them. Two hundred strong South Hill men-at-arms stubbornly brandished their spears and threw everything they had, but the one thousand picked Nicopolans were unfazed. Approaching steadily in good line formation, they endured the punishment and enveloped the enemy. Soon the South Hill's flanks recoiled as the Nicopolans exacted terror upon them.

Like ants, the Nicopolans swarmed over the smaller and already exhausted force, which could do nothing else but form a circle and brandish their swords and spears in vain.

Sir Harold

The opponent's cavalry and vanguard were baffled by the appearance of a large army surrounding the village. Before they could regroup, Sir Harold and his twenty knights and thirty cavalrymen were already galloping toward the vanguard's position.

While the narrow and winding village streets weren't ideal for cavalry, Sir Harold knew he needed to crush the vanguard to prevent them from regrouping with the main army. He only needed to break this single column and stop South Hill from struggling further. If he failed, then the opponent might attempt to break out, prolonging the fight and possibly resulting in unnecessary casualties on both sides.

The thought of a decisive victory lingered heavily in his mind as he latched his visor shut. Through the narrow iron slits, he watched as the opponent was running away from him.

The South Hill vanguard, numbering around one hundred, had panicked at the sight of heavy cavalry bearing down on them. The combination of being surrounded by an unexpected army and now facing a heavy cavalry charge convinced them that their situation was hopeless. They weren't prepared to fight such formidable opponents.

Worse yet, their once advantageous position for a back attack against Sigmund's skirmishers was now completely turned against them. Separated from their main army, they were vulnerable from all sides. The vanguard had no choice but to abandon their position.

Sir Harold's knights gained on them and delivered a punishing blow. The first row of casualties led to an almost instantaneous rout. The vanguard quickly disintegrated, with soldiers discarding their unnecessary equipment and fleeing for their lives.

"Commander, they're breaking up," a fellow knight reported.

"Ah, what a beautiful sight." Sir Harold laughed, unlatching and lifting his visor. "Let's not let them get away. Men, your ransom awaits."

With that simple command, Sir Harold and his cavalry hunted down the vanguard remnants.

Audrey

Watching Sir Harold and the cavalrymen aim at the vanguard, Audrey knew there was a chance that the South Hill cavalry might come to help. Thus, like she had been taught by Lansius, she divided her dragoons into two groups: one as the hammer, the other the anvil. The dragoons were flexible enough to dismount and fight like crossbowmen or footmen, even set up ambushes.

However, the South Hill cavalry didn't react as she had expected; instead of aiding the vanguard, they headed straight toward their main army. Without recalling half of her dragoons, Audrey led the remaining one hundred in a swift race along the outer side of the village, intent on capturing the opponent's cavalry.

Riding with the wind blowing hard against the vents of her visor, the baroness spearheaded the pursuit. Their cavalry was lighter, and only a few of the one hundred dragoons wore heavy armor. Like Audrey, those in heavier armor compensated with better horses, more than capable of matching the speed with the rest.

The South Hill cavalry, stunned by the chase, veered to avoid contact. Yet, the dragoons' warhorses were fresh and well-rested. Moreover, having marched and fought since summer, their speed and stamina had increased significantly.

"Don't aim at the horses," Audrey commanded as they were getting closer and preparing their crossbows.

Finally, Dietrich, who led a separate detachment, managed to block the opponent's move. Bolts were fired, causing the enemy to react with unease and confusion. This distraction was all Audrey needed; her dragoons rushed from behind and moved past the opponent's side, and crossbow bolts were loosed.

Within a few breaths, they inflicted significant damage and spread terror throughout the South Hill cavalry. It was widely known that only Mage Knights were proficient with crossbows on horseback, as they alone could reload the heavy draw using just their arm strength. Thus, the sight of a mass of mounted crossbowmen was unexpected.

Realizing they were facing a different type of cavalry, the remaining South Hill cavalry decided to offer combat. They gambled that crossbowmen on horses wouldn't anticipate close-quarters fighting. They veered and charged into the dragoons' double-file formation.

However, it was a mistake. Lady Audrey and her select riders had already swung their spent crossbows to their backs, trusting the leather slings to hold them, then retrieved their second crossbows from their left waists. They aimed at the approaching cavalry and loosed their second volley. As soon as the crossbows reverberated and the bolts flew true, they pulled their sabers, ready for a fight.

Under the barrage of bolts, the South Hill cavalry broke from the wounded in their ranks. While not all bolts penetrated, it was enough to cause tremendous fear and destroy morale. More than twenty fell, twenty fled, and the remaining thirty who maintained their courage finally tasted defeat in close combat. The lighter and more nimble dragoons were more than a match against their heavy opponents.

Audrey pulled the reins of her horse, and her staff followed dutifully. She lifted her visor and saw that one of her riders was proudly carrying the captured enemy's banner. She had experienced firsthand the power of mounted crossbowmen. Even without the special cranequin crossbow with a spanning mechanism that Lansius had talked about, they were already a powerful addition to their force.

She quickly ranked them a second-best yet more readily available option compared to mounted nomadic archers, who required ten years of practice.

Now, after the South Hill cavalry was nullified, all that remained was cleanup. "Anyone without a hostage, give chase."

Hearing her command, forty riders galloped after the remaining twenty.

Meanwhile, Dietrich approached and reported, "My lady, they're fleeing. We've achieved complete victory."

"How's the situation with Sir Harold?" she inquired, still concerned.

"I saw Sir Harold routing South Hill's column."

Audrey pondered for a moment. "Task our separated hundred to assist. And also, Dietrich, good job blocking their path."

"At your service, my lady."

"Armed men approaching!" one of her lookouts suddenly cried out.

She gave a quick look and replied confidently, "It's Sigmund."

"Watch your aim," Dietrich instructed, squinting to discern whether it was truly Sigmund. The distance was too great for him to see.

After some time, Sigmund appeared, leading his seventy skirmishers and a few horse-drawn carts. The two groups, brothers-in-arms, greeted each other.

"Reporting, my lady," Sigmund announced as his force rejoined with the baroness's column.

"Good work holding them for so long. And who's the little girl?" Audrey asked from atop her charger.

Sigmund brought forward a girl from behind him and presented her to the lady. "She's a peasant's daughter whom I saved. Today, before the battle, she bravely informed me of South Hill's approach."

"Clever girl," Audrey commended.

"G-gratitude, my lady," the girl stammered, still confused about how Sigmund, a self-proclaimed bandit, could befriend a noble.

"Can you read and write letters?"

"A little, my lady."

"A little will go a long way," Audrey mused, smiling. "I can use more attendants. Make your way to my tent and say Lady Audrey, the Baroness of Korimor, invited you. Or you can continue to follow Sigmund."

The little girl's eyes sparkled at the offer. "Y-yes, my lady. I'll do as you say."

The naive answer piqued something within her, and Audrey teased, "You should ask your family first. Don't just abandon them."

"Y-yes, my lady. My apologies, I shall run and inform them . . . But is it safe enough right now?" she asked nervously.

Watching her childish reaction, Sigmund, Dietrich, and the rest of their men chuckled. With their victories, the battle for South Hill was nearing its end.

CHAPTER 25

THE HANDS OF WRAITH

With South Hill's vanguard routed and their cavalry captured, the outcome of battle for South Hill was unmistakably clear. The remaining men under Lord Gunther's command, having fought in vain against much larger forces, finally offered a truce to avoid annihilation.

Servius, Nicopolan column's commanding officer, accepted their truce, recognizing that further bloodshed would be pointless. Their victory was now certain, with South Hill's men no longer desiring battle.

The remaining South Hill troops formed a defensive circle around their lord's armored carriage, agreeing to lay down their spears and crossbows, but keeping their swords. They stood guard, pale and weary, awaiting the arrival of the true victor of this battle. Any flicker of hope had vanished from their eyes.

Approaching from the east, Lord Lansius walked toward the Nicopolan column. His arrival was grand, flanked by his entourage and thousands of men whose armor and weapons shimmered in the sunlight.

Eager anticipation filled the air as everyone awaited the battle's conclusion.

Carla, his squire, guided Lansius's destrier. He could have easily ridden but chose to cover the distance on foot, savoring the moment. The euphoric looks on his men's faces were as unforgettable to him as his was in their eyes. Although it was against his nature to be in the spotlight, he knew it could sometimes be good for their morale.

Such a victory would forge long-lasting memories for them and might pave the way for lasting loyalty to House Lansius. More men reached him, joining from the other side of the village. In a friendly manner, Lansius called out to them "Walk with me" or "Come with me."

His inviting gestures and words prompted everyone to follow him earnestly.

Before long, he was marshaling close to a thousand men before he arrived at the position of the Nicopolan column, where Servius was waiting.

"My lord, South Hill has offered a truce," Servius reported, pride evident in his face and that of his staff.

"Good work, Servius," Lansius responded and offered his hand. The two clasped hands, much to their men's delight. The Nicopolans, craving honor and recognition, were ecstatic.

"What are the terms?" Lansius asked.

"Their surrender, my lord, in return for a private meeting with you," Servius explained.

Lansius nodded thoughtfully. "Let's meet the Lord of South Hill and hope their request is reasonable. Otherwise, more blood will be spilled."

South Hill Side

The South Hill captain and his men watched Lord Lansius's approach as if witnessing a raging storm. The famed Black Lord walked amidst a sea of warriors. Only then did the South Hill men realize the scale of the army they had been battling against.

As they watched the columns of men, everyone from South Hill felt not only defeated but also humbled and outclassed. They couldn't help but view the conqueror with awe. And they weren't alone in this sentiment. Peeking from his carriage, Lord Gunther mumbled, "So this is the man who has humbled half of Lowlandia . . ."

His captain could only nod bitterly, pained by his failure and their defeat.

The Lord gazed at him and sighed. "All our men are battle-hardened, and he dismantled them as if they were nothing."

The Black Lord had completely crushed South Hill's forces, leaving no opportunity to rally. Even the usually stubborn Lord Gunther became compliant. Surrounded and thoroughly defeated, he had no choice but to offer terms.

The Lord of Korelia and his entourage now walked toward Lord Gunther's carriage. His escorts cleared any obstacles and shielded him from visible threats. Behind him, the bannerman proudly carried the blue and bronze standard, its few golden strands sparkling against the sun.

Everyone present watched the banner with a mix of raw emotions. It was the flag that had humbled every major lord in Lowlandia. Many whispered that with the fall of South Hill, it was unequivocally the banner of a united Lowlandia.

The creak of a wooden door was heard as Lord Gunther, assisted by his squire and captain, descended from his carriage. He had spotted Lord Lansius, but Lansius greeted him first.

"My Lord of South Hill, it's a genuine pleasure to meet you."

The words might have seemed insulting, but the tone was free of malice, prompting Lord Gunther to reply courteously. "My lord, I am merely the caretaker of this region. I apologize if I have wronged you—"

"Ah, so you acknowledge your role in the attack on Korelia?" Lord Lansius interjected, speaking freely since they were out of earshot of their men, with only their closest aides nearby.

The directness was unexpected, but Lord Gunther was prepared. "Indeed. At that time, I was merely following the Coalition's urging."

"Will you shoulder the blame?" he asked sharply, his tone filled with impatience and perhaps also a disdain for long political sophistry.

"I have seen the error of my ways, but isn't it excessive to come here unannounced, using trickery, and trapping my troops like this?" the older lord inquired.

"It is excessive, but time is a luxury I don't have," Lord Lansius responded.

"Time . . . ?"

"That issue is for later." He deftly sidestepped the question. "For now, I'm ready to discuss your terms."

Lord Gunther refrained from sighing and motioned to his squire, who offered a lavish silken pouch. Extracting the iron keys, Gunther showed it to Lord Lansius. "This is the key to South Hill Castle. I accept my defeat, but please, show leniency to my House."

"I will ensure a pension for your House. However, due to your past transgressions against the Lord of Three Hills, the fate of your House rests with the Grand Alliance's decision."

Lord Gunther could only offer a weak nod. His face showed strain as he surrendered the key to Lansius.

"Are you injured?" Lord Lansius asked, concern evident in his voice.

"Just an old wound," he responded.

Lord Lansius gestured to his confidant. "Fetch my physician." Then, to Sir Gunther, "I will ensure you receive proper care and treatment. Please return to your carriage; your pain gives me no pleasure."

In the aftermath of the battle, four hundred knights, cavalry, and dragoons, led by Sir Harold, galloped toward South Hill Castle. Armed with a few key hostages, a letter, and the seal of the lord, they hoped to secure the castle's surrender.

Their arrival, like a thunderbolt in clear midday, shocked everyone on the other side. Panic ensued in both the castle and South Hill City. Chaos was only allayed when the cavalry showed no intention of attacking, looting, or sacking the city.

With knights at the forefront, Sir Harold projected an air of order and discipline. Heralds and messengers were dispatched to both the castle and the city to explain their intentions and garner support.

For the castle and the city, witnessing such a large cavalry force and evidence of their lord's capture left them no choice but to request time to deliberate.

Outwardly, they claimed the need to welcome the new lord, while internally, the House controlling South Hill and its supporters grappled with their abrupt loss of power.

Despite their blood ties, the very recipients of Lord Gunther's favor were unwilling to surrender the castle just to save a defeated lord. Ultimately, it was the fear of Lord Lansius, coupled with concern for their captured family members and the sight of the large cavalry force—which hinted at even larger forces behind it—that swayed the House and the castle staff.

Before sundown, they lowered their drawbridge and opened their gates. Following Lord Lansius's instruction, Sir Harold sent Dietrich and his group to take over the castle's defenses. Meanwhile, he and the remaining cavalry camped outside, vigilant against any potential ploys or traps.

They politely declined friendly offers of wine and beer, remaining alert until the arrival of the main army.

As day turned to night and dawn broke anew, Sir Harold awoke with reddened eyes, relieved that nothing concerning had occurred. He promised himself not to tarnish his lord's near-flawless victory.

That morning, Sir Harold began receiving visitors from affluent families, treating them cordially. Most were there to discuss hostages or ransoms, and a few even boldly offered marriage proposals for their daughters, eager to climb the social ladder. He requested that they await his lord's return. The knight's and his staff's non-threatening gestures helped to ease these families' apprehensions.

They didn't have to wait long. Just after midday, the Black Lord arrived at South Hill Castle, accompanied by two thousand of his forces and a thousand camp followers. The officials and castle staff nervously awaited outside to greet their new lord.

"Behold, you are in the presence of the Lord of Korelia, Protector of Korimor, and the leader of the Grand Alliance," a rider heralded.

"My lord," greeted the officials and castle staff as politely as they could.

Unexpectedly, Lord Lansius and the lady chose to dismount and walk with their escorts toward the castle. Whenever informed of important or elderly figures, the lord stopped, exchanged polite greetings, and conversed briefly about the castle or city.

This gesture left a favorable impression on his new subjects. Being conquered by an educated gentleman seemed more appealing than the rule of another brash warlord.

While the powerful family of knights, squires, and their servants accepted defeat and prepared to adapt to their new master, the townsfolk remained fearful.

The shock of their troops' defeat, compounded by the recent failure at Korelia, was still fresh in their minds. Many among the populace had fled since yesterday, fearing that Lord Gunther's capitulation wouldn't suffice to appease the Black Lord's wrath.

However, the Lord of Korelia and the Lady of Korimor chose to conduct a quick procession. The transfer of power was completed smoothly, without any show of force or a parade. It was marked only by a symbolic gesture: the staff silently lowered Sir Gunther's banner, which had adorned South Hill for over ten years, and replaced it with the blue and bronze standard.

Behind closed doors, ransom and negotiation talks proceeded peacefully.

The absence of military maneuvers and harsh decrees allowed the townsfolk a measure of relief. There were no indications of retribution from the Lord of Korelia, despite South Hill's involvement in the Coalition against his fief. No punitive actions seemed imminent against the populace.

Furthermore, the lord's decision to camp his large army away from the city, allowing only the camp followers to establish camps and trade, was reassuring.

Another day passed in South Hill. Despite some persistent skeptics, the feared aftermath did not materialize: There were no customary three days of looting, no gallows erected for executions, and no open courts set up to punish select individuals.

For the Lowlandians, this was as favorable an outcome as they could have hoped for—an almost bloodless transfer of power.

Gradually, the residents of South Hill began to reconsider their views on the Black Lord. Contrary to the dire rumors, he might not be as terrible as they had believed. Some even started to believe that he could be a better lord, or at least that he was a competent warlord who might bring peace to their region.

Lansius

The day was turning to dusk, and the wind carried a certain chill along with an earthy scent. Despite having secured the castle, Lansius chose to stay with his troops.

He had ordered Sir Harold and his knights to occupy the castle while allowing the cavalry and skirmishers to rent inns and celebrate the victory as they wished.

The remaining issue was the Nicopolans. Owing to their large numbers, Lansius couldn't allow them to enter the city, as they might cause problems. This was why he stayed with them, celebrating in his own fashion.

"Servius," Lansius called, seated in his wooden chair on the platform erected for the feast.

"My lord," Servius answered cheerfully, while the thousands of men around them buzzed with anticipation.

"Light the fire and bring out the food. It's time to feast," the lord instructed, and three thousand men cheered in unison.

"At once, my lord," Servius replied, signaling his staff to light a large camp-fire. Before long, the encampment was filled with the glow of lanterns and long torches, taller than a man, designed to last for hours.

Then, the cook's assistant brought out the food they had prepared. Only now did the men see the roast meats and other dishes, their tantalizing scents and aromas having tormented them for hours.

Observing their eager reaction, Lansius commanded with a grand gesture, "Bring everything out, even the duck."

Everyone was astonished. A roast duck, the size of a small horse, was being hauled on a cart by no fewer than six people. Duck meat was a rarity, not so much for its expense, but because it was challenging to raise, with only the brav-est venturing to breed them.

Moreover, due to their size, ducks were hard and time-consuming to cook properly, and most cooks shied away from the task. Fortunately, they had cap-tured a bold squire who, upon ransom negotiation, revealed that his family excelled in this unique skill.

Beside Lansius, a certain baroness also drooled in anticipation.

Lansius stifled a chuckle and, despite understanding that the servants were doing their best to be quick, he couldn't help but rally his men. "Well, what are we waiting for? Cut the meat and share it with everyone."

At the lord's instruction, the Nicopolans surged forward. Higher-ranking individuals attacked the duck, helping the servants in carving the big, juicy meat. After securing the best cut, they hurried toward the high table, presenting the finest cuts to the lord and lady before distributing the rest to their men, who had formed a queue.

"Form a line," their officers shouted to those yet unorganized, arranging them into six orderly lines.

"Everyone will get a share! There's enough for all," Servius reassured those at the back.

Meanwhile, at the high table, Carla tasted the food and approved. Afterward, Lansius ate a small portion and drank from his goblet, signaling everyone else to start eating.

Like a race, those with filled plates began to eat. Audrey went straight for the roast duck, and Lansius couldn't blame her. The meat, with its strong odor, was lean yet tender, slightly chewy or gamey but satisfyingly rich and filling. The skin was crisp, the fat juicy, and the sauce—a blend of vinegar, honey, herbs, and mustard—masked the odor and enriched the flavor.

"Eat well. I'm going to help with the line," Lansius announced to Audrey as he stood up.

"But the duck, it's best eaten hot," his wife said, gazing at him, baffled by his culinary transgression.

Lansius leaned in closer to her ear. "I'll let you in on a secret."

She furrowed her brows in curiosity.

"There's another duck, and it's even fatter."

Audrey's eyes widened, shimmering with affection.

"Make sure to get the best cut. That's an order," Lansius said with a smile, to which Audrey responded with an approving nod.

Escorted by Carla, Lansius made his way to the middle of the long lines. As he walked, his men bowed their heads and greeted him, some cheering or weeping upon seeing him in person.

I just can't get used to this . . . Is this what famous actors went through each day?

Their reaction to his presence was overwhelming.

"My lord," Servius greeted.

Lansius patted the older man's back and then gazed at the hundreds who were lined up. "Rest assured, there's plenty of food today, and everybody will get a piece."

"I hope it's not a small piece, my lord," one man commented, eliciting laughter from the others.

Lansius playfully retorted, "If anyone doesn't get a full plate, I'll invite him to my table."

The men cheered at the lord's promise.

Lansius did this strategically to maintain their support and to ensure order. Since it was risky to allow them to enter the city, he needed to keep them confined here until he could formulate a proper plan. Besides that, he also had an ulterior motive.

They can have slices of duck egg . . .

Apart from ducks, Lansius had also acquired duck eggs as gifts from the duck tamer family. Before his staff could use them to prepare broth for him, he chose to distribute the eggs directly to his men. He had sent five hard-boiled eggs to the infirmary as gifts for those injured in battle, and he planned to distribute the rest here.

"My lord, may I have a word in private?" Servius called out suddenly.

Lansius nodded at the request. The two, followed by his escort, moved to a quieter area.

"I've just received word from the kitchen staff," Servius said, his tone grave. "A portion of the supplies we have is compromised."

"Compromised?" Lansius echoed in surprise.

"It's Sergio," Servius revealed with a bitter expression. "He must've mixed dirt and sand at the bottom of his supplies to make them seem larger than they actually are."

Lansius couldn't even sigh. His mind already raced to find a solution, his heart pounding and hands shaking with rage. He was incensed that even in death, the Tarracan man could still cause disaster.

Servius continued carefully. "I thought my lord should know that if we stop rationing, there's likely only enough grain for about ten days."

"What about the harvest?"

"I'm not a farmer, but they have said that the harvest in South Hill has been delayed each year. They say it will need at least two to three more weeks, perhaps even longer, before it's ready to harvest."

"That's almost a month . . ." Lansius murmured in disbelief.

"My lord, we should continue with rationing until we can find a solution," the former mercenary leader suggested. "The men have had their fill tonight. Tomorrow, we can tighten our belts once again."

"How many know about this?" Lansius asked. Without waiting for an answer, he added, "We need to work quietly. Perhaps I could turn this into an opportunity."

CHAPTER 26

HALF VICTORY

Several weeks before Lord Lansius's battle in South Hill, Sir Michael and the White Lake cavalry had arrived safely in Korelia. The city celebrated their victorious return from the Korimor campaign. As Korelia's leading authority, Sir Justin promptly organized a celebration to honor their allies and commemorate House Lansius's latest victory in Korimor.

After resting for three nights, Sir Michael and his contingent resumed their march back to White Lake, eager to return home before the harvest season.

Their all-cavalry force swiftly covered the distance, arriving in White Lake just in time for the harvest. Sir Michael's triumphant return to the city, laden with spoils that sparked envy among many, quickly became the talk of the town.

The stories of their battles against the Nicopolans captured the admiration of the populace. Even the nobility, who had previously disgraced him, began reconsidering their stance, impressed by the spoils he secured and his exploits in battle. Moreover, the fact that he had fought alongside the Lord of Korelia, a rising power in Lowlandia, indicated that Sir Michael had made a significant name for himself and was likely in favor.

Subsequently, talks began about restoring his reputation or at least amending their relationship. The once-fallen marshal was now viewed as a redeemed figure.

Watching this unfold, the most pleased was Lord Robert. He had gambled on sending Michael to Lansius, hoping for a positive outcome, but he never expected such a turn of fortune.

The viscount's belief in Michael had been vindicated. He had always known that Michael possessed the necessary qualities. Maybe not as a general, but certainly as a competent knight and an able nobleman.

And now, fulfilling his daughter's wish, Lord Robert had allowed Sir Michael to meet her in the castle's garden for a quiet chat.

* * *

"Sir Michael," Lady Astrid called as she saw him at the garden's entrance.

The knight, who was the talk of the city, broke into a smile. "Lady Astrid," he greeted as they approached each other.

For a moment, they both smiled, unable to hide their feelings.

"I've returned," the knight reported warmly.

"I pray that you're not injured. How is your eye?" the lady asked with concern.

Michael adjusted his eye patch as he reassured her, "It's not painful, and it doesn't hinder me anymore."

"Michael," Lady Astrid began, her tone filled with excitement. "I've talked to Father."

"Yes?" the knight responded, full of anticipation.

Astrid blushed and, instead of giving a direct reply, asked carefully, "Do you still want my hand in marriage?"

"The sky is my witness," he quoted a memorable line he learned from the nomads. "I didn't fight battles in faraway Korimor for myself. The glory and prestige are dedicated to you, my lady."

"Michael . . ." Astrid gazed at him affectionately before revealing, "Father has agreed."

Michael's lone eye widened as he raised his voice, "The lord agreed to our betrothal?"

Astrid nodded, her sweet smile gracing her lips.

Michael's wide grin was accompanied by clenched fists as if he were ready to leap for joy. Yet discipline kicked in, and instead of jumping, he knelt and asked for her tender hand.

Astrid happily extended her hand, and Michael vowed, "I will be a good and loving husband. I shall be loyal, protect you, and bring honor to your House."

Astrid, blushing red, turned her face away. "You've already brought honor to my father's House. He's pleased with your triumphant return. Now, no one in the court can look down on you."

Standing up, he said, "The court may need more time to accept me back. Only after they're comfortable can we arrange our marriage. Perhaps a season or two will be necessary."

Astrid let out a small grin. "A wise approach. But unfortunately, the marriage needs to take place as soon as possible."

Michael blinked in surprise. "I have no complaints, but won't it cause issues for your father's standing?"

"There will be no issues. The letter you gave to Father has already solved that problem."

"The letter from the Lord of Korelia?" Michael was surprised. "What did it say?"

"The Lord of Korelia expressed his desire to take you under his wing."

Michael was stunned by the unexpected answer.

Astrid continued. "It's prudent not to waste this opportunity. The Lord of Korelia is the biggest name in Lowlandia right now."

"The Lord of Korelia actually said that?" he muttered, still in disbelief.

"He wrote it in a letter with his seal on it. Sir Michael, it seems you truly did a commendable job," she said with pride in her eyes.

"But, my lady." Michael was hesitant. "If I am to be under the Lord of Korelia's command, then you'll have to accompany me to Korelia or even to Korimor."

"Likely to Korelia," she answered lightly and without hesitation.

"You don't mind leaving White Lake?"

Astrid gazed at the garden around them. "I love this place, but I am no longer a child. We are about to unite our Houses, and I will do my part. Whether it's Korelia, Korimor, or elsewhere, I'll go with you."

Michael was dazzled by his change of fortune and could ask for nothing more.

"Besides," she whispered, turning to him, "Father is also moving to Korelia."

Michael was again surprised and lowered his voice, asking, "The Grand Alliance, has it been approved by everyone in the council?"

"Almost, but with the Lord of Korelia's victory over Korimor, those opposed are losing ground fast." Astrid then added, "Father will risk it and support the Grand Alliance wholeheartedly. Our House won't let anyone steal our initiative."

Riding the wave of Sir Michael's popularity, the castle officially announced his marriage to Lady Astrid, to the delight of the people. The ceremony was scheduled to take place at White Lake Castle, just six days after the knight's triumphant return. Lord Robert had acted swiftly to solidify his standing by welcoming a victor into his House.

One day before the wedding, father and daughter chatted while walking through the castle, now adorned with decorations for the upcoming event.

"Astrid, remember that it won't be easy. After the marriage, you must accompany Michael wherever he's stationed."

"Yes, Father. I understand. I'll dutifully follow my husband, riding beside him and donning armor if need be."

Robert sighed. "I've provided you with the best tutor and assigned the best lady-in-waiting, yet you seem to have grown into a shield maiden."

"But, Father, people everywhere admire Lady Audrey, who followed the Lord of Korelia into battle. Isn't that also a noble way to bring honor to our House?" Astrid teased.

"The Lady of Korimor is an exception. Please, don't emulate her path in life."

"Father, I have my own path," she reassured him. "I'm a proud Lowlandian, the daughter of the Lion. I will not tarnish my father's name."

Robert looked at her proudly. He knew that despite her ladylike demeanor, she could endure hours of riding without a hint of fatigue. Riding had been her favorite hobby before reaching marriageable age led her to a more cloistered life in the castle.

Upon arriving in the lord's spacious study, Astrid took a seat as her father gazed out the small window, overlooking a golden expanse of land covered with ripened crops.

Their entourage closed the thick oaken door, leaving them in privacy. Lord Robert turned to his daughter. "Astrid, I still feel that you would be better suited to marry the Lord of Korelia."

"But, Father, you've said yourself that Lady Audrey is a unique individual. And now she holds a barony. I surely can't compare to her."

Lord Robert found himself recalling memories of Lady Audrey, who was fierce beyond competition and exuded the aura of a powerful yet loyal companion. Yet, he couldn't resist teasing, "Well, a second wife isn't—"

"Dad!" Astrid rose from her seat.

The viscount chuckled, turned to her, and opened his arms wide.

She recognized the gesture and wrapped her arms around her father. They embraced, their bond uniquely strong, as Robert had no other children.

"Promise me you'll stay safe in Korelia."

"Yes, Father."

"And oversee the construction of our House's manor in Korelia," he added instructively. "Ensure it's not lesser than the Lord of Three Hills' manor."

Astrid giggled at her father's competitive spirit.

The White Lake region soon found itself amid a series of jubilant celebrations. In sharp contrast to the previous year's somber mood, the grand wedding, coupled with the victory in Korimor, captured the people's hearts and imaginations. This joy was further amplified by a bountiful harvest that swept over the region, bringing more reasons to rejoice.

The people organized a large harvest festival, dedicating it to Lord Robert's House and the newly married couple. However, the couple themselves were unable to attend the harvest ceremony.

Heeding the Lord of Korelia's offer, the newlyweds, after their brief honeymoon and escorted by fresh cavalry, were already en route to Korelia. There, they were set to embrace their new roles and responsibilities.

Nicopolan Encampment, South Hill

After pacifying the Nicopolans with a great feast, Lansius ordered the castle to send him documents for study. Sir Harold quickly complied, sending the scrolls and parchments along with the record keeper and his aide, all under escort. Lansius wasted no time in perusing the documents.

While his troops enjoyed a relaxed day, going hunting for small game or fishing, Lansius was busy interviewing the record keeper, learning about the South Hill region. He had a plan in mind, but he wasn't sure if it would be applicable.

After all, a solution that was effective in his world might not necessarily be suitable for the problems of this one. Lansius understood that each world, culture, and its people was unique.

Burning the midnight candle, Lansius read through the scrolls and noticed something peculiar. He compared the numbers between harvested yields and military campaigns involving South Hill. The correlation was more than just severe. Every time there was a campaign, the harvested yield dropped significantly.

While a decrease was natural due to lesser manpower, in South Hill's case, it was severe enough that some years saw the yield almost halved compared to the previous year.

"This doesn't make any sense," he muttered to himself.

"What . . . no . . . making se—" Audrey mumbled from the bed before dozing off again.

Lansius looked at her, asleep with a book in her hand. Audrey had tried hard to stay awake, reading just to keep him company as he studied. While she had fallen asleep, he felt blessed to have someone like her by his side.

Returning to his scrolls, Lansius pondered the erratic harvest of the South Hill region. With incomplete data, there were various possibilities for the loss of productivity. Then he recalled the South Hill column he had faced in the western plains of Korelia this summer.

He remembered a field of grass, the wind over the tiny vents on his helmet, the weight of a heavy lance in his arm, and charging through a wall of humans.

Suddenly, he had an epiphany.

They're relying too much on levies.

He sighed as he put together the pieces of an unexpected puzzle. While using a large number of peasants as levied troops was common, South Hill was mustering an abnormally large number. So much so, that it disrupted their agriculture.

Lansius searched furiously through the scrolls for population numbers and found them beside the lantern on the table. He saw the figure and muttered, "Less than seven thousand in the city and all the villages combined."

The last survey was done a decade ago, but it was clear that the population was marginally small. Lansius became worried. South Hill's last campaign for Korelia had been a disaster. Out of the two thousand who had set out, only several hundred returned. The rest were either captured or died on the run.

If even a small campaign could damage their harvest to such a degree, then their recent loss in Korelia could cause a catastrophe.

The South Hill region was unknowingly heading toward an agricultural disaster.

Rising from his chair, Lansius quietly headed out of his field tent. He encountered Carla sitting with the guards. Lansius motioned for them to stay seated and said to Carla, "Get me Servius."

It was the middle of the night, but Carla didn't ask questions. She knew it must be urgent.

Lansius waited in the front section of the command tent where he usually held council. He didn't have to wait long.

"You summoned me, my lord?" Servius asked as he arrived at the entrance, escorted by Carla.

"Please enter," Lansius said and then added, "I apologize for summoning you so late, but this matter is dire."

"I'm here to serve," he replied as he approached.

"We have a problem. The records indicate that South Hill didn't have enough men."

"Men, my lord?" Servius inquired.

"They might have cultivated enough land in the spring, but they don't have enough men to harvest."

Servius gave Lansius a sharp look as he pondered. "How much manpower are we talking about?"

"This summer, the previous lord levied two thousand for a campaign. Only four hundred returned."

"By the Ageless."

Lansius exhaled deeply. "You asked about the amount of manpower we need. I'd say at least a thousand farmers, ideally closer to three thousand."

Servius's face turned grim. "My lord, I have farmers in my ranks, but not three thousand."

Lansius walked closer and whispered, "We need to solve this. Otherwise, we can only expect half of the region's annual harvest. I've checked the numbers, and they don't bode well for us or the populace."

"My lord," Servius pleaded with an anguished expression. "I've already followed your instructions. I've secured the men who uncovered Sergio's ruse. The dirt and sand at the bottom of our supplies have remained untouched. So please, I beg you, don't let another famine befall us."

Lansius could see the horrors of famine reflected on the former legion leader's face. Even veterans of countless conflicts bow down in the face of hunger threatening their men and families. "I haven't abandoned you. We'll overcome this."

The legion leader grasped Lansius's hand and knelt. "Please give me instructions. Command me."

"Servius," Lansius began, pulling him to his feet, "at first light, gather all Nicopolans who have experience in farming. Don't give up yet. We still have a chance."

Lansius watched Servius leave and was about to return to the rear section where he slept when he noticed a figure waiting for him, standing silently in the dim glow of a lantern. "Sorry to have kept you awake," he said apologetically.

"Do you need someone to talk to?" Audrey offered a waterskin. "I might not be able to help solve the issue, but I can keep a secret. Or I can pretend that I hear nothing."

Lansius took the waterskin and drank from it. Afterward, he revealed, "South Hill's harvest is in big trouble."

Audrey pondered for a bit before responding seriously. "It's related to those men you captured and kept in Korelia, isn't it?"

"Yes, almost all of the South Hill column are peasants," Lansius confirmed.

"Still." She hesitated for a bit. "I imagine there will be a lot of issues if we free them before they've finished their work. Besides, the harvest is not even a month away."

"Indeed, there's no time to transport them here."

Audrey sighed. "I feel like we're going from one famine to another."

Lansius could only nod weakly. "This is what warfare does. In their quest for power, the nobles use peasants to fight, and thus the farms get neglected."

"Crippled men make poor farmers," she commented, then stared off into the distance before turning to look at him. "So, what is the Lord of Korelia planning?"

Lansius had nothing and shook his head. "Only some rough ideas. But I'm not sure if any will work or if it will cause a riot."

Audrey closed the distance between them and hugged him tightly. "You know, I wish I could help more."

"You're already helping," he reassured her. "I bet if I married another lady, she would pester me with castle decorations, winter furs, and perhaps even jewelry."

Audrey chuckled and teased, "Is it a bad time to ask for a decoration for my armor?"

Lansius chuckled and lifted her. All his armored exercise and riding had paid off—he could do it with ease. Carrying her in his arms, he went to the sleeping section and laid her on the bed, but refrained from joining her.

"You sure you don't want company?" she asked again.

"I'm perfectly happy seeing you asleep."

"Then, I'll be here when you need me. Just wake me up," Audrey said, closing her eyes.

She must be weary.

Despite her status, Audrey took charge of the cavalry, their training, equipment, and maintenance. With their numbers reaching four hundred, it was no small task.

Lansius returned to his seat and a small table.

Time passed, and despite his thorough study, only one solution continually came to mind. Initially, Lansius had favored a Roman model to aid the harvest, but now the situation called for something more drastic.

The problem was that fully implementing military-agricultural colonies would take years to develop. However, he could extract the essence for a more immediate, crash course solution.

Thus, he wrote in his native Earthen language: *the Han dynasty's tuntian strategy?*

While unsure, Lansius began to lay out a heavily modified yet simplified version because he didn't have multiple years to develop it.

The next morning, Lansius was awakened by an unforeseen development. Unexpected reinforcements had arrived.

CHAPTER 27

SAPERE AUDE

Nicopolan Encampment, South Hill

As dawn broke over the camp, Lansius, still bleary-eyed from a night spent poring over scrolls, was roused by activities outside his tent. He had just taken his first sip of water when Audrey entered.

"Oh, you're awake," Audrey said with a smile, already clad in her stylish black brigandine.

"Did I hear someone mention reinforcements?" Lansius inquired.

"Indeed. We've just received twenty cavalrymen, freshly trained, and fifty men from Korelia," Audrey informed him as he began to settle down for breakfast. "They're escorting two hundred South Hill men, along with several cartloads of bolts, crossbows, and barrels of salted meat."

"More than I ordered and faster than expected," Lansius praised.

"Indeed, the marshal has proven to be reliable. However, this doesn't help our current issue," said Audrey, sitting down beside Lansius and taking a bite of freshly baked bread.

"The situation has changed, but those two hundred men will be useful."

Audrey gazed at him. "Why do you want them anyway?"

"At first, I planned to use them to turn the villagers to our side. Possibly for making ambushes or traps. But as it turns out, our little merchant and bandit circus was quite successful."

"Ah," she exclaimed, understanding. "So, what do you want them to do now?"

"I want them to be my little heralds."

"Heralds?"

Lansius gave a nod and explained, "I have to create a new policy to solve this issue. The problem is, a policy means nothing if people either don't know about it or fail to understand it."

"I see, so you're using them as your speakers," said Audrey.

"Something like that." Lansius glanced at her. "They're locals, and I hope they can bring the peasants into our fold."

The two continued with their breakfast. As they neared the end of their meal, Audrey spoke up. "There's one more thing, or two," she informed.

Lansius gazed at her, waiting.

"The reason the reinforcements arrived so fast is that Sir Justin arranged for them to use nomad guides."

Lansius pondered for a bit. "I still doubt that nomad guides and our nascent market post route could be this fast."

"They don't. They're fast because they used a shortcut."

"A shortcut to South Hill?" Lansius blurted out.

"It turns out there is one. They don't need to go through the Three Hills area to reach here."

"We need to look out for this new route; it would be beneficial."

Audrey chuckled. "Unfortunately, they sort of warned everyone not to use it. The route is treacherous, with little water, and hard to navigate, with only the stars as guidance. Also, it ends in a large forest with only a goat trail."

Lansius thought about the hardship they must have endured to get here. "Must have been hard. They're lucky to have gotten here at all."

"Well, they were almost lost, but fortunately, one of our lieutenants who led a hunting group found them by chance."

"Ah, a reward is in order then."

"The name is Farkas. He's a young lieutenant under Sigmund."

Lansius nodded, making a mental note of the man. With his top retinue holding his fiefs, he would soon need new staff.

Sir Harold and Sigmund arrived at the encampment upon Lansius's summons. Together with them, Lansius led a meeting with the two hundred South Hill men. He wanted to cross-check his findings, but in the process, he uncovered a whole different issue he hadn't anticipated.

"My lord, the problem with the harvest isn't the peasants. We are willing to work. But the previous lord gave a lot of the land to his relatives," one of the farmers told him.

Another man added, "They told us to treat it like the baron's land. We had to work on it first, even before our own."

"How much land are we talking about?" Lansius inquired.

"It's spread unevenly, but combined with the baron's land, it accounts for almost half of all the fields."

Lansius was astounded. The law stated that the peasantry retained 70% of the yield while the baron took 30%. However, in the case of South Hill, they circumvented this rule by adhering to the law in letter but not in spirit, forcing the peasantry to work on land that was not part of the baronial estate—land privately owned by knights, esquires, or rich merchants. He glanced at Sir Harold and commented, "I never imagined this region was so poorly managed."

Sir Harold gave no verbal response but sighed, his jaw hardening.

Emboldened by the reaction, the peasant continued. "My lord, the previous lord's relatives expect us to work their land as if they were little barons. And as if that weren't enough, they also send us on campaigns."

Murmurs of agreement echoed from the others.

"We can confiscate the land," Sir Harold suggested firmly.

"Pardon me, lord and sir," another man interjected. "Confiscating their land wouldn't help. Even before harvest, they've already sold the produce for cash."

This new notion piqued Lansius's interest. "Please explain," he instructed.

"The former lord's relatives are always cash-strapped and often sell their harvest in advance. So, the actual owners of the yield are always the merchants."

"Forward contracting," Lansius muttered. He understood the practice, which, although not inherently bad, could be highly deceptive and predatory, especially against the poor and financially illiterate.

Sigmund, standing beside Sir Harold, asked, "Does this mean we can't confiscate the land?"

"We can confiscate the land," Sir Harold explained, "but this year's harvest is already in the merchants' hands."

Sigmund exhaled sharply, muttering curses under his breath. The skald was clearly in league with the peasant.

Meanwhile, Lansius looked unsure.

Sir Harold leaned toward him. "My lord, we can handle the merchants. A little coercion goes a long way."

"No," Lansius said, shaking his head. "We need something more potent."

Sigmund stood at the ready. "My lord, we await your command."

Lansius pondered the consequences. Given its involvement with merchants, he recalled his observations of trade in this era: Trade was predominantly local, with merchants primarily sourcing goods from nearby farms to sell in the city's market.

Meanwhile, trades between baronies, where major merchants sold goods to the next domain, were infrequent and irregular. These transactions typically occurred unannounced, often as a one-time affair, with no expectation or promise of a return the following year. A merchant might simply choose a different city or route for their next annual trade.

After assessing the risks associated with the merchants, Lansius spoke with a determined tone, "Let's organize a military parade and gather all the city representatives. It's time to introduce a new policy."

* * *

As the guests arrived at his encampment, Lansius intentionally kept himself exclusive, letting only his retainers greet the representatives. As they waited, the guests naturally inquired about their host. For this reason, Lansius had posted Sigmund there to subtly spread hints about his motives, preparing them for the new policy.

Before the atmosphere could grow stale, a military parade performed by a thousand men and a two hundred cavalry soon captured the guests' attention. The archery display from the crossbowmen and the thunderous hooves of the cavalry sent a raw message about the host's military strength. It was a show of force, subtly coercing them not to be on the wrong side.

Lansius wanted to cut through the unnecessary politics and get straight to business. He had little time, and the harvest was fast approaching.

In a display of military prowess, Lord Lansius and his impressive entourage rode against the parade as the columns split in half and saluted their lord and commanders. The lord then veered toward the command tent where the guests were waiting. As he dismounted, a subtle signal from him was all it took for thousands of his men to abruptly halt the parade.

The representatives gulped, fully aware of the Black Lord's absolute control over his military. No herald announced his arrival, as if such formalities were unnecessary.

Truthfully, his presence alone could be felt even with eyes closed. As the lord, clad in his strikingly deep blue brigandine, entered the tent, there was an eerie silence while his retinue and guardsmen briefly tensed, standing ramrod straight.

More than just fear, there was respect in their eyes. The guests observed this with mixed feelings. Initially, they had viewed the meeting as an opportunity to advance their agendas. However, upon witnessing the lord in person, their ambitions gave way to relief, grateful simply to be spared his wrath.

"My lord," they addressed him respectfully.

"Gentlemen, please be seated," Lord Lansius instructed.

The city and merchant representatives, who were also wealthy landowners, took their seats in front of a long mahogany table. At the opposite end, the lord sat, flanked by his knights and squires. Select members of his retinue stood at attention to his left, right, and behind him.

"Today I am enacting a new policy," the lord announced.

The representatives, dressed in fine silken robes, velvet, and fur coats, appeared guarded yet nodded in acknowledgment.

"This new policy isn't designed to harm anyone. There will be some loss of profit, but it won't affect your capital," he reassured them. Then he signaled for the scribe to begin writing.

"From this day forward, I designate South Hill as a Military Agricultural Colony."

The guests looked at him, unsure of what the name change implied.

Lansius continued. "Therefore, I am abolishing the South Hill Barony and all its holdings."

Understanding dawned on everyone. Their eyes bulged, and their throats felt parched. They wanted to ask questions but dared not, choosing instead to wait for a more appropriate moment.

"As such, all lands under the baron's holdings will now be managed by the new military council," the lord explained. "Now, what does this mean?" he asked, echoing the guests' unspoken concerns.

Like an experienced mentor, he clarified, "Aside from the legal changes, not much will radically change. The peasants will continue working their land and the communal land. The harvest from their land will remain theirs, while the harvest from the communal land, previously for the baron, is now held by the military."

The guests remained silent, absorbing the information.

"The biggest change is that all land gifted by the previous lord is now null and void." Lansius looked around the room, meeting the eyes of his audience before continuing with a stern warning, "Anyone challenging this rule will trigger an official investigation. We will scrutinize whether they are liable for violating Imperial law by illegally forcing the peasantry to farm on their privately owned land."

The guests' faces turned pale at the announcement. Yet, one guest, dressed in finely decorated red clothes, stood up.

Lansius motioned for him to speak.

"My lord, pardon my intrusion, but what will happen to those farmlands? Many of them are already under contract to provide us with their harvest yield."

"Make no mistake, the owner of that land is violating the law, and anyone in cohort with them is also punishable. But . . ." Lansius paused, capturing the room's attention. "I am not heartless. This was a decision made by the previous lord, so I am willing to turn a blind eye."

The guests murmured in agreement and visibly uplifted.

The guest in red clothes, still standing, asked again, "Then, my lord, what about those farmlands?"

"Only the affected farmlands—and only those involved," Lansius emphasized, concerned about potential misunderstandings, especially since there were other privately owned lands. Combined, these lands—knights' estates, esquires' lands, and holdings of rich merchants and landlords—could be comparable to a quarter of the entire barony.

Lansius knew if he stepped on too many toes, then his rule would be in jeopardy.

Having gained their nod of understanding, Lansius continued. "Anyone who has no involvement in this can continue as usual. Meanwhile, for those who are involved, you should know that those lands will be taken over by the military. The peasantry will no longer work them. They will be harvested by the army, and the yield will be used as military supplies. As such, all contracts related to those farmlands are considered void."

The guests were shocked and immediately turned livid. The man in red was about to speak, but Lansius raised his palm, stopping him. "Void does not mean worthless!" he asserted strongly, managing to maintain control.

No one challenged him, so Lansius continued. "To show my appreciation for your support of this policy, those who can provide legally binding written contracts to purchase grains from those lands will be reimbursed at their inception value, either in cash, commodities, or through tax exemptions."

Relief washed over many, with a few wiping sweat from their brows, relieved to know that at least they would regain their initial investment and not lose it all.

A guest in green velvet clothing rose up and asked, "My lord, what about verbal contracts?"

"Verbal agreements and accords will be addressed through the judiciary," the lord replied without hesitation.

The guests seemed pleased with this arrangement.

Then Lansius added, coldly, "Any attempt to cheat will result in prosecution, with the perpetrator's assets confiscated and their family reduced to peasantry."

Hearing this, the guests straightened their backs, visibly uncomfortable and fearful.

Lansius leaned back in his chair, and Sir Harold stepped forward, asking, "Any other questions?"

The man in green seized the opportunity. "My lord, your decision seems fair to us. But what about the owners of those lands—the knights and esquires whose yield you will confiscate for this year?"

"They can pay for their crimes, or they can join me in my next campaign. If they perform admirably, then I'll allow them to take their land back. I'm only interested in this year's yield to avoid the risk of famine. Nothing more. I have no interest in confiscating other people's land unjustly."

He nodded and allowed someone else to speak. "My lord, you mentioned that the new military council will manage the farmland and holdings. Does this mean that you really intend to use your men-at-arms for hard labor?"

"Indeed, the situation demands it," Lansius confirmed and looked around. "Gentlemen, I'm trying to avert famine, not gain benefits. The records show that South Hill is heading toward a famine. I'm sure you're all aware that each time the city is involved in a campaign, there's always a steep decline in harvest yield. And this past summer, South Hill faced its biggest loss ever."

The guests nodded nervously. The losses in South Hill during the failed Korelia campaign were nothing short of disastrous. Even in the city, they had lost many friends and relatives.

"But, my lord, what about next year? I doubt you will station these many men here indefinitely as farmers."

Lansius chuckled. "Despite what the rumors say about me, I'm not a seer," he jested, prompting chuckles from his entourage. Returning to the issue at hand, he said to his guests, "Let's not overthink this. Let me evaluate my plan, and when it's appropriate, I'll unveil it. But right now, let's focus on securing a good harvest in this region."

After his meeting with the representatives, Lansius addressed the two hundred freed men and the thousands of Nicopolans.

"Men," he began warmly, noticing smiles on his men's faces. The easy victory and the great feast still had an effect on them.

"We ventured to South Hill to settle my issue with the previous lord. That objective has been fulfilled. However, there's another objective: securing a good harvest for everyone. But as it turns out, we've made a mistake."

The smiles on his men's faces changed as they realized the gravity of his words.

"We expected South Hill to be ready for harvest. And yes, thanks to the hard-working people, the region is well-cultivated. However, due to their past defeat, they lack two thousand able-bodied workers to tend to these fields. I don't want to say this, but this region is unknowingly skirting close to famine."

Murmurs broke out among his men at the mention of famine.

"Gentlemen, don't be afraid," Lansius said, gazing upon the thousands of Nicopolans. "Fortunately, we are aware of this in advance. Though there's little time, we can make enough changes to avoid the issue."

His men listened attentively to his explanation.

"Servius has informed me that we have able farmers among you. Thus, we will form groups consisting of farmers and soldiers to work the fields. Some will work in the communal fields. Others will provide help to villages or families in need."

Seeing his men's confused reactions, Lansius added, "Even if you know nothing but how to hold your spear, this region can use your help. We need able bodies to fix granaries, hunt pests, repair roads, sharpen farming tools, maintain carts, and escort grain transports safely."

His explanation prompted a wave of nodding and murmurs.

"We can do that," one man said, followed by a chorus of agreement from his colleagues.

"The bottom line is, we can't be idle and expect food to be available," Lansius paused, allowing his words to sink in. "We need to assist the people of South Hill. Otherwise, famine and winter will end us all."

The grim warning left everyone uneasy. Silence fell as the lord exited the stage.

Sir Harold then took the stage and commented, "Well, unfortunately, we can't beat famine in a fight. If it were a person, I assure you the Lord of Korelia and I would find a way to beat it senseless."

Some burst into laughter, releasing the tension that had been building in their nerves.

"I thought Famine was scared of the Lord of Korelia," someone shouted.

"No," Sigmund chimed in, standing beside Sir Harold, "Famine is afraid of the Lady of Korimor."

"Ooh, the eyes!" someone exclaimed, and laughter erupted again.

Despite the threat of famine, morale was high. In the eyes of the Nicopolans, their new master had yet to make a mistake.

Sir Harold continued. "The lord has decreed exemptions for those who can smoke fish, also for individuals who can hunt big game. For those, please report to me afterward. If you think you can contribute in other ways to secure provisions, let us know."

After midday, Lansius supervised the formation of the work groups, proactively gathering various input from his retinue. He took all their suggestions into consideration. As expected, food and supplies quickly became an issue.

"There's no other way," Servius advised during their private meeting inside the command tent.

"I share his opinion," Sir Harold voiced. "I will share the castle's provisions and also reach out to the merchants for additional supplies."

Lansius sighed, realizing they had exhausted all their options. "We just enjoyed a feast with roast duck. I don't have the heart to tell them that we must return to rationing."

Audrey stepped forward, offering, "Let me handle that announcement."

Just as Lansius was about to respond, Sigmund interjected. "Um, my lord, my lady, this might sound foolish, but Agatha might have some ideas." He brought the girl forward.

CHAPTER 28

THIRD'S SHADOW

The Lord of Korelia's Command Tent

The girl Sigmund ushered forward was becoming the center of attention. She had her hair in a ponytail and wore a simple brown garb, marking her peasant background.

"Sigmund," Sir Harold called lightly. "This area is off-limits."

"I know," Sigmund replied. "But her ideas are quite convincing."

"Who is she?" Lansius asked, while Audrey approached the girl.

"Her name is Agatha," Audrey revealed, guiding her in front of him.

Lansius glanced around and caught Sir Harold's gaze. "It's the girl Sigmund found in the village," the knight informed him.

"Ah, the one who warned him of the impending attack," Lansius recalled, remembering a story from two days ago.

Audrey patted the girl's shoulder and turned to Lansius, saying, "She's joining us as Carla's assistant. Without Sterling around, she needs help from time to time."

"I see . . ." Lansius nodded.

Audrey noticed the girl staring at Lansius in awe and quipped, "Lass, if a noble hero you seek, look elsewhere."

The remark made Lansius chuckle. "That's uncalled for," he protested in jest.

The rest of the council members chuckled as well.

Agatha was surprised to find that the famed Black Lord and his top retainers had a sense of humor.

"Can you keep a secret?" Lansius suddenly asked Agatha.

She nodded eagerly.

"Alright, I'll tell you one." He then whispered, "I'm actually a nice person."

Audrey and the others stifled their chuckles while the girl, not recognizing the jest, looked confused.

"How old are you?" Lansius asked.

"I'm twelve, my lord."

Lansius frowned as the girl looked much older than twelve. Still, he continued. "So, Sigmund says you have something to say. Can you tell us?"

Agatha furrowed her brow in thought, then remembered. "About food. Families in the village have plenty, and nobody wants to keep old grain for another year."

"Go on," Lansius encouraged.

"If your lord's men help us with the farm work, the villagers will gladly help with food. Just remember to bring something to eat with. We don't have cheese, but we have plenty of grain and vegetables."

Lansius looked at his retainers. "This is an interesting find."

Servius, who had been silent, spoke up. "My lord, let me investigate this."

"Do so quietly," Lansius instructed.

Servius nodded and left the tent.

Meanwhile, Sir Harold, towering over Agatha, knelt down and asked, "Lass, we're talking about feeding many people. I'm sure the villagers can't cook for us all."

"Cooking is hard, yes. You'll need to help with that. But there's plenty of grain."

Lansius became curious. "Is the grain good to cook?"

"It's brown, but it's good for winter soup. You'll need salty bone broth and fat, though."

Lansius nodded, intrigued by this unexpected development.

"Is your father hiding the grain from bad men?" Audrey inquired tenderly.

"No, my lady. Nobody wants it, not even the bad men."

Audrey looked at Lansius. "Must be leftover legumes, peas, and rye."

"In short, horse bread," Sir Harold commented as he stood up. The girl gazed at him in awe, and the tall knight scooped her up, carrying her like a toddler in one arm.

"Given the situation, I doubt the Nicopolans will complain," Sigmund suggested.

Audrey's face looked disturbed, while Agatha giggled. "But they're delicious."

Before long, Servius confirmed the girl's statement. "It's true, my lord. The villagers seem to have plenty of leftover grains that nobody wants. But they are of such poor quality that grinding them would take too much time and labor."

"If we use the city mill, can we produce flour for bread?" Lansius inquired.

"We can, but don't expect all of it to be suitable for bread-making," Servius reported.

Lansius scratched his head. "We need a culinary breakthrough."

Agatha, seated beside Audrey, suddenly spoke up. "That hunter knows how to make good gruel. His was tasty."

"Where is this hunter? Do you remember his name?" Audrey asked.

"Fanther? Fafner? Furkus?"

"Farkas . . . ?" Audrey ventured.

Sigmund's eyes widened, recognizing the name of his lieutenant.

"That's the one! He visited my house, and my father gave him some of our brown grains. He mixed them with his blood sausages to make a tasty gruel."

Without needing instruction, Sir Harold, Sigmund, and Servius headed out.

South Hill, the Lord's Command Tent

A young man clad in camouflage attire, with a crossbow slung across his back, was escorted into the tent by a group of guardsmen led by Sir Harold.

Upon seeing who awaited him inside, the young man panicked and exclaimed, "I'm innocent! I took a little extra, but I was the one who hunted that deer!"

The lord and lady appeared disturbed by this revelation.

Spotting Sigmund entering the tent, Farkas pleaded, "Captain, please."

Sigmund raised an eyebrow and grinned. Turning to the lord, he explained, "This lieutenant is a rather energetic fellow, but I'd trust him with my life in a fight."

Farkas had just sighed in relief when a child suddenly exclaimed, "Yes, that's the one!"

"D-don't say that. I don't even know you," he recoiled, thinking it was an accusation.

"But I know you," the girl insisted.

"By the Ageless, spare me . . ." Farkas groaned, almost comically.

Watching the pair, the lord burst into laughter, even the lady giggled.

Farkas left puzzled, watched as Sir Harold approached and patted him firmly on the shoulder. "Relax. We're not here to punish you."

The young hunter nodded gratefully.

"The girl said you visited her family two days ago and received some grains. Is that true?"

Farkas seemed to remember and exclaimed, "Ahh, you're the farmer's daughter."

The girl grinned. "Yes, you cooked a good meal. And my lord wishes to know more."

The lord clarified, "We need to know what kind of grain you used and how you turned it into a decent meal."

"It's mostly rye, along with bran and peas," Farkas revealed, seemingly unsure why the lord and his staff were inquiring about his meal.

Noticing their serious demeanor, he continued. "They're too coarse, not good enough to be ground into flour. But, if you soak them in water for a quarter day, the hard parts will soften. Then you can boil them over a roaring fire in an iron cauldron, pressing it tightly with an iron pan and weights on top."

The lord and lady nodded in understanding.

"Where did you learn this?" the lord inquired.

"My father taught me," Farkas replied, a hint of nostalgia in his voice. "He also advised mixing in fat or blood sausages for flavor."

The lord turned to the tall knight. "Have you ever heard of such a meal?"

Sir Harold mulled for a moment. "I've seen it, but never really knew or tried it."

"Sir, it's unlikely anyone would dare to offer such a humble meal to a knight. It's mostly a hunter's meal," Farkas explained.

"Why is it a hunter's meal?" the lady asked.

"Well, one can buy such grain cheaply in the market. And hunters usually have plenty of leftover blood sausages, since the butchers rarely pay us all in cash. Also, almost everyone prefers meat."

The lady seemed satisfied with the answer.

The lord finally motioned for Farkas to approach. When he did, the lord handed him ten silver coins.

"Eight for aiding the reinforcements stuck on the goat path, and two for the information about the meal."

Farkas was overjoyed. And it wasn't over yet. The lord handed him a quiver, explaining, "These bolts fly far. Use them for hunting and bring us good meat."

After further deliberation, Lansius's staff agreed to experiment with the available peasants' grain. They formed a group of hunters to show and teach the Nicopolans how to cook the brown grain. To enhance the otherwise unsavory, bland, and bitter gruel, they added blood sausages and salted meat to the rations.

Servius encouraged his men to eat what the locals had to offer and began reducing the grain rations. Fortunately, he faced little rejection, as the portions of salted meat from Korelia kept the men content.

With the food issue partially solved, Lansius and his staff quickly organized the first wave of approximately seven hundred people. They were divided into a dozen groups to be sent to neighboring villages. Each group included locals from the recently freed two hundred South Hill men, ensuring that the policy was well received and didn't cause confusion.

These groups were tasked with assisting in work, particularly on the baron's communal lands. Men of war they were, but they would temporarily adopt the lifestyle of farmers.

As the first wave set off to their assigned locations, Lansius and his staff watched somberly. They placed their hopes for the upcoming harvest squarely on these men's shoulders.

Korelia City

The cold winds had prevailed over the summer sun as Korelia celebrated its harvest season. Despite lackluster harvest results due to the past siege, the people held a modest celebration.

Yet, life in the growing city continued to be exciting, thanks in large part to Sir Anci and Lady Felis, who were seen everywhere in Korelia.

A few weeks ago, Sir Anci, the Champion of the Imperium, had returned from Korimor riding alongside the White Lake cavalry. Since then, he had been staying in Korelia, seemingly enjoying all that the city had to offer. His remaining task was to escort Lady Felicity, who was scheduled to return home.

With Sir Anci's presence, Lady Felis became even more adventurous. She explored everywhere and tried everything she desired. Every place they visited soon became popular.

Recently, she had dedicated her time to the newly opened orphanage. Felis arranged for a field kitchen to introduce the orphans to a variety of foods, hoping that good meals would inspire them to learn cooking and grow their own vegetables.

Lady Felis initially funded the project with her own money, but Calub quickly reimbursed her, feeling it was the right thing to do. The field kitchen's success, and the joy it brought to her heart, encouraged her to extend similar support to the neighboring complex housing veterans.

The veterans and their caretakers warmly welcomed them, grateful for the visit. Lady Felis was a popular figure, and the appearance of Anci, as the current Champion of the Imperium, made their visit even more special.

As the field kitchen prepared the meal, Anci engaged in conversation with the veterans. Initially reserved and sympathetic toward the crippled veterans, he came to deeply respect them for their laughter and positive attitude.

After these events, Lady Felis was on the brink of organizing an archery competition for the city's defenders when a large group of officials entered the city. Among them were two carriages, escorted by armed cavalry and bearing red banners with twelve silver dragon insignia, unmistakably the Imperium's royal envoys.

Lady Felis knew the envoys were here to bring Lord Lansius's official patent of baronage. And they would also serve as her escort home. Her fiancé, Lord Arte, had confided in her the importance of winning their hearts to garner more support for Arvena's cause.

Lady Felicity and Sir Anci quickly collaborated with Calub and Cecile to welcome the royal envoys. As was the custom, they organized a feast on behalf of the Lord of Korelia.

Sir Justin

While others were busy welcoming the royal envoy from the capital, the marshal was expecting a different carriage.

"Boss!" a member of a particularly armed group called out, escorting a carriage and cart.

Just then, the cart's door swung open, and a young girl burst out, running toward Sir Justin. "Father!" she exclaimed excitedly.

"Eleanor!" He embraced her tightly, lifting her up. "Where's your brother and Mommy?"

"Brother chose to stay, and Mother is taking care of him. I'm the only one who cared enough to come for you." The child spoke rapidly. "See, am I not your best child?"

"Indeed, you are my bravest and best," the knight affirmed, holding her close. "But to travel to Korelia alone, accompanied only by thugs and violent criminals . . ." He shook his head in pity.

"But, Daddy, I trust them. They're good company. Tradesman One-Ear has the funniest stories, Maester Red-Face cooks the best meals, and Funny-Baldy is so thorough with his cleaning."

Sir Justin chuckled, looking proudly at his men, who grinned back.

"Sir, she'll make an excellent little boss," One-Ear remarked.

"She's not stingy with money either," the bald one added, prompting laughter from the rest.

"I almost bought you guys a drink. Almost . . ." Sir Justin jested.

The crew groaned, then laughed even harder, knowing Sir Justin was too generous to let good work go unrewarded.

Korelia Castle

The next day, before the banquet honoring the royal envoys, Sir Justin met with them privately. He had previously deliberated with Lady Felis, Sir Anci, Calub, and Cecile.

The envoys, middle-aged men weary from travel, spoke as though they had journeyed continuously from the capital to Korelia. However, Sir Justin, informed by Sir Anci, knew this was just an act. The messengers had actually been in Midlandia for months, stalling as they anticipated a battle.

It was only after Lord Lansius emerged victorious at the Battle of Korelia that they begrudgingly made their way to the city. Their intent now was to exploit the situation, hoping to extort Lord Lansius for his patent of baronage.

Unfortunately for them, upon their arrival, they learned that Lady Audrey had taken over as the Baroness of Korimor. Her claim was legitimate, as she shared blood ties to Omin, the previous Lord of Korimor.

This turn of events lessened the importance of the official patent of baronage. With Audrey as Lansius's wife, he could legally hold Korelia even without the peerage.

Consequently, after brief negotiations, Sir Justin suavely persuaded the envoys to settle for a small sum of gold as a token of appreciation. While some might view it as wasteful, Lord Lansius had confided to him that their House couldn't afford another front to wage.

Instead of provoking enmity, Lord Lansius had encouraged Sir Justin to promote their commodities, particularly the unique shawls of the nomads, refined by the Korelians to suit noble tastes. In a stroke of ingenuity, the marshal invited the envoys into the bathhouse and presented them with these shawls as luxurious bathrobes.

The materials were not only soft to the touch and comfortable to wear, but also remarkably warm despite their lightness. Their lustrous sheen and delicate yet strong texture immediately captivated the envoys.

"Is it imbued with magic?" one joked, admiring the fabric.

Sir Justin laughed. "It's our most unique product, only made in winter and in small quantities. What we sell to the market is of lower quality, but what you're wearing is the purest form. We reserve it only for the most distinguished individuals."

Intrigued, the envoys coaxed Sir Justin for more. After feigning reluctance, for a price, he promised to secure another shawl for each of their lovers back in the capital.

That same week, following a short ceremony, the royal envoy officially confirmed Lord Lansius's status as the Baron of Korelia. A royal patent signed by the High Lords Council served as proof. With this, the legality of Lord Lansius's hold over the city and his noble status were affirmed.

While it was only a legal matter, when the Korelians heard about it, they spontaneously threw a modest but citywide celebration to commemorate their lord's achievement. Even in his absence, the people of Korelia continued to feel Lord Lansius's presence.

Soon, the burgeoning city would witness the arrival and departure of more important figures as it evolved into the de facto capital of Lowlandia. With sections of its city walls completed, operational windmills, watermills, vast agricultural projects, and a thriving market, Korelia had become a magnet for traders and migrants seeking better lives and opportunities.

While this city in faraway Lowlandia was enjoying a peaceful season, outside the province, in Tiberia, a large-scale war was raging. After several pitched battles with inconclusive results, the Imperium forces, led by the High Lords, were losing ground.

The ambitious Lord Gottfried of Brigandia, emboldened by Midlandia's favorable reaction, was exerting his utmost efforts to breach the capital's outer defenses before winter's onset. His northern army was besieging towns and cities, forcing the populace to flee westward.

With the losing battle against the western nomadic incursions in Centuria, the Nicopola famine disaster, turmoil in Elandia, and now a raging rebellion disguised as a civil war in Tiberia, the crisis had fully engulfed the Imperium.

CHAPTER 29

FRUGES HIEMALES

Korelia City

The city buzzed with celebration, honoring Lord Lansius's official confirmation as the baron. It was during this festive atmosphere that Sir Michael and Lady Astrid arrived, accompanied by their new household and entourage. Everyone was pleasantly surprised to learn that the newly married couple had pledged their service to House Lansius. Their arrival provided even more reasons for the Korelians to celebrate.

The merriment and festivities masked the arrival of master masons. These highly skilled and experienced builders hailed from Midlandia and White Lake regions. They had returned with their team to fulfill a contract for building vital infrastructure projects.

While discussing their plan and contract, the conversation often turned to the lord and lady of the city. Last season, several had the opportunity to meet and talk to them in person. Despite the rumors, they found the lord and lady to be down-to-earth and reasonable, even outright likable.

They fondly remembered how the Lord of Korelia emphasized a functional and cost-effective design for a new Great Keep. His goal was not self-glorification or a display of power, but to provide a practical abode for his retinue. He envisioned the Great Keep as defensible, yet equipped with necessary amenities, including heating and plumbing.

Following the lord's wishes, the master masons designed a structure based on proven, robust, and maintenance-friendly concepts. The contract stipulated that ornamental pieces be kept to a bare minimum. This pragmatic approach earned the master masons' respect.

While other nobles favored grand archways, alabaster marble, and fine sculptures, the Lord of Korelia prioritized defensive capability. This aligned with the master masons' passion for constructing robust defensive structures.

For them, building a castle was akin to a defense game, using a mazelike layout to bewilder attackers. Corridors led to false exits with arrow-slit windows on the defenders' side, enabling them to counter with impunity. The gates were deceptive, appearing as main entrances, but were actually wooden gates set against sturdy walls.

Their focus wasn't solely on trapping and countering attackers; they also prioritized the occupants' survival. The design included large warehouses, divided into several chambers, ample water storage, and innovative methods for replenishing fresh water from rain or underground sources.

The master masons fondly recalled their surprise upon completing the blueprint, realizing the Lord of Korelia aimed to construct not just a Great Keep, but a formidable fortress.

Now, they had returned to bring the design to life. They began laboring on the crucial sections of the city wall and the construction of the new Great Keep. Their commitment would bind them to Korelia for a few years, until the final stone was correctly placed.

Korelia Castle

It was a pleasant morning at Korelia Castle, with clear skies above and a calm wind gently stirring the air. In the courtyard, a bustle of activity unfolded. Coaches and lesser carriages lined up in orderly fashion, attended by a diligent array of escorts. Half of them bore the emblem of twelve silver dragons on a red banner, while others flew the banner of Arvena, featuring a riverbank and a white castle.

From inside the castle, Lady Felicity emerged first, dressed in her traveling attire, followed by the knights and then the squires. The crowd engaged in light-hearted chatter as they walked toward the courtyard. The discussion was filled with smiles and chuckles.

During their conversation, the lady paused in front of the coaches and looked back at the castle. "I can't believe it's already been one year," she said, her voice tinged with nostalgia.

The others around her responded with sympathetic smiles.

"I hope this isn't the last time I set foot in Korelia," Felis added, without sounding bitter.

"Lady Felis, you're always welcome here," Sir Justin reassured her. "Next time you visit, the new Great Keep will probably be finished."

"When that time arrives, I hope to see a little Lans or a little Drey running around," the lady said, her eyes sparkling with hope.

Sir Justin chuckled. "I'll be sure to mention that to the lord and lady."

Lady Felis shifted her attention to the newlyweds, Sir Michael and Lady Astrid, who had recently joined Lord Lansius's retinue. "Alas, Lady Astrid, we haven't had the time to know each other."

"It's a most unfortunate situation, my lady."

"Please make sure to let Cecile know if you need anything. The weather in Korelia can be challenging at times. Do remember to keep yourself well-quenched with beverages and use herbal balms for your skin."

With a courteous smile, Astrid bowed her head. "I shall keep your advice at heart, my lady."

Lady Felis then gazed at the knight with the eyepatch, who likewise bowed his head in response. "Sir Michael, I expect great things from you. But remember that you also have duties to your wife."

Sir Michael responded with a respectful nod. "Indeed, my lady. I am wholly committed to taking care of Lady Astrid with utmost diligence. Her well-being shall always be paramount in my mind."

Satisfied with the answer, Lady Felis's eyes moved to Calub and Cecile, offering them a warm, acknowledging smile. "I'm going to miss you both."

"I as well, Lady Felis. Please take care out there, Midlandia isn't safe even for someone like you. Always watch your back, and remember to ask Hannei for help," Calub advised.

"Will do, old friend. But really, I wish I had your help just like in Progentia."

Calub chuckled. "When you truly need me, send a rider. I'll be sure to pack my gear and head your way."

Lady Felis smiled but shook her head. "I can't do that. You must be a responsible husband to Cecile and soon father to your children."

Calub and Cecile exchanged smiles. Their wedding had been set for two months' time, just before the onset of winter, when work would subside. At present, everyone was busy and couldn't afford distractions. Should they marry now, every party involved—the guilds, the master masons, Sir Justin, and the castle staff—would be drawn in, inevitably delaying their work.

Lady Felis then beckoned Cecile and Lady Astrid for a private chat.

While the ladies engaged in their extended farewell, Sir Michael conversed with Calub. Meanwhile, Sir Justin approached Sir Anci. "Are you all set?"

"Should be. My squire and servant are quite the combo," Sir Anci replied with a smug grin. Today he was wearing a bold red brigandine.

The older knight nodded before asking more seriously, "So, what will you do after returning to Midlandia? What is our lord planning?"

Sir Anci grinned. "Lord Arte? Can't say for sure, but I sure wish I could bring Lord Lansius. Even just as a guest, he would be a powerful ally." Then he looked at the older knight, asking, "What about you, sir?"

Sir Justin whistled a tune. "My family estate in Arvena is vast but rocky and stubbornly not fertile. Three generations have tried in vain to grow food on it."

"Ah, I understand that feeling. Still, we could use an advisor."

"Certainly, I owe a lot to your master, Sir Peter. When Lord Lansius returns, my hired company and I shall pay a visit to Lord Arte. I'm no longer his retainer, but for old times' sake, and to settle our blood dispute with Gottfried, I'll do my part."

The two men grinned and clasped hands firmly.

"Gratitude, Sir Justin. I'll let them know about this."

The marshal then pulled something from his pocket. "A favor, if you will, to Lord Arte?"

"Easy. I shall make sure the lord receives it." Sir Anci accepted Sir Justin's sealed letter and tucked it into his purse.

As Lady Felis concluded her farewells to Cecile and made her way to her carriage, the atmosphere subtly changed. Noticing this, Sir Justin took the opportunity to say his final words to Sir Anci. "Please safeguard the young lord and Lady Felis. And if things get dicey with the Midlandians, you can always find refuge here."

Before the sun grew hotter, the coaches, carriages, and cavalry escorts began their journey back to Midlandia. The castle staff, guards, and townsfolk cheered and prayed for their safe journey.

Along with Lady Felis and Sir Anci, the official envoys also returned to Midlandia. They had been briefed about the ongoing crisis in Elandia and how the seneschal had led his troops to pacify the unrest. The envoys planned to wait in Midlandia until the situation was under control. However, they weren't aware of another war breaking out in Tiberia.

South Hill, Lansius

Midday arrived in one of the villages surrounding South Hill City. The sun cast a mild, gentle warmth over the scenery. A cool breeze, playful and light, gently swayed the golden crops that dotted the landscape. The peaceful lull of the view contrasted with what Lansius was feeling.

With an uncertain late harvest, his schedule for the next campaign had been compromised. He couldn't help but feel that he was going against time. Worse, his men, who should have been resting to recover from their march, were working in the field.

There's only so much I could do . . .

The previous day, Lansius had dispatched his first wave of seven hundred men to help with the agriculture production. And today, he was marching with the second wave, sending more men to locations where help was most needed. With the risk so high, he had decided to get involved directly.

Lansius was well aware that there was no method to improve the grain yield. What would be harvested now, had been planted in early spring and matured slowly through summer and early fall. Thus in a sense, the yield had been predetermined.

However, they could still make sure that all cultivated grains would be harvested with minimum loss. In this case, workforce availability was paramount, as well as the correct tools, storage, and transportation.

As support, Lansius had selected three hundred men who had experience with construction to build temporary storage in strategic locations. They were also to maintain the vital road to the city. To assist these groups, he also contracted skilled masons and seasonal laborers from the city.

Guarded by his light cavalry, Lansius wore a humble straw hat and conversed with the village chief, elder, and villagers. He wanted to ensure that his policy was well received.

"For this season only, I free you from working on the communal land," Lansius explained to a crowd of villagers surrounding him.

"My lord, does that mean we don't need to harvest the baron's land?" the village chief asked carefully.

"Yes, just this once, you can focus on your own patch of land. My men will take care of the baron's land. But be sure to assist them if they need help. After all, most aren't as experienced farmers as you are," Lansius answered lightly. He had been giving a similar explanation today multiple times already, and he would need to repeat the line many more times.

It was a tedious job, but his presence kept the morale of his men and new subjects high. While the villagers were at first fearful and guarded, Lansius's demeanor and favorable policy had won them over.

On every occasion, Lansius tried to listen to any problems or suggestions that might arise. He was also checking the brown grain and was relieved to find an amount that could sustain his men until the harvest.

From their interaction, Lansius also took advice about winter crops.

"You know about how to grow winter wheat?" Lansius asked in sheer disbelief.

"We do, my lord. Several generations have successfully planted them, but we lacked the seeds," the village chief explained.

Lansius mulled his response. While the winter crops wouldn't directly aid his campaign this year, their success would ensure South Hill's future food security. This, in turn, would enable him to take more for this upcoming campaign. "Where do you get the seeds for winter wheat?"

"The merchants brought them from Three Hills City, my lord," the elder replied. He added, "The mark of successful farmers in South Hill is when they are able to buy winter wheat seeds and harvest them in late spring."

"And then switch back to summer wheat after harvest."

"Indeed, my lord. You seem very knowledgeable about this," the chief said, clearly pleased.

"I'm aware of the practice, but I won't force you to do this. Cultivating and harvesting twice a year is surely taxing on the body."

Not to mention, it might cause a peasant rebellion.

Lansius didn't say the last bit.

"It is, my lord, but in case of famine, we can endure it, as long as you don't expect all of us to do it every year."

Lansius gazed upon the villagers and declared, "I shall put it in writing that peasants can be taxed only once per year."

The villagers around them cheered, albeit in a subdued way, out of fear of offending their new lord.

"A question though." Lansius returned to the village chief. "Why doesn't Midlandia practice this?"

"My lord, Midlandia is fertile. If they grow winter wheat and harvest twice, then the price of grain will become worthless. Meanwhile, South Hill and most of Lowlandia are not so fertile. When harvest yields so little, sometimes we need to do this just to survive."

Lansius nodded like a student listening to his teacher. Afterward, he said, "I still need to check with the other villages, so I shall take my leave. But tomorrow I shall return to seek your advice."

The village chief, feeling honored, politely bowed deeply. His fellow villagers followed suit.

Lansius gazed at the Nicopolan group who were stationed in this village and instructed, "Treat them well, or the skies and the trees will whisper to me."

The footmen-turned-farmers straightened their backs and replied crisply, "Yes, my lord."

Lansius rode his horse and rejoined Audrey and his entourage, who were resting at a forked dirt road underneath a cluster of old trees. They weren't joining him in the village because they acted as a security lookout and also because Audrey was feeling tired.

Yet, she had insisted on accompanying him, citing that anyone who wished otherwise should be prepared to draw their swords.

"How is she?" Lansius asked Carla as he dismounted.

Carla took the horse's reins and replied, "The lady just needs a bit of rest. She just had a light snack and has—"

"Has recovered without anything to worry about," Audrey declared as she approached.

Lansius smiled. Meanwhile, sensing it would turn into a private affair, their entourage quickly moved elsewhere and faced the other way.

"So, what does it feel like to return to the farms?" Audrey asked.

Lansius smiled warmly and gently guided her toward a nearby tree, ensuring its broad canopy provided a cool shade over their heads. "Well, it reminds me of Bellandia."

Audrey took a deep breath. "You know, sometimes I feel guilty for bringing you into this. Perhaps it would be better if I let you be in Bellandia."

Lansius drew a deep breath and shook his head. "No," he declared firmly. "I wouldn't trade you for anything."

Audrey wasn't expecting such an answer, and her cheeks were slightly flushed. Yet she teased, "Not even for Felicity?"

"No, no, no. I prefer to keep my head attached to my neck."

Audrey giggled. "I doubt Lord Arte will dare to do anything to you. Now that you're a big power in Lowlandia."

Lansius shrugged and then returned to his main concern. "My dear baroness, I have my sword ready. Shall we duel so I can send you to rest?"

Audrey gave a mischievous grin. "Even in fever, I could still beat you."

Lansius sighed, leaned closer, and then went to check her forehead. "Doesn't feel like a fever . . ."

"Yes, so let's ride again and finish this inspection tour," she urged.

"You sure nothing is wrong?"

Audrey left him and went to mount her horse.

Carla brought Lansius's horse and said, "I'll make sure to watch her closely."

"Gratitude. I'm counting on you."

As they were about to ride off, a group of horsemen approached, their banner revealing them to be led by Sir Harold.

Lansius and Audrey paused as the knight rode up to them, greeting, "My lord, my lady, we've reached several breakthroughs."

"Do we have the blacksmiths' support?" Lansius asked.

"Yes, my lord. We can expect good prices for the farming tools."

"Excellent," Lansius responded. "We're going to need those tools as loans for the farmers. Were there many difficulties?"

"Not as many as we expected," replied the tall knight. "Sigmund believes everyone is keen on building good relations and has acted accordingly."

Lansius nodded thoughtfully. Audrey then asked, "So, aside from farming tools, what are they willing to offer us cheaply?"

"We can expect shipments of blood sausages, pickles, turnips, carrots, and cheese," Sir Harold reported.

"That will certainly boost morale," she commented, gazing back at Lansius, who then asked, "What about my other request?"

"It's being prepared as we speak," the knight assured. "But my lord, is it really necessary?"

Lansius mulled for a moment before saying, "Food security has more aspects than just production and storage. There are other aspects we need to fix. Otherwise, South Hill could become a thorn in our side."

This piqued Audrey's curiosity. "What aspects are you talking about, and what's being prepared?"

"A banquet." Lansius then added with a lower voice, "A gray banquet."

CHAPTER 30

LONG SHOT

As the sun leaned toward the western horizon, Lansius, Audrey, and their entourage rode toward South Hill City. Instead of heading to the castle, Lansius stopped at the gates, pulled his hood down to conceal his face, and then proceeded to walk to the market. Audrey and half of their entourage followed, similarly disguised.

With plans for the farming villages taking shape, Lansius now focused on another aspect of rulership: establishing order.

This would be his first time doing so. In Korimor, the Nicopolans had forced them and the Korimor people together, negating the need for such actions. However, the situation in South Hill was different. Though their army had been defeated, the castle, the city, and its inhabitants remained intact.

The situation presented a certain danger and questions of loyalty. Despite having troops stationed in the city, Lansius was determined to ensure South Hill remained under his control, and he had a plan.

Lansius found a suitable place, a modest inn, and he instructed Carla to handle the arrangements. She paid for three people, after which they ascended to the upper floor, leaving the guards outside.

Reaching the second floor, Lansius noted the communal sleeping space was vacant. He hurried to a window overlooking the market.

"Why are we here?" Audrey inquired, peeking through the window.

Absorbed in his thoughts, Lansius replied offhand, "Because it has a view of the market."

Audrey's dissatisfied expression prompted Lansius to add, "I want to . . . wield my authority."

"Wield what . . . ?" she began, furrowing her brow, but raised her hand to stop him. "Never mind, it's probably complicated. But aren't we supposed to attend a banquet?"

"This is more important than the banquet. Besides, we're not the stars of that event," Lansius said, smiling.

"Interesting . . ." Audrey mulled.

At that moment, Carla approached. "My lord, my lady, your drinks?" she offered, extending a wineskin filled with ale and a waterskin.

Audrey chose the ale, while Lansius continued to watch the market. Spotting a familiar figure, he asked, "Isn't that the hunter from yesterday?"

"Yes, that's Lieutenant Farkas," Audrey confirmed, offering Lansius the wineskin.

"I envy your eyesight," Lansius remarked, accepting the drink. He then instructed Carla, "Fetch Farkas discreetly. And bring Sigmund, but ensure he keeps a low profile."

South Hill Market

The sun had sunk low in the west, but the market was still abuzz with activity. Peddlers occasionally shouted, selling their wares, sellers invited passersby into their shops, and various food stalls offered snacks or a full meal experience.

Captain Sigmund, accompanied by two guards, attracted everyone's attention. Their movement indicated it was a formal occasion, not a mere shopping errand.

The three ascended to the elevated platform usually used for morning auctions.

"Hear ye, hear ye," Sigmund began, addressing the crowd gathered in front of the platform. "I hold a letter from the new City Council."

He displayed a parchment with a wax seal, drawing the crowds closer.

"The City Council decrees: Whoever brings this basket to the guardsman at the gate and takes the receipt will be rewarded with a basket of coins."

Hearing this, the crowds laughed and shook their heads in disbelief. Their laughter grew as many made jokes about it. It was a simple task, yet the reward was so substantial that no one took it seriously. Everyone thought it was clearly a joke, a mistake, or worse, something sinister.

Many tried to persuade their friends to accept the task, but ultimately, no one dared to take the basket from Sigmund's hand.

Sigmund waited patiently. Some inquired about the basket's contents and weight, and he revealed it was filled with simple blood sausages. This further puzzled the crowds and fueled their laughter.

Suddenly, a girl, slightly older than Agatha and wearing miserable, dirty clothing, ascended the platform. She appeared nervous and seemed to anticipate being ousted at any moment. However, Sigmund motioned for her to approach.

The girl cautiously walked closer, and Sigmund asked, "Do you understand the assignment, or should I repeat it?"

"Yes, master. Deliver this basket to the guardsmen at the gate and take the receipt from him."

"And then return here with the receipt. Good." Sigmund nodded and handed her the basket. Meanwhile, Sigmund's guard nailed the letter to a wooden pole, marking that the job was taken.

The crowd watched in anticipation, thinking they were in for another jest. As the girl descended with the basket in hand, the crowd followed enthusiastically.

She strolled nervously to the gate, the crowd around her eager to see what this was all about.

Before long, she reached the gate and handed the basket to the guardsman. Farkas, who was there, counted the sausages and gave her the receipt.

The crowd followed her until she returned to the platform. Many chuckled, ready for the finale of this absurd joke. Some had guessed what would happen, and bets had been made.

With a trembling hand, the girl handed the receipt back to Sigmund, who gazed upon it and confirmed it. He then said sympathetically, "Place the basket on the floor. It's about to get heavy."

The girl did so, and Sigmund motioned to one of the guards, who opened his thick canvas rucksack and poured copper coins into the basket.

The shimmer of polished copper under the waning sun, the sound of coins trickling down, and the way they poured like water into the basket, left everyone shocked. Mouths agape, jaws dropped. The laughter ceased.

"Enough," Sigmund commanded, and the guard stopped as the wicker basket was filled with coins.

"A basket of coins. The reward is now complete," he announced to the stunned crowd. Almost everyone in the market needed time to process what had just happened. The amount of copper coins they saw was probably worth several months of their salary.

The skald looked at the girl, still amazed at her fortune, and urged her, "Take the reward."

"May I go now?" she asked nervously.

"Certainly. But with so many coins, do you need someone to protect you?"

She shook her head. "No, I have friends, and I'm going to share it with them."

"An excellent idea. You may call them now if you wish."

The girl smiled, tears in her eyes. She turned and called for a dozen of her friends, who eagerly ran toward her. They were similarly aged children in ragged clothing and dirty appearances, the lowest of society, living in the slum and working as small laborers, beggars, or pickpockets.

In an unexpected twist, Lansius's mysterious request had likely guaranteed their survival for the winter.

Lansius watched the entire situation unfold from a prime spot, comfortably seated, as Carla had borrowed two chairs from the innkeeper.

"Well, that's unexpected," he remarked.

Audrey expressed her surprise. "You didn't foresee someone like that girl winning?"

"How could I have anticipated a thing like that?" Lansius chuckled. "Still, it's a fortunate coincidence."

Noticing Audrey's puzzled expression, he elaborated, "I mean, they needed the coins more than mere peddlers."

"What are you trying to achieve by giving a basket of coins? It's a large amount."

"What I have in mind is worth more than even a basket of gold coins," Lansius stated confidently, piquing Audrey's curiosity.

The sound of footsteps from below caught their attention. Carla appeared. "A message from Sir Harold. Your presence is expected at the castle."

"It's time to leave," Lansius declared.

Audrey stood up, and Lansius noticed her wincing. "Do you need to lie down?"

"No, no need. I'm just a bit hungry, that's all," she replied lightly and went on her way, leaving Lansius scratching his head.

South Hill Castle

The lord and lady entered the Great Hall, where a banquet was being held.

"Behold, you are in the presence of the Lord of Korelia, Lord of South Hill, Protector of Korimor, and the leader of the Grand Alliance," his herald announced proudly.

In contrast to his grand titles, Lansius wore a milky-white tunic that had little to show.

Ever perceptive, Lansius noticed the subtle looks, ire, and smirks. Yet he said nothing. With Audrey by his side, he walked toward the high table as their new subjects slightly lowered their heads.

Before taking a seat, Lansius turned around to face them. "Gentlemen and ladies. My gratitude for your presence. Please accept my apologies for my attire. In my defense, the inspection of the farmland took more time than expected."

The nobles seemed pleased, offering subdued chuckles.

"South Hill is a fine place, long mismanaged, but I am hopeful we can rectify this. Through my policy, which many of you have supported, I hope we can start with a clean slate." Lansius took a goblet from Carla and raised it high.

Sir Harold led the nobles in raising their goblets. "To a new start," the knight announced, and they echoed in unison.

Lansius took a drink, followed by the others. Then, the lord and lady took their seats, and the banquet continued with an assortment of snacks.

"A banquet while we are on the verge of famine," Audrey remarked, her voice nearly lost in the music.

"Occupying a land involves more than just garrisoning it with troops," Lansius explained. Seated apart from the rest, they conversed without being overheard.

Audrey listened intently. "I see, so we're keeping them happy. But what about the plan you, Servius, and Sir Harold have concocted?"

Lansius smiled. "It's the same objective: ensuring our food security."

Her gaze sharpened. "But they're not farmers."

"Audrey, food security lies not only in the fields but also at the tables of the rich."

She looked surprised at the notion before becoming thoughtful, trying to understand its meaning.

Lansius continued. "When people discuss the food situation, they usually think of production or storage. However, there is one other equally important aspect, and that is consumption."

"But these are landowners," she argued. "Wealthy as they are, they only number a fraction compared to the thousands of people living in this region."

"You are correct. But you see, there are only two actors in consumption: the gentry and the commoners. Naturally, if we want to save on food, it would make more sense to address the commoners' consumption."

Audrey nodded, agreeing with the notion.

Lansius then grinned unexpectedly. "Audrey," he called her, feigning disappointment.

"What?" she frowned.

"That's how the noblemen think. To address the commoners' consumption: Do you want to ration the poor while the rich feast at their leisure?"

Surprised, she blinked several times. "I didn't mean that."

Lansius chuckled. "My dear squire turned baroness, you're starting to think like a noble."

She pouted. "I'll reflect on that. But then, if we can't fix the commoners' consumption, what should we do?"

"It's quite a hard issue. We could order the populace to eat less, but we could risk a rebellion. Meanwhile, it's also a useless move."

"Useless, how?"

Lansius chuckled. "The commoners, they're just like us several years ago, but worse. Commoners in Lowlandia mostly only eat just enough to get by. Compared to Arvena or Midlandia, they have it worse."

"True, our Lowlandian-born troops are easily contented. A bowl of hot gruel can make them happy," Audrey recalled from her experience.

"Exactly. So, we can't ask the South Hill commoners to eat less. It would be like ordering them to starve."

"I understand now." She exhaled sharply. "Earlier, you mentioned food security also lies at the table of the rich?"

"Indeed. We need to focus on these wealthy people. Look at this banquet. They expect nothing less than a feast. I told Sir Harold to ask the castle staff to prepare an ordinary banquet, as we're not celebrating anything special, yet here we are."

Audrey observed the Great Hall, filled with an array of food including two roast ducks, fruits, and ales. "It is rather excessive."

"They're accustomed to abundance. Ironically, the fall of House Gunther made them more powerful. After all, land and food production go hand in hand with wealth and power."

"But they feared you. A decree might be enough."

Lansius put a slice of honeyed milk bread pudding on her plate and explained, "A decree would only alienate them. We've already asked them to support the new policy, pitting them against Sir Gunther's associates."

"True, we've already asked that of them. Demanding more might provoke trouble," Audrey said as she stared at the cakelike pudding. "Also, I believe you don't intend to garrison South Hill with such a large force indefinitely."

"Indeed. That's why we need to address the elephant in the room," Lansius said, recalling a crude drawing of the big Caladanian creature from a book as he took a bite of egg custard.

Audrey put her plate aside. "What is the reason behind the basket of coins?"

"That one will take time to fully mature." Lansius pondered, finding it difficult to explain. "It's to coax the populace to our side, and there's also a different benefit you'll learn about later."

"So, naturally, it was more than just giving away a basket of copper coins." She nodded thoughtfully.

Sir Harold, dressed in an exquisite gambeson tailored to fit his height and stature, approached the high table. "I apologize for the interruption, but my lord, Servius is ready."

"Servius?" Audrey asked.

"He's the star of this show." Lansius chuckled and then added, "Now, it's time to go on the offensive."

With Sir Harold by his side, Lansius stood in front of his table, capturing the attention of everyone in the Great Hall.

The musicians stopped their gittern and lute. Lansius then addressed the chamber. "Gentlemen and Ladies, I'm sure you have met my acting captain and host of this banquet, Servius." He gestured toward the man.

Servius, dressed sharply in striking yellow and black, bowed to the audience.

The nobles nodded, acknowledging Servius.

Lansius continued. "You may have discussed various topics with Servius: politics, mercenaries, even perhaps food production. He knows it all. As the commander of a condottieri legion, I'm sure you all feel safe in his presence."

Many nodded their heads in agreement.

"Now that we've established his credibility, we have an important story to share," Lansius said, motioning for Servius to take the lead.

"I apologize, as what I'm about to reveal may be unsettling," Servius began. "It happened this summer in Nicopola. Just like the previous year, there were rumors of famine. However, such occurrences had happened so often that frankly, nobody gave a damn. After all, it was all too common for the poor and peasants to die. 'Such is the law of this world,' they say."

The guests nodded, each sharing a similar sentiment.

"As for the better members of society, well . . . It was only expected for us to have enough to weather the storm. Being a legion commander, I had more than just land and money. I also had connections and armed men at my disposal. Securing food for myself was all too easy."

The landowners looked captivated by his story. As Lansius had expected, Servius, who had wealth, power, and commanded men, served as a relatable figure for these people, almost a role model, embodying what they aspired to be.

"That summer, I expected food prices to rise, but I wasn't worried. If prices doubled, I would simply pay more. If they tripled, I would use my men to negotiate a better price. But I was wrong," Servius said, his tone turning grim.

The guests could sense something was about to be revealed, and their expressions hinted at fear and discomfort.

"Prices rose tenfold for a week, and then there was none to be found. The markets closed; the stalls . . . empty."

Small gasps emerged from the female guests.

Servius paid no heed. "When it became so dire, I sent armed men to 'borrow' grains. But unlike usual, even the timid merchants begged fervently, fought tenaciously, and wept profusely, declaring it was all they had left for their families. Only then did I realize that my city was doomed."

As Servius's tale unfolded, a heavy silence fell over the Great Hall. The guests, who had indulged to the point of excess as was customary, now felt a wave of nausea washing over them, their faces painted with concern. While Lowlandia was accustomed to lawlessness and armed conflicts, it had never faced total societal collapse.

Their relatively small population and reliance on herding had shielded them from the worst outcomes. But now, Servius's story brought the horrors of famine to their minds, starkly contrasting with the abundant leftovers from the feast still on their table.

Lansius observed calmly, eyeing the room for even the subtlest shifts. He needed to ascertain whether his subjects bought the story. If not, he would have no choice but to resort to more radical measures to curb their excessive consumption. Such measures, he knew, could eventually provoke attacks against his lieutenants and captains.

A knife in the back, or poison in their drinks—such were the risks. And when that happened, even Lansius feared what he would do to them. Thus, for everyone involved, this evening would be a turning point.

CHAPTER 31

GENTLE GIANT

South Hill, Great Hall

The banquet halted as Servius recounted the fall of the Nicopolans. From their high table, Lansius and Audrey noted how intently the entire chamber listened, with even the castle staff and servants straining to hear.

"There was no more food in town. The baker had closed, and everyone kept a watchful eye for chimneys billowing smoke," Servius continued. "For the first time in my life, I had no choice but to gather what I had and venture out in search of food. I was fortunate to have my men with me. Like nomads, we raided villages and manors for food. Without my men, my family and I would likely have ended up dead."

The guests were visibly uneasy, gripped by their insecurities. Lansius understood that, despite the guests' earlier merriment, they felt vulnerable. After all, he had just toppled their previous lord, who had reigned for over a decade. And it had all happened so suddenly, without even a warning.

"Many stragglers followed us, starving and desperate. Initially, my men chased them off, but eventually, even that became too much effort. They were too numerous. Like vultures, they scavenged the places we had raided, searching for leftover crumbs. Yet, even for us, there was hardly anything to eat." Servius paused, his sharp yet somber gaze sweeping over the guests, who sat at long tables still laden with leftover food.

"Some resorted to eating insects, rats, lizards, and even young tree bark. When those ran out, they boiled leather from pouches and shoes collected from the dead. Some hallucinated and ate wild grass," he recounted, his gaze piercing the audience. "Many died en masse. I witnessed people killing each other over worn boots found in gutters, eaten as if they were a duck's liver."

The guests were deeply unsettled. Servius hesitated for a moment before continuing. "Then, I found help."

Almost everyone in the chamber breathed a sigh of relief.

"We encountered a large group who persuaded us to travel east through the mountains into Lowlandia. They had a large cache of food from raiding bigger manors and estates."

The guests exchanged uneasy glances. It dawned on them that they, as owners of similar manors and estates, could easily have been the victims of such raids.

Servius continued, unfazed by the guests' reactions. "I thought my men and our families were saved, but it turned out we were deceived. They wanted men to fight their war, thinking to become lords and nobles." He sighed. "A war at the height of famine? To even attempt this foolishness was just unthinkable. However, we followed because the group, against all odds, was able to provide food. Unbeknownst to us, they fed us with a mixture of horse meat and human flesh."

The chamber was filled with horrified expressions and gasps, some guests turning pale. Some looked to Lord Lansius, imploring him to intervene.

One man spoke up. "My Lord, please, this is too much."

Lansius didn't budge. "You should know that all three thousand Nicopolans under my command have tasted human flesh. If I had lost the battle in Korimor, I might have been eaten," he said with a scornful laugh, maintaining the pressure. "Everyone here would do well to listen, so the tragedy that befell these Nicopolans doesn't occur in South Hill."

With the lord's support, Servius took center stage again. "Even before crossing into Lowlandia, the situation had become dire. We saw more and more corpses with missing limbs on the road. Fleeing groups from other towns said they witnessed how the weak and the unfortunate were butchered. But the poor had nothing left but skins and bones, and so these cannibals began to target the wealthy and nobles as if they were livestock."

The grim tale managed to instill fear, especially among the wealthy.

"Servius, enough. They've learned the lesson," Lansius finally declared, and the man in yellow and black turned and bowed.

A guest quickly asked, "My lord, why are you telling us this? Is this meant as a warning?"

"A warning . . . ? Not quite," Lansius remarked. "Did you know that the Nicopolans came to Lowlandia and laid waste to Umberland?"

The guests started to murmur among themselves, having heard nothing of this predicament.

"Servius, tell them how many of you attacked Umberland," Lansius instructed.

Servius took a deep breath and replied, "Eight thousand crossed into Umberland and raided the communities. We found food, but not enough, so we ventured farther to Korimor."

The hall was in disbelief; such a large number was hard to fathom.

"In Korimor, I encountered Lord Lansius, and our two armies battled. Fortunately, Lord Lansius defeated the vile group and freed my men. It was a great victory, one I still cherish. However, Umberland, the gateway to Nicopola, remains open. The lord and lady have defeated one group, but more are on their way. And on this side of Lowlandia, there are only Three Hills and South Hill."

The revelation left the guests, especially the wives, even more disturbed.

A man in his late fifties, plump and well-dressed, retorted, "My lord, forgive me, but we in South Hill have never experienced such extreme famine. Perhaps—"

"Yes, Lowlandia is more robust because we have a large number of herders. However, do you think it's feasible to survive by only eating meat alone?"

His simple question left the guests troubled.

Lansius pushed his point further. "Are there enough lambs, ducks, and, the Ageless forbid, horses for us to eat and survive winter and spring?"

Most guests could only stare down, some with defeated looks.

"Gentlemen and ladies of South Hill, some of you will think of my captain's story as no more than a veiled threat. A way to scare you and to deceive you. But let it be known that I'm merely trying to save this region, its people, and all of your families included."

The shift in tone prompted the guests to look upon Lansius with renewed spirit.

"I'm sure there have been rumors about me. So let me make it clear: I don't take what isn't mine by law. I don't want to impose complicated rules. And I certainly have no right to order you to eat less. By the Ageless, I believe that everyone is entitled to freely buy what they want and to eat what they want, as long as it's not detrimental to society."

The guests' expressions lightened. One of them asked, "Then, my lord, what do you want us to do?"

Lansius smiled. "All I'm suggesting is: Maybe we could feast with less. Perhaps, we don't need to eat this many loaves of bread or this many plates of lamb chops. Maybe some of this fruit would even taste better if dried or preserved in honey to be eaten during winter? And surely cheese is finer when aged."

Nods of agreement followed. The idea wasn't hard or taxing to implement and in some cases had some benefit.

"The next harvest is uncertain, and even if it appears abundant, it is wise to conserve. Ensure you stock up and try hard not to waste food. I'm sure you're aware that increasing food production is challenging. However, we can save a little on food. Even a little savings will be useful and might save this region from famine. If we achieve this, my troops will have a free hand to retake Umberland and prevent another incursion into Lowlandia."

With these words, the guests seemed to be swayed to Lansius's cause.

After Lansius's speech, where he encouraged his subjects to consume less, the banquet continued with lively conversation. Servius and Sir Harold remained as co-hosts, while the lord and lady excused themselves to rest after an earlier, lengthy inspection tour.

"I'm surprised you didn't threaten them to eat less or face famine," Audrey commented as soon as the door closed behind them. Here, in the privacy of the lord's chamber, they could speak freely.

"Threatening them with new laws or rules wouldn't do us any good. They'll find a way to circumvent the rule or just hide their feasts," Lansius said, scanning the colorful room, which was more spacious than those in Korelia or Korimor, though Korimor had better furniture and taste.

She gazed at him. "Can't we use punishment to deter them?"

"Unfortunately, we don't have a reliable way to enforce the rule, unless you want to create an armed group whose job is to break into people's banquets and check whether they're eating too much," Lansius chuckled. "And really, just how much is too much?"

"Ah, true. That would be hard to do," Audrey muttered.

"Impractical and also unpopular," Lansius added.

A soft knock was heard, and then the door cracked open slightly. "My lord, my lady, Sterling just arrived from Three Hills City," Carla reported.

"Ah, I'll meet him in the council room, then," Lansius said to Carla. He was eager for news from Three Hills. And then, to Audrey, he asked, "Do you want to come?"

"No. Not this time. I'm all sticky from the heat; I'd better clean up while there's still some light, or I might ruin the new bedsheet."

Lansius nodded. "Indeed, the linen looks new. Then I'll be heading to the council room."

"Lans, can you ask Carla to enter on your way out? I need to check this chamber."

"Checking for venomous traps?" Lansius asked, observing the room.

"Yes, we'd better be vigilant," Audrey replied. "One vengeful servant with a snake can wreak havoc. Even with Sir Harold's and Dietrich's assurances, I won't rest easy until I've checked things myself."

Council Chamber

"My lord," the young squire greeted as soon as Lansius entered.

"Sterling, when did you arrive?" Lansius asked.

"Just in time for the banquet. I must say, that was an unexpected speech."

Lansius chuckled and gestured for him to take a seat. "What do you think about Servius's story and my speech?"

"Captivating, my lord. But you did ask them to stock up for winter. Wouldn't it raise the price of grains?"

"Oh, I'm expecting that."

"You want the price of grain to rise?" Sterling asked, baffled.

Lansius chuckled as he understood Sterling's confusion. "Unlike in Korelia, South Hill has a different situation. Here, more than half of the people are farmers."

Sterling gave no response but listened intently.

"Usually, prices go down at harvest so that the farmers barely make a profit. Thus, for them, high prices mean great benefits. It'll empower them to buy tools, winter clothes, oxen, or draft horses for ploughing. But more importantly, it'll give them more incentive to plant winter wheat."

Sterling looked surprised. "Winter wheat? The farmers here can do that?"

"Indeed, it's surprising that they are familiar and willing to do it. South Hill farmers are more advanced than I expected. Or it might have something to do with their climate," Lansius mused, remembering that South Hill was close to Corinthia, which had access to the Middle Sea.

"But what about the poor and the seasonal laborers?" Sterling inquired.

"It's unfortunate that they won't enjoy cheap grain this season, but at least at the end of spring, there will be another harvest. For this region, my aim is to guarantee grain availability. Price will follow availability. Besides, it's not like the price won't come down at all."

Sterling nodded, trying to comprehend the new concept.

"So what happened in Three Hills?" Lansius changed the subject. "Are there any difficulties?"

Sterling took something from his inner pocket and revealed a leather wrap. "My lord, the letters and reports from Three Hills."

Lansius took them, broke the seal, and read some of them. "Did we make it?" he asked.

"Yes, my lord. After we received news of your victory in South Hill, the Lord of Three Hills quickly rallied his supporters to back our campaign to Umberland."

Lansius exhaled deeply. "I'm relieved, but I'm surprised it took another victory to convince them."

"Lady Daniella and I wish to offer our apologies; perhaps our incompetence was the cause—"

"No, don't be. You did well. These letters, proof of purchases, and reports of winter provisions, prove that you two worked hard. Perhaps, I underestimated the complexity of the politics in Three Hills," Lansius considered. "Tell me, how's the harvest in Three Hills?"

"I heard it's not their best, but still a good harvest, my lord. Unexpectedly, they're doing well. One more thing. I also received news that Korimor also enjoyed a good harvest."

Lansius rested his back on the seat and felt a lot of weight lifted from his shoulders. He couldn't resist chuckling.

Watching his lord brighten, Sterling smiled. "I heard people say that every land my lord has graced has produced a good harvest."

Lansius responded with a small grin and shook his head. "That's a dangerous idea. If next year's harvest is bad, then they'll blame me."

Sterling chuckled and then, adopting a more serious tone, spoke. "My lord, since I'm here, and Lady Daniella didn't specify for me to return, may I have my old post back?"

"You want to be my squire again?" Lansius wanted to confirm.

"Every youth in Lowlandia wishes to be your squire, my lord."

Lansius was pleased with the praise. "Then I'll gladly have your service back."

South Hill Market

The next day, before midday when the market was slowing down, Sigmund and several men appeared with a donkey cart in tow. Their appearance triggered a wave of onlookers who crowded around the market's elevated platform.

"Hear ye, hear ye," Sigmund addressed the crowd. "I hold a letter from the new City Council."

He displayed a parchment with a wax seal, and the crowd looked on with intense anticipation.

"The City Council decrees: Whoever brings the donkey and the goods to the village north of the city, will receive a house and a sizable farmland."

Instead of racing toward Sigmund to accept the order, the crowd burst into laughter. The reward seemed too good to be true. Many were convinced that the council was trying to make a joke out of them.

A few approached the donkey, trying to get a feel for the beast's temperament, but were subsequently kicked or bitten. This led the crowd to laugh even more; many were brought to tears by the hilarity of the scene. Some offered encouragement, while others made jokes, as the donkey turned out to be unexpectedly fierce and strong.

When they were all defeated, the crowd called upon one name, the market's champion, Robart.

Robart emerged from the workshop where he worked. Towering over the crowd, he was a strong but gentle man with a simple mind. He wasn't interested in the commotion, finding it amusing but not for him, until the crowd convinced him to give it a try.

With his maester's encouragement, Robart went to the wooden platform and accepted the challenge.

Sigmund asked, "Do you understand the assignment, or should I repeat it?"

Robart nodded, saying, "Take the donkey and the cart to the village north of here."

"Excellent!" Sigmund replied and motioned his men to give the donkey's reins to Robart.

Sigmund then nailed the letter to a wooden pole himself to mark that the job was taken.

The crowd watched in anticipation. As expected, Robart easily wrestled the donkey and guided the beast and the cart to the city gate. Many followed him eagerly as if it were a parade.

As Robart and the cart left the city, the crowd returned to their work, thinking this was nothing more than just an amusement.

Sigmund also left the market, leaving only one man in the general vicinity to keep watch.

As the sun reached its zenith and then slowly descended to the west, people began to rest from their daily labor. That's when Robart returned with the donkey cart. His return was hailed like a hero's, with people and kids crowding around him.

Before he even reached the market, people were already laughing at this apparent foolishness. "A house and a sizable farmland, just for taking a donkey to a village? What mad jest the new council has concocted."

Nevertheless, people flocked to see the end of this spectacle, expecting a punchline. Many had placed their bets against Robart, with most betting that the council would give nothing more than a small guardhouse and a garden with a single tree beside it. Some even bet that the council would give a toy house and bags of soil.

Oblivious to the laughter directed at him, Robart lumbered happily to the market; he even effortlessly carried two small kids in one of his arms, all the while guiding the donkey with the other. Meanwhile, the empty cart had become a playful ride for the poor kids who worked and grew in the market.

Soon, Robart found the guard and handed over the donkey's reins, which the guard smilingly tied to a fence.

"Please wait a moment. On behalf of the lord, the new council shall send their men with your reward," the guard said. The crowd didn't have to wait long before the sound of hooves echoed in the distance.

CHAPTER 32

AGRARIUS

The City Council official, Sigmund, and his men returned to the market, riding their horses. Upon seeing the donkey and the empty cart, Sigmund asked Robart, "Do you have the receipt?"

Robart gently set the kids down from his arms and rummaged through his pocket to produce a small parchment with a seal on it.

Sigmund took the parchment, examining it with a smile. He then turned to face the crowd and declared, "I hold the contract fulfilled."

Robart's face broke into a happy grin while the kids in the cart erupted into cheers and claps. Meanwhile, the crowd watched on, their faces full of anticipation.

Sigmund gazed at Robart and said, "Please follow me. I'll show you to your new house and the land promised by the new council."

Hearing that, the crowd turned dead silent. They exchanged doubtful looks, and skepticism was in the air. Driven by curiosity, they followed Robart and the lord's men. Soon, the market was nearly empty, as shop owners, stall keepers, peddlers, and even innkeepers joined the procession, all eager to see whether the council would keep its promise.

Sigmund rode at an easy pace. He conversed with Robart and traded banter along the way.

Not far from the city gate, they found a good house surrounded by good land for crops, vegetable plots, or orchards. Many were familiar with the house as it was one of the most coveted properties. The previous lord demanded a high price for it, and so far, none had been able to rent or buy it.

Sigmund dismounted as the crowd gathered around them. He held an official parchment sealed with the lord's stamp. "As promised. A good house and good land." He then surrendered the document, a key, and three silver coins. "For the repairs, should it be needed."

At first, the crowd shook their heads in disbelief, murmuring in confusion. Soon, however, a chorus of congratulations overtook them. They cheered for Robart. While feeling the prize was excessive, they also believed the gentle giant was probably the most worthy recipient of the house, as he had helped many, countless times without asking for anything in return.

When someone attempted to buy the house from Robart, Sigmund intervened, saying, "The council only recognizes Robart as the owner. Only the lord of the city can change the arrangement."

The mere mention of Lord Lansius was sufficient to deter anyone from exploiting Robart's simple nature.

After ensuring everything was in order, Sigmund and his men departed, leaving Robart and the onlookers to examine the property to their hearts' content.

As the sun began to set, many gathered at Robart's new house, bringing meals, small gifts, and ales to celebrate the unexpected boon. Some even introduced their daughters to Robart. The evening unfolded beautifully, with plenty of warmth and joy.

Throughout the feast, one topic dominated their conversations: the lord and his new council's commitment to keeping true to their words. Despite numerous rumors questioning their motives, the general sentiment was overwhelmingly positive.

Castle

While the scene in the market unfolded, Lansius was busy sorting the affairs of the nobles. In the morning, Lansius held his first official court and formally received guests who came to pay their respects. Many were ransomed knights or notable men-at-arms who pledged their loyalty to House Lansius.

With their pledge, Lansius received an additional 20 knights, 50 light cavalry, and around 100 men-at-arms, whom he subsequently integrated with Servius's Nicopolan regiment to ensure their loyalty.

Lansius welcomed the new cavalry, as his own had been campaigning with him since summer. His riders had marched and fought for far more than the normative forty days.

Unlike his commoner-based light cavalry, dragoons, and men-at-arms, whose contracts were year-round, the knights and their followers were only obligated to serve for a limited time. After their victory in South Hill, laden with honor and spoils, they expressed a desire to return home.

Sir Harold, as their senior commander, reported that some enjoyed South Hill and its different climate, while others wanted to build houses in Korimor, as Lansius had given them a parcel of land as promised. However, most wished to return to Korelia, as many were native to the area between Korelia and White Lake.

Since the campaign in Umberland would mostly be fought in the mountains, Lansius didn't mind sending his heavy cavalry home. He had already calculated that it would be a mostly infantry affair with few opportunities for cavalry action.

After the formalities ended, his staff tallied the records and found that almost all the captured knights had agreed to join in order to receive a lighter ransom and retain their previous status. Those who did not join were either financially struggling to pay the ransom or were among Sir Gunther's top enablers, whose illegally acquired lands had been repossessed.

With the new policy gaining wider acceptance from the peasantry, commoners, and landlords, the lands of South Hill were transformed. The policy brought structural change that overruled every land grant and corruption that the previous House had done. In a sense, this was a mini agrarian reform without bloodshed.

Instead of confiscating one by one and causing lengthy feuds, the policy provided South Hill with a clean slate.

Lansius understood that he could only do this because he had achieved military victory over the reigning House and captured most of the influential knights. He was under no illusion that everyone would willingly accept the policy. He knew that sooner or later, he would face resistance.

Council Chamber

"The previous lord's top enablers had been living an easy life like mini barons for a long time. It's likely, they wouldn't take to a hard life willingly," Lansius commented as he and his staff convened in the council chamber for a morning meeting.

"Do you expect an armed rebellion?" Audrey, who sat next to him, asked.

"Well, not now while we have thousands of troops, but later on when we go on a campaign."

Sir Harold sighed before suggesting, "We could capture them again and hold them indefinitely."

Lansius shook his head. "We could, but we have no proof, only hunches and suspicions. Also, it would give us a bad name, since they just paid their ransom in full."

Sterling, who was back on the job, looked at the documents and commented, "Indeed, they paid in full."

Lansius nodded and gazed at Audrey, saying, "They're certainly rich and could raise a mini army if they want to."

"We could leave a sizable garrison to counter them," she proposed.

"That is one strategy to deter them. But I'm thinking of sapping their strength," Lansius proposed.

Everyone looked at him with anticipation. "What do you mean by that?" Audrey asked.

"Does it have to do with the struggling knights?" Sir Harold ventured.

"Indeed." Lansius smiled. "I'm thinking of curbing their power further. Let's extend our hand to the struggling knights."

Sir Harold rubbed his chin. "Does that mean, my lord, you are willing to loan them money?"

"No. That would set a bad example. At most, I'm willing to forfeit my share of the ransom." According to the law, the one who captured a person was entitled to half the ransom, while the other half went to the lords—in this case, directly to Lansius's coffers.

Audrey looked puzzled. "But what if they still can't pay even after you forfeit your share of the ransom?"

"Easy, I'll accept their property as collateral until they prove their valor in the next campaign."

Sterling quickly made notes as nobody voiced any objection.

The discussion carried on until Dietrich arrived with new reports about South Hill. Lansius then made several decisions, focusing on billet housing and the maintenance of carts, which had been used extensively during the march from Korimor. Additionally, he addressed a number of other issues requiring attention from his staff.

"Make sure to invite one of the duck breeder families and the orchard master to Korelia. Their expertise would be invaluable," Lansius instructed.

"Noted," Sir Harold remarked, while Sterling made some notes.

"How about Sir Gunther?" the knight inquired.

"Yes, he accepted the move to Korelia. So, arrange for his household to be included in the convoy. Our knights and cavalry should be a good escort for him."

Everyone nodded, agreeing with Lansius's decision.

Audrey looked around and asked, "Anything else, or can we take a break?"

Dietrich shook his head. Apart from the reports he had collected, he was mostly dealing with security, and there was little to be concerned about with such a large army garrisoning the region.

"Perhaps one more thing?" Sir Harold asked.

"Please, feel free," Lansius replied.

"The staff and I were a bit perplexed as to why, my lord only purchased so little winter gear. Wouldn't we need a lot of them for the upcoming campaign?"

"Ah," Lansius exclaimed. "Well, first, we already stockpiled a good amount in Three Hills. Second, I'm afraid that if I purchase more in South Hill, the price would rise so high that the commoners who need it for winter would suffer."

His explanation was well received, and Lansius continued. "There's also another concern. I don't want to make the price rise so high that making winter gear becomes profitable enough to take workers from the farms."

Sir Harold nodded, satisfied with the explanation.

Seeing that nobody else had anything to say, Lansius rose, and the rest of the council members followed. "Then, let's take some rest until the sun is more forgiving, and then we'll do a round of inspections of the villages."

That concluded the council morning meeting.

Lansius

As the midday sun passed, the lord and lady, escorted by cavalry, went to inspect the farming communities again to ensure that nothing was amiss. Lansius was gladdened to see that some changes had already taken effect.

The farmlands were noticeably less grassy, and the work areas for processing and storing grains were also being cleaned and repaired. Some of the villagers were repairing fences to protect the ripe crops from animals, some started to hunt for pests, and a few were making scarecrows.

The Nicopolans were also adapting better than expected, starting their work on the communal plot by weeding, replacing broken fences, and fixing the dirt road so carts could move more easily. Their only complaints were about the bitter grain, and they asked for more ale and sausages.

Lansius jokingly told them to wait, pointing out that the harvest was near and it would be wasteful to drink now without a celebration. However, he promised to deliver them fresh batches of sausages from the hunt as soon as possible.

In other villages, some vegetables had been harvested, and Lansius witnessed that the Nicopolans and the locals could work hand in hand.

After spending time with the village chief, the lord and lady rode back to the castle. Lansius was scheduled to sign some trade contracts, one of which was a purchase order for winter wheat seeds.

As was the custom, the negotiation had been dealt with beforehand, and the merchant, a plump man in his fifties, was given an audience as a formality.

"My lord, my lady," the merchant greeted. "It's an honor to be in your esteemed presence once again."

"We are honored as well," Lansius replied warmly and then motioned for Sterling to proceed.

Sterling approached the merchant and gave him the freshly stamped document. The merchant accepted the scroll politely.

"Is everything alright on your end?" Lansius asked from his seat.

"Everything seems fine, my lord. Although, your subject has a question."

"I don't mind," said Lansius, gazing at Audrey, who looked tired. "But keep it short," he added.

"Certainly. Your subject only wanted to ask, why is my lord buying winter wheat seeds?"

"Ah, that. I suppose I could tell you. As I have done with farming tools, I intend to give the seeds to the farmers."

The merchant couldn't help but ask, "For free?"

"Indeed. The whole strategy is to increase production by lending tools and seeds to the peasantry," the lord explained.

The merchant nodded, saying, "My lord is too generous. The peasants will be pleased."

"It's good business to keep them content," the lord replied. "With the situation in Lowlandia and the Imperium in general, I fear that in the near future, money will be worth less than grains. We'll do well to prepare in advance, lest we become victims of the turmoil."

"Wise words, my lord. I shall take them to heart." With nothing more to say, the merchant allowed Sterling to escort him out.

With the audience session concluded, Lansius rose and stretched his arms.

Audrey smiled at him. "Tired?"

"Yeah." Lansius took her hand and helped her up. "We have some free time before supper. But perhaps we could have a private dinner if you wish."

Audrey looked at him with a smile. "Do I look that pale today?"

"Hardly, suntanned even," he jested.

She chuckled and replied, "A private dinner sounds nice."

"That's settled then," Lansius declared.

Behind them, Carla and Sterling made mental notes about what to arrange for the evening.

Grand Chamber

The Grand Chamber, situated on the second floor, was a smaller hall compared to the Great Hall. The place was a functional room for the lord's family, used either to dine, listen to music, or receive guests in private.

That evening, Sigmund had come and reported the event at the market.

"Robart . . ." Lansius mulled the name as if trying to memorize it. However, he had no intention of meeting or inviting the gentle giant. He only wished for him to live in peace.

"Is the reward really necessary?" Audrey asked after finishing half her meal.

Lansius smiled. "A good house and good land might seem excessive."

"Then why?" she asked.

Lansius chuckled. "You'll find out in a week or so."

"You're going to do more?" Audrey blurted out.

Lansius laughed, finding it hard to explain. Even he himself struggled to recall the exact historical case he had read only once or twice. Fortunately, he was able to grasp the underlying idea and concept well enough to attempt to apply it.

For reasons unknown to him, before he arrived in this world, aside from games, history was all he had or was interested in. Lansius gazed at Audrey to reassure her, "There's no point if I don't follow up. But I understand your concern. I don't intend to waste any more of our precious assets."

"Well, it's not like I don't trust you, but sometimes, I'm worried, since Calub isn't around." There was a hint of guilt in her voice.

"We have Sterling," Lansius said, and the squire bowed his head, adding, "I'll do my best to live up to your expectations."

"Make sure the lord isn't wasteful. He has three baronies to run," she said with concern.

Lansius couldn't help but quip, "It's a mark of a good wife to be concerned about her husband's spending."

Audrey chuckled, took her goblet of pale ale, and drank it straight. Her eyes were already drowsy.

"These past few days have been exhausting," Lansius remarked.

"Indeed, it's best if we take care of ourselves. Else miasma might catch us."

Lansius nodded. The miasma concept was false, but he felt that the weather was quite different here compared to Arvena, and that might cause problems. Even Audrey was having trouble. "Let's head to the bedroom then. Might be a good idea to rest early. I don't feel like reading books or scrolls tonight."

"I agree," Audrey replied. She then turned to Carla. "Let's skip sword training tonight."

"Of course, my lady," Carla replied, and then piqued by their unusual condition, she poured the ale from her wineskin into another cup and took another sip from it.

Observing her, Sterling approached the table and sniffed at the ale.

"Something in the ale?" Lansius asked, observing the mixture of water and ale in his goblet.

"Perhaps the ale is a bit too strong," Sterling ventured.

"Nah, we're probably just tired." Audrey dismissed their concern.

Once inside the chamber, Lansius unbuttoned his doublet and hastily cleaned his face using clean water in a copper basin. He noted a scent of iron and couldn't help but look around.

"What's the matter?" Audrey inquired.

"I smell blood," he said with a sharp and alert gaze, his hand ready on his hilt.

"Well . . ." Unexpectedly, Audrey didn't look alert but rather awkward.

"You're injured! When?" Lansius stormed toward her, believing she was hiding an injury.

"Easy, it's not—"

Lansius grabbed her arm and started to look for wounds.

Annoyed, she gazed at him strongly. Her eyes glowed a faint golden hue. Lansius recoiled and blinked in pain, almost taking a step back. "Why did you do that?" he complained.

Audrey moved around him and hugged him from behind. "Because you're too forceful. You should treat your wife gently," she said with a pout.

Hearing that, Lansius chuckled. "Can't I at least check your injury?"

Audrey nestled her face into his back and said, "It's not an injury."

Lansius furrowed his brow. "Not an injury?" And then he realized, "Oh . . ."

"It's that time of the year," she explained. "The time when I usually get a bit moody."

Lansius recalled their past experiences during the fall season: the bitter reunion at Toruna Manor and their awkward relationship at Korelia Castle.

"Does that mean . . . ?" he ventured.

Audrey gave him a sweet smile and whispered, "Hannei told me about fertility. If it's true, then next month . . . Well, I believe Korelia and Korimor deserve an heir."

CHAPTER 33

THE WIND OF HARVEST

Agatha

Like the previous year, this year's harvest season was also late, but it was slowly inching closer. The cool wind from the northwest, beyond the mountain separating Nicopola and the Great Plains of Lowlandia, began to make its presence felt. Even at midday, one could easily notice the subtle change in the air.

The farmers of South Hill were laboring hard in the fields. Despite the late harvest, the lack of manpower due to the failed campaign against Korelia had left them ill-prepared. Worse, the lord's men were forcing them to prioritize work on the communal land, which yielded crops belonging to the lord and his cohorts.

The situation was dire until a short battle drastically altered the region's political landscape. Overnight, a new name emerged as the Lord of South Hill.

This change in power came as a surprise, but the new lord immediately worked to pacify the region. As the victor and new lord, he could have easily confiscated any land and wealth he wanted, using any pretext he liked. However, he ultimately refrained from doing so. Instead, he opted to engage in trade rather than demanding food for his large army.

For the villagers, Lord Lansius's arrival was a bittersweet moment. Along with him came two hundred men who had been freed from Korelia. Their return provided much-needed relief to the community. Through their stories, the villagers, including Agatha, learned about the fate of their relatives who had been captured.

These men shared that those from South Hill who had been captured were treated fairly in their captivity. While it would be years before they could return, their situation was deemed far better than being sold into slavery.

Unfortunately, those who returned also confirmed many deaths. A large number had perished during their hasty retreat to the Great Plains. Many became widowed, old parents were left childless, and brothers mourned their siblings.

Such was the harsh reality of war in Lowlandia. However, instead of being drowned in mourning, those who survived carried on with their lives.

Yet, as Agatha had witnessed, life also brought unexpected helping hands. The farming communities around South Hill were greatly surprised when Lord Lansius, for this year, exempted them from obligatory work on the communal land.

Confusion and disbelief initially surrounded the policy, but these were swiftly resolved as the lord himself visited the villages and gave his words of assurance.

His benevolent policy and personal approach quickly made him popular. Although some held him responsible for the loss of their loved ones in the Battle of Korelia, the majority were inclined to support his nascent rule.

With the new policy in effect, the farmers could focus on their crops. However, this change also brought an unexpected development.

The lord was bringing in his men, the Nicopolans, to work on the communal land. Each village received dozens of men, who would pitch tents, live in barns, and work alongside the villagers.

Despite giving them a warm welcome, the communities had mixed feelings. While they appreciated the Nicopolans, who would tend the communal fields in their stead, there was suspicion that this arrangement might be a ploy to claim a share of the villagers' crops as payment for their help.

Such suspicion was not exaggerated, as it had been common for Lowlandia lords to station troops in villages and demand food in exchange for "protection."

However, these doubts dissipated when the villagers observed the lord regularly supplying his men with provisions from the city, including a bounty of meat from hunting expeditions. Moreover, the Nicopolans gladly shared, bartered, or traded what they had with the community.

With no remaining suspicions and only some lingering fear, the villagers found no reason not to accept the Nicopolans fully. After all, it was easier for them to trust a third party than the Lord of Korelia. Even those who had lost loved ones and harbored resentment toward the lord couldn't extend their bitterness to the Nicopolans, who had caused them no harm.

With the Nicopolans' assistance, the villages and farms buzzed with activity. Weeding the farms to remove grass was the top priority, followed by fixing wooden fences around the fields to deter animals from the forest. Scarecrows were also erected in many places, while another group actively hunted rodents and pests.

In the village center, the communal granary underwent repairs in preparation for the upcoming harvest. The area designated for drying grains was also cleaned and maintained as needed.

At first, the Nicopolans worked only on the communal farm, but they were ready to extend their help to anyone in need. The lord only required the person in need, along with the village chief, to formally register their request for assistance. He would then, through his lieutenant, assign his men to help on the designated farm. If necessary, additional men could be requested.

In exchange for this assistance, the lord asked for a percentage of the yield as payment, which was certainly fairer than a failed harvest.

The Nicopolans' presence also solved many problems unrelated to the harvest. Streams were cleaned, wells repaired, and obstructed roads were cleared.

Some of the Nicopolans were sophisticated, educated city folk. Thus, they were able to help with carpentry, masonry, and even mending clothes. Some taught basic calculations and alphabets in their spare time.

A few respectable individuals shone as informal leaders, helping to organize work and other events as necessary. Because of their presence in the community, several local troublemakers were subdued, and some were even conscripted into the army. This deterred more youths from following in their footsteps.

In another case, a wolf pack that had been troubling the villages was driven deeper into the woods after an elaborate ambush.

Everywhere Agatha looked when she returned home from her training, she saw progress and improvement. She had never seen her village so ready for harvest. For the first time, the fences were in good shape, the fields cleared of grass, and there were new scarecrows that could move their limbs at the slightest touch of wind.

The roads were now widened and clear of potholes, allowing carts to travel fast and without fear. The forest, too, had become a safe place for gathering wild berries and firewood. She never expected that Lord Lansius would be able to bring about so much change in such a short time.

People she met on the road appeared happy. Even her parents were smiling, grateful for the two new scythes loaned by the new City Council. Agatha was relieved to see that things had turned out so well for her village. She came home to friends, relatives, and parents who, for the first time in a long while, dared to believe there was more to life than just toiling endlessly to enrich the nobles.

Lansius

One week had passed since Lansius's meeting with the grain merchant. As he had predicted, the market responded well to the news that he was purchasing winter wheat seed. The merchants, initially puzzled, also reacted positively to his genuine intention to provide the seeds to the peasantry without charge.

Because of these developments, the grain price dropped two notches. The market was becoming confident that South Hill peasants would plant their winter wheat.

Despite Lansius's upcoming campaign to Umberland, the introduction of winter wheat led most merchants to expect a steady grain supply in the region throughout the next year, thus diminishing any incentive to hoard.

However, Lansius wasn't going to gamble with the merchants' speculative tendencies. He knew that mere gossip could upset the market and undo much of his hard work. Furthermore, the grain price issue was just one among a myriad of other challenges that he needed to address before the South Hill region could be deemed secure.

Thus, in the privacy of the council room, Lansius summoned his staff to discuss their situation.

"The question is: How do we secure South Hill without leaving a large garrison?" Lansius asked his staff.

Audrey remained sitting and listening, Sir Harold pondered with arms crossed, while Dietrich was observant but quiet.

It was Sigmund who pondered, "Without a large garrison, is it even wise?"

"It is if we could," Lansius replied, leaning back in his seat.

"It's unfortunate that we can't rely on our cavalry as quick reinforcement," Audrey lamented.

"Indeed, South Hill is far from Korelia, also having no direct route but to pass through the Three Hills region. Even with a horse relay, a message will need at least seven days to reach Korelia, and then another nine or eleven days to reach South Hill with an all-cavalry force."

Sir Harold drew a sharp breath. "Eleven days of rapid march through the Great Plains. Unless they're nomads, the riders will be too tired to fight upon arrival."

"Indeed, that is a correct assessment," Lansius confirmed.

"Can't we use the nomads as a quick reaction force?" Audrey asked.

Lansius let out a stiff smile. "We can, but their numbers aren't that big either. Also, I don't want to use the nomads in South Hill as there are frictions between them."

"Frictions?" Audrey furrowed her brow.

"My lady, many from South Hill who were routed in the Battle of Korelia died in the Great Plains while on the run from the nomads," Sigmund replied.

"Ah, why didn't I think of that?" Audrey remarked.

As the discussion slowed down, Dietrich asked, "A question, my lord. Just how many men do you think are needed to keep South Hill from rebelling?"

Lansius pondered for a bit before answering, "Aside from fifty in the castle, perhaps two to three hundred would be prudent."

His staff reacted by sighing or nodding deeply.

"Is such a large number really necessary, my lord?" Dietrich asked again.

"Two or three times the size of an army that the rebels could raise is the norm," Lansius explained. "The city alone has close to four thousand people, while the surrounding towns and villages have at least another two or three thousand. Theoretically, someone with charisma and gold might convince a percentage to rebel."

Sir Harold looked at Dietrich. "What the lord said is true. Remember that Omin started as a knight and only had clout with a dozen guards. But he managed to convince the commoners and organized a successful coup."

Dietrich nodded thoughtfully.

"Losing three hundred of our force seems large, and it'll hurt us in our next campaign, but since we have so many . . . can't we afford that?" Audrey tried to suggest.

Lansius gazed at her with a small grin. "That is true, we have two thousand men. But remember, they are Nicopolans."

Audrey seemed to realize her error and massaged her head.

Lansius continued. "While the Nicopolans, especially Servius and his band, are loyal to our cause, the rest have only followed us due to their need for food. Thus, I have no confidence in their loyalty in my absence."

The council chamber turned quiet, with only an occasional wind from the tight vertical window whistling in the background.

"So, we can't rely on our cavalry or our allies at all. Then we are truly in a predicament," Audrey lamented.

Lansius smiled and leaned forward. "What if I tell you there's a way to raise a large number of armed men who are obedient to your cause and don't cost you money to feed, to arm, or to maintain?"

His words attracted everyone's attention.

"Is it even possible?"

"Such a grand plan will certainly require a lot of time, and at most, we only have two weeks before harvest."

"Oh, but the plan is already ongoing," Lansius revealed, much to his staff's astonishment and skepticism.

Sigmund finally spoke up, "My lord, is such a grand plan possible without our knowledge? Surely, we would have noticed such an undertaking."

Lansius's smile widened. "But Sigmund, you are the one who completed the preliminary stages."

South Hill City

The next morning, Sigmund and his guardsmen returned to the market once again. The people at the market welcomed the officials' arrival and quickly gathered into a crowd. Everyone, from the common folk to the rich, followed, all looking to him expectantly.

Sigmund climbed the steps of the wooden platform and gazed at the crowd looking at him intensely. The market had come to a standstill.

"Hear ye, hear ye," Sigmund addressed the crowd. "Today, under the command of the new City Council, I bring you a series of decrees."

The crowd gasped when they saw that Sigmund was holding a stack of parchment, each sealed with wax. Anticipation was running high.

"The City Council decrees: Whoever assists the city in harvesting, collecting, and storing grains safely and timely for seven days without fail, will receive no toll, market levies, or tax for the next year."

Upon hearing this, everyone cheered loudly, looking around in excitement. Many were seasonal laborers who were more than able to help. In fact, they had always wanted to help, but for years the villagers had so little to offer that such arrangements couldn't happen. Nobody wanted to work for minimal gains.

But now, the lord was offering them tax exemption for the next year. This meant that traveling merchants could journey without paying tolls, peddlers could vend their goods free from levies, and shopkeepers were exempted from market taxes.

"There's more," Sigmund declared as his men nailed the first parchment to the wooden board post.

Hearing this, the crowd momentarily subdued their celebration, eager to hear more.

"The City Council also decrees: Price manipulation is a serious crime. Therefore, all involved, nobles or commoners alike will be imprisoned in the dungeon for a minimum of one year. Furthermore, half of their family wealth will be confiscated."

There were murmurs of disbelief, but they knew that the new council was committed to their word, no matter how absurd it sounded.

Sigmund continued. "Any crimes related to grains and food that harm the common good will be punished with one year of hard labor on the communal land."

His men took another parchment from Sigmund and nailed it to the wooden board post.

"The City Council decrees: Should a coup arise against House Lansius, the perpetrator henceforth loses their noble status. As such, any commoner or peasant can capture them, with a bounty of twelve gold coins for a knight, two gold coins for a squire, and ten silver for each man. The bounty can be shared."

The crowd recoiled at the announcement, but instead of fear, they were thrilled by the prospect of a large reward, enough to propel them into landowners. They also welcomed the possibility of participating in preventing a coup.

Sigmund continued. "In light of the previous decree, the new City Council allows each household with an untarnished name to possess two spears or one crossbow."

The crowd turned ecstatic. The previous lord had been so fearful of his own people that even daggers were confiscated upon entering the town. Now, the council permitted them to arm themselves, providing them leverage against troublesome nobles.

"Furthermore, when harvest is done, the City Council, on behalf of the lord and lady, wishes to invite everyone to a festival. Everyone who wishes the lady well will receive two mugs of ale and a copper coin."

The people cheered loudly, praising the lord and lady in unison. The last decree was as good as offering free ales and a large meal to everyone who came. Knowing the City Council's reputation for keeping their word, the people were overjoyed.

As Sigmund concluded his announcements and his men nailed up the final parchment, a spontaneous celebration erupted in the market. Despite the early hour, the scent of ale filled the air as the crowd celebrated.

Ten days later, in the second month of Autumn 4425, South Hill finally welcomed its late harvest. Despite considerable effort and rising anticipation, the harvest results had proven to be only marginally adequate. Each grain had yielded just over half its expected potential.

Once again, the climate and weather, untamable as ever, had asserted their supremacy in dictating the results of human labor. The winds of uncertainty quietly swept through the region.

CHAPTER 34

SPYMASTER

South Hill City. Ten days before the harvest.

As soon as they rode out from the city, Audrey, dressed in dark hooded garb, asked with a blushing face, "What's with that last decree?"

Lansius, riding a common horse and dressed similarly, chuckled. "Why? Don't you like well wishes?"

"It's embarrassing," she protested as they trotted along a quiet road. Carla, Sterling, and the rest of the guards in disguise rode in front and at the rear.

She continued in a low voice. "Besides, what's with the twelve gold coins for a knight? That's way too expensive. I know we had plenty in the baggage train, but this will put a hole in our coffers."

Lansius laughed. "You're forgetting a small but important detail."

Audrey guided her horse closer. "Twelve gold coins for a knight . . . what did I miss?"

"Yes, we'll pay them twelve gold coins for a knight. But guess who will take the captured knight's manor, land, warhorse, and armor?"

"Ah!" she exclaimed, her mouth agape.

"Also, don't be stingy with rewards, especially against a coup. I could offer more, and it would still be profitable, but it might make the local knights nervous."

"I see . . ." Her voice trailed off as she got lost in thought.

Lansius smiled as a gust of wind blew around them, bringing a certain scent of autumn.

Riding slowly, Audrey turned to Lansius again. "I think it's time for you to explain what this plan is all about. Yesterday, you talked about raising numerous armed men who are loyal, don't cost money, don't need feeding, or arming. But all I've seen are some basic rules and allowing people to have spears or crossbows."

Lansius chuckled, while Audrey added, "We've already given away a basket of coins, and a house with land. Now you're planning to give away barrels of ale and coins."

Lansius responded by asking, "Drey, do you know how to make an army follow commands?"

"Good payment, punishment, and the law stating they must obey," she answered.

Lansius nodded, sensing she grasped the idea. "That's how you make an army follow commands. And how do you make commoners follow commands?"

Audrey's gaze sharpened. "Use commoners as an army?"

"Yesterday, I mentioned armed men," he reminded her. "For peacekeeping, you don't have to rely on the military."

Audrey appeared doubtful.

Lansius smiled and pointed out, "We're drawing from the same pool for men: the populace. Rebel or us, the source is the same. Now, if we draw the populace to our side, promising great rewards for catching rebels, what do you think will happen?"

"But how will they dare to go up against rebel knights? Just having weapons isn't enough," she argued.

Lansius had anticipated that question. "That's why I'm offering absurd rewards for simple tasks."

Audrey recalled the events in the market, her eyes flickering with realization. "You're training them."

"Conditioning them," he corrected her with a smile. "The basket of coins, the house with the land, all are a demonstration of authority."

"Authority . . ." she mulled, as their horses trod upon the familiar route.

"Just like in the army, merely being a lord isn't enough to control the men. One must be able to show that he is in control and has the power to reward, enforce rules, and give punishment. That is called: having authority."

She seemed to follow, so Lansius continued. "When we show that our words are true, people will listen. And there's no better way than giving them ridiculously simple tasks and giving big rewards. That demonstrates authority."

Like a good student, Audrey listened intently.

"When you show authority and demonstrate it effectively, titles become unnecessary. From mercenaries to bandit kings, their leaders operate without formal titles."

"That is true," Audrey remarked.

Lansius finished off by correcting a misconception. "Controlling the commoners is not only possible, but it's always been done. Nobles levy the commoners for wars. So, the notion that we can't rely on them in peacetime is rather absurd."

The horse neighed as another wind blew, sending dry leaves around them.

Audrey removed the dry leaves from her hair and clothes and asked, "But I've never heard of anyone using commoners to resist coups."

"Because most nobles aren't comfortable sharing power with commoners," Lansius revealed without hesitation. "And do you know why they aren't comfortable?"

Audrey pondered seriously and ventured, "Fear?"

"Not quite. The correct answer is morals."

She furrowed her brow. "Morals?"

"If a lord is cruel and dishonest, the populace is likely to oppose him, not providing help. As for me, I hope I'm good enough."

Audrey reached for Lansius's hand. "You're a good lord," she reassured him warmly.

Lansius smiled. "This is why to rule without making anyone miserable is a good cause."

The lord and lady, accompanied by their entourage, continued their way toward the villages. To their left and right, the ripened farmland welcomed them.

After midday, when the sun was more merciful, the Lord of Korelia returned to the castle, having completed his weekly inspection.

Waiting in the courtyard were Dietrich and the page boys. The lord and lady dismounted, and after completing the necessary formalities, they were escorted to the inner part of the castle.

"Any tidings, Dietrich?" Lansius asked.

"My lord, the knights and squires will return to Korelia tomorrow morning."

"And Sir Gunther?"

"His House has confirmed they will join. Their carriages are being loaded as we speak."

Lansius nodded as they continued walking to the Grand Chamber where they could discuss more freely.

They reached the Grand Chamber and took their seats to wind down. The servants promptly brought drinks and refreshments. Yet, it was Carla and Sterling who poured drinks for the lord and lady.

"How's the local knights' reaction to this morning's council announcement in the market?" Lansius asked.

"Still quiet, no reported movements."

He nodded and then leaned into his seat. "Unless the lady wishes to ask anything, that would be all for me."

Audrey gazed at Dietrich. "Anything else you want to report?"

Dietrich knitted his brow. "None in particular, Cap—I mean, my lady."

"Don't sweat it," said Audrey. She then picked a fruit from the silver platter and offered it to Dietrich. "They tell me it's from the previous lord's own orchard."

Dietrich politely accepted the aromatic fruit. "Gratitude."

"Something to keep yourself from boredom. Guard duty in the castle can be really dull."

Dietrich let out a grin before turning to Lansius, bowed his head a little, and took his leave.

Audrey sipped her cup of water, her gaze resting thoughtfully on Lansius, who seemed lost in contemplation. "What's on your mind?" she asked gently.

"Just a thing or two about South Hill," he said.

"You know, Lans, I'm still curious about giving no market tax or toll tax for next year. Won't it deplete South Hill's income next year?" Audrey asked.

"It was intentional," he revealed. "First, it would deter a coup as anyone who tries would face strong opposition from the commoners and esquires who benefited from the one year tax-free policy."

Audrey found it interesting and listened with her back straight.

Lansius continued. "Second, it would take a chunk out of the region's income for a year. That'll reduce the region's ability to raise an army. Even if a coup is successful, they would only have a small army."

"That is a lot of use from just a single policy," Audrey mused.

"There's more. Offering less tax is also a good incentive to win the people's hearts without much effort. Furthermore, for a small city like South Hill, with limited scribes and clerks, suspending half the taxes for a year will allow them to focus on the big issue—ensuring that the region's bookkeeping is accurate. Mind you, the previous lord left messy records."

"A plan within a plan," Audrey commented in astonishment.

Lansius smiled and drank from his goblet.

"Have you decided who'll govern the city after we leave?" she asked.

Lansius glanced at her before answering, "Ideally, Lady Daniella, but she's technically your knight, and also she's in Three Hills."

"Three Hills as an ally is doing us a disservice," Audrey said, voicing her disappointment.

Lansius leaned to one side, resting his elbow on the armchair. "Three Hills is a big city with big politics. Perhaps, this is the best Lord Jorge could do."

"Well, whoever you pick, make sure it's not Sir Harold."

Her request piqued Lansius's curiosity. "Any reason why?"

"We're going on a campaign, and we need his expertise," she explained.

"Ah," Lansius mumbled. Then he added, "You don't need to worry. Sir Harold has made his stance clear. He wants no part in governing a city."

Audrey breathed a sigh of relief. "So, there's only one name left," she ventured.

Lansius took his goblet again. "I guess, it's time to summon."

Grand Chamber

"My lord," Sigmund greeted Lansius as he entered the Grand Chamber. They were alone; Audrey had retired to her room with Carla. Only Sterling remained, sitting in the far corner.

"Please take a seat. I have news for you," replied Lansius.

The skald took a seat and prepared to listen.

Lansius remained standing and spoke. "As you know, I'm going on a campaign to Umberland. However, I need someone to lead the garrison in South Hill."

Sigmund seemed prepared and replied, "I believe Sir Harold would be the best candidate."

"I agree with you, but the knight already made his stance clear. That's why I'm thinking to let you govern the city."

Sigmund blinked and shifted in his seat uncomfortably.

Lansius didn't say a word, observing the captain's reaction.

"Is this why you sent me to the market as a herald?" Sigmund finally reacted.

"One of many reasons," Lansius explained casually. He forwent mentioning that from the start, he had refrained from addressing the people directly because he wanted Sigmund to be the face of the authority he had planned.

Sigmund looked uncertain, pondering. "But what about the Orange Skalds and the skirmishers?"

"Farkas will be the new leader."

"I see . . . So, my lord, has confidence in him."

"Not as much as I trust you or Dietrich. And his gittern play is still lacking."

Lansius's words drew chuckles from Sigmund.

"But, at least, the men respect him, and he's morally acceptable," Lansius continued.

Sigmund raised an eyebrow. "Morally? How can you tell, my lord?"

"I already know how he behaves with the prey he hunts. So, I asked the hunters how Farkas behaved with other hunters' slain prey. They told me Farkas only takes a small cut if he didn't contribute to the kill, even when he's technically their lieutenant."

Sigmund nodded thoughtfully.

"Showing restraint and respecting others despite your status is a good trait for command. However, I'm not sure about his tactical ability, but you have twenty days to prepare him."

"My lord, I can vouch for that. In twenty days, I shall drill Farkas in what I know, including the gittern play."

Lansius was pleased with the declaration. "One more thing," he said. "Even if you're in South Hill, the Orange Skalds should continue."

"But they'll be under Farkas."

"Farkas will lead but one group. I wish to have more, ideally one in each city in Lowlandia," Lansius revealed.

Sigmund nodded in understanding. "To serve as your eyes and ears."

Lansius approached Sigmund and placed a leather pouch on the table, revealing it to be filled with gold and silver coins. "The funds for the skalds. Try to make it work."

"My lord, with this much, even if it fails, we'll have enough musicians to entertain several cities."

Lansius chuckled and tapped on the skald's shoulder. "Lowlandia and the Grand Alliance will face many enemies. I need someone who can walk in bright disguise and in the shadows."

"Then, I'll strive to be the perfect candidate," Sigmund replied with a determined nod.

As part of the capitulation, Sir Gunther, the previous lord of this region, had forfeited his family manor for a price and followed the group of returning knights to Korelia. Sir Gunther and his House were to be accepted as a minor member of the Grand Alliance. Lord Lansius promised to provide them with a pension in exchange for their loyalty and support.

To guard the manor, the lord had sent skirmishers to the area, which also served as a reward, given the surrounding ripened orchards and abundance of food.

For the skirmishers, life was good. Their injured could recuperate in peace while the healthy could rest their weary bodies. Emboldened by the situation, they even dared to anticipate great things in the coming harvest. Unfortunately, fate could be a cruel mistress.

When the crops were finally harvested, the mediocre results dampened the mood in South Hill City and Castle, knowing the effort the lord and the Nicopolans had made.

Everyone was affected by the mood, and even the upcoming harvest celebration couldn't lift their spirits. The only one who was unfazed was the lord and his closest retinue.

The castle staff whispered about the lord's response. Some argued that the lord had done what he could and chose not to be affected by the bad news. While most agreed, a few even dared to suspect that the lord simply didn't care.

"In two weeks, the lord will depart with his big army," one whispered, triggering nods from the other servants.

"They'll need a lot of grain," another replied, followed by, "Probably will leave us with barely enough to pass the winter."

A few sighs were heard. They had big expectations for Lord Lansius, but now all of it seemed to be undone. Nobody in South Hill had the illusion that the lord would cater to their needs more than his own army. Thus, morale began to drop.

Lansius, Council Chamber

"My lord, the people are getting restless. The price of grain has steadily increased despite the harvest," Dietrich reported.

Lansius remained quiet and motioned Dietrich to give another report, as if unbothered by the grain price. Audrey, seated next to him, betrayed slight concern.

Sir Harold, placing his arms on the table, added, "My lord, this harvest result may jeopardize our campaign to Umberland."

"I doubt it's that bad," Lansius responded lightly. Then he glanced at Sterling, asking, "What's the story on the street?"

"There are all kinds of baseless rumors flying around the city," Sterling reported. "Things aren't looking good, my lord. If we depart next week, Sigmund will probably face trouble. Should I summon him for you?"

"No," Lansius disagreed. "I want him to train Farkas. Let's not bother him with this market panic. The people's expectations are simply unjustified. Harvest results are almost a gamble, so there's no need for excessive worry."

"As long as the farmers and the people have done their best, then any result that isn't famine is acceptable," Audrey commented.

"Wise words," Lansius praised and poured some light mead into her silver goblet.

She accepted the goblet but, despite the rich honey aroma, refrained from taking a sip. "Three days have passed since the harvest ended. People, even the castle servants, looked concerned with the result. Perhaps something needs to be done."

Lansius gazed warmly at her. "I know."

"A false rumor might ruin a barony. Perhaps a statement to calm the people would be prudent?" Sir Harold suggested.

Lansius nodded at the wise counsel and said, "It's a correct response, but in our case, let's just wait."

"But the price is rising, my lord," Dietrich voiced his concern.

Lansius let out a chuckle that drew everyone's attention. "I'm actually waiting for that."

Everyone in the chamber looked at him, puzzled.

Then, with a sly smile, Lansius quipped, "Want to see my magic trick?"

CHAPTER 35

THE LORD'S GRAIN GAMBIT

It was still some time before the sun reached its zenith when the lord and lady, accompanied by their entourage, arrived at the city granary, situated a fair distance from the market. The caretaker of the place was taken aback by their visit.

The sudden activities and sightings of horsemen and guards piqued the crowd's curiosity, and they soon gathered. Once they knew who had arrived, the anticipation was high. Rumors spread that the lord was catching big thieves or rounding up those who stole the harvest. People were expecting to see men dragged out from the granary in ropes.

However, despite all the rumors, the lord's visit was mostly ceremonial. He simply conversed briefly, looked at the storage personally, and confirmed what the people of South Hill already knew: This year's harvest yield was lacking.

With the granary still reeling from last year's failed campaign, this year's mediocre harvest results, and Lord Lansius's plan to campaign against Umberland, South Hill's food security was put in doubt.

While aware that the farmers would plant their winter crops, the community's outlook had changed. Previously, the winter crops were seen as a hopeful promise of abundance next spring. But now, they were seen as a necessity; without them, they would certainly face famine.

And they knew that the one who would decide their fate was Lord Lansius.

"Just how much will the Black Lord take from the granary?" many asked in hushed whispers.

Due to the market's situation, the merchants, ever driven by profit, had begun to keep a larger stockpile than usual. Despite the lord's harsh stance against price manipulation, the merchants didn't believe they were breaking any laws. In their view, they were merely preparing for the worst. As a result, the price of grains continued to rise, and the poor were increasingly concerned about the coming winter. Their only hope was for a helping hand from the lord.

A few dared to ask, "Unlike the rich and landowners, why are we still untouched by the lord's benevolence?"

Others argued, "We helped with the labor, yet we see no benefit from the free market tax or toll tax."

The poor, surviving through begging or doing odd jobs whenever possible, found themselves in no position to benefit from the tax-free policies.

The lord's inspection of the granary was brief and uneventful, ending as swiftly as it had begun. Contrary to the crowd's expectations, the visit resulted in no tangible action. No one was brought to justice, there was no address to the people, and no alms were distributed. The lord and his entourage simply rode away.

Barely raising more than eyebrows, the visit left the crowd dissatisfied. They dispersed, continuing with their day as the fear of winter continued to weigh heavily on their minds.

The next day at dawn, as the first shop in the market barely opened to receive its daily goods of vegetables and milk, there was a commotion in the streets. Even though the roads in the city were still empty, traffic was already building up. Many city dwellers woke up surprised to see horse and donkey-drawn carts lining up the streets leading to the market.

At least thirty carts were already there, and then another ten arrived, further clogging the city's narrow and winding streets.

"Officer, what's going on?" a few daring individuals asked the guards, who appeared to be patrolling the streets.

"Nothing to worry about. We're just escorting the farmers to sell their grains."

"Farmers, selling grains?" They couldn't believe their ears.

"Yes, apparently, unlike last year, they have plenty of surplus this year," the officer explained.

"They have?" another neighbor who just joined asked in surprise.

The officer gave a stiff smile. "I don't know the details myself. We're ordered to escort the farmers safely, and I'm expecting further instructions later. Gentlemen, until then," he said, before walking away with his group in brigandines and sallets. They continued patrolling the area, aware that a large number of horses and donkeys could be troublesome.

While the people in the city were still processing what had happened, the market situation was approaching a near frenzy. The various shops worked as diligently as they could, purchasing the grain at yesterday's market price.

More carts of grain arrived from the surrounding villages, greeted by an ever-increasing number of shops opening, each vying not to be outdone by their competitors. Everyone was seizing the opportunity for profit. Gaining such a high quantity of grain felt like a boon; they were convinced they were securing a tremendous amount of profit, even before the morning had fully dawned.

Little did they know just how much grain they were actually dealing with.

The sun rose higher, bathing the city in its golden light, yet the market remained paralyzed by the convoy of carts that had gathered in the busy area. These narrow carts, loaned by the City Council, filled the streets, each one waiting its turn to offload grain. Buckets of hay and water were scattered here and there, as coachmen tried to keep the burdened beasts in good condition.

The sheer number of carts crowding the streets leading to the market affected everyone. This congestion showed no signs of resolving soon. As it turned out, the farmers were not only selling but also purchasing goods with their hard-earned money, loading them into their carts and thereby further slowing down the process.

This unforeseen development was followed intensely by everyone. While almost everyone didn't fully understand how the market set its prices, they knew instinctively that scarcity drives prices up, and abundance drives them down. So they watched with great excitement, hoping that the price would come down.

After close to forty carts had been unloaded and processed, and with forty more still lining up in the streets, the merchants began to worry and decided to meet in secret. Many shop owners had just been awakened by their workers or helpers, having had no expectation of large market activity so soon after the harvest and so close to the harvest festival.

"Forty carts followed by another forty," one exclaimed as soon as they gathered.

"Where do they come from? Outside of South Hill?" another asked.

As he sat down, an old balding merchant shared, "My men report that they saw another group coming from the other villages. At least twenty carts, likely more to come."

"How could there be this many? Is the lord somehow behind this?"

"My fellow merchants, please remain calm. I have conducted a small investigation," the host said calmly, relaxed in his seat.

"As expected of the richest man in South Hill," one of the guests quipped.

The man in the bright red doublet smiled and continued. "The situation is caused by our own negligence. We've miscalculated."

"Miscalculated? How?" one asked on behalf of the group.

"This year, the lord allowed the peasants to exclusively work and harvest their own land," the host responded.

"Yes, we know that, but that doesn't mean they could produce that much more."

"Indeed. The problem lies in our faulty measurement," he revealed. Before anyone could react, he asked, "Tell me, how did you find out that the harvest result was meager?"

The young merchant pondered, then shrugged and confessed, "I know from other fellows. They raised their prices, so I raised mine."

The host gazed at the rest, and one answered, "With just a few drinks everyone can ask the granary workers. They can see with their own eyes just how much is stored in the building. I even know some who bribed the clerk to learn the actual tally in the records given to the lord."

Many nodded their heads.

"This is where we got it wrong," the host surmised. "We were too focused on the granary and failed to see the real situation."

"Failed? But we have men, neighbors, and relatives who took part in the harvest. They all tell us that the harvest yield was lower than last year. Surely, they wouldn't lie," one retorted.

"I'm not suggesting they're lying," the host clarified.

"Then how could this happen? Combined, we've already processed probably more than fifty cartloads of grain."

"Gentlemen, bear in mind that we overlooked the issue of distribution." The host leaned forward. "Let me explain. By law, the lord could only take crops from communal land, and that is what gets delivered to the city granary."

The guests followed intently, voicing no objection.

"The issue is, as I said before, for this year, the lord allowed the peasants to work exclusively on their land. Under the previous lord, the peasants usually lost many crops due to pests or animal attacks that gathered as soon as the harvest season started. However, this year, they could harvest their crops to their hearts' content."

The merchants nodded their heads slowly, beginning to understand.

The old merchant commented, "That is true. Twenty years ago, when my father was still alive, we usually purchased grains directly from the peasants. But since the Three Hills conflicts, the farmers had so little we didn't bother to travel there anymore."

"For more than a decade, we've been so accustomed to relying on the communal land, on our private farms, and those of the nobles, that we forgot the peasants were also suppliers," the host lamented. "The harvest did indeed lessen, but the distribution made it seem worse than it actually was."

Many sighed or shook their heads in disbelief. They had been misled by the stockpile of grains in the granary and were unaware that this year, the farmers had their own stockpile. Only now did they remember that the lord had made his men, the Nicopolans, available to assist the peasants with their crops. Thus, it became clear how the peasants could achieve optimal results, even in a low-yield situation.

Deep down, the merchants were aware that in their greed, they had cornered themselves into painful losses. Usually, whenever a surplus happened, they could sell it to Three Hills for profit. Even when the previous lord forbade it, they smuggled it for even more profit. But now they dared not gamble against the Black Lord.

One who remained standing headed to the door. "Please excuse me, I have stocked up plenty. I need to tell my store not to buy anymore."

Another rose from his seat. "Thank you for the explanation. I'll also stop trading."

"How about the price?" the young merchant asked his colleagues.

The old merchant, donning his hat as he prepared to leave, advised, "Better to sell at your purchase price from several days ago."

"But that's a loss."

The host rose and tapped the young man's shoulder. "At this rate, everyone will feel a loss. Better to drop the stock now before the winter wheat harvest next spring. At this rate, the beggars will be eating white bread."

Many chuckled nervously as they left. The idea that the price of white grain would drop so low that beggars could eat wheat and oats instead of rye, barley, legumes, or bran, was laughable. But the possibility now existed, and if it happened, the merchants knew they would face a tremendous loss.

With heavy hearts, the merchants raced to stop their shops from buying grains and began to offer lower selling prices. A few even quietly showed willingness to offer lower prices to anyone with money and willing to speculate on bulk purchases, out of fear of further loss from their vast grain storage.

Midday was still far off when the market rejected the remaining grain carts, leading to a serious disturbance and loud shouting between the farmers and market workers. The situation soon worsened as some frustrated farmers began to sell their grains on the street at lower prices than the merchants, causing a ruckus and further aggravating the disturbance.

Unable to intervene effectively, the merchants attempted to bribe, but not all were willing to accept such measures.

The merchants considered using thugs to enforce their will, but the presence of the lord's men deterred any such actions. Seeing the Nicopolans armed and the lord's men positioned with crossbows on windows and rooftops, nobody dared to escalate the conflict. They were acutely aware that the Black Lord had his eyes on this situation.

Nobody wanted to forfeit their lives and wealth, and thus the farmers reigned in the market. The narrow streets of South Hill turned into a surprise grain market, flooding the city with cheap grains for everyone to buy. The farmers also proved to be generous, each giving a free bowl of grain to beggars and children in need.

The situation ceased only when the lord, via his captain, directed the farmers to the granary, offering to buy their remaining grain out of benevolence. Thus, the story circulated that on the first harvest under Lord Lansius, despite the low yield, the farmers were flooding the city with grain.

The commoners, not privy to all the information, attributed the situation to the new lord being blessed by the Ancients. Any earlier skepticism toward his House had now vanished, replaced by fervent trust and submission. The poor were particularly heartened; the sacks of white grain they had gained at such low prices seemed nothing short of magical in their eyes.

This harvest season, everybody, even the poorest, had plenty to eat, and they directed their gratitude to the new lord.

South Hill Castle, Audrey

"My lady," Sigmund and Sir Harold greeted as they entered the council chamber.

"Sir Harold," Audrey responded, then turned to Sigmund, "Apologies for bothering you during your training," she said, motioning them to their seats.

"This is my duty, my lady. I cannot imagine not participating in this," said Sigmund, taking a seat.

Carla diligently poured drinks for the guests. Inside the council room were only four people: the lady, Sir Harold, Sigmund, and Carla.

Audrey nodded and asked, "How's the situation out there?"

Sir Harold smiled and reported, "Servius did everything smoothly. The plan is flawless, so our part in the scheme was minimal."

"The early farmers got their money, and the food prices dropped significantly," Sigmund added.

Audrey let out a breath of relief. "Well done," she praised.

Outside, the problem seemed solved. The price of grain had dropped, and as a bonus, the farmers gained money to improve their lives. However, the staff suspected that not everything was as it seemed.

"A question," Sir Harold said, drawing everyone's attention. "On behalf of the other council members, while we understand what was happening, we're not sure how this could happen."

Audrey nodded. "It would be wiser to wait for the lord, but I can try to explain."

"Indeed, my lady, an explanation from you would be much appreciated," Sigmund said.

Audrey took a deep breath and began. "What happened in the market today was a diversion. We take the merchants as the enemy and the grain as our troops. To achieve victory, we need to corner the merchants until they refuse to buy more grain."

She continued. "The first strategy was to appear as having a larger army than the opponents. While we had the farmers' grain, it was only worth around eighty cartloads. Thus, we used narrow military carts and didn't allow the farmers to load bushels of wheat directly into the carts and load them to the brim as usual. Instead, we used wooden barrels."

Sir Harold commented, "It's safer but less efficient. Each of our carts could carry slightly more than half of an ordinary wide merchant cart."

"The use of wooden barrels was also intended to slow the process," Audrey added. "The plan was to cause chaos in the market. The lord mentioned that by creating the illusion of an abundance, we could reassure everyone about the grain supply."

Sigmund nodded quietly, looking impressed.

"By utilizing narrow carts and wooden barrels, we successfully distributed grain equivalent to eighty cartloads across over a hundred carts. However . . ."

Sir Harold interjected, "It still wasn't enough."

"Indeed, with just around 110 carts, the lord was still skeptical that he could convince the merchants. So, the cornerstone of the second strategy was to increase the cart number to more than 140. To reach this number, only 70 carts at the front were fully loaded with white grains. The rest had white grain on top, but brown grain at the bottom."

"It was a risky move. But it worked." Sir Harold chuckled, amused. "The market seized up after processing forty carts and refused to buy more."

"The lord explained to me: Just like on the battlefield, if one side sees the other receiving large reinforcements, one column after another, they would be more inclined to flee."

Sir Harold chuckled again. "It amazes me that we treated the grain price and the merchants like we were on a battlefield."

"Indeed, it's unthinkable," Sigmund added with a small grin.

"If everything is clear, then, shall we proceed with the report?" Audrey asked.

Sigmund straightened up. "Currently, the carts with white and brown grains are returning to the camp. As planned, they didn't unload at the city granary. We have the captain to relay another order that the grains should be transferred directly to the Nicopolan camp outside the city."

"Good. Let's keep the brown grains for emergencies," Audrey instructed.

"Actually, my lady, some Nicopolans have grown fond of brown grain and blood sausages. So, we can treat the food like any other." Carla, standing next to Audrey, spoke up for the first time.

Audrey chuckled at this revelation. "Now, I'm curious. Perhaps I should give it a taste."

Carla furrowed her brow. "We dared not cook such food for you."

Audrey shifted in her seat and glanced at her. "Last year, I was still a squire. A meal is a meal. If it's good enough for them, it's probably good enough for me."

"Count me in for a bowl," Sir Harold commented with a smile.

The mood in the chamber lightened.

"My lady, there's another development," Sigmund reported, as all crucial matters had been reported. "One of our agents heard that some merchants are willing to part with their grains at a low price if anyone agrees to purchase in bulk."

Audrey drew a deep breath. "Just as the lord predicted."

"What did the lord tell you, my lady?" Sigmund asked.

Audrey chuckled and muttered, "He said: That'll teach them not to play with grain prices again."

The guests responded with a wave of subdued laughter, pleased by the justice delivered. Afterward, Sigmund repeated, "Should we entertain the offer?"

"Of course, more grains are better for the upcoming campaign," Audrey replied without hesitation. "Also, the lord wanted to appease the nobles and landlords who will join us in the upcoming campaign."

"Ah, I see, a strategic gift of grains," Sir Harold mused.

"Exactly. It's also to keep them from messing with the prices," Audrey explained, then turned to Sigmund. "Can you handle the negotiation?"

"Certainly. I'll play them hard first, ensure we get a better price."

With that, the council marked the grain issue as resolved. Ironically, by utilizing the Tarracan man's notorious strategy of faking abundance, Lord Lansius had brilliantly safeguarded South Hill's harvest, convincing all that the city had more than enough grain, thus averting the high price.

Now, only one matter remained—the preparations for their departure in just three days. This would be their fourth campaign of the year. Despite a string of victories, there lingered a fear among everyone that they might be overreaching. For them, battle and war were akin to a gamble, and Lord Lansius had cast his dice so often that many feared his streak of luck might be nearing its end.

CHAPTER 36

FOURTH MARCHES

South Hill Castle

While Audrey led the council meeting, Lansius immersed himself in strategic planning within the confines of his study. He had learned enough from the village elders and the Nicopolans under Servius about how to proceed with South Hill.

Seated behind a large desk, Lansius scrutinized this year's harvest records. Even in a low-yield situation, a baron like him still secured a fair share of the harvest. The harvest collected by the Nicopolans from the communal field would be kept in the city granary and, as was the norm, sold whenever needed to maintain food prices.

Aside from the grains in the city granary, from which he would allocate a portion for his campaign, Lansius also received a share of grain from the peasants who sought the Nicopolans' assistance. Moreover, the villagers sent a few more carts of grain to the camp as a gesture of gratitude.

In his hand, he held a small letter from the village elders.

We, the elders of the Northern Villages, on behalf of our fellow villagers, humbly wish to convey our deepest gratitude for my lord's benevolent policies. They have brought an abundance of harvest and joy to the community. We, your humble servants, wish to offer what meager supplies we have, in hopes it could be used for my lord's future campaign.

May the Ageless One and the Ancients protect my lord and my lady from all harm.

- Signed, the elders of the Northern Villages

Lansius felt overwhelmed by the farmers' generosity. As he looked at the donated amount, he mused, "They're really confident in their winter wheat."

Aside from the first source, the communal land, and the second source, the farmers' share, Lansius also had a third source: his purchases.

Due to the weak harvest and merchants' price gouging, the market had been in a state of shock. However, it also provided Lansius an opportunity to counter the market dynamics. After today's gambit, he was confident that the next day prices would plummet, leaving him as the sole buyer in the region.

This situation would undoubtedly dent the merchants' pockets, but he viewed it as a necessary lesson to humble the rich, making them think twice before profiting from others' suffering. With everyone having enough to eat for the winter, Lansius hoped it would strengthen South Hill against possible rebellion or coup, as potential perpetrators would not be able to secure enough men to rally for their cause.

Returning to the grain issue, Lansius estimated that, with all three sources combined, he would have more than forty days of supplies, with some room to spare. Yet, the situation in Umberland remained a source of concern.

He kept it to himself, but he was deeply troubled. Early reports brought by Sterling from Three Hills were especially damning. From these, Lansius learned that Umberland's countryside had been ravaged and was now devoid of its peasantry.

Defending a region with scarce food production is a death trap.

Thus, as preparation for such dire circumstances, he needed to acquire as much grain as possible without causing his allies to suffer. To achieve this, he planned to buy grain in Three Hills but needed to keep this part of the plan secret. He didn't want anyone to speculate that he was planning to purchase a large quantity of grain from Lord Jorge's domain.

Lansius glanced at the numbers, calculating how many carts of grain he had. Fortunately, he found the number to be sufficiently large.

"It should be grand enough," he muttered to himself, sure that the supply carts would be sufficient to deter anyone from speculating.

With the supplies for the campaign largely secured, Lansius stored the parchments in his drawer and took a moment to lean back in his chair. Gazing around the room, he couldn't dismiss the bright colors used in the study, yet had purposely kept the place mostly unchanged, knowing his stay in South Hill would be brief.

Lansius then picked up another parchment marked "Plans for South Hill." The first item on the list was the road project. Despite the challenging topography, he wanted to ascertain the feasibility of a direct route to Korelia. With South Hill potentially becoming a breadbasket, a faster direct route to Korelia would significantly benefit his domain.

Next on the list was the plan to send an envoy to Corinthia. But first, he needed to learn more about them.

"Sterling," he called.

The squire quickly rose and approached with hurried steps. "Yes, my lord."

"Can you summon Sigmund for me? He should still be in the castle after the council meeting."

"At once." Sterling bowed and exited the study.

Even without Sterling at his side, there was no risk to Lansius's safety. Guards stationed outside the door were loyal men from Korelia and Midlandia who had followed him since his battles with Lord Robert. It was said that competition to be his guard was so fierce that they spent their own money on appearances, including trimmed beards, perfumes, brightly tailored brigandines, and even polished accessories.

Lansius dismissed the thought of investigating further, choosing to trust his staff and his men. While curious, he preferred to avoid micromanaging his men unnecessarily.

As long as they don't cause issues, I see no harm.

Unlike gambling, there were only benefits to having well-motivated guards with a good appearance. After a brief respite, Lansius returned his attention to the current issue: Corinthia. Although the city was part of Lowlandia, its distance and terrain rendered the barony largely independent, often keeping it uninvolved in the Lowlandia conflict.

Despite many considering the barony to be little more than a poor fishing village, Lansius saw the potential for an ally or the opportunity to learn about the Middle Sea, locally known as the Narrow Sea.

However, expectations for Corinthia to transform into a bustling trading city were generally dismissed. The Narrow Sea was treacherous, characterized by cliffs on both sides or endless inhospitable marshlands, leading to frequent accidents even for experienced Navalnia seamen. Consequently, the southern trade route remained mostly inactive.

After taking a sip from a goblet of water, Lansius turned his attention to the last on the list. It was South Hill's most pressing issue: manpower. He recalled the elders' words and his discussions with Servius.

Good or bad, this year's result is due to the Nicopolans' assistance.

And next year, there won't be Nicopolans in South Hill.

For this harvest, Lansius had implemented a modified version of the Military Agricultural Colony with some success, inspired by the tuntian system from the Han dynasty. Unlike the Roman practice of allocating land to veterans as both a reward for service and a means to create strong outposts and recruitment sources, the tuntian system used soldiers to directly produce their own food during campaigns.

Implementing a full tuntian model in the Imperium was impractical due to the forty-day campaign limit and the reluctance of levies to engage in such hard labor on a campaign. However, since Lansius maintained a year-long payroll for his army and they were in the midst of a real threat of famine, he believed it might be feasible to adopt this model to some extent.

Yet, its use for South Hill had come to an end. Lansius needed to move his army to Umberland before winter.

Thus, there was a real concern for South Hill's food production in the absence of the Nicopolans. The question was whether the region could still thrive and produce a surplus with the current manpower shortage.

Medieval agriculture was inherently prone to risks. Without pesticides, over-cultivating but failing to harvest could lead to rodent infestations, or worse, locust swarms that could devastate the entire province.

Thus, drawing on his extensive knowledge of history—a subject he once vaguely considered unnecessary—Lansius dipped his quill pen into the ink and began drafting his plans. He aimed for a strategy that might enable Sigmund to govern the region with relative ease and lessen everyone's burden in the long run.

While he could simply accept the situation as it was and leave the farmers to their work, Lansius aspired to do more. He aimed to improve the odds, even slightly, that next year would be better, even without his troops around to assist.

Soft knocking was heard from the door, followed by, "My lord, I'm here with Captain Sigmund."

"Ah, let him in," Lansius responded. He had been waiting.

The skald, dressed in a fine crimson doublet, entered the study chamber. "My lord, you summoned me?"

"Please, have a seat," the lord motioned, quickly adding, "Sigmund, what do we know about Corinthia?"

The skald's gaze sharpened as he sat down. "Not enough," he mused, pondering what Lansius's question really was.

Lansius chuckled, satisfied by the skald's sharp intuition.

Sigmund added, "I think I could fathom just a slight hint of my lord's intention. I shall send two of my best agents to Corinthia."

"Other than a small cost, there's no harm in gathering information, and the benefits from it will be worth their weight in gold." Lansius voiced his support.

"But, my lord, what has piqued your interest in Corinthia?"

"Hopefully, a potential ally and trading partner. If things go well, I might even invest in ship design or sea trade," he explained.

"I see." Sigmund nodded thoughtfully.

There was nothing else to say about Corinthia, so Lansius moved to the next issue. "While you're here, do you have any requests regarding your upcoming governorship?"

Sigmund breathed a sigh of relief. "I'm glad my lord asked. I need advice on managing the nobility. How can I rein them in, especially when two factions are at odds?"

"Which factions concern you?"

"The knights that opposed you might be in bed with the merchants, and the landlords."

Lansius nodded, seemingly unperturbed. "Not everyone will openly support us while the situation remains undecided. Currently, we enjoy popular support, so it's natural for people to wait and remain neutral before pledging their support to any faction. Thus, the best strategy is to maintain our neutrality."

Sigmund listened intently, so Lansius continued. "If you remain steadfast and keep military power free from their influence, you should emerge unscathed. More-over," Lansius paused briefly, "you can always rely on delay tactics to defuse tensions. Tell them you're awaiting my discretion. I can always respond with a stern no."

Sigmund nodded, seemingly satisfied with the advice. "Then, my lord, how about managing the land for next year? Without the Nicopolans, South Hill lacks a thousand men to work and tend the farms."

Lansius handed him a neatly folded letter from the table, which Sigmund accepted politely.

"Memorize this letter, take it to heart, and then burn it."

"My lord, is that necessary?"

"No, but it sounds dramatic," Lansius quipped, prompting chuckles from both.

"In this letter, you'll find a framework for a Civilian Agricultural Colony," Lansius explained.

"Civilian Agricultural Colony?"

"It shouldn't be surprising," Lansius remarked. "We're currently using the military. However, there's another way to do it."

"By civilians, is my lord thinking about the commoners?"

"Anyone, even the unfortunate," Lansius clarified. "Seasonal laborers, land-less farmers, orphans, the poor in the market. Any capable but unfortunate farmer should be invited to work on the communal farm."

"But wouldn't that compete with the private farms and landowners? They also rely on the same labor pool."

"Tell them we need to increase crop production no matter what to avoid famine. Stick to that point, and they'll quiet down eventually. After all, this will likely just force them to offer decent wages to their workers or to employ them year-round instead of seasonally."

"So, just a minor inconvenience for them," Sigmund commented.

"Indeed. They wouldn't stage a coup over mere pocket change," Lansius reassured him. "Also, I will allow two hundred camp followers to settle, so you're not starting completely from scratch."

"My gratitude, my lord. But what about the payment system?"

"I have outlined the details in the letter. Divide the communal land into two parts: one half to be managed by the peasants as part of their tax, and the other half to be worked by the new labor force. You'll need to compensate the laborers, but consider it an investment."

"Will the region have enough cash, especially since my lord has promised to waive tolls and market taxes for the next year?"

"It will. I'll abstain from claiming my share from South Hill for a year or two, until the situation stabilizes." Lansius paused, then added, "Frankly, don't worry too much about coins. We're facing a potential famine, and I fear grain will become more valuable than silver."

They heard the chirping of a bird passing by the narrow window, seemingly announcing the fair weather. "It will be a lovely week for marching," Sigmund commented.

"Hopefully, the weather will remain this good," Lansius replied with a smile. "Also Sigmund . . ."

"Yes, my lord?"

"Could I ask you to create something for me?" Lansius's eyes brightened. "I've always wanted to try something to make the march less painful."

South Hill City

The harvest festival was planned for the next day, after everyone had completed the harvest, stored the grains, and cleaned the land sufficiently to avoid pest growth. As it would be a two-day event, extensive preparations were necessary.

From morning to noon, across the village and city, everyone was busy setting up tables and chairs, and slow cooking had already started to ensure the various meals would be ready by the next day. It was a community event where the lord was expected to donate liquor, cooking ingredients, and musicians to ensure merriment.

Street performers had prepared a new act, dubbed "The Rise of the Black Baron and the Magical Grain." People were eager to watch the performance on the city's main street, or wherever patrons were willing to pay.

The city buzzed with decorations of all sorts. Children gathered berries and wildflowers, while others brought fruits from the orchards and fresh vegetables from the gardens.

While the community prepared for the festivities, the lord's military was gearing up to march. Footwear was repaired, fresh woolen socks distributed, and carts received their last major maintenance before heading to Three Hills.

The main army would march one day after the two-day harvest festival. Although he could have ordered them to march now, the lord decided to boost their morale by allowing them to enjoy the festivities.

Meanwhile, Sigmund had quietly dispatched a small team of skirmishers, disguised as wandering minstrels, on a fast cart to Three Hills. This was the reason the lord had allowed them to rest to their heart's content at the previous lord's manor—so they wouldn't begrudge being sent out before the harvest festival.

Once again, the minstrels would serve as his forward eyes and ears. His scouts in bright clothing, falsetto voices, and thrilling music.

The next morning, the city came alive with music, dances, and all kinds of festivities. There were small archery competitions, fishing contests, a baking contest, running contests, and of course, a drinking contest.

The baking contest was especially phenomenal, filling the city with the aroma of freshly baked bread for the entire day. Because it was a competition, butter and aromatic herbs were used generously, giving the air a sweet, milky, and rich scent.

The lord and lady were present, providing the crowd with barrels of liquor from his castle, along with flour, butter, and, special for this year, Korelian salted meat. In turn, the city offered the lord and lady the best cuts of roast duck, slow-cooked since the night before.

Entertainment was everywhere, with folk dances, theatrical plays, and music. The highlight was a trained horse that took part in a drama play, behaving as if it understood its role and could act as well as any human.

The lady was enchanted and spent an hour playing with the horse. Seeing an opportunity, the lord extended an invitation for the horse owner and other actors to perform in Korelia, which was graciously accepted.

"Korelia next year should be a great place to be," Audrey remarked excitedly as they rode home.

Lansius chuckled. "I'm sure it will be. Let's just hope we can resolve the Umberland issue before the harvest season."

Audrey offered a small grin. "With you leading, I doubt we can fail."

"That's high praise. But really . . . we should prepare for the worst. After all, there are many unknown factors in Umberland."

Audrey nodded, understanding that to underestimate the danger in Umberland would be foolish.

"My lord, my lady, apologies for interrupting," Sir Harold said as he rode closer.

"Please, speak," Lansius said openly.

"Your presence is requested again," Sir Harold conveyed.

Lansius looked to the skies. "But it's still early for supper."

"It's not the city. This request came from the village elders. They've begged me to extend an invitation for my lord and lady to the northern villages," the knight explained.

Lansius chuckled and looked at Audrey, who nodded with a smile. "I don't mind," she said.

"Well, then, let's enjoy a drink or two and a light bite," Lansius declared, his entourage readily agreeing.

As the festivities carried on, the air of merriment rejuvenated everyone's spirits. The usual doom and gloom were momentarily forgotten, swept away by cheerful cries and laughter. Individuals from various factions set aside their differences, united in joy, sharing laughs, meals, and drinks. That day, South Hill was reborn anew.

South Hill

Two days after the harvest festival, at dawn, the castle buzzed with activity. All its chandeliers and lanterns were lit, signaling the lord and lady's preparations to march. The kitchen staff busied themselves preparing breakfast and lunch for the road.

"Are you ready?" Audrey asked Lansius, who was already dressed in his traveling clothes, belt, and sword.

"Ready," Lansius remarked, his gaze lingering on the master chamber that had been their abode for the last several weeks. He noticed Agatha, assisting with packing their clothes. Catching his gaze, she looked up.

"Yes, Master?"

"Agatha, please take care of this place for us," Lansius said gently.

The girl hesitated.

"What's the problem?" Lansius inquired, not expecting any other response than affirmation.

Audrey, standing by his side, giggled and approached the chambermaid in training. "She's torn. Half of her wants to come with us, and the other half wants to stay with her family."

Lansius offered a gentle smile. "Is that true, Agatha?"

The girl nodded. "It's true, my lord."

"Then continue your training. Once Umberland is safe for travel, we can invite you to join us, either there or in Korelia," Lansius reassured her.

"Really?" The girl's excitement was palpable.

"It's a promise. But in exchange, do me a favor."

"Anything, my lord," said Agatha with a wide grin.

"Look after Sigmund for me. Offer him counsel from time to time. While he undoubtedly knows more about everything, being asked for advice and confided in is valuable and will make him wiser," Lansius confided in her.

The girl nodded earnestly. "I'll offer as much counsel as he needs."

A knock on the door interrupted them.

"My lord, my lady, do you need more time to prepare?" Sterling inquired from outside.

Lansius looked at Audrey, who shook her head as she donned her traveling cloak. "If it's time to leave then, we should act quickly."

Thus, the lord and lady bid farewell to the castle staff and the people who had gathered on the street outside. Marching in formation with their select guards and cavalry, they headed northeast, taking the route through the northern villages and toward Three Hills.

They had been there for just slightly over a month, yet the parting was bittersweet for the populace who had come to recognize the lord's leadership during these turbulent times. Many wished he could stay and rule the city for a bit longer, but they knew that the lord was shouldering the responsibility for the entire province.

As the formation moved away from the city, Audrey glanced back and caught sight of the castle's colorful glass window, shining like a miniature sun amidst the orchards on either side. "I'm going to miss this place," she murmured.

"Indeed," Lansius echoed, retrieving a small earthen jug from his saddlebag and offering it to her.

"What's this for? Are we celebrating something?" she inquired before taking a sip.

"To our victory over South Hill and to saving so many troops from hunger," Lansius declared, proud of his achievement.

"To victories, past and future," Audrey toasted. Their smiles broadened as they shared the sweet mead.

Grateful villagers lining the road waved them off, catching one last glimpse before the couple embarked on an eight-to-nine day march to Three Hills. Beyond Three Hills lay the plateau leading to the mountain pass where Umberland was situated. There, the fate of Lowlandia would be decided.

CHAPTER 37

MULI MARIANI (MARIUS'S MULE)

Korelia

Undisturbed by the distant march of war, the Korelians celebrated the marriage of Calub and Cecile with joy and festivity, marking the culmination of the city's celebrations since the harvest's arrival.

The first celebration was the harvest festival itself. Despite the recent Battle of Korelia disrupting planting seasons, this year's festivities shone brighter than usual. This was due to the stable food prices that allowed everyone to partake in the celebration. This stability was achieved through a trade agreement with the merchants of Eastern Lowlandia and grain surpluses from White Lake.

Next came the celebration in honor of Lord Lansius's official recognition as the Baron of Korelia. Upon hearing the news, the people threw a spontaneous citywide celebration to honor the Imperium's decree. This celebration was prolonged after news arrived that the lord had secured another great victory over South Hill, creating a euphoria never seen before.

The marriage between two well-loved figures brought the season's festivities to a close.

Calub, the alchemist, was an honorable treasurer whose diligence ensured that wages and payments were disbursed on time and without any mischief. His work ethic and integrity endeared him to many. Similarly, Cecile, the late Sir Callahan's daughter, was cherished by the Korelians. Her House's contributions and gallant sacrifice were still fondly remembered.

The townsfolk enthusiastically organized a banquet for the newlyweds, with Sir Justin, serving as the marshal, officiating the marriage in Lord Lansius's absence.

The year 4425 would be long remembered in Korelia as a season full of celebration and joy.

As autumn deepened, life in Korelia resumed its tranquil pace. Shepherds led their flocks to graze on the harvested fields, preparing the land for the next season. The sound of shearing signaled the start of wool work, which would continue through the winter. The breeding season brought a promise of renewal and growth, particularly important for sheep, ducks, donkeys, and most notably, horses.

With Korelia's growing importance, an increasing number of breeders established trade posts in the city, leading to the emergence of a bustling market. The volume of horse trade, which included horses for farm work, burden beasts, leisure, and warhorses, increased dramatically. With every transaction, the city levied modest taxes to attract more businesses.

Sir Justin was at the forefront, ensuring horse breeders felt comfortable and encouraging collaboration with the nomads. He believed that sharing knowledge between the two parties would work wonders.

As efforts to further improve Korelia City continued, the community was busy in the barns, gathering and storing hay. This task was crucial to ensuring there would be ample feed for the horses and livestock throughout the harsh steppe winter.

Amidst the work and preparation for the cold months, a wave of excitement washed over Korelia, sparked by the newly operational bathhouse. Word of this oasis of relaxation quickly spread beyond the city's boundaries, drawing curious visitors from the surrounding villages. They came in droves, eager to immerse themselves in the soothing waters that promised respite from their daily labors.

Behind the scenes, four individuals elevated the bathhouse to new heights. Initially, it was Lady Felicity's presence that drew the women's populace to the bathhouse. They were eager for their daughters to bathe in the same waters as her, believing it would bring good luck, or at least, offer something to boast about to friends and relatives.

Now, with Lady Felicity having returned to Midlandia, the bathhouse continued to be graced by more beauties. The newly married Cecile often visited with Claire, her sister. Frequently joining them were Lady Astrid, the daughter of the Lion of Lowlandia, and Eleanor, the marshal's daughter, who was now her lady-in-waiting.

The four were busy preparing a branch of the school for commoners and landless gentry, finding a weekly respite in the bathhouse's newly built warm water section.

Their influence helped turn the bathhouse into the city's top attraction. This influx of visitors injected new life into Korelia's economy. Around the bathhouse, a vibrant community of inns, taverns, and food stalls sprang up, catering to the needs and desires of the guests. Each new establishment added to the city's allure, transforming the area into a bustling hub of commerce and social gathering, further driving its economic impact.

The operational and profitable bathhouse also elevated the city's prestige in the eyes of the Midlandian guilds, eager to expand their influence and business. More guilds sent their laborers to offer projects to the City Council or to sell their services directly to the masses.

The first newcomers were a cobbler family from Midlandia, who set up their shop near the bathhouse. They were soon followed by a textile workshop and a tailor. Then, a bakery opened, enticed by the prospect of securing firewood at favorable prices due to the bathhouse's demands.

Following this trend, a wealthy merchant from last year's salt trade constructed a temporary kiln. Using rejected firewood from other sources, he began to supply basic pottery, bricks, and even clay roofing to the locals—items that had been previously imported and were prohibitively expensive for most Korelians.

The leftover materials from the kiln, including the ashes, aided in the construction of mud houses for the thousands of captured laborers. Previously, the marshal had allowed them to enjoy some form of harvest festivities in their camps. Now, refreshed and well-rested, he directed their efforts toward completing the mud housing and winter-proofing other facilities.

He aimed for them to withstand the harsh winter of Korelia without falling ill and risking delays in the various projects, especially the construction of the city wall and the new eastern keep.

The fair and humane treatment left the laborers mostly at peace. Being Lowlandians, they had expected worse treatment. Moreover, since they were either from Korimor or South Hill natives, they were reassured with the knowledge that their families were aware of their situation and were waiting for them at home.

They were also content, knowing their families were in good hands. Despite initial skepticism, the news from travelers from Korimor and South Hill was uniformly promising. They began to view the Lord of Korelia not just as capable but as fit to rule, and perhaps even as the leader the Lowlandians needed to end the region's long history of bloodshed.

Despite Lord Lansius's obscure background, there emerged a general willingness to submit, not born out of fear or helplessness but out of admiration and acceptance. This sentiment persisted even in his absence, as Korelia, and everyone within it, whether free or not, continued to forge new paths independently.

Such progress was only possible because Lord Lansius had laid a solid foundation. He had done more than construct buildings; he had assembled a team of capable and trustworthy personnel to oversee and manage the various aspects of the city, ensuring its continued growth and well-being.

More importantly, the staff members, armed with his vision, did not shy away from investing in and engaging in mutually beneficial business relations. They also extended fair treatment to captured laborers, understanding they were not enemies but another part of Lowlandia to be embraced. With these elements in place, the city and its people thrived.

House Arte

Far from Lowlandia, in the village of Brunna near Midlandia, a concentration of troops was building up. Three hundred Arvenians were in training, supported by two hundred Midlandians.

After returning from their visit to the capital, Sir Archie, or Lord Arte in disguise, had been steadily growing his power base in Brunna. The small but wealthy estate had previously been owned by a baronet involved in slave ownership in Sabina Rustica.

The punishment for this crime was death. Furthermore, the late baronet's seditious act against Lord Arte constituted another high crime, warranting a more serious capital punishment.

In desperation to avoid execution, the late baronet struck a deal to adopt Sir Archie into his House in exchange for his silence. The baronet thought he had outwitted death, but Sir Archie made certain the man lived only until the document and patent were signed and the necessary ceremonies concluded.

Officially, the baronet passed away due to old age. Unofficially, it was a lethal combination of a high dose of an aphrodisiac and a surprise visit from a courtesan that led to severe heart problems for the old, yet lustful, man.

As the baronet had no direct heir, only several bastards with little claim to the estate, Sir Archie inherited the entire Brunna estate and village. This inheritance provided him with a manor, a source of income, and land to build his forces—a stroke of luck, especially since no Midlandian nobles would have willingly granted him land that offered such independence.

Many had hoped to turn him into their henchman. Arte knew he was fortunate to have Lansius, whose remarkable performance significantly boosted Arte's standing among his Midlandian peers. Furthermore, Lansius's success opened the door for Arte to gain support from Sir Stan and Seneschal Bengrieve, two of the most influential figures in Midlandia.

Their influence shielded Arte from other nobles across the vast Midlandian territories who might have sought to entangle him in their ongoing succession crisis.

In military matters, learning from Thomas's insights about Lansius's strategy against Lord Robert, Lord Arte invested heavily in crossbows. Instead of building expensive cavalry units, he doubled down on creating a force of competent men-at-arms, augmented by crossbowmen.

In Brunna, they trained hard until Thomas felt confident they could replicate Lansius's success against the Lion of Lowlandia. Due to his competence, the bearded axe man was subsequently appointed captain.

His superior, Sir Peter, an able diplomat, became Lord Arte's trusted right-hand man, while Sir Anci was named cavalry captain.

Leda, the freed Rhomelian slave from Sabina Rustica, quickly proved her worth by meticulously maintaining the records and ensuring the finances were balanced. This allowed the burgeoning force to remain independent and not indebted to other Midlandian nobles who might use them as their private army.

Thilde, a female Arvenian squire who had been captured and tortured in Sabina Rustica, became another rising star in House Arte. Despite her injuries, she learned to walk again and trained harder than anyone, earning immense respect from her comrades and becoming the embodiment of Arvenian courage and stubbornness.

While Brunna was focused on military preparations, it was also gearing up for another significant event: a noble wedding. The anticipated day arrived with Lady Felicity returning from Lowlandia in a procession befitting a high noble, flanked by armed guards and cavalry.

With Imperium officers in attendance, the couple tied the knot. It was a merry affair with a sense of grandeur, despite their nature in disguise. Although subdued, the week-long party and celebration quickly became the subject of widespread discussion among the neighboring villages and towns.

The revelation that a mere knight, now an adopted baronet, had accumulated such vast wealth, manpower, and influence left everyone in awe.

Contrary to expectations of a tranquil fall and winter, the newlyweds, just a week after their honeymoon, donned their armor and fur clothes. Without hesitation, they led their army out of Brunna. A fierce determination shone in the eyes of the Arvenians as they marched, united in their resolve. They were intent on exacting vengeance upon Lord Karius and Lord Gottfried.

Lansius

The army and their camp followers marched under fair weather and covered a good distance each day. Their preplanned route and knowledge of where to camp greatly aided their travel.

By midday on their fourth day from South Hill, they took a rest, using tents atop the carts as makeshift shades. It was then that the scouts reported the arrival of dozens of allied horse-drawn carts from Three Hills.

Just as Lansius had been informed by his budding network of spies and long-range scouts, the goods he had been awaiting had arrived.

Everyone was eager to see what the dozens of carts contained. It turned out that almost all were filled with bags of various models and materials, though they were roughly the same size.

At the lord's command, his staff quickly distributed the bags, with the lord himself taking one.

Sir Harold, Servius, and Farkas, who had just returned from forward scouting, were amused by the double-strapped backpacks. Although they had seen them before, they had never considered them to be more useful than the simple bags carried on the shoulder or pouches on their belts.

They quickly noticed that with these backpacks, instead of relying on various smaller bags or pouches, each man could carry more goods. They were akin to saddlebags but for humans.

"With these, we can reach Three Hills in under three days," the lord declared confidently as he inspected the bags.

His words were met with chuckles from his staff and others within earshot. The fact was, they were still four to five days away from Three Hills. Even if they could march that fast, the burdened beasts in the supply and baggage train would collapse from exhaustion.

"My lord, it isn't wise to risk our supply line," Servius advised.

"This is to help with the supply line. With these bags, we can pack as many goods as possible to lessen the beasts' burden," the lord explained. Before anyone could complain, he had loaded his bag with various goods and carried it comfortably on his back.

"This is manageable," he remarked after some tries. "Let's march this way."

"You wish to march on foot?" Sterling asked, puzzled.

"Yes, why not? After all the festivities, we need some training. Otherwise, we might face a nasty surprise in Umberland," the lord replied without hesitation.

The staff exchanged looks before Lady Audrey stepped forward, addressing the command staff. "Tell the men to pack all personal belongings in their bags, along with goods they can carry. Let the carts carry less. Let's aim to cover as much ground as we can today."

The lord looked at his wife and started, "You don't have to walk—"

Ignoring the interruption, Audrey continued. "My lord, I believe it's best to explain the reasoning behind this. I doubt these bags are merely for training."

"Of course," Lansius reassured her and then addressed the rest of his men. "These bags are greater than you might think. Two of the most crucial factors in the military are speed and freedom of movement across terrain. And with the help of these bags, we can achieve it."

Everyone listened, not expecting a humble backpack to carry such significance.

"In Umberland, we'll be fighting in dense forests and mountainous terrain. Relying on horses, donkeys, or oxen for our supplies will limit our speed, choice of routes, and more importantly, our ability to conceal movements. It also exposes our vital grain supplies to the enemy," Lansius explained.

The idea that someone might try to take their hard-earned grain away incensed the Nicopolans. The trauma from their hunger under Sergio's rule would take years to heal.

"Now, imagine if everyone carried their own supplies," he ventured. "It would free us to move wherever we want, climb steep hills, or traverse forests without concern for our supply line. Yes, it's tiresome, but it's doable. It's nothing compared to the backbreaking work of tending to crops."

Nods of agreement came from the circular formation around him.

With everyone's attention, Lansius continued. "Each person should carry spare clothes, a blanket, warm attire, foot wraps, and flour. Depending on their group, they're also to share tent gear, along with a cauldron, cooking utensils, medicine, and other mending tools."

The men were surprised at the volume of items they were expected to carry, items that would otherwise typically be loaded onto the group's dedicated donkey or mule.

Noticing the men's reluctance, the lord added, "This practice is well-known in my birthplace. A trained man will carry a bag twice this size, filled to the brim with food, water, and equipment, allowing him to march independently of any supply line for weeks."

Now, it was the command staff's turn to nod their heads. They were the ones who truly understood how such mobility and freedom of movement could impact warfare.

By not being tethered to a slow-moving supply line, a group could more easily set up ambushes, move faster to secure advantageous positions, impede the enemy's movement, or flank them unexpectedly. Along with the mobile dragoon forces, this agility and freedom would prove invaluable when utilized correctly and with synergy.

"This setup also enables you to cook and survive on your own if you get lost, or if need be, when we are defeated and you find yourselves in a rout," the lord added, ever so casually.

The notion of facing defeat spurred protests from the men. After the initial shock, expressions of warm support poured in.

"We're with you, my lord. There won't be a rout with you in the lead," one shouted.

"We might not be Korelians, but the Nicopolans will prove their worth in battle." Another man beside Servius voiced his determination.

Lord Lansius offered a stiff smile. As he chose not to intervene, Sir Harold stepped forward and, with a single loud clearing of his throat, managed to silence the men.

"Gratitude, sir," Lord Lansius said to his knight. Then, addressing his men, he continued, "Gentlemen, there's no harm in discussing defeat. Just like fear, we must embrace and understand it. Do you know that defeat and retreat are the greatest strategies of them all?"

The lord's unexpected question caused everyone to ponder. To them, defeat and retreat was such a taboo that nobody dared speak of them. The noblemen were especially sensitive to these words, fearing they would destroy morale or lessen the men's bravery.

Yet, ever unorthodox, Lord Lansius broached the subject of defeat and retreat with a straight face and calm demeanor. Expectation and anticipation ran high; many believed the lord aimed to impart something valuable for the upcoming campaign.

CHAPTER 38

GREAT GENERAL

En-route to Three Hills

Lansius climbed atop a horse-drawn cart to make himself more visible. Despite wearing only a simple white doublet and a wicker hat on his head, the lord had a commanding presence. "Gentlemen, let me tell you a little secret: defeat or losing a battle is not the end."

His words of simple truth echoed, meeting with various reactions.

He pressed on, explaining, "I have studied how great nations in the past have prevailed despite losing major battles again and again. You might not know this name, but to me, it's as close as home. In Trebia, 20,000 lost their lives; in Trasimene, another 20,000; and in Cannae, 70,000. They were disasters, yet the nation not only survived but prevailed!"

The claim put everyone in either shock or disbelief; they had never imagined a kingdom could survive such disasters without collapsing.

"The Imperium is no different," Lansius pointed out. "The western part and the Centuria province have faced defeat after defeat for more than twenty years against the western nomads, yet the Imperium is still standing."

The men nodded in unison, finding similarities between the two and feeling rather proud of it.

Raising his voice, Lansius called, "Fellow Lowlandians and Nicopolans. Let their resilience be our lesson. Do not fear defeat, for true defeat lies only when you cower in fear and give up."

Even with doubt painted on their faces, the men voiced no rejection.

Lansius followed with an analysis: "Defeat in battle is but a condition when multiple unexpected things happen all at once. Failure to learn about the enemy's superior force is one of the usual factors, followed by failure to acknowledge our own troops' situation and morale. Bear in mind, courage is a fickle thing. One moment you feel brave, the next, you feel tired and would prefer running over fighting."

Like a good mentor, Lansius calmly surveyed his students. "Other factors might relate to the physical situation. While terrain can be scouted, rain or snow remains beyond our ability to predict. Then there's the role of equipment—whether we've carried the right tools for the job, thick woolen blankets and socks for winter, waxed leather for rainy days, or long pikes to counter cavalry."

Everyone nodded in agreement with the lord's assessment.

"And last, provisions: flour for bread, grains for gruel, cheese, fat, blood sausages—everything. Without food, defeat is almost guaranteed. However, one defeat does not equate to losing everything. Remember the Imperium and its resilience."

Audrey intrigued, raised her hand. "My lord, then how should we react when defeated?"

"Good troops should act like fighters. Even when beaten down, you should never give up and must stand up again."

Audrey nodded; the analogy to a fighter was easy to understand.

Lansius looked at the rest of his men and decided to gamble on a lesson. "I do not fear defeat. And as such, I do not fear Umberland."

The unexpected bold words made the men's faces brighten with smiles and grins.

However, Lansius raised his hand to recapture their attention. "Yet, it's what comes after Umberland that I fear."

Seeing puzzled looks from the men and staff, Lansius elaborated. "If you do as I've instructed, and if the fair weather holds, conquering Umberland will not be too difficult. However, taking Umberland means facing refugees, armed or not. How should we answer them? With open arms or with unsheathed swords?"

Grim expressions appeared on everyone's faces.

The issue wasn't new or groundbreaking; the Nicopolans had suspected such a situation would arise, pitting them against another group of Nicopolans, but they had never given it real thought until now.

"For certain, Lowlandia has no more grain to spare. And you know I'm not lying about it. You farmed it yourself in South Hill."

A heavy silence fell until Servius raised his hand to interrupt.

"Speak." Lansius motioned.

"My lord, may we learn what your plan for Umberland is?" Servius asked.

Lansius gazed warmly at the older gentleman who prided himself as a condottiere leader. "Unfortunately, that answer I do not possess," Lansius admitted without hesitation. "I can only promise that I'll do my utmost to make a decision that we won't regret."

The words of reassurance helped to pacify the Nicopolans' worries.

Just then, Sterling stepped forward, offering a cup of water to the lord. After a brief pause to drink, Lansius turned back to his men. "All this talk about war, defeat, and strategy might sound confusing."

He garnered smirks and chuckles from the men around him.

"A long time ago, a wise man wrote that war isn't hard. He also said that victory is easy, but defeat is never easy. And I wholeheartedly agree with him."

Everyone watched with raw anticipation. For the poorest of Nicopolans who had made it this far, just to be in the presence and witness this exchange was already the highlight of their lives. They would cherish this memory like an heirloom.

"Reflecting on it, in strategy, we understand that a good lord or general knows how to win, but a great one knows how to retreat."

The words puzzled his men, and murmurs erupted. Some quickly agreed and nodded, while others looked skeptical and shook their heads.

Fully expecting such a reaction, Lansius waited patiently until they calmed down. "Tell me, who is the better general, one who retreated twice and lost half his troops, or one who retreated ten times and lost only a quarter of his troops?"

The question sparked realization among his staff members and their men.

"Everyone can lead an attack. Any one of you can take a group of brave youngsters and attack a bandit hideout. Ensuring you have more men than the bandits isn't complex planning. However, what about organizing a retreat in order? What about retreating without causing a rout? Is any one of you capable of doing that?"

Understanding dawned on the men's faces. Even Audrey, Sir Harold, and Servius nodded openly.

"A proper retreat is the hardest maneuver to learn. The best general is not one who could win wars, but one who could retreat without damaging his troops. He then could regroup and attack at a better time and place."

Witnessing the nodding heads, Lansius continued. "If one can achieve this, then even after facing a dozen defeats, he would eventually emerge victorious. This is what I wanted to achieve."

Despite its audacity, the statement held an undeniable truth, and the men were swayed further.

"Gentlemen, I don't mind losing battles, and I want you to maintain the same mindset," Lansius declared, trying to instill seeds of fearlessness in his men. "No one under my banner should fear losing, defeat, or retreat. Our only goal is to win the war! So, cast aside your fears. Trust that even in defeat, we will prevail."

Servius turned around to face his comrades, feeling their resolve in the air, and shouted, "You heard what the lord said. No matter what, we will prevail!"

A thunderous chorus of responses erupted from the men. Spears and shields banged in a cacophony of agreement.

"Ever victorious!" one roared, followed by another's cry of "Unstoppable!" Others chimed in with their own battle cries, a wave of fervor washing over the ranks.

Lansius watched the reactions with a wide smile, adjusting his wicker hat due to the heat while waiting for the commotion to subside. "Fellow comrades-in-arms, now you've heard of my troubles and learned more secrets of warfare."

His men happily nodded in agreement.

"The burden of planning and governing is mine to shoulder; let my staff and I take care of it. Meanwhile, all I ask of you is to shoulder a different kind of burden."

Most knew what the lord was hinting at, and smirks and chuckles formed on their lips.

Lansius took another bag from the cart and held it up. "This will help us achieve victories. Learn to use it, train with it, depend on it, and soon we will show the world what rapid marches are."

Just as parents reveal their burdens and business to their children to foster understanding, Lansius employed a similar psychological method to influence his troops. He openly shared the grim challenges and responsibilities he faced, compelling them to recognize the gravity of their situation. This, in turn, made them more cooperative and less inclined to resist demands and changes than usual.

Achieving their compliance was precisely Lansius's goal. He aimed for his troops to quickly adapt to marching with backpacks.

There was no doubt that it could be done. The real challenge lay in convincing them.

Historically, although Roman legionaries marched with their bags, the Medieval army, due to its tradition and training, was generally unwilling to carry the burdens on their backs. Instead, they depended on donkeys, mules, or solely on the lord's baggage train for sustenance.

Lansius considered this approach too far from ideal, as it placed significant burden on his limited logistical capabilities. Furthermore, it compromised his troops' mobility, since medieval horse-drawn carts and unpaved roads were inadequate. While they could navigate the Lowlandia steppes, Umberland would be a different game.

He understood that he must either transform his troops or face continuous difficulties in the future. Thus, while marching in peace to Three Hills, Lansius had decided to take action.

Although it seemed like a straightforward task, he was aware of the historical resistance from the military. Even the Romans, who initiated this practice, faced strong resistance. The reforms enacted by Gaius Marius led people to openly mock the new army as *Marius's mules*, because the legionaries were now carrying their supplies instead of relying on mules.

However, this change allowed the new army to move rapidly without depending on roads or favorable terrain. It enabled them to march farther, venture beyond the Roman road network, and set up ambushes in unforeseen locations. After securing a great victory, no Roman ever questioned the benefits of soldiers carrying their own rations.

Fortunately, Lansius's situation was much better. He had demonstrated just how effective a leader he was: capable and also compassionate, thus making his troops more agreeable.

"If the lord wishes us to become his mules, so be it," many complied with minimal complaint.

Others felt content carrying their own supplies, thinking that, even if they were defeated or in retreat, they could still survive with the food on their backs.

As they prepared to resume their march, further instructions came from the chain of command. First, they focused on how to properly load and manage the straps across their shoulders and torsos. Second, the lord required each person to carry at least a week's worth of food. Additionally, depending on their group, each member was also responsible for sharing the burden of the group's essentials, including the canvas tent, bedrolls, ropes, cauldron, and even a wooden pole.

Carrying this load, especially in gambeson or ringmail, was a heavy burden, but they trusted their lord's judgment that it was achievable. Moreover, they were eager to meet the lord's expectations, especially since he was leading by example, marching also on foot.

True to his word, Lord Lansius, flanked by his most trusted men and following a signal from a buccina, led the march. With his bags loaded, a shield in his left hand, a spear in the other, and his helmet strapped to his chest, the lord marched steadfastly.

Watching him, all remaining doubts dissipated, and soon, three thousand men and camp followers, arranged in multiple columns, followed. They were trying hard not to disappoint the lord, who in their minds was a better leader than any nobles they ever knew.

Lansius

This is more tiresome than I expected . . .

But no matter, better a little pain here than paying the blood price.

It had been a good one-hour march, and Lansius felt it in his feet, hips, and shoulders. However, he found solace in the distance they covered. Compared to before, they were progressing faster.

As they marched, Lansius kept a watchful eye on his surroundings, aware of his cavalry on either side of his flanks and front.

Under Sir Harold, the dragoons were to keep a perimeter in case something went undetected by the layers of forward scouts.

The sound of a horse trotting from the side alerted him. The horse and rider approached until exactly at his right side, providing Lansius with good shade from the sun. He gazed at the rider and, unsurprised, found his wife on the saddle.

"It's been an hour," Audrey commented.

"I can still go for another three," Lansius quipped, much to the chuckle of his men around him.

"My lord, you can leave this training and bag demonstration to us," Sterling chimed in.

"I'm sure everyone wouldn't mind. You've shown us more than enough that it's doable," Servius added.

"Shall I fetch the horse, my lord?" Farkas, the hunter turned minstrel, offered.

"No, it's good exercise. Otherwise, I'll be getting weak," Lansius responded lightly.

His men chuckled. Meanwhile, Audrey gazed at Sterling. "Squire," she called.

"Yes, my lady." Sterling approached her.

Audrey didn't say anything but gave him two waterskins, obviously for Lansius's needs. Then back at Lansius, she said, "Since you won't let me march on foot for some reason, at least allow me to provide you with some shade."

He let out a wide grin, followed by the chuckles of his men.

"The lord marches under the auspices of his great wife," Farkas quipped, garnering laughter from them.

"No shame in it, for my wife is indeed great," Lansius praised. "And it's always good to march under shade, be it from the clouds or from a benevolent wife."

His men chuckled again. The joy gave them respite from the monotony of marching.

Audrey let out a sigh, but a smile formed on her lips. "You're not born Arvenians or Lowlandians, yet the stubbornness is the same."

Lansius had no response but to chuckle.

Watching the lord said nothing, Farkas quipped, "But my lady, you're also not born Midlandians, yet you're prettier than most of the ladies in Lubina Castle."

Audrey raised her brow and retorted, "I heard you're Korelia born and never left the city. Then how can you tell that I'm prettier than the ladies in the Midlandia court? Who taught you all these, Sigmund?"

"Indeed, my lady, Captain Sigmund has convinced me as he has confirmed it with his own eyes. Your face, your waist, your form—"

Lansius deliberately cleared his throat, stopping Farkas from continuing a popular ballad.

Servius tapped the minstrel's shoulder. "Perhaps, it isn't a bright idea to woo your baron's wife."

"Does the new minstrel wish to lose an eye or have a shorter tongue?" Sterling teased to add more pressure.

"I assure you that I didn't mean—" Farkas tried to explain nervously, thinking he had overstepped, but Lansius raised his hand to stop him.

"Farkas, I think now's the time," the lord said rather ominously.

"The time? What time, my lord?" Farkas asked nervously.

Next to him, Sterling made a not-so-subtle throat-slitting gesture.

Lansius chuckled at his staff's antics. Their way of welcoming a new staff member was unprofessional, yet it fostered camaraderie. "Farkas, I'm sure Sigmund has taught you about my request."

"Ah, the marching song?" the minstrel turned bright.

"Indeed, I think the time is right. Let's see if we can march farther with the help of a song."

Farkas raised his hand to gather his subordinates, the so-called Black Bandits unofficially, though the name fit, as the rhymes they made were also rebellious in nature.

Farkas started the cadence, quickly garnering attention.

"Citizens, watch your wives, we say,
Black-haired rogue's coming your way!
Lion's gold from White Lake's day,
Stashed away, oh stashed away!"

Then, his men in bright clothes joined in the chorus.

"He's the Black Lord, strong and bold,
Vanquished foes on steppes so cold.
From Korimor to South Hill's hold,
Triumphs now in tales retold!"

Encouraged by the joy on the men's faces, Farkas continued.

"Western lords, they felt his might,
All three armies lost the fight.
Omin, Sergio, Gunther's plight,
Faced our lord and lost their right."

His fellow minstrels then sang the last part.

"Into Umberland, we march with pride,
Lowlandians by the Black Lord's side.
Shepherd's tunics we've set aside,
For bright doublets, worn with pride!"

Hearing this for the first time, Lansius chuckled to mask his embarrassment. Everyone around them chuckled too, finding it vulgar but unapologetically refreshing.

"That's a lively song," Audrey commented with a grin.

"Sigmund is really one crazy bastard," Lansius muttered. Yet, he noticed the men naturally catching on to the lyrics and beginning to ask for more.

Before long, his column marched to the lively song. Then the column next to it started to learn the song, followed by another column.

By daybreak, three songs had circulated and were well-loved by the men.

While Lansius felt slightly embarrassed by the lyrics, which aggrandized him, he couldn't deny the results.

"We've camped farther than planned?" he inquired of his scout as his command tent was being erected.

"Yes, my lord. We've not stopped at the planned site. This is the spot we intended to reach by midday tomorrow."

Lansius grinned and chugged from his waterskin. "Then in two days, we'll probably be dining in Three Hills City."

CHAPTER 39

NIGHTFALL'S GUEST

For tyrants, no sensation surpasses the thrill of wielding power over others and seeing their commands carried out. Yet, this intoxicating sense of control is exclusive to the tyrant. For everyone else, this concentration of power and its rampant abuse proves to be detrimental, even to those closest to the despot. This dynamic makes the situation perilous for all involved.

The inherent human desire for freedom means that inevitably, all those under the tyrant's rule seek to break free, striving to overthrow the despot. Ironically, this often leads to them becoming the new tyrants, perpetuating a never-ending cycle of power and resistance.

Despite a similar concentration of power, the situation in House Lansius was strikingly different.

After a grueling two-day march, burdened with heavy bags, the troops caught sight of the outer walls of Three Hills City, arriving almost three days ahead of schedule. Despite their exhaustion and discomfort, the group was buoyed by smiles and laughter, astonished at their own marching speed.

For them, there was no greater validation for the lord's plan than the outcome itself. Moreover, there was no greater feeling for the troops than knowing the ones in power were thoroughly competent in their planning and decision-making.

While power was concentrated in one individual in both scenarios, House Lansius's volunteer-based army presented a stark contrast to that of a tyrant's household.

The men were not fearful but were instead grateful and appreciative of the opportunity to serve under such a competent commander. Furthermore, Lansius's approach to leadership was distinct from that of a tyrant. Before implementing any major changes, he spent time explaining his plans to his men, convincing them with sound reasoning and arguments, and even leading by example.

The troops felt they were in good hands, governed not with a leash and whip but by wise counsel and a guiding hand.

Now, with the sun low on the horizon, the vanguard had reached the city, where formalities ensued between the officers. More surprisingly, when the main army arrived, they were greeted by a sea of tents just outside the city wall.

"No need to pitch tents today," many exclaimed excitedly, pleased with the arrangement.

Soon, there were arrangements for a feast from the Lord of Three Hills, welcoming the victorious army from their conquest of South Hill.

Externally, everything seemed to progress flawlessly. However, the machinations behind the scenes were more complicated.

While Lansius had allowed the Nicopolans to sleep in tents outside the city wall, he instructed his dragoons to camp farther away in a much safer location. Even in the failing light, Servius and Farkas were building a security network of scouts as their eyes and ears.

The lord had commanded that he wanted no surprises, and while Lord Jorge was friendly, there was no guarantee that the rest of the Three Hills nobility was in line with their lord.

A woman in traveling attire entered the command tent. "My lord, my lady," she greeted quickly.

"Lady Daniella, it's good to see you again," Audrey replied, seated beside Lansius, who slouched, looking too weary to engage.

"My apologies, the preparations I made were not adequate. I had anticipated two more days before the army's arrival."

"No, that's not on you," the lord muttered. "You could even claim that it's because of your efforts that we arrived early."

"I never expected that equipping an army with bags would yield such results," Daniella mused.

Lansius looked as though he was about to explain something but changed his mind at the last moment. Instead, he drew a deep breath and rested his head on a folded chair with supple, cushioned head support—one of the luxuries he had acquired from the last war.

Seeing Lansius so fatigued, Audrey decided to play his part. "Dame, you mentioned the preparations were inadequate. Yet, we've seen tents erected for the army, a feat I believe was orchestrated by you?"

"Indeed, my lady, but the accommodation must be insufficient. Isn't that why, my lord and lady, didn't sleep in the provided tents?"

Lansius mumbled something, and Audrey smiled understandingly. "Yes, I'm aware. Let me handle this."

Turning to Daniella, Audrey explained, "We decided to camp here for security reasons. Lord Jorge's failure to provide aid or support for our campaign to South Hill has led us to question his motives."

"But my lady, the Lord of Three Hills sent words of congratulations, which I believe I forwarded to you through Sterling."

"Indeed, we received such a message from Sterling, but it arrived only after our victory, not before."

Daniella nodded, understanding the situation. "I regret my inability to fulfill my role. I couldn't rally the council of Three Hills to our cause."

Audrey offered a stiff smile. "Don't blame yourself. Even the lord believes Three Hills' politics might be too intricate for anyone, even for Lord Jorge. This is why we let the main army camp closer to town while the cavalry and command structure stayed farther away."

Daniella nodded deeply. In contrast to Lansius's previous approach, which kept his troops away from Three Hills to avoid disrupting the city, he now camped his main army directly outside the city gates, a visible show of force likely aimed at the nobles who might be deluded into thinking they could still do as they pleased.

"It's a wise move," Daniella said, then added, "I apologize for not thinking that far ahead and not being cautious enough."

"Don't be. Perhaps we're simply overreacting, but the lord felt it was better to be prepared. Even with a large army, we shouldn't become overconfident."

Daniella could only nod again.

"Well, how about your other reports?" Audrey inquired.

"Yes, my lady, the dealings for grain are—"

Lansius's snore suddenly caught everyone's attention. With smiles and grins, they motioned to end the meeting, allowing their lord to rest without interruption. For his retinue, the politics in Three Hills held little significance, as their loyalty was squarely with Lansius himself.

Outside the command tent, Audrey gestured for Daniella to walk with her.

"Please excuse the lord. The march has left him utterly exhausted."

"Understandably, fast riding indeed wears on the body."

"The lord wasn't riding," Audrey corrected gently.

Daniella furrowed her brow for a moment before her expression turned to one of surprise. She had connected the dots on how the lord could convince the troops to march faster while carrying heavy bags. "My lady, it's unthinkable that the lord would march on foot."

Audrey chuckled. "He insisted on inspiring his men. And he didn't just march. Like everyone else, he also carried one of the bags you procured."

Daniella shook her head in disbelief, yet her grin was undeniable. "It seems the lord continues to do the unexpected."

"For a good reason. After today, no one can deny the results."

"Indeed." The dame then shared what was on her mind, "Perhaps this is what the wise mean when they talk about the mark of a good leader."

"Undoubtedly," Audrey affirmed. "The lord confided in me that it's ideal to lead by example. He always advised never to demand of your men what you wouldn't do yourself."

"One should never ask another to bear a weight one is not prepared to lift oneself," Daniella echoed, citing her mentor's words.

Audrey nodded, then stopped to face Daniella directly. "One question."

It was a brief statement, but Daniella understood from Audrey's gaze that it carried significant weight. "Please, my lady. As a knight of Korimor, command me," Daniella said, kneeling before her in the middle of the camp, conscious of the onlookers.

Audrey grabbed her arm and helped her to her feet. Unlike Lansius, who was unaccustomed to such formalities, Audrey was more prepared for her role. Without missing a beat, she asked, "Do you trust Lord Jorge?"

Daniella answered without hesitation, "I trust him as a person, but not his judgment or his cohorts. However, I might be biased, having worked with him before serving Lord Lansius."

Audrey valued her candor. Then acting on her own judgment, she suggested, "Perhaps, it might be wise for Lord Jorge to act to regain Lord Lansius's favor."

"Leave it to me, my lady. I'll do my utmost," Daniella pledged, inspired by the lord's willingness to march with the men.

Dragoons' Camp

After ensuring that everything was in order and that Sir Harold, along with the last of the supply train, had joined the camp, Audrey returned to the main tent. Her hair was awash in the light of the golden sunset, momentarily casting her in the visage of a noble northern queen. The look was so captivating that Carla paused her chores just to stare at her master.

Audrey quickly noticed and returned her gaze.

"My lady," Carla greeted her hurriedly, realizing her lapse.

"Has the lord awoken?" Audrey inquired, walking toward the inner part of the large command tent.

"Yes, my lady. I have also brought the meals for you both," replied Carla, following behind her.

"Gratitude. You should take a break and go eat," Audrey suggested.

Carla silently bowed her head and retreated to a corner near the entrance, where she could dine in peace while still keeping watch over the tent.

Meanwhile, Audrey entered the inner section and was greeted by Lansius with a casual "Yo."

His carefree attitude brought a smile to her face. "Feeling better?" Audrey asked, hanging up her traveling cloak.

"Yeah, a bit. Oh, sorry for falling asleep earlier. I hope Dame Daniella wasn't mad or anything."

"There's no need to worry. Everyone is grateful. Because of you, we arrived in Three Hills faster than expected. The men are highly motivated and proud of this achievement," Audrey said, changing into fresh attire.

Feeling his gaze on her, she looked back at him, catching his look of admiration. "But you're exhausted," she reminded him.

"Duty never ends," Lansius quipped, sending Audrey into giggles.

"You should carry fewer goods in the bags. You're not a mule."

"Well, Sterling also carried a lot, and he just had his leg fixed. I can't do less than him."

"And you claim I'm the stubborn one," she remarked with a grin.

Lansius smiled and gestured for her to sit. "Come, let's eat before the stew gets cold."

Audrey quickly finished changing into a loose black tunic and took a seat on a small folded chair. She broke her bread and dipped it into the stew.

The aroma of the stew and bread mixed with the sweet scent of honey wax—a distinction from the nobles' quarters from lesser establishments that used tallow-based candles.

They ate in peace. The rigors of marching and leading had been so taxing that the quietness became something to cherish. Without needing to say anything, he offered her a forkful of tenderly boiled vegetables, glistening with a hint of butter. She, in turn, passed him a slice of crusty bread, richly slathered with young cheese.

Only after they were half-full did Audrey speak up, "You seem to enjoy marching. But I hope you'll reconsider. Umberland is still another eight to nine days away."

"It shouldn't be that far," Lansius replied thoughtfully. "Servius mentioned it's closer than what the map conveyed, though the roads are poor and the terrain steep."

Audrey gave no response, choosing instead to continue with her meal.

Lansius drank from his goblet of water and suddenly admitted, "Don't tell anyone, but I regret my decision to walk."

The admission and shift in tone made Audrey giggle, and Lansius couldn't resist joining her.

"Oh, Lans, I told you—"

"You know me; I'm used to walking everywhere, but damn, those bags can carry a lot."

Audrey put her plate on the table, unable to resist laughing. Lansius, too, laughed at himself.

Afterward, she rose and proceeded to hug him. "My dear poor husband. Next time, you should be riding next to me. I'll figure out some excuse."

Lansius chuckled. "No need for an excuse. It was a demonstration, not a new routine, at least not for the command staff."

She returned to her spot and said, "You should get more rest. I'll take care of the camp."

"Has Sir Harold—"

"Done. We have all the supply train accounted for."

"Excellent. And the night watch?"

"No need to worry. Since we camped with the dragoons, everyone is relatively fresh."

Lansius nodded, pleased. "That's great to hear. I don't feel like doing anything but sleeping."

"I bet. You must be aching all over," Audrey ventured.

Lansius squinted his eyes and asked, "You don't look surprised?"

Audrey smiled. "You reminded me of my first hunting expedition. Wearing ringmail everywhere inside a forest, trying to keep up with Isolte. I still remember vomiting my breakfast and lunch."

Lansius chuckled at hearing that.

"It's good that you didn't vomit."

"I'm not that weak anymore. Just a bit surprised by the weight."

Audrey finished her meal and said, "Anyway, you should be proud. The troops were celebrating this fast march. They liked it and came to understand their newfound ability."

Lansius chuckled. "Well, we cheated somewhat. I told Sir Harold to guard the slower supply carts so we could advance faster."

"Yet, you have proven that rapid march is achievable."

Lansius nodded while slurping more of his vegetable stew.

"I think you'd do better with duck egg broth," she suggested.

Lansius swallowed and looked her dead in the eyes. "No duck egg," he stated briefly but firmly.

Audrey grinned at his reaction. "How about if I spoon-feed you?"

"Interesting idea, but no." He shook his head.

They finished their meal and kept the leftover bread for next day, in case they encountered a late breakfast or someone got hungry at night.

As they prepared to rest, the conversation turned to their situation with their ally.

"The problem is Three Hills," Lansius stated. "I want to know where they stand . . . I wish I had someone as capable as the late Sir Callahan."

Audrey poured him some watered-down spiced wine to dull the aching. "The dame is trying hard. I'm sure she'll improve with experience."

Lansius mulled. "Maybe it's my fault. She's adept with army management, but diplomacy might not be her forte."

"I'm afraid we have no one else, especially not one with experience. Unless you're considering recruiting Lord Robert."

"Ah, the Lion of Lowlandia," Lansius said with respect.

Noticing his tone, Audrey suggested, "Perhaps it's time to summon Sir Michael."

"Oh, I've heard he's newly wed. I wouldn't want to bother him."

Audrey sighed deeply and quipped, "Yet our honeymoon has been ruined. You owe me another."

"Tonight is as good a day as any to start. Let's call Carla for some mead," Lansius quipped back.

Audrey chuckled at his audacity and retorted, "I doubt you're up for much with those sore legs."

Before they could continue, a voice announced, "My lord, my lady, an important guest has arrived."

Audrey cleared her throat, while Lansius rose and stepped outside to greet Carla, asking, "Who is the guest?"

"It's Lady Daniella, my lord."

Lansius furrowed his brow. "Why is she here again? Did something happen?"

"Ah, she has returned," Audrey commented, as if she had been expecting her.

"My lord, she's brought someone else with her."

From Carla's tone, Lansius sensed the importance, quickly donned his doublet, and headed to the entrance. Audrey followed.

"Is our staff with them?" Audrey asked as they walked.

"Sterling and Sir Harold are with them," the squire informed them.

At the entrance, they saw Lady Daniella, Sir Harold, Sterling, and a figure in a brown hooded robe.

"My lord, my lady," Lansius's retinue greeted, while the robed figure revealed a handsome face with lighter brown hair.

Lansius gasped, "Lord Jorge."

The Lord of Three Hills offered a stiff smile and greeted him. "Lord Lansius, it's good to see you in person again." The air crackled with anticipation. His unexpected presence undoubtedly heralded a shift in the status quo. Lowlandia was on the brink of change, and nothing would be the same anymore.

CHAPTER 40

MASTERS OF THREE HILLS

Dragoon's Camp

At Dame Daniella's urging, the Lord of Three Hills had traveled incognito to meet with the leader of the Grand Alliance. His arrival signaled the winds of change to the status quo. Doubts within Lansius's camp about Lord Jorge were quickly dispelled, placing the initiative firmly in his hands.

"My lord, why are you here?" Lansius approached Jorge, with Audrey following behind him.

The honored guest offered a broad smile and declared, "I'm here to show my sincerity."

Lansius glanced at the entrance. "I don't see your escort."

Hearing that, Jorge chuckled. "Lord Lansius, you're not the only one with bold ideas," he retorted, eliciting a polite chuckle from Lansius.

Knowing his counterpart still had questions, Jorge clarified, "I came here of my own volition. I don't need an escort; I have your protection after all. I doubt anyone would dare harm someone under the Lord of Korelia's protection."

Lansius smiled and responded, "Your words are too kind." Then, noticing his staff had arranged seats and a table, he quickly motioned for Jorge to be seated. "Please, my lord."

"After you, my lord, my lady," Jorge replied.

The three sat simultaneously, and Carla promptly served everyone pale ale. Lansius took the initiative and drank first to assure his guest of the ale's safety.

Jorge nodded and took a sip from his silver goblet.

Meanwhile, the rest of the staff were watching from a distance. Sir Harold and Sterling were whispering with Dame Daniella, likely inquiring about the current situation. They understood that when the time came, their lord would seek their advice and opinions.

After they had taken their drinks, Audrey spoke up. "Have you eaten, my lord?"

"Indeed I have, my lady. Thank you for the offer," Jorge replied with a dazzling smile. While most ladies would be charmed, Audrey's attention was focused on ensuring the guest didn't carry any concealed weapons.

"It's time I explain my visit," Jorge began. "I'm here to apologize for my court's indecisiveness. We have factions, some of which, I must admit, probably still wish me dead."

"I'm not sure it's that dire," Lansius replied with concern.

Jorge appreciated the concern. "This is why I came without an escort. I want you to know I wholeheartedly support the Grand Alliance, despite my court being filled with people who resist change."

Lansius nodded deeply.

"However, that should no longer be an issue," Jorge hinted.

Audrey and Lansius exchanged glances, prompting Audrey to ask, "Is there a breakthrough?"

"I want to say yes, but it's going to take more time. The way my lord has stationed your troops outside the wall hasn't gone unnoticed. However, my court tends to be overly slow to decide, which could make matters worse. Thus, I decided to act on my own," Jorge said.

"What kind of act?" Lansius asked cautiously.

The noble guest hesitated at first before explaining, "After the Battle of Korelia, my House's grip on power has weakened. As I've said before, my council fears a coup. Worse, Sir Arius is currently defending against a Nicopolan incursion, and the few Black Knights stationed in the city are stretched thin."

Lansius took a deep breath, acknowledging the situation.

"If I send troops to join your campaign, they'll be my loyalists. We believe the opposing factions will wait for this opportunity, especially if you purchase a significant amount of grain. Even after the harvest, the food situation hasn't returned to normal, and I fear a large purchase might spell trouble for the populace. That would be the right moment for them to instigate a coup."

"A coup while you're at your weakest and lacking popular support," Lansius summarized.

"Exactly," Jorge exclaimed, seemingly unworried.

While Lansius pondered, Jorge declared, "Thus, I feel it would be better to declare my support and join this war in person."

Jorge's declaration surprised everyone. Audrey and the rest of the staff looked to Lansius, who stared at Jorge momentarily before gazing back at them. It was unexpected but a significant boon.

Lansius couldn't conceal his gratitude but remained wary. "My lord, why offer your support despite your predicament? Wouldn't this risk your House and family?"

The charming lord paused before stating softly, "This might trouble you, Lord Lansius, but I'm planning to take my family. We'll follow closely behind your main army. Consider us as a reserve or whatever you need."

"But, my lord, we're headed for battle. It will be dangerous," Audrey warned.

Jorge met her gaze, his gesture showing appreciation for her concern. "Here or there, my family and I are at risk." Then he turned his gaze back to Lansius. "Frankly, I'd rather be surrounded by my loyalists and allies, even on a battlefield. At least in there, I'll know who the enemy is."

Lansius closed his eyes briefly, masking his reaction. Then, putting his hand on the table, he rose, and extended a hand toward Jorge. "My lord, it would be an honor to have you and your family join our campaign."

Jorge, ecstatic, rose quickly and clasped Lansius's hand. "Shogun," he addressed Lansius, "then I am in your care."

"It is my duty," Lansius responded seriously, before adding with a lighter tone, "although I have some concerns that people might interpret this as me keeping you hostage."

"Nonsense. They will see it as two lords of Lowlandia uniting to address a serious threat," Jorge countered.

Lansius chuckled, nodding in agreement. He looked to Audrey, who also showed her support, while Sir Harold and Sterling voiced no objections.

As if on cue, Carla refilled everyone's goblets. Seizing the moment, Lord Jorge raised his silver goblet. "To Umberland. May we rescue the nobles still holding out there."

After the agreement was put on paper, Lord Lansius ordered Dame Daniella to summon Sir Morton to his camp. While waiting for the escort, Sir Harold entertained Lord Jorge with their detailed account of the South Hill campaign. Carla and Sterling were also there, assisting in taking care of their honored guest.

Meanwhile, Audrey conversed with Lansius on the inner side of the camp.

"Don't you fear that the opposing faction would deliver a coup while Jorge and all his loyalists are marching with us?"

Lansius drank from a goblet of water and massaged his temple. "Everything seems possible. I can't be sure." He leaned back in his chair and explained, "If the opposing faction is ambitious and stupid, then they'll do just that. However, if they're ambitious and smart, they'll wait for news of whether we're successful in Umberland before starting their plan."

"That's true." Audrey nodded in understanding. "Indeed, if we're successful, then I doubt they'll want to oppose us directly."

Lansius's gaze turned sharp, and he looked annoyed.

"Is that hatred I see on your face, darling?" Audrey quipped.

"I just don't like the way they play this game. All this risk of a coup while we're facing a big crisis. This is horseshit!"

"I can understand that. We're going to rely on Three Hills' support for our supplies." Audrey let out a sigh. "Then what are you planning to do?"

"That's the frustrating part," Lansius slumped in his seat. "Just like in South Hill, we have no evidence, only suspicion."

Audrey glanced at him before deciding to say, "I held back before, but I might need to remind you that this is Lowlandia." The firmness in her voice caught Lansius's attention. Audrey quickly added, "If you wait for evidence, by then, everything will be too late."

Lansius leaned forward in his seat, gaze locked with Audrey. "Do you want to strike first without evidence?"

Audrey knelt in front of him and said softly, "Sometimes, you're too inflexible for your own good."

"But punishing the wrong people could cause long-term resentment and spread the seeds of instability and rebellion," he explained.

Audrey let out a smirk. "I'm not saying to punish them."

"Then?"

"You know, you can just summon them and ask."

Lansius's brow furrowed momentarily before musing, "That is true. I can investigate them."

"That's not what I meant, but you're also correct. That's a role you can play. After all, every noble is also the local judge. Moreover, you're the leader of the Grand Alliance," she pointed out.

"That is true, it's within my jurisdiction." Then he gazed at Audrey, asking, "But what did you mean earlier?"

"Well, I'm trying to say that we don't have to make it too complex. We're dealing with subjects, not an army maneuvering into battle. Summon them, bring them out from the safety of their walls. Show them who's in charge. And then, we can see what kind of people they are."

Lansius nodded thoughtfully. "Iron fist in a velvet glove. This is a workable approach."

"Glad to be of help." Audrey then rose with a smile. "Then, if you come up with a plan, I'll be glad to hear it first."

As evening turned to morning in Three Hills City, the market sprang to life, buzzing with energy more than ever before. The lord of the city had granted Lansius's army free entry, attracting camp followers and off-duty troops into the city's welcoming arms. Despite the initial surprise and caution regarding the presence of a large army, the locals could not turn away the influx of customers, and so far, there had been no problems.

They flocked through the gates, their footsteps echoing on the cobblestones, drawn by the promise of leisure and commerce. Instead of fear, the atmosphere was charged with excitement and a sense of camaraderie. The aromas of fresh bread, spices, and smoked meats from the food stalls tantalized the nose.

Laughter and chatter filled the air, mixing with the calls of merchants hawking their wares—from shimmering fabrics to intricate trinkets that caught the morning light.

While most Nicopolans hadn't been paid as per their agreement in the fields of Korimor, they were given their share of plunder from their victories in South Hill. Although it wasn't a significant amount, it was more than enough for them to indulge themselves.

Many, having already secured what they needed in South Hill, chose to eat heartily. Others, in search of sturdier or correctly sized footwear, were drawn to Three Hills' renowned cobblers' alley. This bustling lane was lined with shops displaying boots of all sizes and styles, from repaired second-hand work boots to new, finely crafted riding boots. The air was rich with the smell of leather and wax, as cobblers and apprentices busied themselves with their craft, offering not just new footwear but also repairs and custom fittings to all who had cash in their pockets.

Meanwhile, behind closed doors, Lord Lansius's staff arrived early to purchase winter seeds for South Hill. The group, consisting of the city's biggest merchants, had entertained Dame Daniella and Sterling, who acted on their lord's behalf.

As soon as pleasantries were over, they got down to business. As they went through the list approved by the Lord of Korelia himself, the merchants were surprised to learn that Lord Lansius wasn't going to buy a lot of grain for the upcoming campaign.

"Just winter seeds? Not even flour for the upcoming campaign?" one of the merchants, clad in a silver fur coat, said with surprise.

Dame Daniella furrowed her brow, looked him in the eyes, and deftly replied, "We have enough grain and flour in South Hill. What made you think we need to purchase more?"

Another merchant, more plump but with better articulation, quipped, "Surely, it's a good approach to stock more food in case the campaign goes, say, unexpectedly?"

The dame smiled. "We have assurances from the Lord of Three Hills that the city's granary has enough if we need assistance. Furthermore . . ." She looked around to ensure they were the only ones in the chamber and no servant was in sight.

Her reaction prompted Sterling to head to the door, exit, and close it behind him. Noticing this, the merchants grew anticipatory.

"My lord has confided in me that the campaign will likely be a brief one," Daniella hinted.

The merchants shook their heads in utter disbelief. Many of them had thought to make a profit after learning that the Lord of Korelia was heading to Umberland. Due to the unexpected good harvest in Three Hills, they had quite a surplus this year. And because Lord Jorge's administration lacked effective oversight, many landowners retained a significant portion of the harvest for themselves, resulting in these surpluses ending up in the merchants' holdings.

Until now, they had kept this grain surplus to themselves to prevent prices from plummeting. Ironically, they had pinned their hopes on Lord Lansius to purchase their grain and get rid of the surplus. However, it turned out Lord Lansius had more than enough and that the campaign was only expected to be short.

"Unbelievable," one of the merchants commented weakly.

"But it's the Lord of Korelia we're talking about," the plump merchant joyously chortled.

Other merchants, both old and young, could only exhale nervously. Lady Daniella's presence prevented them from freely expressing their frustration.

Noticing their troubled looks, Dame Daniella offered a diplomatic suggestion. "Look, Lord Lansius is not only a good warlord; he's also a businessman at heart."

Her words attracted everyone's attention. They had heard rumors about the lord making sound business decisions and started to feel a bit of hope.

The dame continued. "I'm sure you've heard that Lord Lansius never treats merchants with contempt. He never confiscates merchants' wealth or gets jealous of their profits. He often says: profit makes the world go round."

"Not to offend you, Dame, but this sounds too good to be true," the plump merchant commented lightly.

"You can ask him yourself if you want. I think I can arrange for two people to meet the lord personally," she suddenly offered.

Everyone glanced at each other. The chance of meeting with the most powerful man in Lowlandia was a great opportunity.

The plump merchant stepped forward, locking gazes with his comrades, and declared, "As your representative, I will go—"

"Fat chance. You have no business that the lord will need," a wise-looking old man retorted. Turning to Daniella, he added, "Others here will, at best, be intermediaries. You would be better off inviting me, as I have—"

"Your product quality will embarrass us all, old man." The plump man's friend supported him.

"I am sure—" The plump man attempted to reclaim the discussion but was quickly silenced by his now rivals.

"The old man is right. Your selection of goods is even inferior to mine," another merchant interjected.

Then, another merchant stood, boldly declaring, "It is I who am fit to accompany the old man."

"Nonsense! You are not even a guild member!"

Dame Daniella let out a deep sigh as if troubled. However, in reality, this was exactly what she had wanted.

Dragoons' Camp

Since morning, Lansius's army of clerks and scribes, recruited from Korelia, Korimor, and now South Hill, had been working diligently. This was the first time they did not need to march, so they returned to their work, calculating, keeping records, making payments, and managing inventory.

They were the ones who worked tirelessly to ensure that everything was accounted for. Lansius's demand for year-round payments was making good record-keeping a necessity.

And they were the ones who made this possible. The corps, originally formed by Servius and Dame Daniella, was now under Lansius's supervision.

Their work and their lord's full support kept their troops in good shape. Desertion was minimal, even among the Nicopolans who had taken an oath at the plains of Korimor not to seek payment, in exchange for food, safety, and shelter.

After the victory in South Hill, Lansius instructed that payments be made to units that had proven themselves in combat. This was as much a reward as it was Lansius's strategy to maintain his influence over his men and ensure their loyalty. After all, as Lord Arte once told him: *People fight for their own interests. A man who asks for nothing cannot be trusted.*

While Lansius oversaw their work from afar, Sterling entered the tent. "My lord, my lady," he greeted.

"Ah, you've returned," Lansius said from his seat inside the command tent.

"The merchants' representative is here to see you."

"Well done. Was it difficult?" Lansius asked.

"Not at all. They're very pleased with this opportunity."

Lansius nodded, delighted. "Then, tell them to wait. I'll send word when I'm ready to receive them."

Sterling bowed his head and left the command tent.

Audrey took a sip from her goblet and said, "Let me handle this."

Lansius gazed at her. "Pardon . . . ?"

"You heard me," she replied lightly. "You don't need to do everything by yourself. Lady Daniella will be there, and since this is merely gossiping about the nobles and landlords, I'll be more than capable."

Lansius was surprised but pleased by her initiative. "You're a better reader of character than I am. I think you'll do just fine."

"Gratitude for the praise," Audrey smiled. "Then, when will I need to meet them?"

"Let them wait a little . . . We don't want to seem as if we're desperate to see them," Lansius explained. With that matter settled, he returned to his scrolls at the table, reviewing them. Audrey, too, returned to her reading—a compilation of wise words she had been trying to memorize to avoid looking like a country bumpkin in front of her subjects.

Just as they were about to take a break, Sir Harold entered the tent with an ominous tone. "My lord, my lady."

Lansius could sense trouble in his voice. "What's the matter?"

"It's the Black Knights' captain, Sir Morton. He's asked for a private audience," the tall knight explained.

"Sir Morton?" Lansius asked, turning to Audrey.

"I wasn't aware of this," she explained, then gazed at Carla.

"No one was, my lady. Yesterday, when he came with the guards to escort Lord Jorge to the city, he said nothing beyond pleasantries."

Lansius looked at his knight. "What do you think he wants from us?"

"I tried to pry, but he said it's a private matter," Sir Harold stated, without concealing his disdain.

Lansius glanced at Audrey, who nodded in understanding.

Rising from his seat, Lansius decided, "Well, we need to kill some time; might as well entertain Sir Morton." He then muttered to himself, "Oh feared Mage Knight, what tidings will you bring to us?"

CHAPTER 41

MENTOR

The Lord of Korelia's Camp

Sir Morton, the Black Knight captain, clad in a stylish black brigandine, was escorted to the lord's command tent. His request for an audience had been granted.

Walking at a leisurely pace and flanked by several guards, the Mage Knight entered the Lord of Korelia's command tent. "My lord, my lady, gratitude for granting me this opportunity," he said formally.

"Sir Morton, it's good to see you again," Lansius responded warmly.

Audrey added, "May we ask, for what reason do we have the pleasure of your presence today?"

"My lady, as I promised before in Korelia, I'll be introducing a good mentor."

Lansius and Audrey exchanged glances. Audrey nodded once, and Lansius motioned for his squires and guards to take a break.

When they hesitated, Audrey reassured them, "Go on, I'll be more than enough."

The guards and squires bowed their heads and exited the tent, joining the corps of scribes and clerks who had already taken a break from their duties.

Now alone, Lansius asked, "This mentor, is she a mage?"

Sir Morton answered, "The mentor will be under disguise; she always is. You can regard her as an educator, and none will suspect anything."

Lansius exhaled deeply, aware of Audrey's gaze on him. "Pardon me for being blunt, Sir Morton. But do we have any guarantee she will cause us no harm?"

"Unfortunately, only indirectly, my lord." The guest paused, gauging Lansius's reaction before explaining, "The Mage Guild seeks to foster good relations with a rising star of Lowlandia. They even wondered if my lord would become a patron in exchange for a mage in your service."

"So I am a potential client," he mused.

"I believe the guild wanted to be at your side, my lord."

Lansius nodded and turned to catch Audrey's glance. Despite her neutral expression, he understood her thoughts. "Very well, Sir Morton. Arrange for her to meet us, hopefully soon, as we are departing in two days."

"She's already in the city. It would be best if my lord wrote an invitation letter for her, so she could make her way here and introduce herself."

Lansius nodded, and Audrey stood, walking halfway to the entrance and calling for a scribe while keeping an eye on Sir Morton.

Instead of a scribe, Sir Harold dashed inside, hand on his hilt. "Yes? Oh, a scribe, just a moment," he said, managing a smile.

The Mage Knight smiled at this, commenting, "You have plenty of loyal men at your side."

"Gratitude and I apologize for my men's reaction."

"Think nothing of it, my lord."

As Audrey was dictating the invitation letter, Lansius suddenly asked his guest, "Tell me, what is she like?"

"I've only known her briefly, but she is among the most experienced in the guild."

Lansius leaned forward. "Sir Morton, I do not wish to sound rude, but are there any quirks, a short temper, or anything else I should be aware of?"

Sir Morton smiled. "She bears the demeanor of a mentor, not a fighter. Also, I've heard she wishes to retire to a vineyard and still needs quite a sum to achieve that."

Hearing such a hint, Lansius felt somewhat relieved. *At least now I know where her goal lies.*

Before midday, Sir Morton had returned to Three Hills City. His audience was brief, yet it sparked considerable gossip. While most speculated it was likely an official errand on behalf of the Lord of Three Hills, others speculated that the Mage Knight was on a mission of atonement for his actions in the Battle of Korelia, where he had slain the famed Sir Callahan.

While the dragoons and cavalry were busy gossiping during their downtime, Lady Audrey presided over a meeting with the merchant representative. No deal was to be made, just a simple meet and greet.

In the baroness's presence, Dame Daniella skillfully inquired about the nobles and landlords of Three Hills. With just a hint of encouragement from the lady and the aid of hard liquor, the merchants were more than willing to share their extensive knowledge of connections.

As she had little knowledge of Three Hills, Audrey relied on Daniella to cross-check the information she obtained from the merchants. The dame's stay and past dealings in Three Hills had been invaluable, as she already had a good understanding of the hierarchy of Three Hills' landlords and their factions.

Before midday, they had completed their meetings. With Lady Daniella by her side, they returned to Lansius to deliver their reports.

"So, what did you learn from the merchants?" Lansius eagerly asked.

"There are lots of knights and esquire families, but according to the merchants, only three stand out," Audrey began, then turned to Daniella. "I am sure the dame could explain more about them."

"Of course, my lady." Then to Lansius, Daniella reported, "They are, respectively, the moneylender, the winery, and the jeweler."

Lansius nodded. "I assume their profitable businesses enabled them to amass private lands for crops."

"Indeed, my lord. These three always show up when I talk about powerful nobles in the city besides the ruling House. The person who controls the winery is—"

Lansius raised his hand to stop Daniella. "It might sound odd, but in this process, the less I know, the better."

Daniella looked puzzled but nodded. Audrey chose to trust her instinct and listened attentively.

"From those three, which one is showing grand ambition?" Lansius asked.

Daniella pondered for a moment before admitting, "It is rather hard to tell."

"Which of them is currently building, or has recently completed, an opulent residence that rivals the lord's palace?" Lansius guided her. "Which one was mentioned by the merchant as wearing dresses to rival those of the nobles, or whom the merchants spoke of in high regard or with a hint of fear? Who among them exhibits jealousy toward the ruling class?"

Daniella paused, reflecting on her thoughts, before responding, "The House engaged in moneylending fits your criteria. The merchant shared tales of their family manor, lavish with fine marbles, bronze sculptures, and gold ornaments. I've also heard that their banquets are always decadent."

Lansius took a moment before asking, "Did the merchant describe the current House leader as smart and industrious?"

Daniella's eyes flickered, trying to recall the conversation. "Despite their fear of him, the merchants seem to regard him as a rich fool, one who fancies only leisurely pursuits like collecting horses and exotic foods."

"Ambitious, not bright, and lazy," Lansius profiled the moneylender House.

The two noted the three criteria Lansius mentioned.

"Then, what about the winery House?" he inquired.

Audrey decided to answer, "The winery House also shows some ambition. He is successful and keeps expanding the family business. The merchants talk about his new manor and vineyard."

Lansius squinted his eyes. "I was not aware that Three Hills has suitable land to grow grapes."

"They do not. Their vineyard is located farther from town, near the plateau that leads to the Umberland mountain pass," Audrey clarified.

"Ah," Lansius muttered. "So, the winery House leader is ambitious, smart, and industrious."

"He is probably the most competent of them all," Daniella agreed. "Well spoken, well connected, and people like him."

"You're implying he's the most dangerous one?" he asked.

"It might be just my intuition, but I believe he is the most influential and possibly the most likely candidate to lead a coup."

"Not so fast." Lansius broke a smile. "How about the last House?"

Daniella exchanged glances with Audrey before reporting, "We keep hearing that the jeweler House is the worst. The current head abandoned his training after his father's death and now only bothers with poetry, drinking, and gambling."

Lansius rubbed his chin in contemplation. "What do his peers say about him? Do we know anything about him being ambitious?"

Audrey pondered but shook her head. Daniella reacted the same and said, "We do not have any clue about his ambition."

Lansius crossed his arms, and Audrey ventured, "I daresay, he's not ambitious. The merchants seem to have nothing good to say about the man."

Hearing that, Lansius leaned back in his chair.

This prompted Audrey to ask, "Does that mean everyone with ambition poses a threat?"

"Not necessarily. It's just that people without ambition generally do not cause trouble," Lansius paused, then added, "Ambition is good when paired with intelligence." He looked at Dame Daniella. "Being ambitious, smart, and industrious are ideal traits for a command staff."

The dame blushed slightly at the praise but remained composed.

Turning back to Audrey, Lansius asked, "Based on the three criteria, who, in your opinion, poses the greatest danger among the three?"

"The moneylender House is ambitious, not intelligent, and lazy. It is a dangerous combination," Audrey assessed.

Lansius then turned his gaze to Daniella.

"The winery House is ambitious, intelligent, and industrious. I say he is the most dangerous," Daniella gave her view.

Lansius smiled. "Both views are valid. The jeweler poses the least concern, so indeed it's between the moneylender and the winery."

"Shall we summon them here?" Audrey proposed.

Exhaling deeply, he shook his head. "I think not. Ironically, inviting them here will give them more credence." He then turned to Daniella and instructed, "Work with Farkas, and try to get more information about these two Houses."

"Understood," she affirmed.

"Focus on the moneylender House," he added.

The two women raised their eyebrows. Noticing this, Lansius clarified, "I think our fear of the winery is mostly baseless. He might be ambitious, but he is also smart, and industrious. I see nothing wrong with that."

"Why focus on the moneylender then?" Daniella inquired.

"As the lady has said, the moneylender possesses a dangerous combination: ambitious, dumb, and lazy."

Daniella was puzzled. "Smart and industrious isn't dangerous, but dumb and lazy is?"

"A lazy fool without ambition will pose no danger. In fact, a happy fool like me is the fabric of society. We are naturally good subjects, perfect for farmers, servants, footmen, or any other roles."

Audrey chuckled upon hearing his quip.

"My lord, please don't belittle yourself like that," Daniella responded.

Lansius chuckled before turning serious, "However, laziness coupled with ambition is never a good mix. Such a person dreams of grandeur but is too lazy to put forth the real effort required to achieve it. They will look for shortcuts to success. Jealousy, lies, sabotage, and even coups become their tools of choice. We'll do well to protect our House from this kind of person."

Daniella nodded in agreement, and Audrey took it to heart.

"Find out if the moneylender House has in the past tried to arrange a marriage with House Jorge or any of its allies. Also, ascertain the extent of his forces. Does he wield any influence over the city's guards, or have clout with thugs and troublemakers? He'll need muscle if he wants to start a coup."

"My lord, collecting such information will take a lot of time," Daniella warned.

"Indeed," Lansius sighed. He knew he needed patience and time to solve this but had to march in two days. "I dislike this, but it seems this matter will remain unresolved by the time we depart."

Following Lord Lansius's instructions, Dame Daniella gathered information on the two Houses. Early reports revealed that the moneylender House was in its fifth generation of esquires. The current head was known for his ambition, often speaking about how well he could rule if he had been born a high noble.

More concerning was the news that his sister had once been offered to Sir Arius, but the arrangement fell through. Coupled with reports of a large number of armed men and influence in various sectors of the city guard, this information alarmed Lansius enough to assign additional men and equipment to Daniella.

Unexpectedly, Lord Jorge readily gave his permission, and it was decided that Daniella would not join the campaign to Umberland but would instead remain stationed in Three Hills with two hundred Nicopolans.

Lansius had hoped for a larger garrison but was cautious of risking the ire of the populace, who had yet to trust him fully. This situation could potentially be exploited by the perpetrator to rally the crowd against him.

On the last night before departure, Lansius wrote a letter to the money-lender, suggesting cooperation and proposing ideas for lending or banking services among Grand Alliance members.

"Do you think this will work?" Audrey asked after the scribe had left, leaving them with the important letter on the table.

"It's probably futile," Lansius admitted as he inspected the letter, finding it to be of high quality. "Such a man is unlikely to be intelligent and industrious enough to realize the potential. However, I hope it might distract the House enough to prevent them from launching a coup in Lord Jorge's absence."

Audrey patted Lansius's shoulder, saying, "Don't doubt yourself. This letter might be more effective than a large garrison."

Lansius smiled at her comment. "Let's hope so."

"Ah, I forgot to ask." Her gaze fixed on him. "I heard from Carla that you declined the merchants' offer. Are they still quoting a bad price?"

"Not at all. They offered a fair price," Lansius replied.

"Then why refuse?"

"I'm merely acting as expected. If they offered me a price and I readily agreed, then it would seem as though there's a plot at play. I'm simply showing that we might or might not need it. By giving them some doubt, I hope to save us from a price hike later on."

Audrey pouted, reflecting, "True. We still need a lot of grain to defend Umberland."

"Correct. We're not just taking Umberland but defending it through winter and spring. We'll need a lot of grain to survive. That's why securing a solid, long-term contract is crucial, not a half-baked one."

Audrey sighed. "Thinking about the grain situation makes me want to eat even more."

"Permission granted," Lansius quipped.

Audrey chuckled at his jest.

They were having their supper and not expecting anyone when Carla entered the inner part of the tent. "My lord, my lady."

"Yes, what is it?" Audrey inquired.

"Sterling mentioned the guards have someone with your invitation," Carla reported.

Escorted by Sterling, a woman in her forties, decked in lustrous gray attire, entered the tent. She carried no staff or wand, only a traveling bag. A similarly fashionable headscarf covered her brown hair. Her clothing and makeup helped maintain some of her youthful appearance.

She stood and glanced at Lansius only briefly, appearing stunned. The sight of his black hair might have been unexpected or noteworthy to her.

"Introduce yourself," Sterling urged.

"My lord, my lady, I am Ingrid, an educator from East Centuria."

"East Centurian, huh," Audrey muttered before asking, "What subjects do you teach?"

"I am well-versed in etiquette, poetry, and also medicine."

"That's a vast range of knowledge," Audrey said approvingly.

Watching them, Lansius said to Sterling and Carla, "Please prepare a tent for her, and then you can take a break."

After the squires had left, Audrey said to Ingrid, "Sir Morton spoke highly of you."

"Gratitude, my lady. Sir Morton is a prodigy. The guild hoped he has showcased how beneficial a member of our guild can be to your force."

Lansius exhaled sharply. "Indeed, he has, although, unfortunately, it was against my own forces."

"My condolences," Ingrid bowed her head apologetically.

"There's no enmity between us and Sir Morton anymore, so please," Lansius gestured for her to proceed.

"Gratitude, my lord. The guild instructed me to serve as a mentor for the lady, and I'll also be working in a limited capacity as a mage until you decide to become a patron."

"What will happen if I become a patron?"

"Available candidates will be trained for your service."

Lansius and Audrey exchanged glances. Before they could react, Ingrid took something from her purse and offered it with both hands to the hosts. The small object, possibly a ring or a necklace, was inside a small purple velvet envelope. "A gift of a jewel from the guild. A gemstone of might as a token of the guild's confidence in your rule in Lowlandia."

Audrey, out of caution, grabbed Lansius's hand, asking the mentor, "I've never heard of this."

"It is a rare item, only found on the old continent. It will grant the wearer momentary power akin to that of a mage, though only physically."

Audrey took the velvet envelope and opened it, revealing a small, inconspicuous gem-encrusted silver necklace. "Why would the guild readily part with such a valued object?" she asked as she inspected it.

"Because they learned from Sir Morton about your grand plan to pacify Lowlandia. The guild wishes to lend their support to your endeavor."

Lansius was intrigued. "But why? Why would a powerful guild have interest in a no-man's-land like Lowlandia?"

Ingrid seemed troubled by the question. She had the answer but had yet to decide whether she could trust the lord and lady. Unexpectedly, the Lord of Lowlandia wasn't distracted by the promise of a mage in service or even by rare magical items that should appease even the most powerful men.

CHAPTER 42

THE SECRET WITHIN

The Lord of Korelia's Command Tent

Audrey looked at the gem-encrusted silver necklace in her palm, carefully checking it by instinct alone. Meanwhile, Lansius was still waiting for Ingrid's response to his question.

Why would a powerful guild have interest in a no-man's-land like Lowlandia?

The educator exhaled softly before explaining, "There are two reasons, both equally important. One is to support efforts to stop the infighting in Lowlandia for the good of the Imperium. The second reason is that, like any other guild, the Mage Guild is concerned about the situation in the Imperium. Rumors have it that the war around the capital has started. Right now, the guild is seeking allies and looking for possible safe havens."

Lansius felt something was odd. "Why does it sound as if the Mage Guild is responsible for thousands of people?"

"My lord is perceptive. Indeed, while the guild only accounts for several hundreds, we couldn't abandon the people who have supported us."

"I never knew the guild cared so much for commoners," Audrey commented.

"Without the people who supported us, the guild wouldn't survive," Ingrid replied almost naturally.

Lansius pondered the practical reason. While it reassured him to a degree, he couldn't shake a lingering doubt about their motivation.

"Where is your guild located?" Audrey asked as she handed the necklace to Lansius, who for the first time inspected it closely.

"The guild has several branches, but the closest is located near the Nicopola and Halicia border."

"Do you know an old mage-hunter by the name of Isolte?" Audrey changed the subject.

Ingrid tried to recall the name but shook her head. "I can't recall anyone with that name."

Audrey nodded, muttering, "She's probably from another branch."

"The Tiberia branch is indeed larger. Is she a friend?"

"She was my old master. She died on a hunting trip several years ago."

"My condolences," Ingrid said politely.

With Audrey having nothing more to say, Lansius stepped up. "Tell me, what exactly does this gemstone do?"

"In times of need, it can give my lord a few minutes of physical power. Enough to get you out of trouble."

"So, it's for fighting?"

"You may use it as such, but its primary usage is for emergency. When my lord is wounded, the gemstone will react and hopefully close the bleeding without needing to remove the armor."

"That's clever," Lansius commented. "Is there any spell to activate the gem or any other specifics?"

"You don't have to, my lord. It's best to let it work on its own when the time is right. Think of it as a protective charm."

Lansius nodded. "How many times can I use it?"

"Once, my lord."

"And after that?" he followed up.

"It must be returned to us. For a gemstone this potent, the guild will imbue it with magic, but it would take weeks."

So, essentially, a heal with only one effective charge.

"Is there any passive effect when I'm wearing this?" Lansius's curiosity got the best of him.

"Passive effect . . . ?" Ingrid pondered and looked at Lansius with a hint of suspicion as she spoke, "None to my knowledge. The guild has studied such gemstones, and we have yet to uncover any hidden effects."

Putting the mentor's suspicion aside, he asked again, "Allow me one more question. How rare is this again?"

"We are not allowed to discuss it, my lord, but we know several were treated as heirlooms in high nobles' families."

Lansius looked at Audrey, noticing some slight worry, and gave the necklace back to her. "For now, keep it for me."

Ingrid must've sensed their hesitation. "My lord, my lady, if there are no other questions, I'll take my leave. We can begin my lady's education tomorrow morning and mage training at night."

"Is there a particular reason for night training?" Audrey inquired.

"While it's not physical, it can be quite exhausting to the body. So, it'll be best if the trainee sleeps afterward to regain her stamina," Ingrid explained.

Audrey gazed at her squarely. "Would it be dangerous if I had a child in my womb?"

The words felt like a cold bath to Lansius. *Is she expecting? Can she even tell if she's pregnant?*

"Are you expecting, my lady?" Ingrid asked without hesitation.

"I haven't felt the changes," she revealed.

"Worry not, my lady. It has happened before, and many reported that the child grew as normal as expected of them."

Three Hills

Not even a month had passed, yet the recruits from South Hill, who had recently joined, were already comfortable with their new lord. During their brief time marching together, they observed the lord marching as if he were just an ordinary footman, carrying his own bag and subjecting himself to grueling marches on foot.

This action quickly endeared him to the recruits, who had few expectations of their new overlord. They recognized him as a leader who truly knew the weight of his commands. As a result, their feelings for him deepened beyond fear and respect, evolving into genuine trust and affection.

During mealtimes and marches, they expressed hopes that the lord would unite all of Lowlandia, bring peace, and elevate the province to unprecedented heights.

Their arrival in Three Hills City, met with open arms and a welcoming feast, reinforced their belief that a united Lowlandia was within reach, not a farfetched dream.

Driven by genuine joy, the troops and camp followers enthusiastically shared stories of the lord's actions and achievements in every place they visited in Three Hills City. The tradesmen and commoners, hearing these tales, clearly recognized them as expressions of admiration, born out of a desire to spread the joy they felt.

It was easy to see that these men, from various backgrounds and origins, were simply enchanted by their streak of victories and escapes from troubling situations that often seemed impossible to win.

Unsurprisingly, among his men, the Nicopolans quickly grew almost as fanatical as the Korelian recruits. The lord's success in saving thousands from the brink of destruction and hunger was seen as something greater than the work of a mere man.

In South Hill, Lord Lansius had turned the Nicopolans into farmers, yet nobody complained. Instead, they were grateful for the chance to earn their bread instead of taking it from someone else's cold, lifeless hand.

While outwardly they joked that the lord had turned them from armed refugees into beggars, from beggars into footmen, and now, from footmen into farmers, it wasn't mockery. Truthfully, they labored in bliss, knowing from experience that famine and winter treated all equally, regardless of background.

Without food, fire, and warmth, Nicopolans or Lowlandians would be reduced to mere names on wooden grave markers, if they were fortunate enough to have anyone left to bury them.

The lord's success in giving them the chance to settle down, albeit temporarily, tending farms in serene peace and waiting for the crops to mature, was nothing short of a miracle for those who, until a season ago, had eaten gray meat just to survive.

Thus, it was inevitable that a personality cult venerating the lord and lady emerged among them. This shared bond united the men from Arvenia, Midlandia, Korelia, Korimor, and Nicopola. Under such circumstances, the men from South Hill were more than eager to join, convinced they were part of something greater.

In just three nights, these men and their stories had left a lasting impression on the people of Three Hills City. The commoners grew hopeful toward this mysterious lord, now the city's powerful ally. Despite various rumors about the Black Lord, the commoners of Lowlandia respected power and had no issue aligning themselves with the blue and bronze banner.

However, not everyone was swayed. Many powerful families remained skeptical, becoming increasingly wary of the Lord of Korelia's expanding power and influence.

The day of marching finally arrived. The troops arrayed on the open plains outside the city, slowly assuming formation. Divided into columns, the Lord of Korelia's army was soon joined by the Lord of Three Hills' army.

For this campaign, House Lansius & Audrey commanded:

10 South Hill Knights, led by Sir Harold

40 cavalry, led by Sir Harold

30 nomadic horse archers and scouts, led by one of Batu's sworn brothers

50 mounted crossbowmen, led by Dietrich

300 dragoons, equipped like men-at-arms and with crossbows, led by Lady Audrey

50 South Hill men-at-arms, led by Sterling

300 Nicopolan regiment on foot, led by Servius

1,300 Nicopolan army on foot, led by Lord Lansius

700 Nicopolan camp followers

There were also an additional four trained dogs for nighttime security.

Meanwhile, House Jorge commanded:

30 mounted Black Knights

100 Three Hills men-at-arms

300 Three Hills levied troops

After securing his family in carriages, Jorge dismounted not far from Lansius, and the two greeted each other warmly. After scanning the sky and horizon, Jorge said, "It is a fine day to march."

Lansius followed Jorge's gaze, commenting, "Hopefully, it isn't too hot, so we can cover a good distance."

"Knowing the region, I think it'll be a cloudy day," Jorge replied, in high spirits.

The two chuckled and motioned to each other to sit as they waited for the army and its logistical preparations to be complete. Soon, the scouting elements and vanguard marched ahead.

While waiting for the main army, Jorge, seated with Lansius beneath a large field umbrella, asked, "Lord Lansius, if you don't mind satisfying my curiosity, how do you make your men so . . . loyal? They seem happy to march, even with heavy burdens."

Lansius chuckled. "There's really no secret. I think you know more about leadership than I do, my lord."

"Well, there must be something you're doing differently, because it's not something I can simply tell my men to do," Jorge said, referring to how Lansius's army carried their supplies on their backs instead of relying on mules or carts.

"The terrain in Umberland will be difficult, so I need some flexibility in case of opportunity or threats."

Lord Jorge nodded, slightly disappointed with the lack of a detailed explanation.

Noticing this, and aware that Lord Jorge was an open-minded noble who didn't ask questions merely to pass the time but out of genuine curiosity and a willingness to learn, Lansius decided to answer him seriously. "Back in my birthplace, I knew a legendary hero named Chesty Puller. He was the most remarkable war leader I've ever known."

Jorge's eyes flickered, and his face showed attentiveness. "Hearing that from you, he must have been special. How does he compare to you?"

"I'm nothing compared to him. Like a firefly to the sun. He was who I aspire to be."

Intrigued, Jorge pressed, "What kind of leader was he that makes you aspire to be like him?"

"It's simple, my lord. Simple but hard to do . . ." Lansius admitted.

"Tell me more about him," Jorge asked, his curiosity as pure as that of an innocent child.

Lansius gathered his thoughts and said, "Chesty taught us never to let down our troops. Even though he was a leader, he marched, ate, and slept among his men, never asking for special treatment. He even ordered his field kitchen to serve his men first, before himself."

Jorge readily nodded, fascinated by the story.

"He always went to where the battles were. When there was no battle, he fought bandits. When there was a battle, he led from the front, often surrounded and against much larger forces, but he never yielded. When other leaders cowered, Chesty courageously stood up, cockily exposed himself to the enemy, and in that way, he led his men from destruction to victory."

"What a prime example of an ideal hero," Jorge commented heartily.

"Indeed. He was bold, forceful, and aggressive but never reckless. He demanded the best from his men, but they knew they could count on him. Chesty often personally ensured that his wounded men got the best treatment." Lansius then looked at Jorge. "What fascinated me the most is: He always stayed with his troops. Hard pouring rain, frozen snow, knee-deep mud, wet soggy clothes and all. He stayed and fought with them."

Jorge nodded deeply, absorbing what was being told. "And how did his men treat him?"

"They treated him like a devout son to his father. They followed him willingly even in the hardest of fighting. Even when the losses were high, his men never gave up out of respect for their beloved leader."

The Lord of Three Hills' face brightened up, and he humbly said, "There's so much to learn."

"Even I'm still learning," Lansius said. Then, inspired by the story he had just recounted, he looked at his squire. "Sigmund, let someone else walk my horse. Today, I'll walk with my men."

Seeing this, Lord Jorge announced, "Then I shall join you. Let me walk by your side."

The men in formation closest to them were thrilled, and the news quickly spread from the column nearest to them to the furthest. Soon, all the troops were excited, and cheers erupted from both armies at this show of solidarity.

The only dissent came from the baroness, who rode up to Lansius. "My lord, you promised to ride beside me."

"Apologies, my lady, but I think I'll march, at least for this day," Lansius responded.

"But you'll get—"

"I'll be fine. I'm feeling good," he reassured her.

Audrey shook her head and massaged her temple before quickly dismounting. "Then, I'll be walking as well."

The lady's declaration prompted even more cheering from the troops, who found this situation particularly funny but encouraging.

"You can't," Lansius objected.

"Why not?" Audrey asked firmly.

"You might be expecting," Lansius blurted out.

The statement hushed the crowd. Voices stopped. The staff, the knights, the men—everyone exchanged glances and whispered until someone shouted, "The lady is pregnant!"

With hoarse voices, the three thousand around them yelled as loudly as they could, celebrating as if they had just won another victory. Other columns heard and joined in, breaking formation to see the lady they revered. The air was filled with raw jubilation.

Caught in the moment, Audrey could only grin and blush at the overwhelming well wishes.

Audrey gave him *the look*, whispering, "But Lans, I'm not sure—"

"We can't be sure. You can't be sure," Lansius said cheerfully while shouldering his backpack.

Lord Jorge and his knights could only grin as they watched the situation unfold and felt similarly empowered. Thus, with high morale, the two armies marched to Umberland.

Three Hills City

Five days after Lord Jorge and Lord Lansius marched to Umberland, the secret meetings among the city's powerful men intensified.

"We should wait until we know the outcome of their campaign in Umberland," one urged his cohorts.

Facing him was a young gentleman who haughtily replied, "The House that I represent will not entertain such cowardly action. We beseech you all to proceed as planned."

Another person added, "Indeed, we have bribed enough, and they, with no shame, asked for more. I say it's time for us to reap what we sow!"

"He is right," one exclaimed as he stood up. "We have all the support we need. The wolf is gone; now it's time to take the den."

The sound of reason fell mute against the clamor of greed and hubris, masked as glory and honor.

That night, while the commoners slept, three hundred men in several groups launched their coup. One group headed directly to the castle, and another to the gatehouse to prevent news from spreading. The attack took the relaxed guardsmen by surprise. Despite fighting courageously, they were betrayed by some of their officers who had been bribed.

Without the Black Knights, the guardsmen were forced to retreat to their holdout, where fighting continued as doors and barred gates were successively broken into.

As dawn broke, the castle was isolated from the city, with only the main keep and its immediate surroundings remaining under the control of Lord Jorge's loyalists. They fought valiantly, but the betrayal had sealed their fate. Now, the rebels were negotiating with them, offering protection in exchange for surrender.

When this yielded no results, they resorted to threats.

"Do we need to bring your families here? We know where they live," the thugs commanding the attack shouted.

"Wouldn't it be unfortunate if something happened to your wives and daughters?" another threatened, his words followed by echoes of laughter.

Knowing Lord Lansius still had his men there, the rebels, having secured the gatehouse, sent their forces to round them up.

Little did they know what awaited them.

Guest House

"Dame, they're coming for us," Farkas warned, having received the latest intel from his men in disguise who had worked through the night, detecting fighting in the castle and the gatehouse.

Daniella exhaled sharply and rose from the crates of bolts on which she had been sitting. "I think it's time. Ready the men."

Farkas smiled. "With pleasure," he said and ran toward the adjacent stable and other buildings in the vicinity.

Daniella calmly prepared her new custom crossbow, and her men followed suit, grins on their faces. "So, stupid. They're going against the Black Lord with such a half-assed attempt."

That mockery was well received, and many chuckled as they checked their blades and armor.

"It took them long enough to find their courage," one responded as he donned his helmet.

"Five days, I've been eating dry rations with little ale, waiting for action."

"The waiting is just horrendous," another Nicopolan commented amidst the chuckles.

Daniella, clad in armor and looking as beautiful as a marble sculpture of a demigod, gazed at the dozens of men who had crammed into the guest house. "You've endured shit. I have endured shit. Now, let's make them all pay."

The men cheered at her simple yet effective rallying cry.

Just as their spirits soared, the heavy thud of armored boots silenced the room, drawing all eyes toward the entrance.

A group of men clad in imposing black plate armor entered the premises; their presence was unexpected. Yet, as they advanced, the air filled with great anticipation.

And the leading knight delivered on that promise. With deliberate movements, he reached up to remove his hood, revealing handsome yet hawkish features and cold eyes. His slightly curly long brown hair made him look more like a deviant than a model knight. However, the men's voices swelled in a new wave of cheers, recognizing the face of the formidable Mage Knight.

"Sir Morton," Daniella greeted her comrade in arms. "So you've received the word?"

"I have," came his usual brief and almost cold answer. Then his steely gaze swept over the men in the room.

"My men are ready," Daniella reassured him.

A faint smile broke through his otherwise stern demeanor. "Gratitude for the assistance," he said to the Nicopolans and Korelians in the room. Then, he added, "Give these traitors no mercy."

The last word resonated with an ice-cold echo, charged with contained rage. It made the men shudder, yet it also stirred excitement among them. They hadn't known that the Mage Knight, who was always by Sir Jorge's side day and night, had been hiding in Three Hills. This revelation meant they now had ample strength to turn the tide of battle against the traitors.

Sir Morton took his helmet from his squire and turned to Daniella. "Dame, I mean no disrespect, but may I lead the charge?"

"By all means," Daniella replied with a wide smile.

"Don't stray like last time," Sir Morton muttered.

Daniella chuckled, recalling the event in that fateful forest. "You can count on me. This time I have something worth fighting for."

Their exchange did not go unnoticed by their men, who grinned with caution.

The coup had thrust the destiny of Three Hills, the Grand Alliance, and Lowlandia into uncertainty. Stray but a little, and not even history would be kind to them. The fate of their brothers-in-arms, along with the future of the region, rested heavily on their shoulders.

Winter of 4425 was still on the horizon, yet blood was destined once more to stain the chronicles of Lowlandia. House Lansius, the Grand Alliance, and the forthcoming Shogunate would bend the arcs of destiny, seeking peace in a region long forsaken.

ABOUT THE AUTHOR

Hanne is the author of the Horizon of War isekai series, originally released
Royal Road. An avid reader and writer, her "realistic" fantasy stories feature
torical details with military-grade accuracy (i.e., gambesons, poleaxes, logis
and all the intricacies of the feudal nobility).

Podium